WITHDRAWN

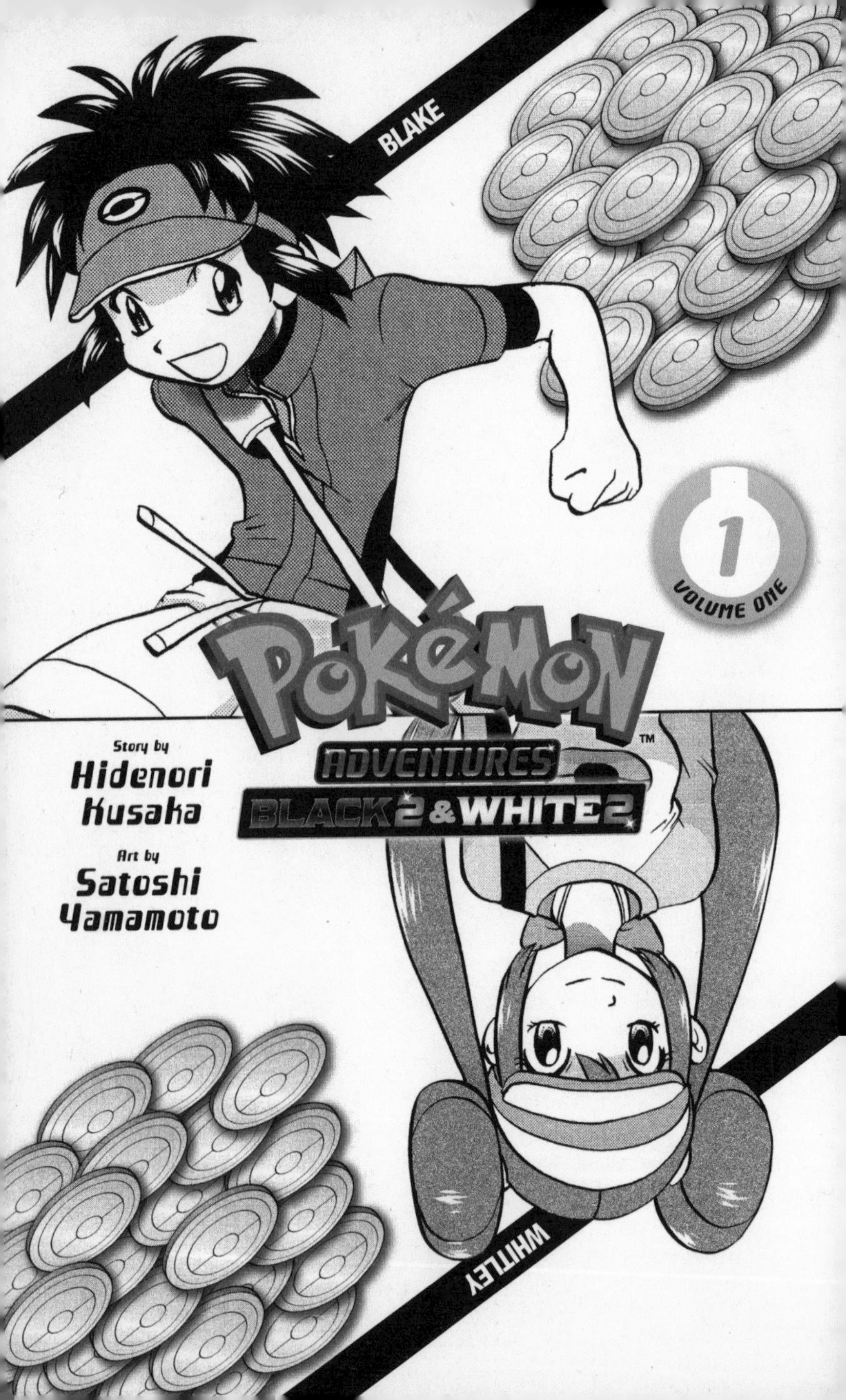
BLAKE
1
VOLUME ONE
POKéMON™
ADVENTURES
BLACK 2 & WHITE 2
Story by
Hidenori Kusaka
Art by
Satoshi Yamamoto
WHITLEY

The Story Thus Far, Tenth Chapter

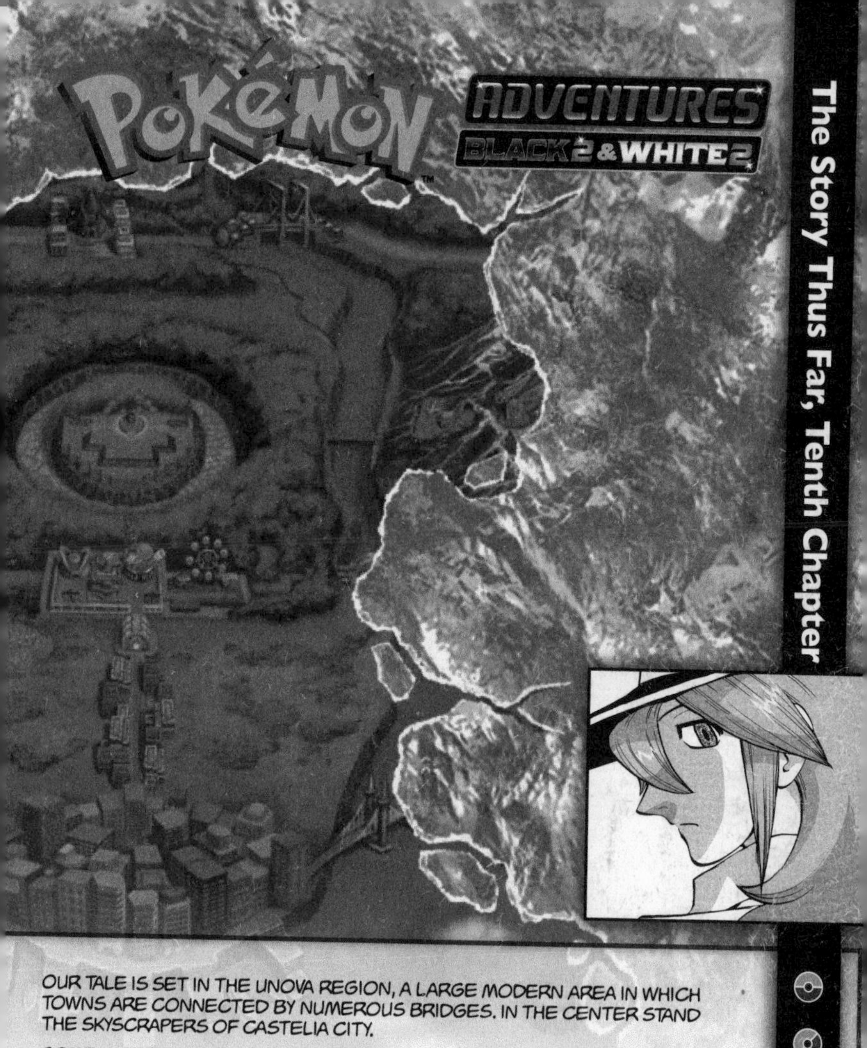
POKÉMON
ADVENTURES
BLACK 2 & WHITE 2

OUR TALE IS SET IN THE UNOVA REGION, A LARGE MODERN AREA IN WHICH TOWNS ARE CONNECTED BY NUMEROUS BRIDGES. IN THE CENTER STAND THE SKYSCRAPERS OF CASTELIA CITY.

SOMEWHERE IN UNOVA, A YOUNG BOY NAMED "N" IS RAISED INSIDE A CASTLE BY AN ORGANIZATION NAMED TEAM PLASMA. N HAS THE ABILITY TO HEAR THE VOICES OF POKÉMON. EVENTUALLY, HE BECOMES THE KING OF TEAM PLASMA.

TEAM PLASMA SPREADS THEIR IDEAL OF "POKÉMON LIBERATION" THROUGHOUT UNOVA. THEY CLAIM TO BELIEVE THAT POKÉMON SHOULD BE SET FREE IF HUMANS TRULY WANT TO COEXIST WITH THEM IN PEACE. THIS PHILOSOPHY SOUNDS REASONABLE AND SOME PEOPLE ARE CONVINCED TO JOIN THE CAUSE AND RELEASE THEIR POKÉMON INTO THE WILD.

N IS RAISED WITH POKÉMON WHO HAVE BEEN MISTREATED BY PEOPLE. HE GROWS UP WITH A STRONG SENSE OF JUSTICE.

EVENTUALLY, N BEGINS TO SEE HIMSELF AS THE HERO OF THE "LEGEND OF THE FOUNDING OF UNOVA." HE WORKS HARD TO FREE POKÉMON FROM PEOPLE.

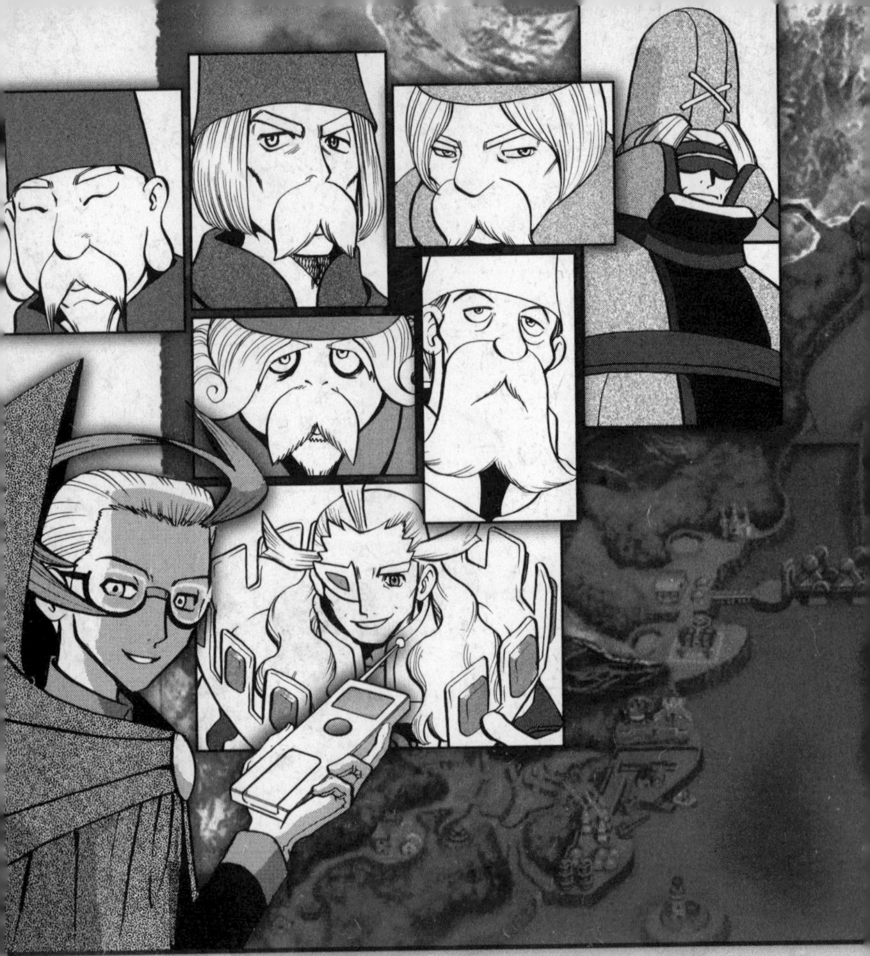

N AWAKENS ZEKROM, THE LEGENDARY POKÉMON OF THE "HERO OF IDEALS," AND EVEN SUCCEEDS IN DEFEATING THE POKÉMON LEAGUE CHAMPION. HE DENOUNCES POKÉ BALLS, POKÉDEXES, THE POKÉMON LEAGUE AND ANYTHING THAT PEOPLE USE TO HANDLE POKÉMON.

THEN TEAM PLASMA ATTACKS THE POKÉMON LEAGUE. IT APPEARS THEY HAVE TRIUMPHED. BUT THEIR TRUE DARK AMBITION IS REVEALED AND STOPPED BY A YOUNG TRAINER NAMED BLACK ASTRIDE RESHIRAM, THE LEGENDARY POKÉMON OF "TRUTH." AT THE SAME TIME, IT IS REVEALED THAT N IS NOTHING BUT A PUPPET RULER PROPPED UP AND USED BY TEAM PLASMA FOR THEIR OWN TRUE GOAL—TO BE THE ONLY PEOPLE LEFT WITH POKÉMON! DEFEATED, ZEKROM, N AND RESHIRAM QUIETLY WITHDRAW FROM THE PUBLIC EYE... THE EXECUTIVE MEMBERS OF TEAM PLASMA, THE SEVEN SAGES, ALL ESCAPE JUSTICE. UNFORTUNATELY, AS RESHIRAM RETURNS TO ITS DORMANT STATE IN THE LIGHT STONE, BLACK IS SUCKED IN WITH HIM...

AS THE UNOVA REGION HEALS, RELATIONSHIPS BETWEEN PEOPLE AND POKÉMON ARE REBUILT. AND THEN, TWO YEARS LATER...

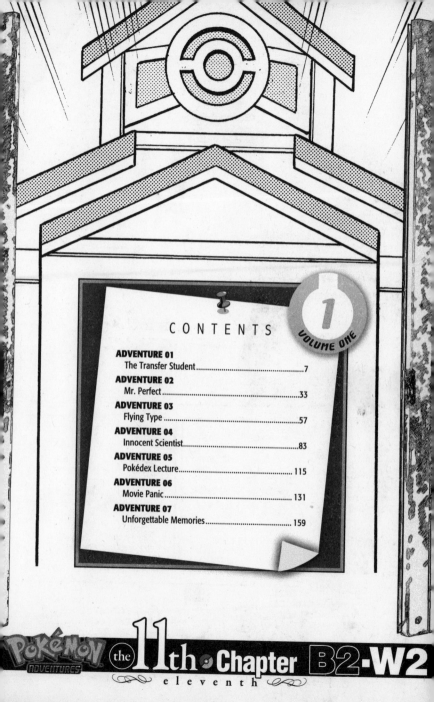

CONTENTS

VOLUME ONE 1

POKÉMON ADVENTURES

the 11th Chapter B2·W2

eleventh

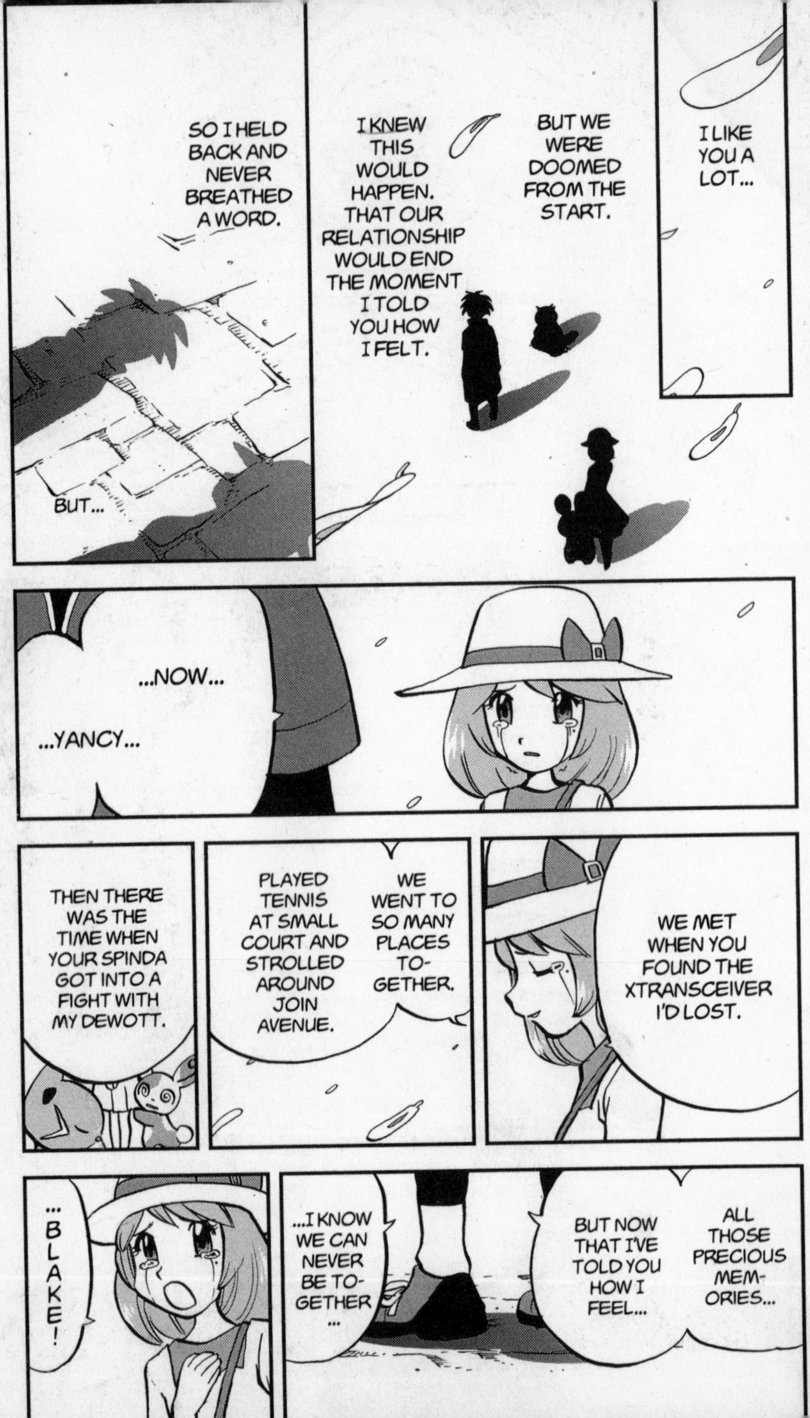
I LIKE YOU A LOT...
BUT WE WERE DOOMED FROM THE START.
I KNEW THIS WOULD HAPPEN. THAT OUR RELATIONSHIP WOULD END THE MOMENT I TOLD YOU HOW I FELT.
SO I HELD BACK AND NEVER BREATHED A WORD.
BUT...
...NOW...
...YANCY...
WE MET WHEN YOU FOUND THE XTRANSCEIVER I'D LOST.
WE WENT TO SO MANY PLACES TO-GETHER.
PLAYED TENNIS AT SMALL COURT AND STROLLED AROUND JOIN AVENUE.
THEN THERE WAS THE TIME WHEN YOUR SPINDA GOT INTO A FIGHT WITH MY DEWOTT.
ALL THOSE PRECIOUS MEM-ORIES...
BUT NOW THAT I'VE TOLD YOU HOW I FEEL...
...I KNOW WE CAN NEVER BE TO-GETHER...
...BLAKE!

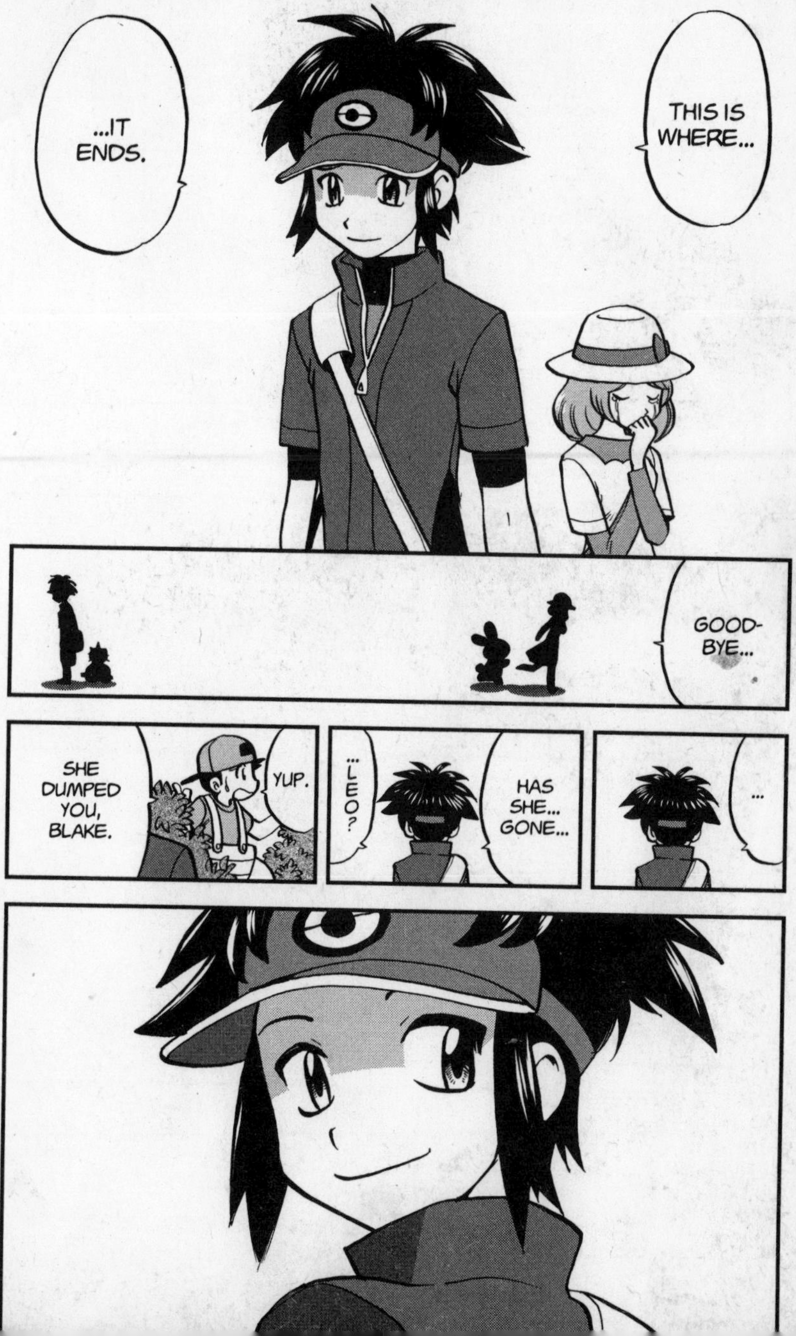
THIS IS WHERE...
...IT ENDS.
GOOD-BYE...
...
HAS SHE... GONE...
...LEO?
YUP.
SHE DUMPED YOU, BLAKE.

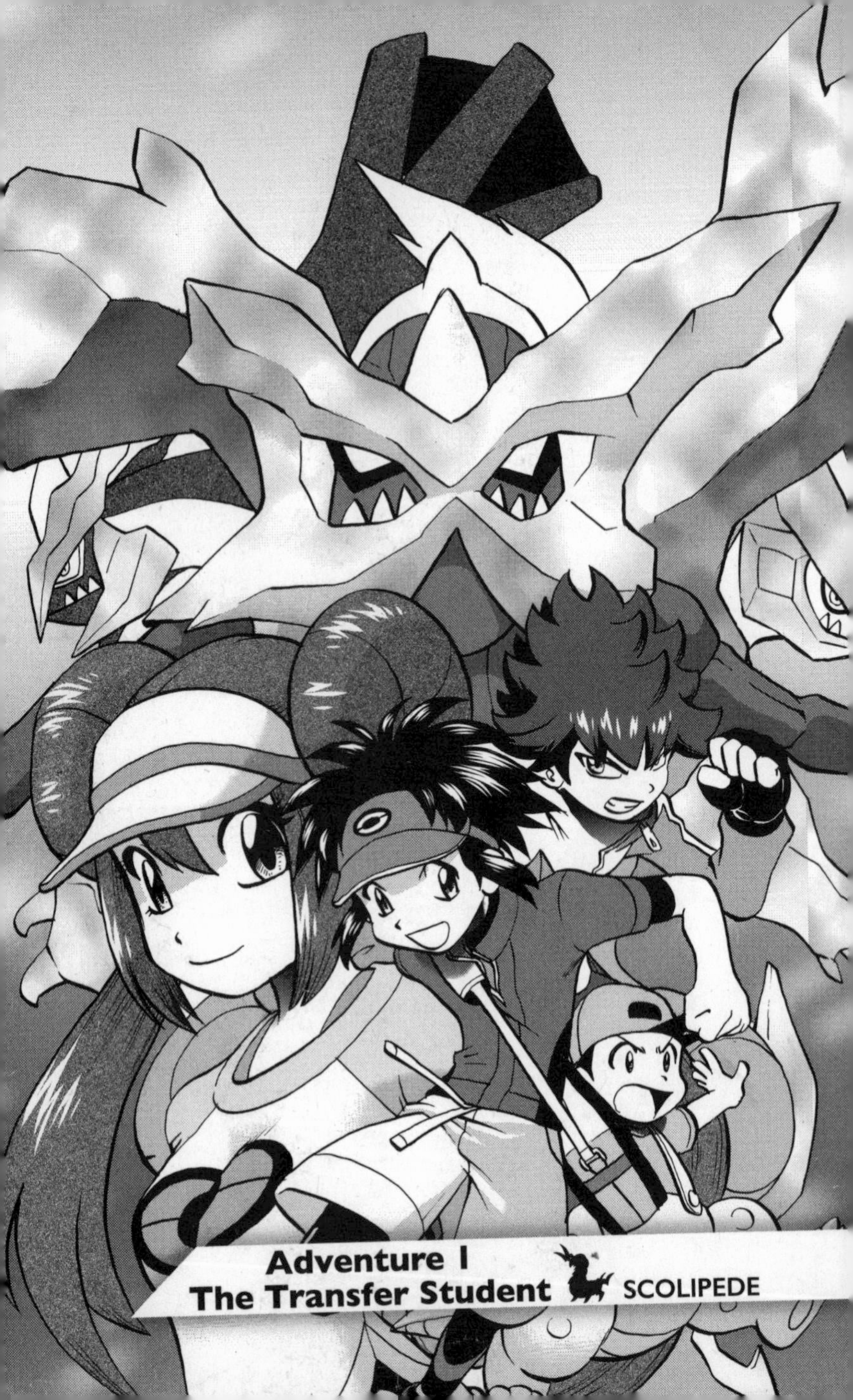
Adventure 1
The Transfer Student
SCOLIPEDE

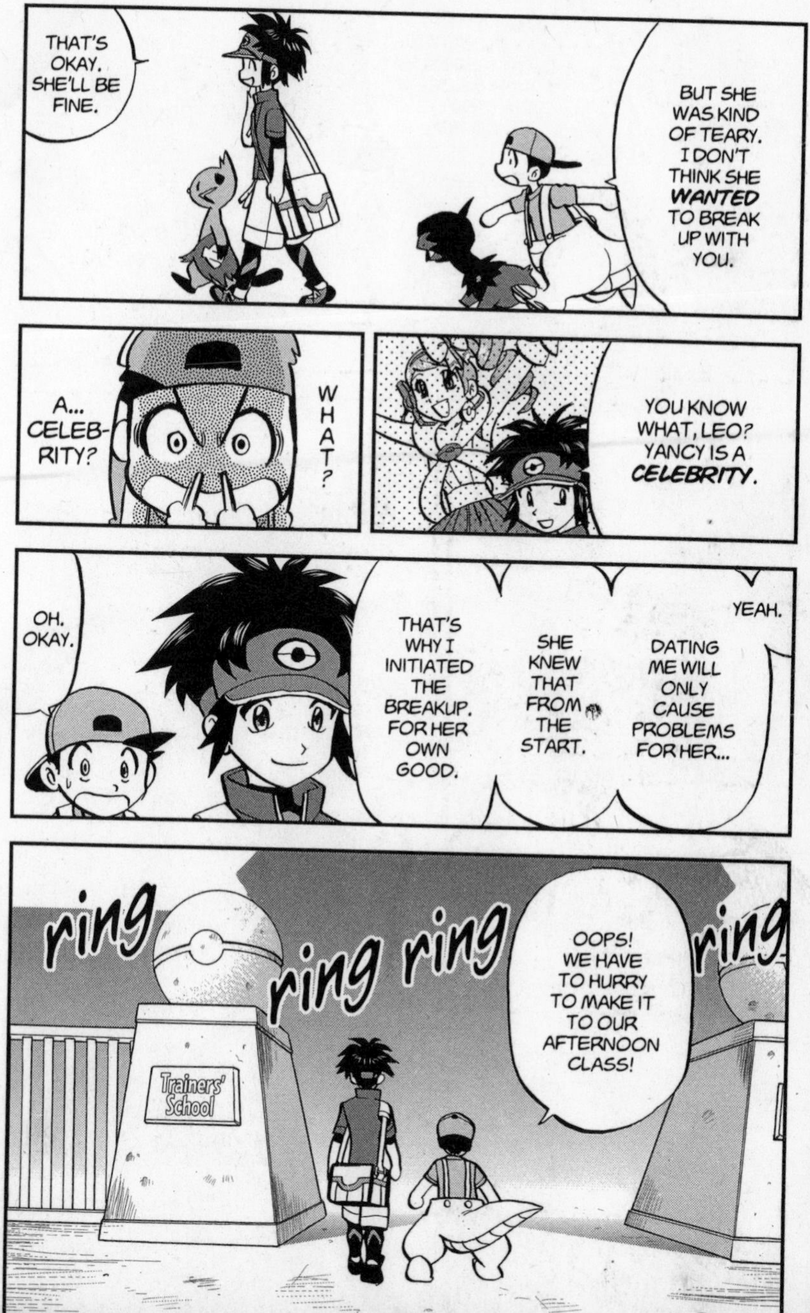
BUT SHE WAS KIND OF TEARY. I DON'T THINK SHE WANTED TO BREAK UP WITH YOU.
THAT'S OKAY. SHE'LL BE FINE.
YOU KNOW WHAT, LEO? YANCY IS A CELEBRITY.
WHAT?
A... CELEB-RITY?
YEAH.
DATING ME WILL ONLY CAUSE PROBLEMS FOR HER...
SHE KNEW THAT FROM THE START.
THAT'S WHY I INITIATED THE BREAKUP. FOR HER OWN GOOD.
OH. OKAY.
ring
ring ring
ring
OOPS! WE HAVE TO HURRY TO MAKE IT TO OUR AFTERNOON CLASS!
Trainers' School

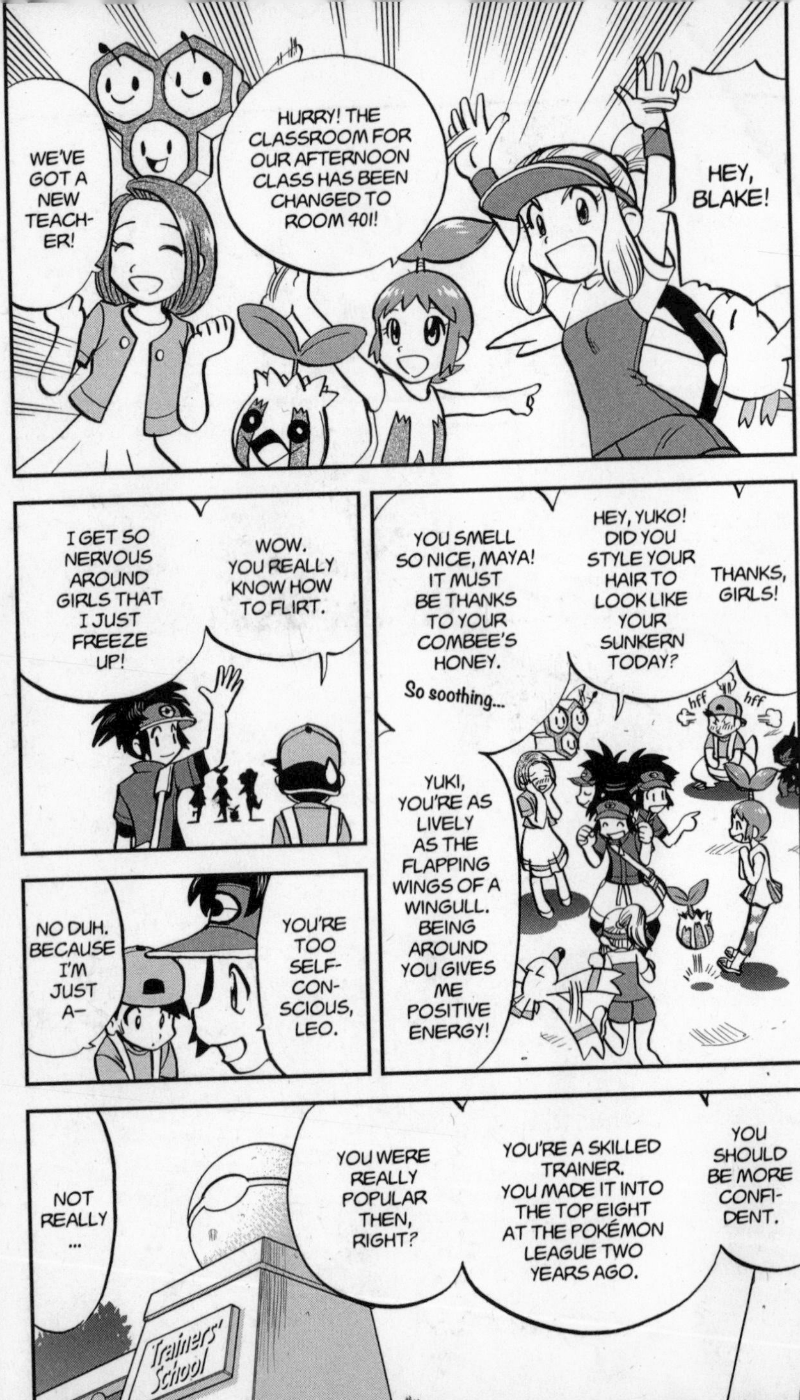
HEY, BLAKE!
HURRY! THE CLASSROOM FOR OUR AFTERNOON CLASS HAS BEEN CHANGED TO ROOM 401!
WE'VE GOT A NEW TEACHER!
THANKS, GIRLS!
HEY, YUKO! DID YOU STYLE YOUR HAIR TO LOOK LIKE YOUR SUNKERN TODAY?
YOU SMELL SO NICE, MAYA! IT MUST BE THANKS TO YOUR COMBEE'S HONEY.
So soothing...
hff hff
YUKI, YOU'RE AS LIVELY AS THE FLAPPING WINGS OF A WINGULL. BEING AROUND YOU GIVES ME POSITIVE ENERGY!
WOW. YOU REALLY KNOW HOW TO FLIRT.
I GET SO NERVOUS AROUND GIRLS THAT I JUST FREEZE UP!
YOU'RE TOO SELF-CONSCIOUS, LEO.
NO DUH. BECAUSE I'M JUST A–
YOU SHOULD BE MORE CONFIDENT.
YOU'RE A SKILLED TRAINER. YOU MADE IT INTO THE TOP EIGHT AT THE POKÉMON LEAGUE TWO YEARS AGO.
YOU WERE REALLY POPULAR THEN, RIGHT?
NOT REALLY ...
Trainers' School

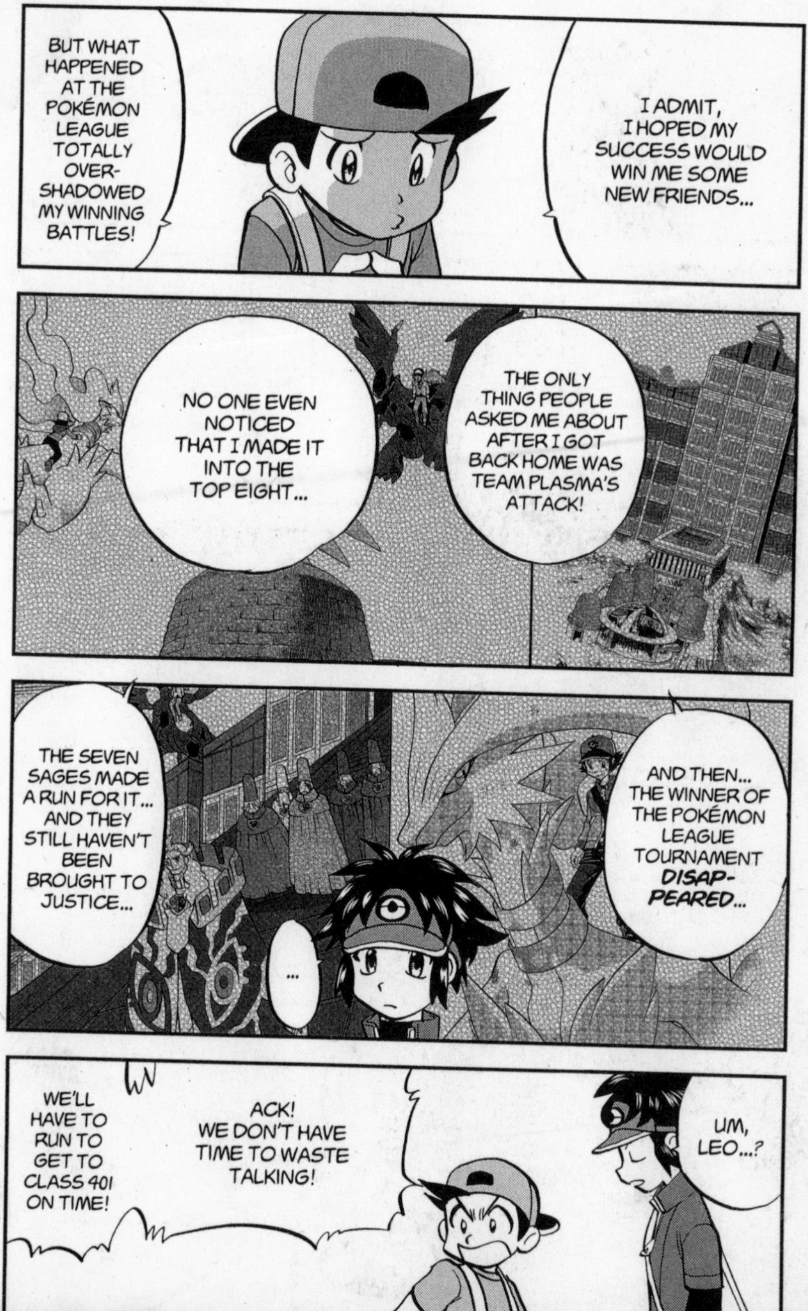
I ADMIT, I HOPED MY SUCCESS WOULD WIN ME SOME NEW FRIENDS...
BUT WHAT HAPPENED AT THE POKÉMON LEAGUE TOTALLY OVER-SHADOWED MY WINNING BATTLES!
THE ONLY THING PEOPLE ASKED ME ABOUT AFTER I GOT BACK HOME WAS TEAM PLASMA'S ATTACK!
NO ONE EVEN NOTICED THAT I MADE IT INTO THE TOP EIGHT...
AND THEN... THE WINNER OF THE POKÉMON LEAGUE TOURNAMENT **DISAP-PEARED...**
THE SEVEN SAGES MADE A RUN FOR IT... AND THEY STILL HAVEN'T BEEN BROUGHT TO JUSTICE...
...
UM, LEO...?
ACK! WE DON'T HAVE TIME TO WASTE TALKING!
WE'LL HAVE TO RUN TO GET TO CLASS 401 ON TIME!

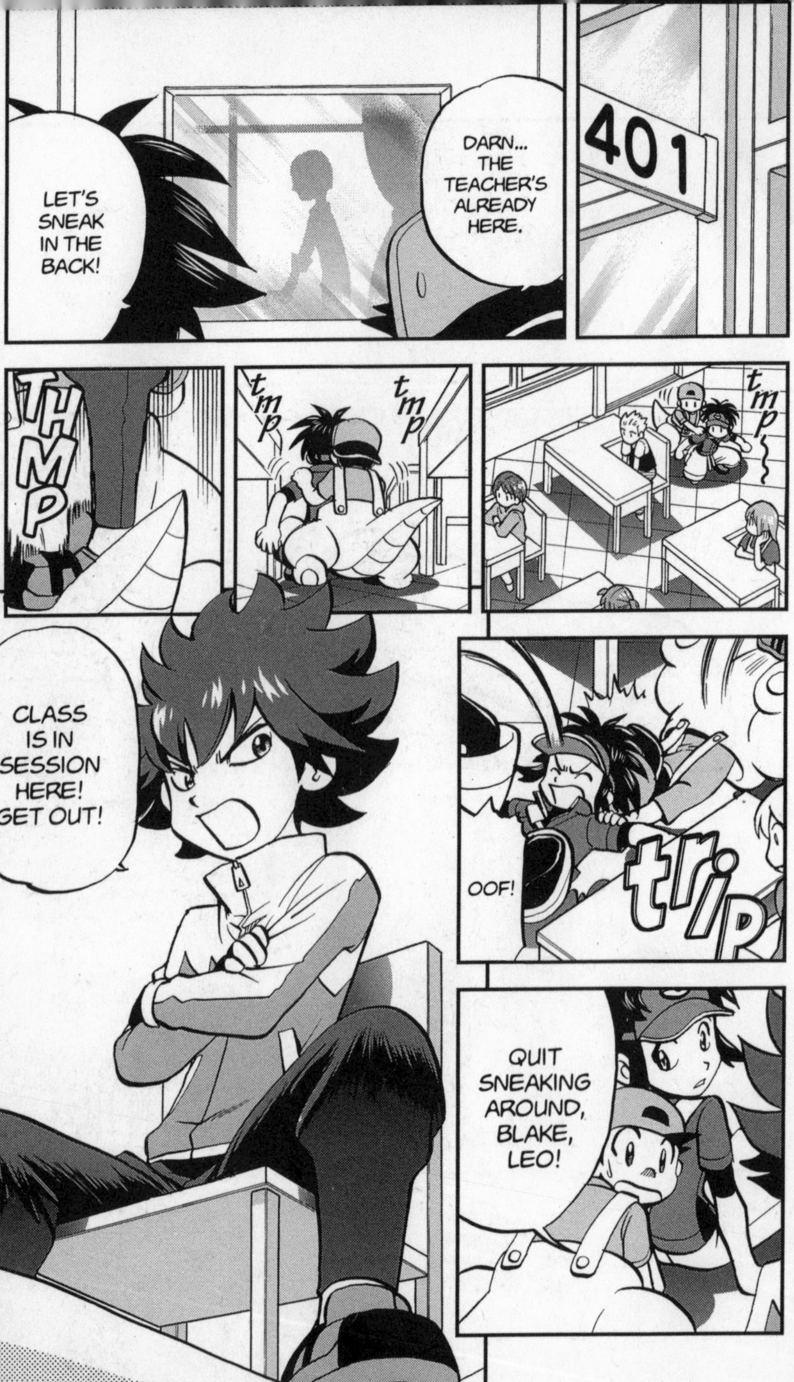
401
DARN... THE TEACHER'S ALREADY HERE.
LET'S SNEAK IN THE BACK!
tmp~
tmp
tmp
THMP
trip
OOF!
QUIT SNEAKING AROUND, BLAKE, LEO!
CLASS IS IN SESSION HERE! GET OUT!

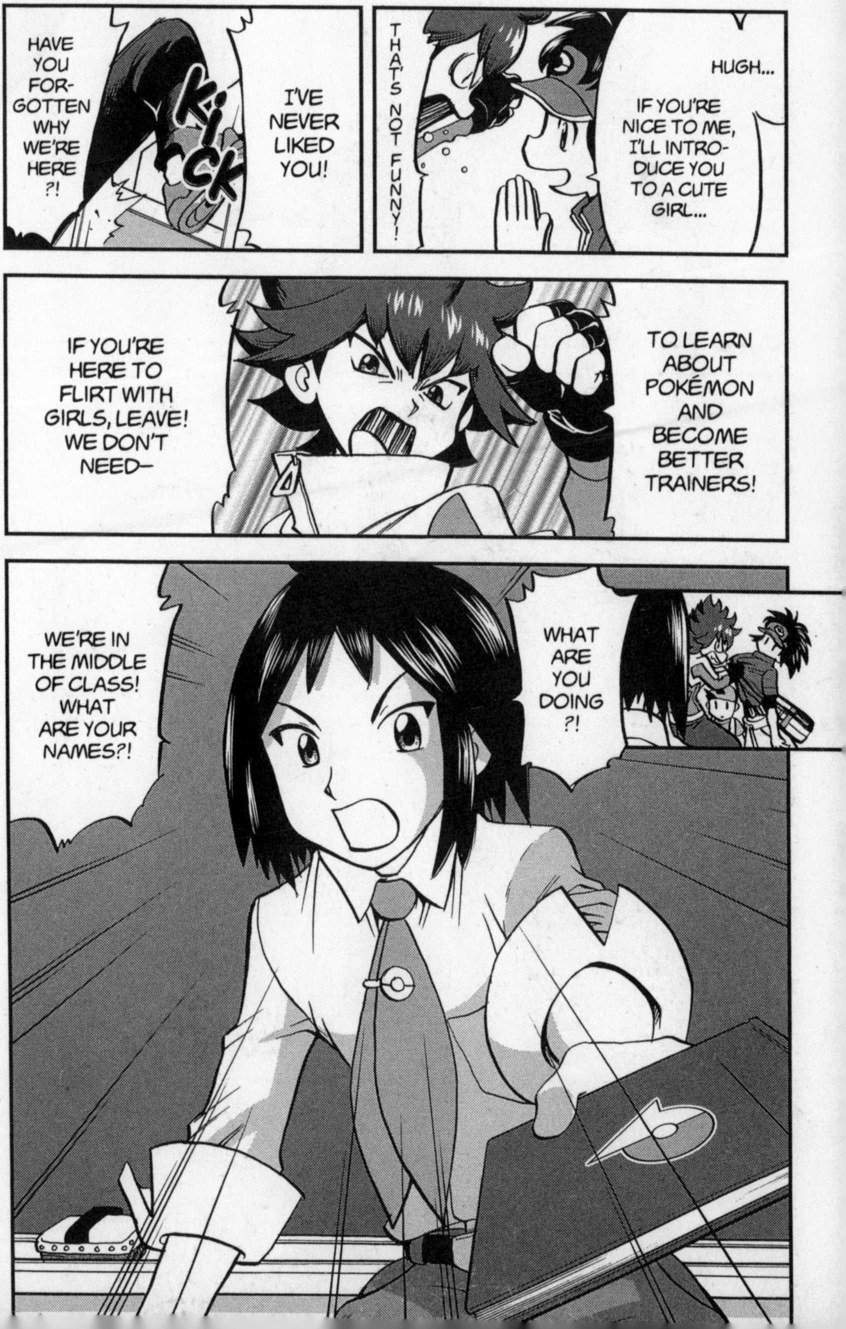
HUGH...
IF YOU'RE NICE TO ME, I'LL INTRODUCE YOU TO A CUTE GIRL...
THAT'S NOT FUNNY!
I'VE NEVER LIKED YOU!
KICK
HAVE YOU FORGOTTEN WHY WE'RE HERE?!
TO LEARN ABOUT POKÉMON AND BECOME BETTER TRAINERS!
IF YOU'RE HERE TO FLIRT WITH GIRLS, LEAVE! WE DON'T NEED—
WHAT ARE YOU DOING?!
WE'RE IN THE MIDDLE OF CLASS! WHAT ARE YOUR NAMES?!

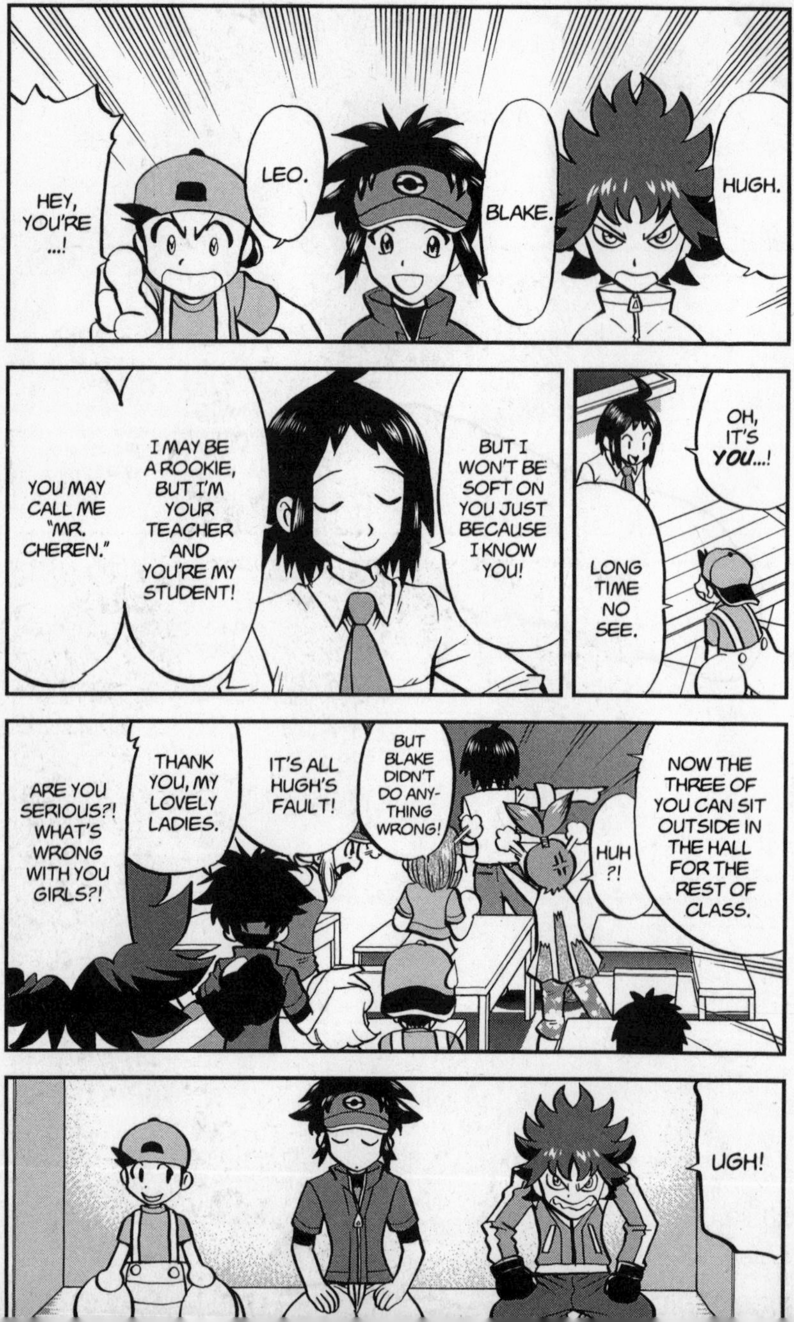
HUGH.
BLAKE.
LEO.
HEY, YOU'RE ...!
OH, IT'S YOU...!
LONG TIME NO SEE.
BUT I WON'T BE SOFT ON YOU JUST BECAUSE I KNOW YOU!
I MAY BE A ROOKIE, BUT I'M YOUR TEACHER AND YOU'RE MY STUDENT!
YOU MAY CALL ME "MR. CHEREN."
NOW THE THREE OF YOU CAN SIT OUTSIDE IN THE HALL FOR THE REST OF CLASS.
HUH ?!
BUT BLAKE DIDN'T DO ANY-THING WRONG!
IT'S ALL HUGH'S FAULT!
THANK YOU, MY LOVELY LADIES.
ARE YOU SERIOUS?! WHAT'S WRONG WITH YOU GIRLS?!
UGH!

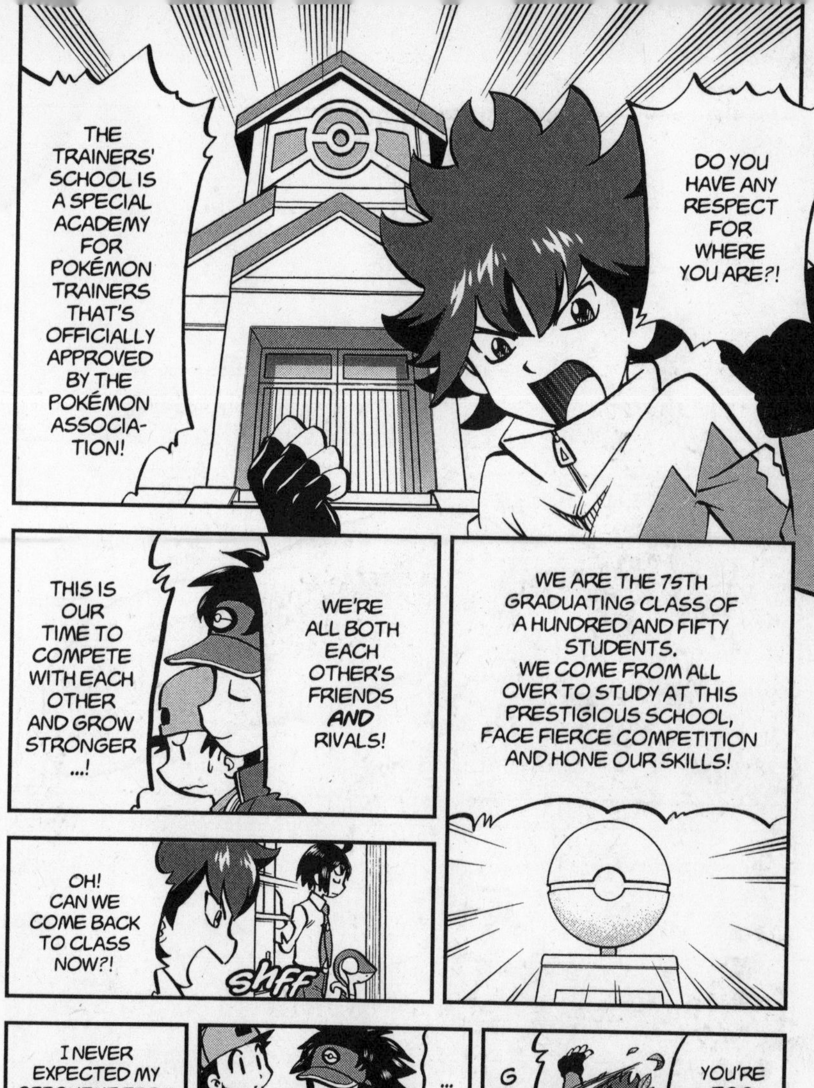
DO YOU HAVE ANY RESPECT FOR WHERE YOU ARE?!
THE TRAINERS' SCHOOL IS A SPECIAL ACADEMY FOR POKÉMON TRAINERS THAT'S OFFICIALLY APPROVED BY THE POKÉMON ASSOCIA-TION!
WE ARE THE 75TH GRADUATING CLASS OF A HUNDRED AND FIFTY STUDENTS. WE COME FROM ALL OVER TO STUDY AT THIS PRESTIGIOUS SCHOOL, FACE FIERCE COMPETITION AND HONE OUR SKILLS!
WE'RE ALL BOTH EACH OTHER'S FRIENDS AND RIVALS!
THIS IS OUR TIME TO COMPETE WITH EACH OTHER AND GROW STRONGER ...!
OH! CAN WE COME BACK TO CLASS NOW?!
shff
YOU'RE TOO LOUD IN THE HALL.
GRRR!
flapflap flap
...
THIS IS QUITE A SUR-PRISE.
I NEVER EXPECTED MY OPPONENT FROM THE POKÉMON LEAGUE TO BECOME MY TEACHER.

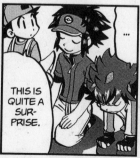

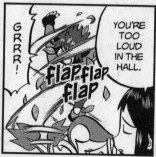

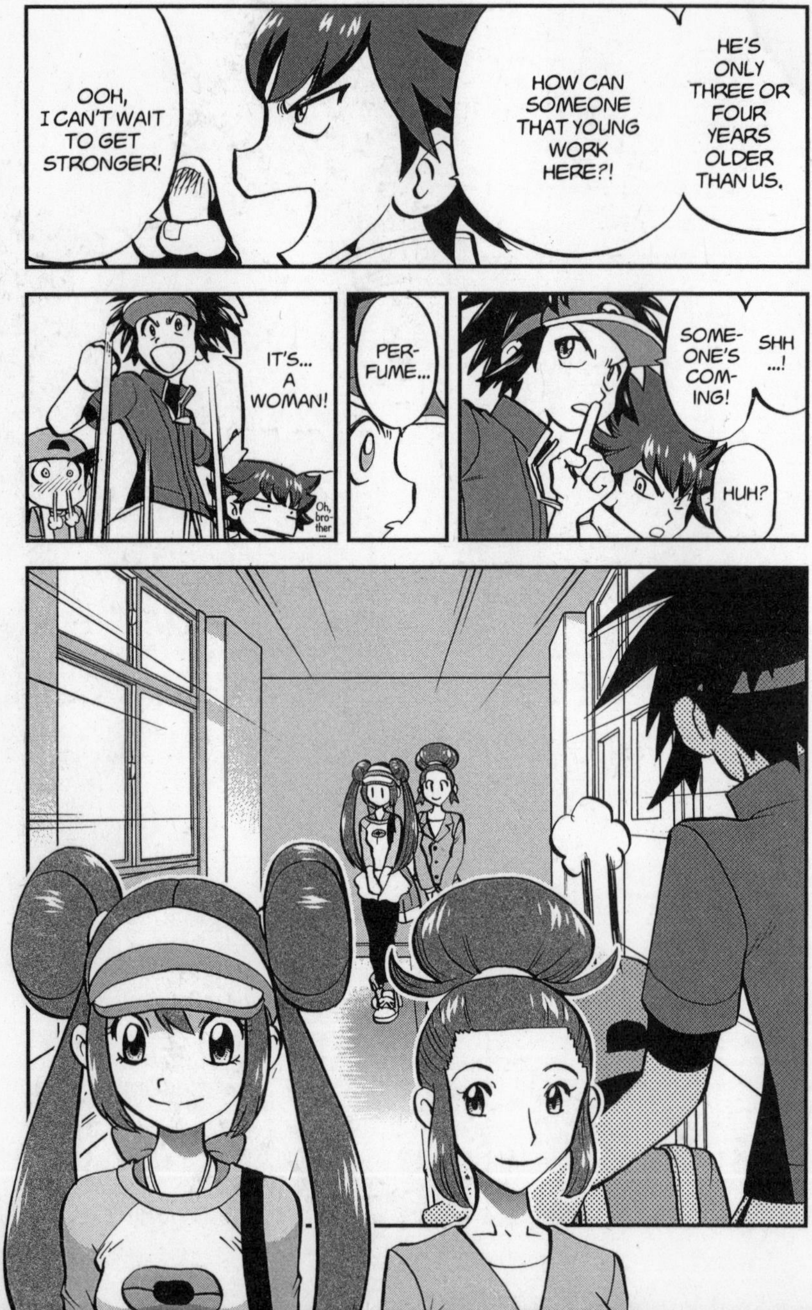
HE'S ONLY THREE OR FOUR YEARS OLDER THAN US.
HOW CAN SOMEONE THAT YOUNG WORK HERE?!
OOH, I CAN'T WAIT TO GET STRONGER!
SHH ...!
SOME-ONE'S COM-ING!
HUH?
PER-FUME...
IT'S... A WOMAN!
Oh, bro-ther...

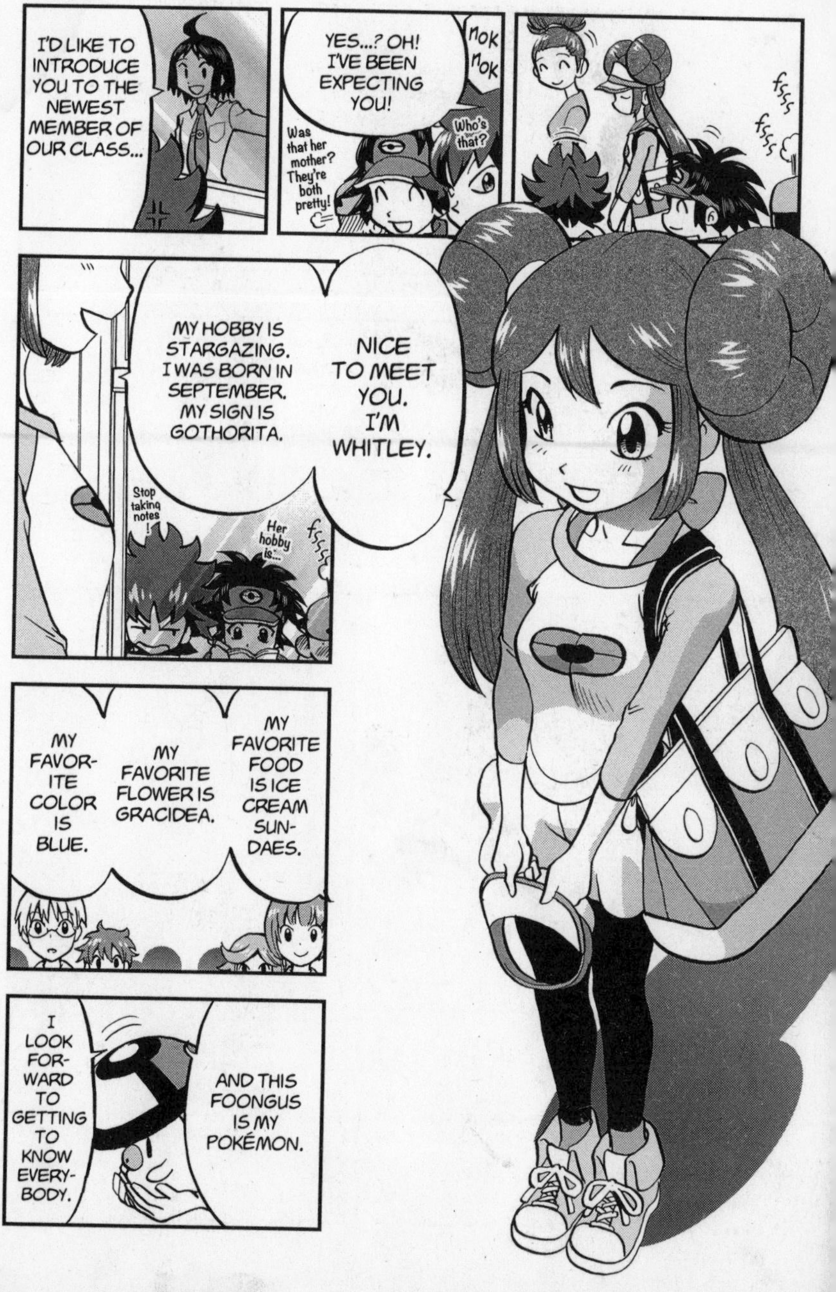
fsss fsss
nok nok
YES...? OH! I'VE BEEN EXPECTING YOU!
Who's that?
Was that her mother? They're both pretty!
I'D LIKE TO INTRODUCE YOU TO THE NEWEST MEMBER OF OUR CLASS...
NICE TO MEET YOU. I'M WHITLEY.
MY HOBBY IS STARGAZING. I WAS BORN IN SEPTEMBER. MY SIGN IS GOTHORITA.
fssss
Her hobby is...
Stop taking notes!
MY FAVORITE FOOD IS ICE CREAM SUN-DAES.
MY FAVORITE FLOWER IS GRACIDEA.
MY FAVOR-ITE COLOR IS BLUE.
AND THIS FOONGUS IS MY POKÉMON.
I LOOK FOR-WARD TO GETTING TO KNOW EVERY-BODY.

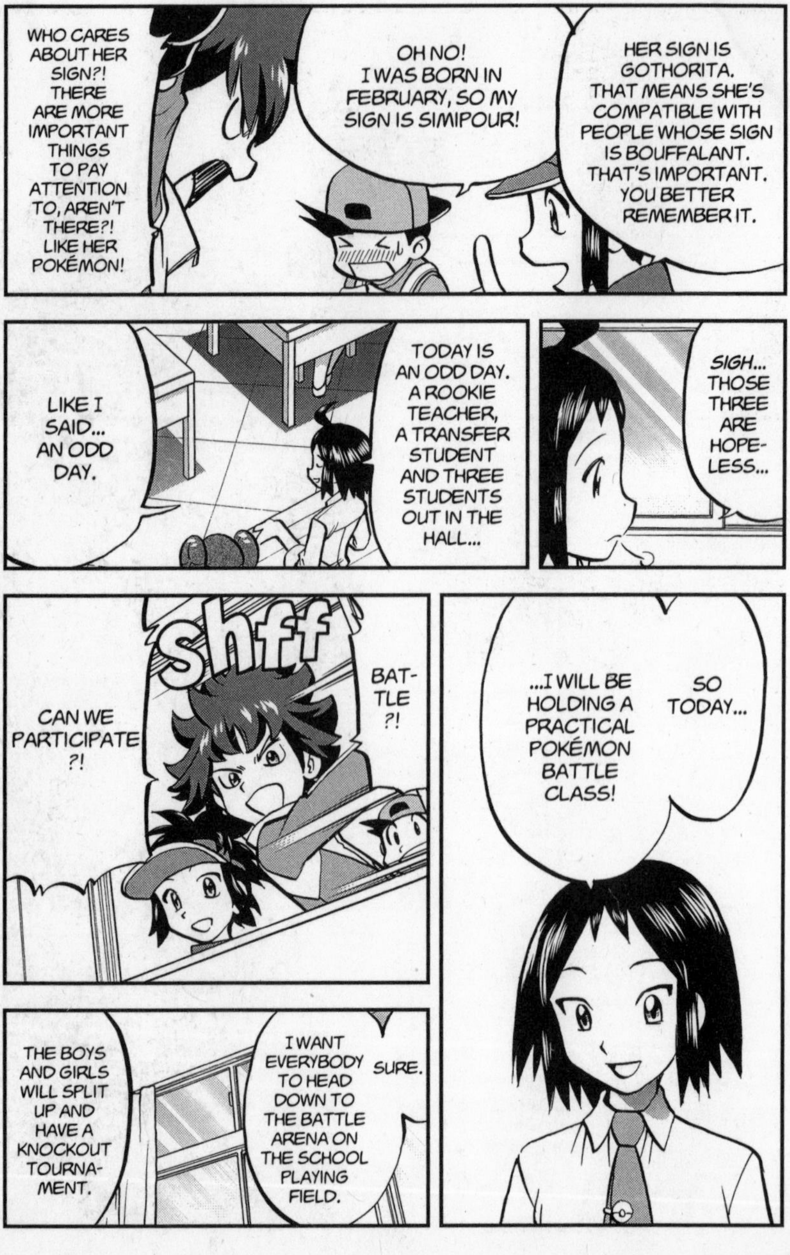
HER SIGN IS GOTHORITA. THAT MEANS SHE'S COMPATIBLE WITH PEOPLE WHOSE SIGN IS BOUFFALANT. THAT'S IMPORTANT. YOU BETTER REMEMBER IT.
OH NO! I WAS BORN IN FEBRUARY, SO MY SIGN IS SIMIPOUR!
WHO CARES ABOUT HER SIGN?! THERE ARE MORE IMPORTANT THINGS TO PAY ATTENTION TO, AREN'T THERE?! LIKE HER POKÉMON!
SIGH... THOSE THREE ARE HOPELESS...
TODAY IS AN ODD DAY. A ROOKIE TEACHER, A TRANSFER STUDENT AND THREE STUDENTS OUT IN THE HALL...
LIKE I SAID... AN ODD DAY.
SO TODAY...
...I WILL BE HOLDING A PRACTICAL POKÉMON BATTLE CLASS!
shff
BATTLE?!
CAN WE PARTICIPATE?!
SURE.
I WANT EVERYBODY TO HEAD DOWN TO THE BATTLE ARENA ON THE SCHOOL PLAYING FIELD.
THE BOYS AND GIRLS WILL SPLIT UP AND HAVE A KNOCKOUT TOURNAMENT.

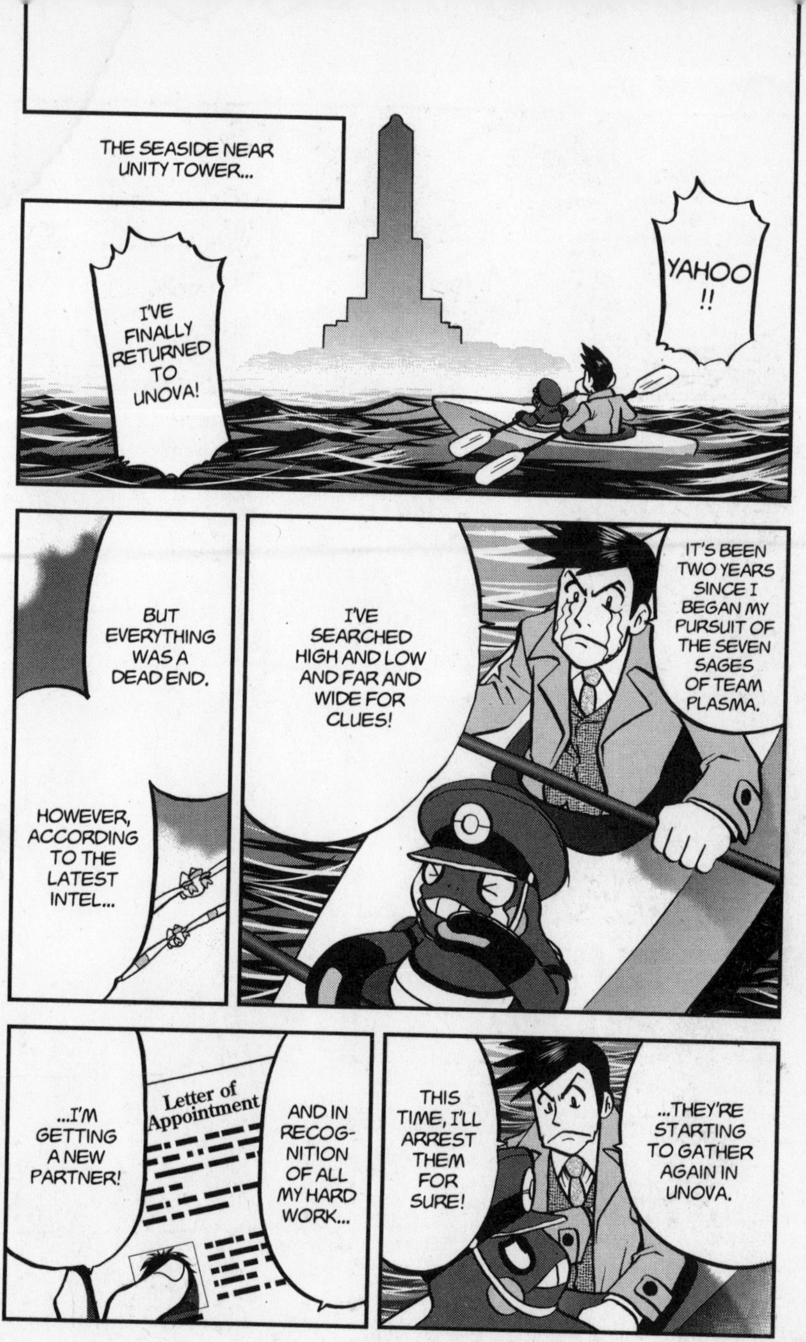
THE SEASIDE NEAR UNITY TOWER...
YAHOO!!
I'VE FINALLY RETURNED TO UNOVA!
IT'S BEEN TWO YEARS SINCE I BEGAN MY PURSUIT OF THE SEVEN SAGES OF TEAM PLASMA.
I'VE SEARCHED HIGH AND LOW AND FAR AND WIDE FOR CLUES!
BUT EVERYTHING WAS A DEAD END.
HOWEVER, ACCORDING TO THE LATEST INTEL...
...THEY'RE STARTING TO GATHER AGAIN IN UNOVA.
THIS TIME, I'LL ARREST THEM FOR SURE!
AND IN RECOGNITION OF ALL MY HARD WORK...
...I'M GETTING A NEW PARTNER!
Letter of Appointment

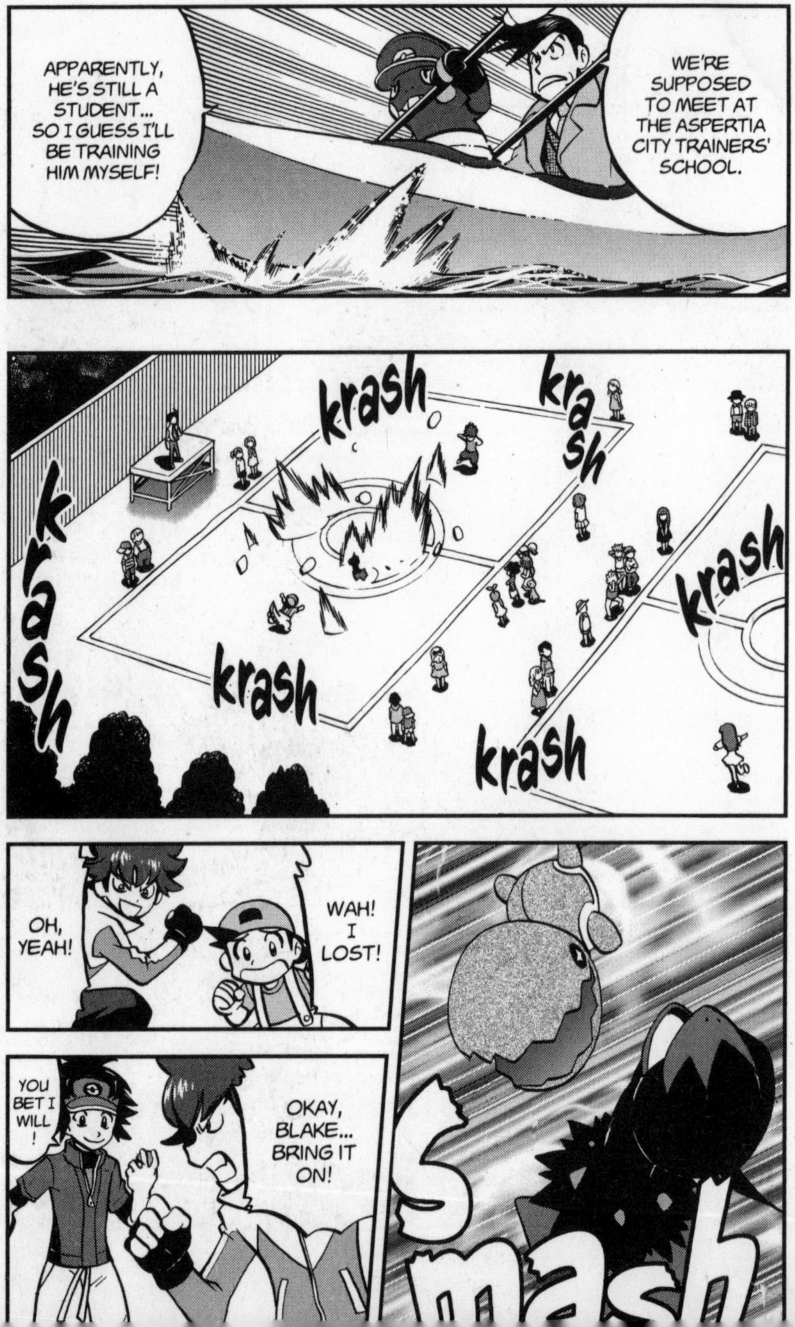
WE'RE SUPPOSED TO MEET AT THE ASPERTIA CITY TRAINERS' SCHOOL.
APPARENTLY, HE'S STILL A STUDENT... SO I GUESS I'LL BE TRAINING HIM MYSELF!
krash
krash
krash
krash
krash
krash
smash
WAH! I LOST!
OH, YEAH!
OKAY, BLAKE... BRING IT ON!
YOU BET I WILL!

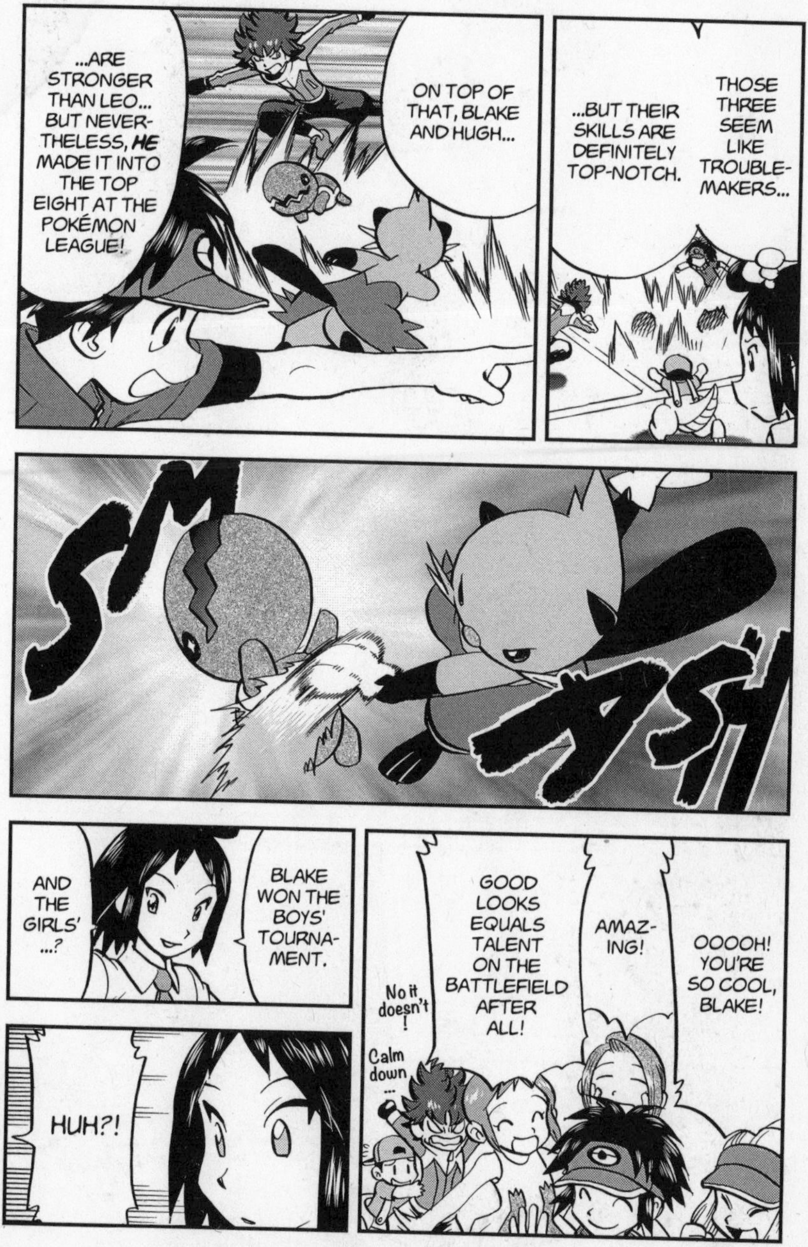
THOSE THREE SEEM LIKE TROUBLE-MAKERS...
...BUT THEIR SKILLS ARE DEFINITELY TOP-NOTCH.
ON TOP OF THAT, BLAKE AND HUGH...
...ARE STRONGER THAN LEO... BUT NEVER-THELESS, *HE* MADE IT INTO THE TOP EIGHT AT THE POKÉMON LEAGUE!
SMASH
OOOOH! YOU'RE SO COOL, BLAKE!
AMAZ-ING!
GOOD LOOKS EQUALS TALENT ON THE BATTLEFIELD AFTER ALL!
No it doesn't!
Calm down...
BLAKE WON THE BOYS' TOURNA-MENT.
AND THE GIRLS'...?
HUH?!

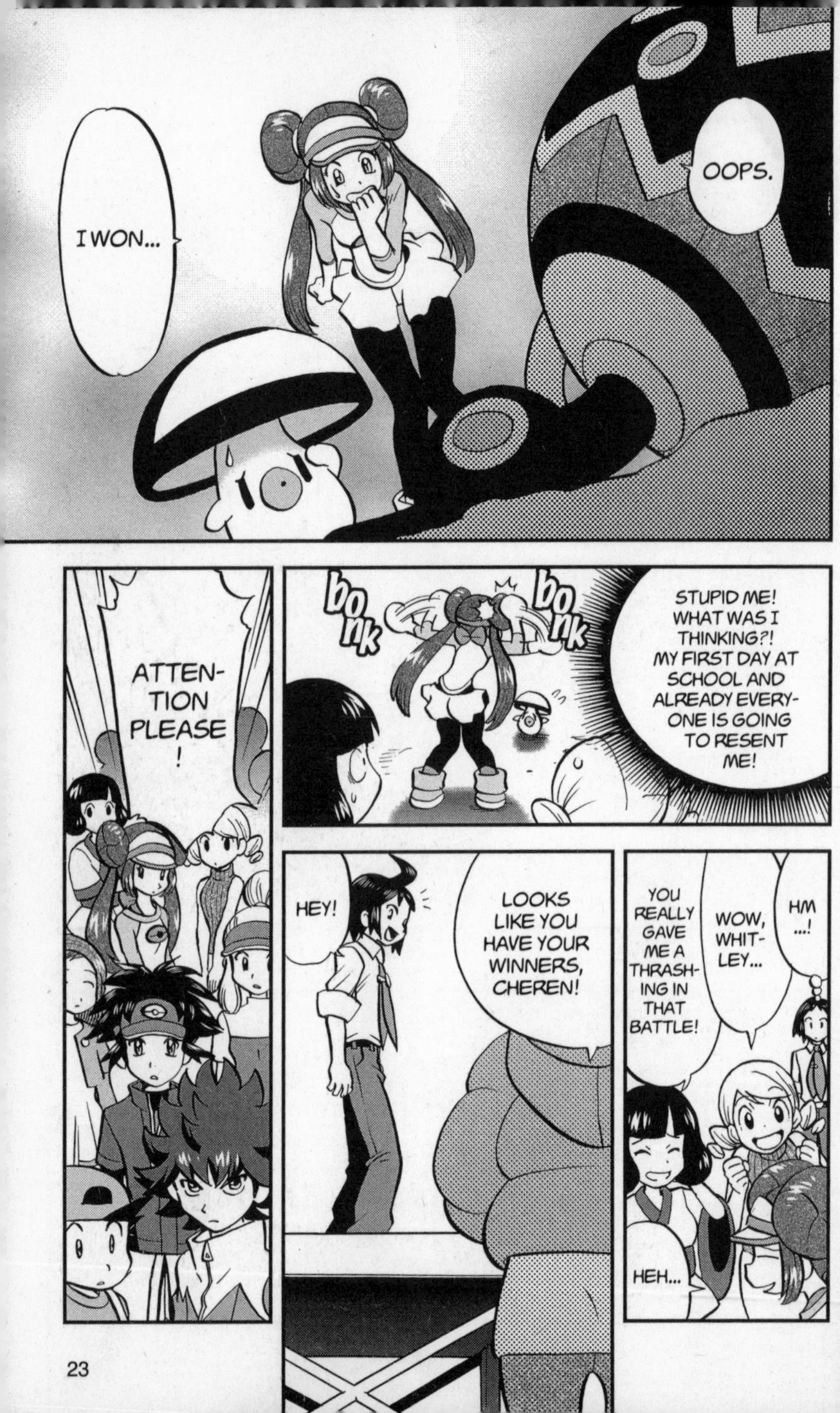
OOPS.
I WON...
STUPID ME! WHAT WAS I THINKING?! MY FIRST DAY AT SCHOOL AND ALREADY EVERY-ONE IS GOING TO RESENT ME!
bonk
bonk
HM ...!
WOW, WHIT-LEY...
YOU REALLY GAVE ME A THRASH-ING IN THAT BATTLE!
HEH...
LOOKS LIKE YOU HAVE YOUR WINNERS, CHEREN!
HEY!
ATTEN-TION PLEASE !

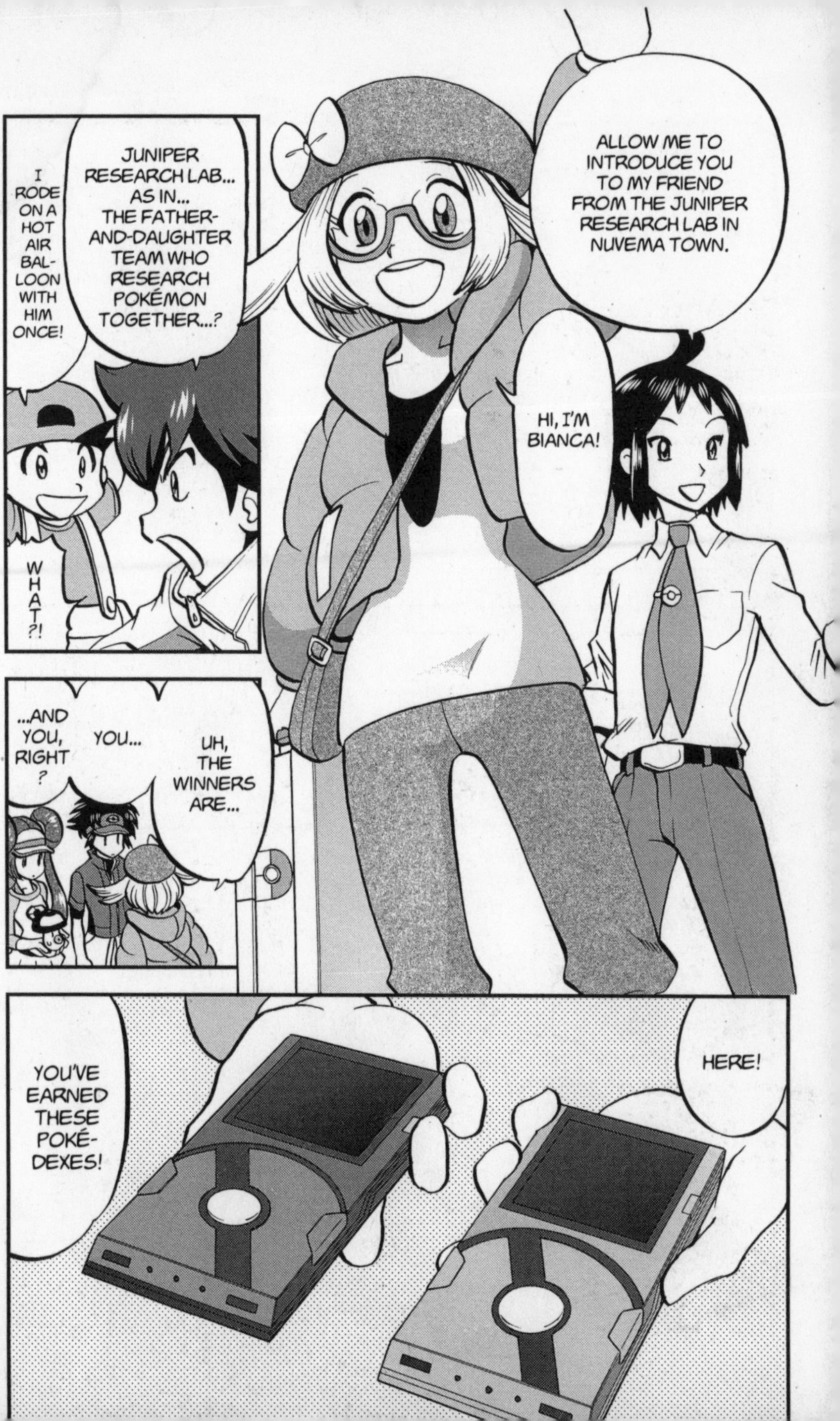
ALLOW ME TO INTRODUCE YOU TO MY FRIEND FROM THE JUNIPER RESEARCH LAB IN NUVEMA TOWN.
HI, I'M BIANCA!
JUNIPER RESEARCH LAB... AS IN... THE FATHER-AND-DAUGHTER TEAM WHO RESEARCH POKÉMON TOGETHER...?
I RODE ON A HOT AIR BALLOON WITH HIM ONCE!
WHAT?!
UH, THE WINNERS ARE...
YOU...
...AND YOU, RIGHT?
HERE!
YOU'VE EARNED THESE POKÉDEXES!

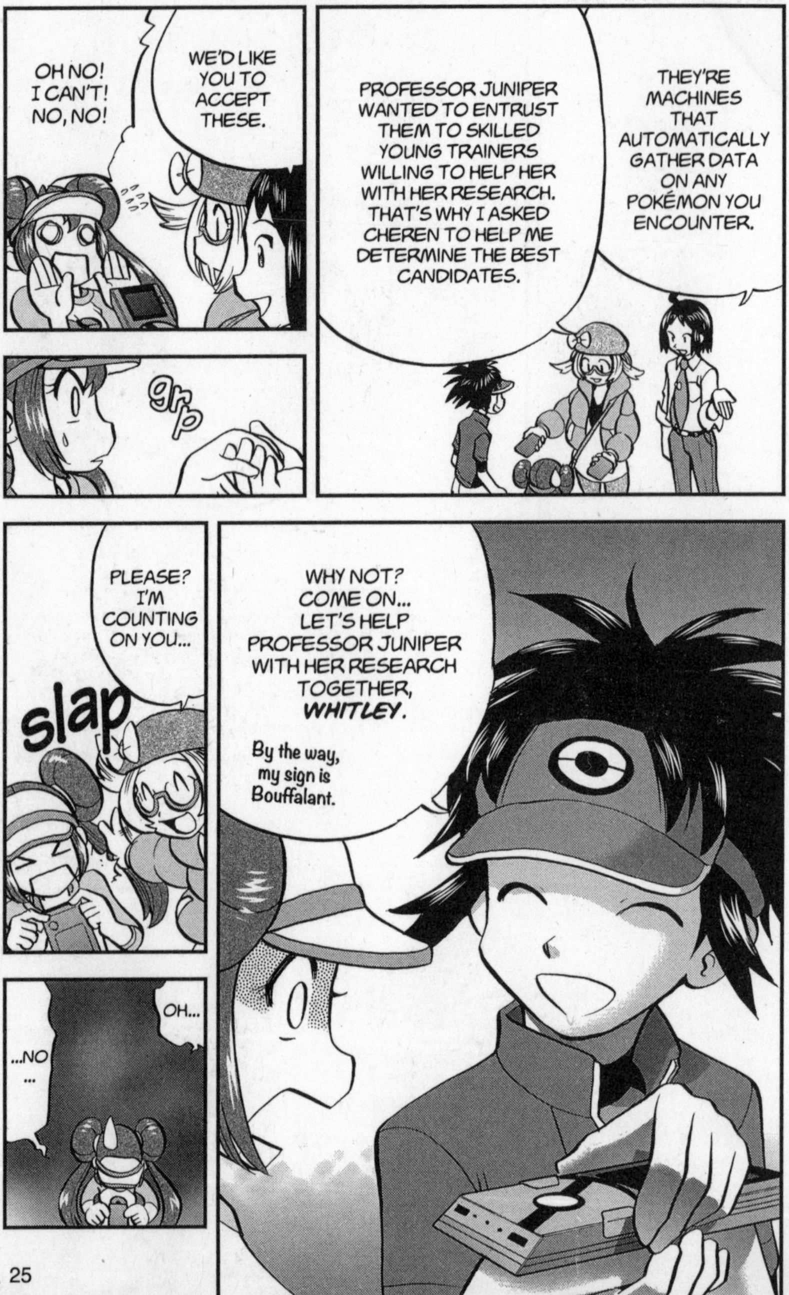
THEY'RE MACHINES THAT AUTOMATICALLY GATHER DATA ON ANY POKÉMON YOU ENCOUNTER.
PROFESSOR JUNIPER WANTED TO ENTRUST THEM TO SKILLED YOUNG TRAINERS WILLING TO HELP HER WITH HER RESEARCH. THAT'S WHY I ASKED CHEREN TO HELP ME DETERMINE THE BEST CANDIDATES.
WE'D LIKE YOU TO ACCEPT THESE.
OH NO! I CAN'T! NO, NO!
grp
WHY NOT? COME ON... LET'S HELP PROFESSOR JUNIPER WITH HER RESEARCH TOGETHER, ***WHITLEY***.
By the way, my sign is Bouffalant.
PLEASE? I'M COUNTING ON YOU...
slap
OH...
...NO ...

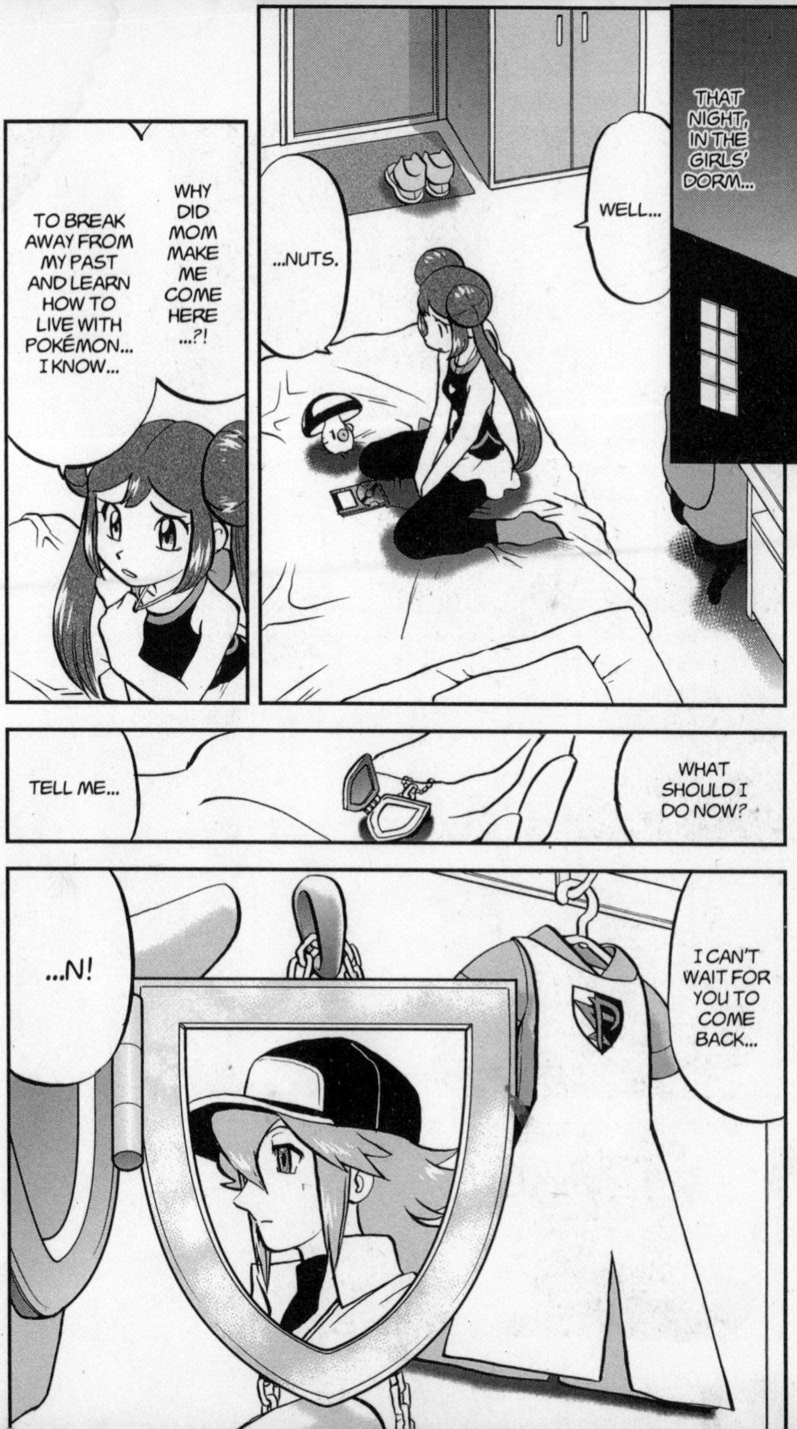
THAT NIGHT, IN THE GIRLS' DORM...
WELL...
...NUTS.
WHY DID MOM MAKE ME COME HERE ...?!
TO BREAK AWAY FROM MY PAST AND LEARN HOW TO LIVE WITH POKÉMON... I KNOW...
WHAT SHOULD I DO NOW?
TELL ME...
I CAN'T WAIT FOR YOU TO COME BACK...
...N!

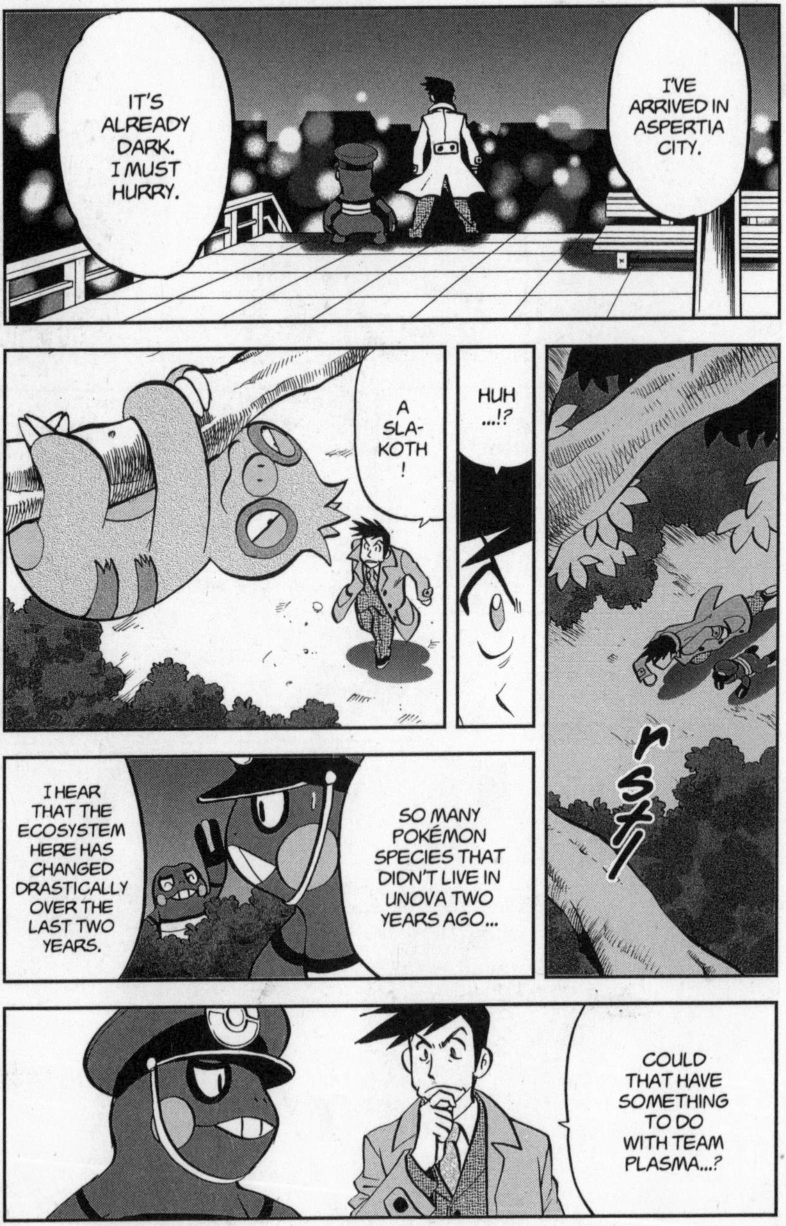

I'VE ARRIVED IN ASPERTIA CITY.
IT'S ALREADY DARK. I MUST HURRY.
rstl
HUH ...!?
A SLA-KOTH!
SO MANY POKÉMON SPECIES THAT DIDN'T LIVE IN UNOVA TWO YEARS AGO...
I HEAR THAT THE ECOSYSTEM HERE HAS CHANGED DRASTICALLY OVER THE LAST TWO YEARS.
COULD THAT HAVE SOMETHING TO DO WITH TEAM PLASMA...?

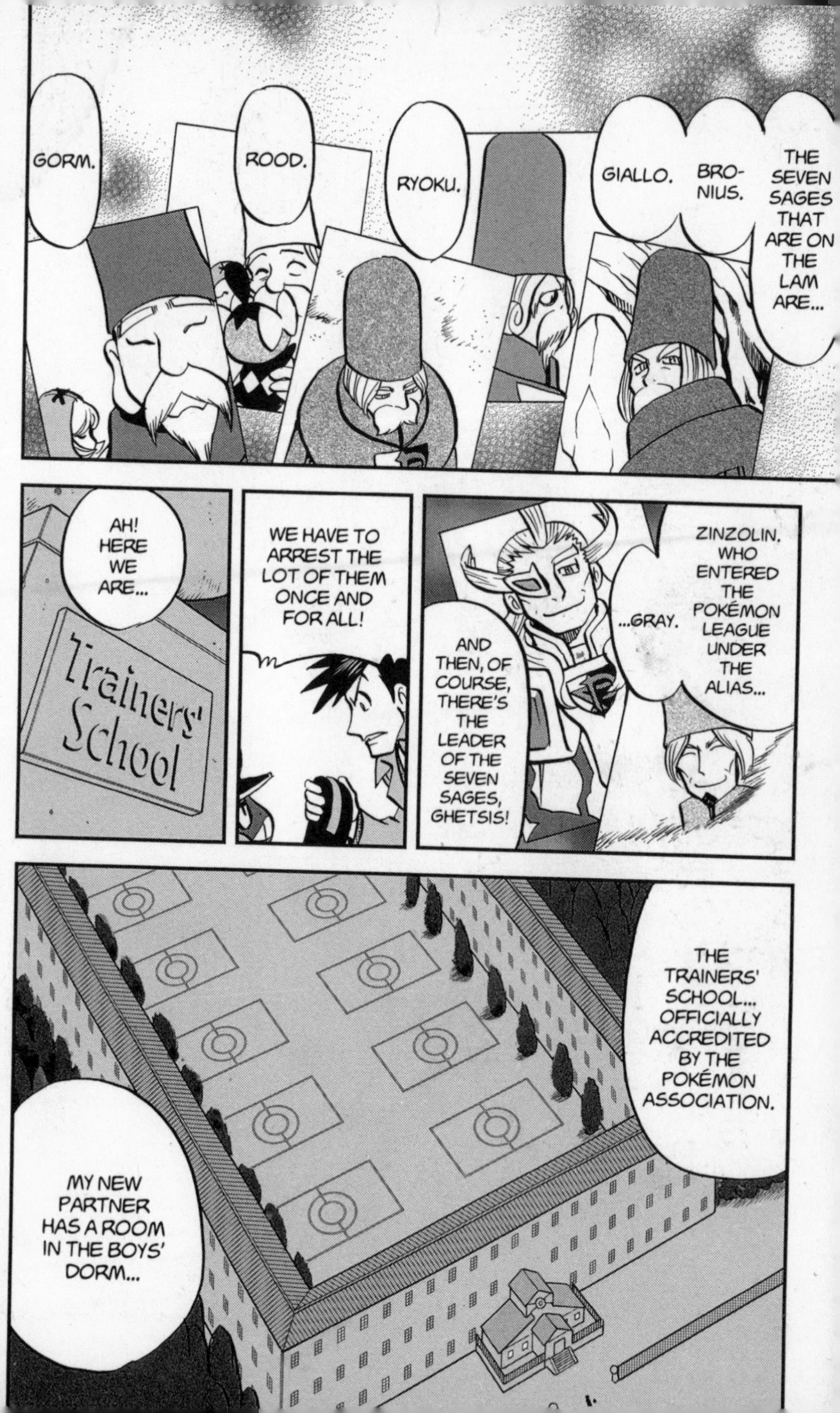
THE SEVEN SAGES THAT ARE ON THE LAM ARE...
BRONIUS.
GIALLO.
RYOKU.
ROOD.
GORM.
ZINZOLIN, WHO ENTERED THE POKÉMON LEAGUE UNDER THE ALIAS...
...GRAY.
AND THEN, OF COURSE, THERE'S THE LEADER OF THE SEVEN SAGES, GHETSIS!
WE HAVE TO ARREST THE LOT OF THEM ONCE AND FOR ALL!
AH! HERE WE ARE...
Trainers' School
THE TRAINERS' SCHOOL... OFFICIALLY ACCREDITED BY THE POKÉMON ASSOCIATION.
MY NEW PARTNER HAS A ROOM IN THE BOYS' DORM...

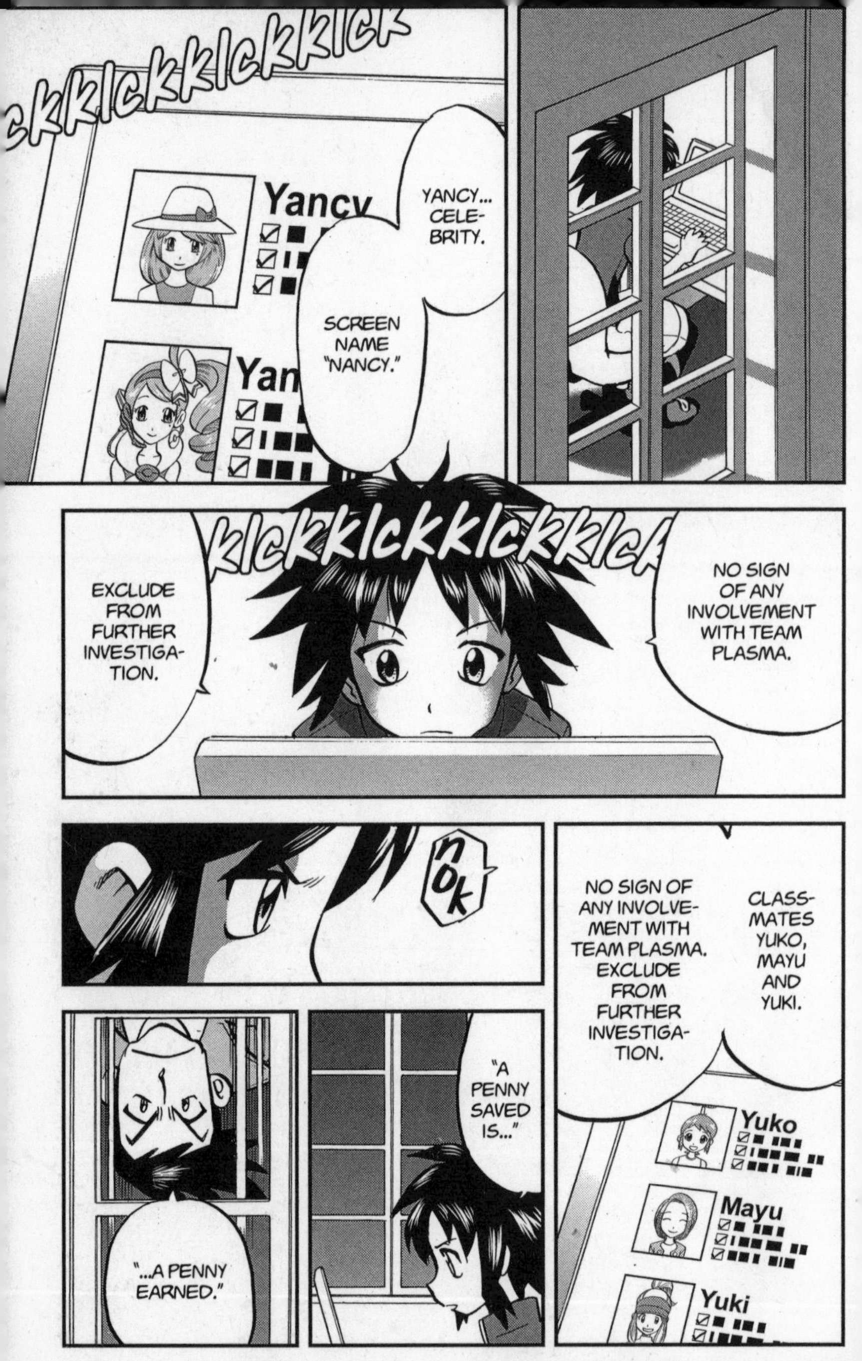
CKKLICKKLICK
Yancy
Yan
YANCY... CELEBRITY.
SCREEN NAME "NANCY."
KLICKKLICKKLICK
NO SIGN OF ANY INVOLVEMENT WITH TEAM PLASMA.
EXCLUDE FROM FURTHER INVESTIGATION.
CLASSMATES YUKO, MAYU AND YUKI.
NO SIGN OF ANY INVOLVEMENT WITH TEAM PLASMA. EXCLUDE FROM FURTHER INVESTIGATION.
Yuko
Mayu
Yuki
nok
"A PENNY SAVED IS..."
"...A PENNY EARNED."

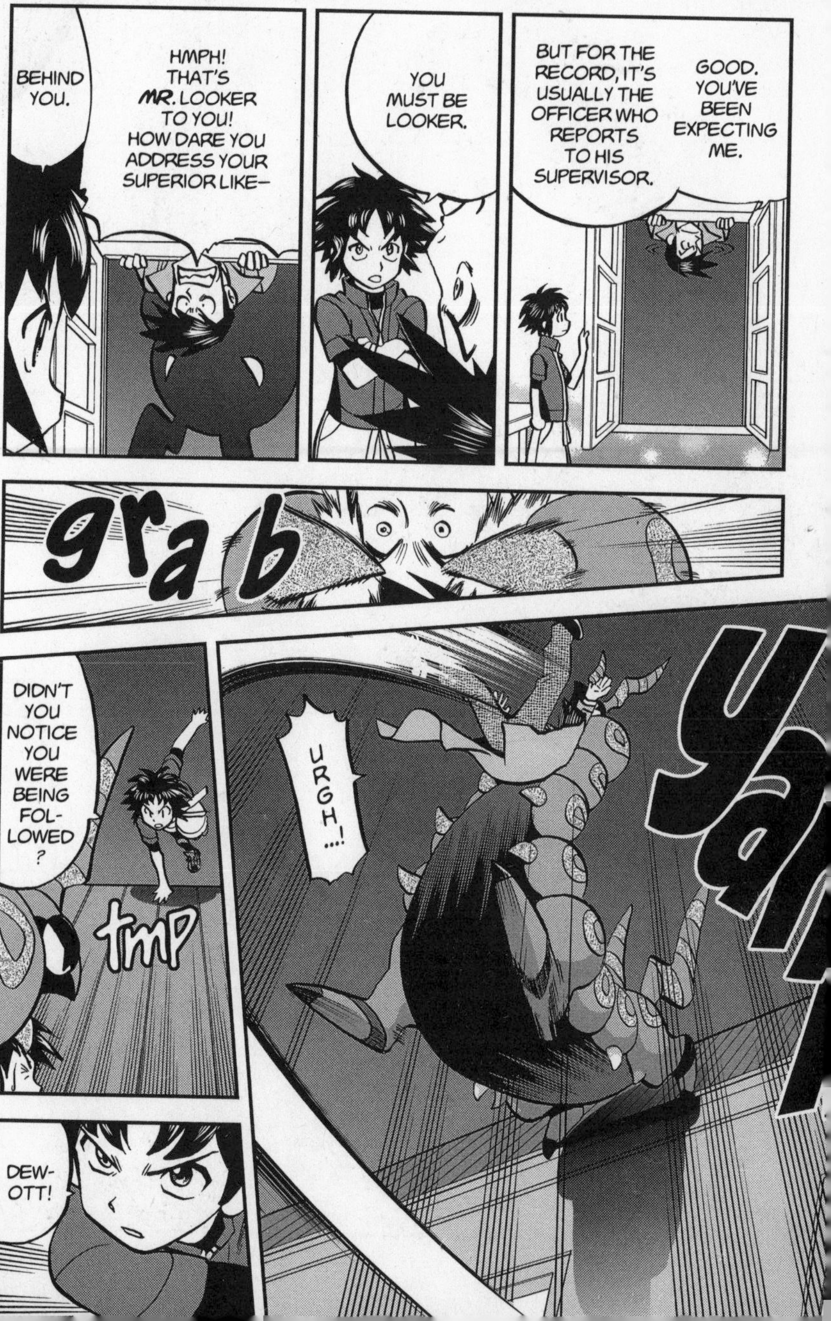
GOOD. YOU'VE BEEN EXPECTING ME.
BUT FOR THE RECORD, IT'S USUALLY THE OFFICER WHO REPORTS TO HIS SUPERVISOR.
YOU MUST BE LOOKER.
HMPH! THAT'S MR. LOOKER TO YOU! HOW DARE YOU ADDRESS YOUR SUPERIOR LIKE—
BEHIND YOU.
grab
URGH...!
DIDN'T YOU NOTICE YOU WERE BEING FOL-LOWED?
tmp
DEW-OTT!

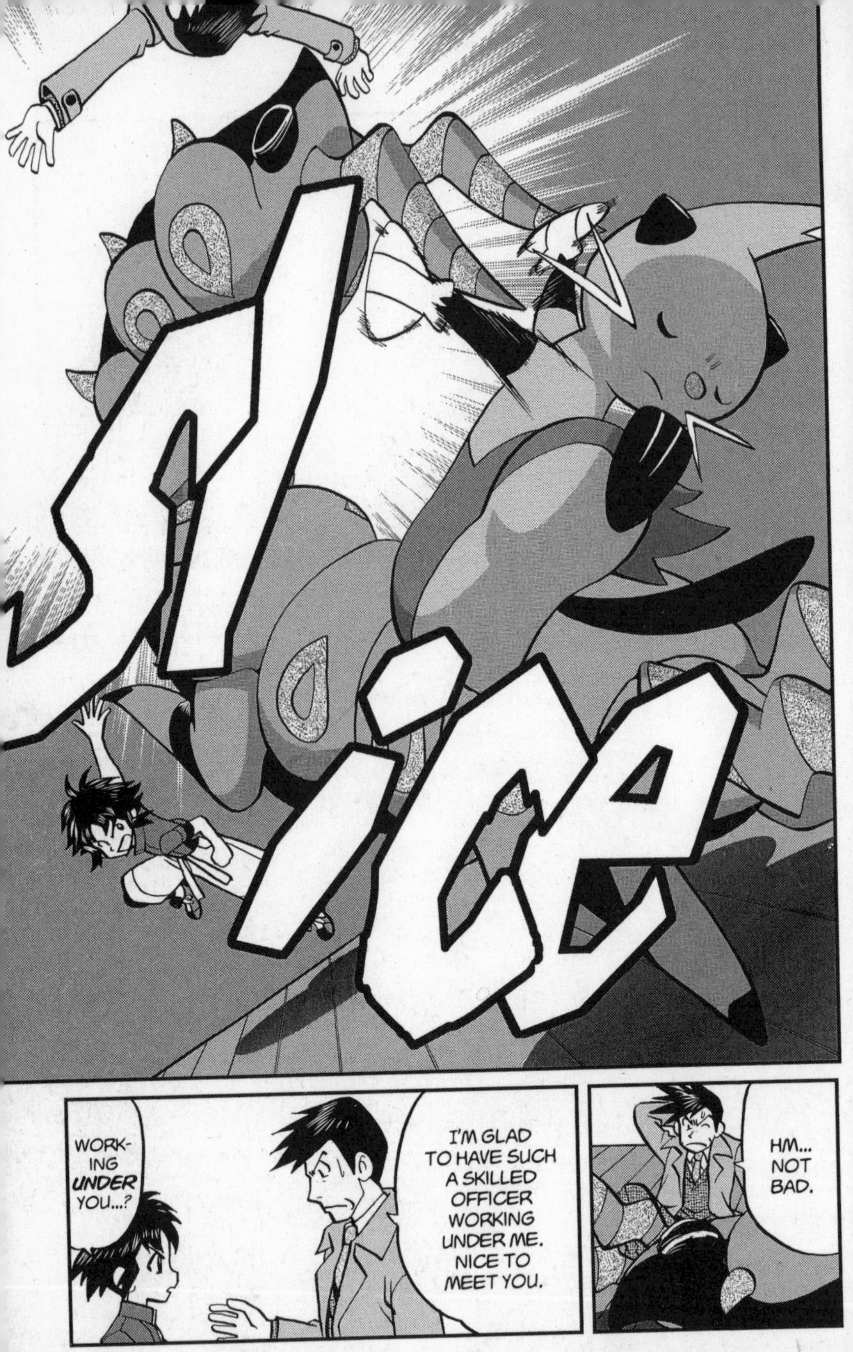
HM... NOT BAD.
I'M GLAD TO HAVE SUCH A SKILLED OFFICER WORKING UNDER ME. NICE TO MEET YOU.
WORK-ING UNDER YOU...?

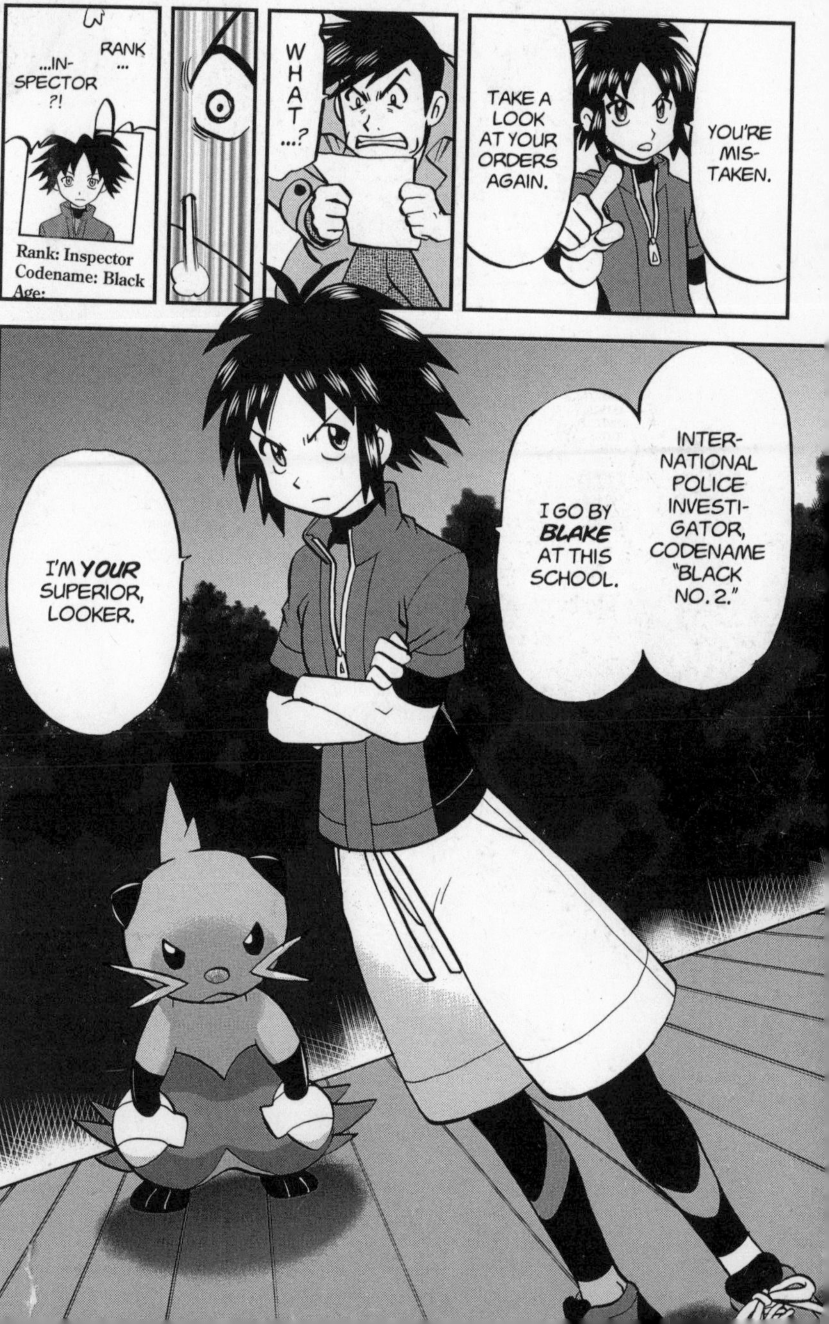
YOU'RE MIS-TAKEN.
TAKE A LOOK AT YOUR ORDERS AGAIN.
WHAT ...?
RANK ...
...IN-SPECTOR ?!
Rank: Inspector
Codename: Black
Age:
INTER-NATIONAL POLICE INVESTI-GATOR, CODENAME "BLACK NO. 2."
I GO BY BLAKE AT THIS SCHOOL.
I'M YOUR SUPERIOR, LOOKER.

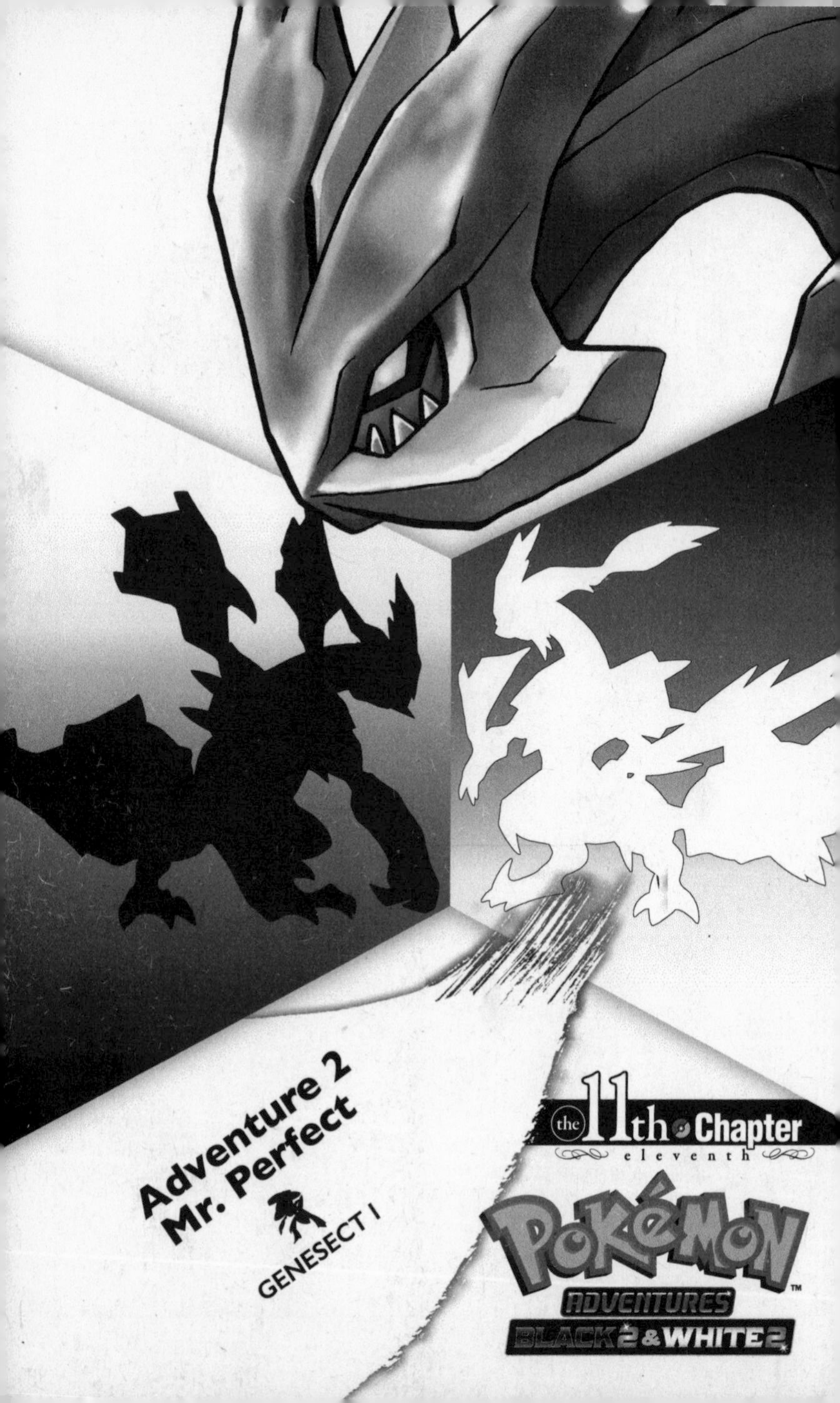
Adventure 2
Mr. Perfect
GENESECT I
the 11th Chapter
eleventh
POKéMON
ADVENTURES
BLACK 2 & WHITE 2

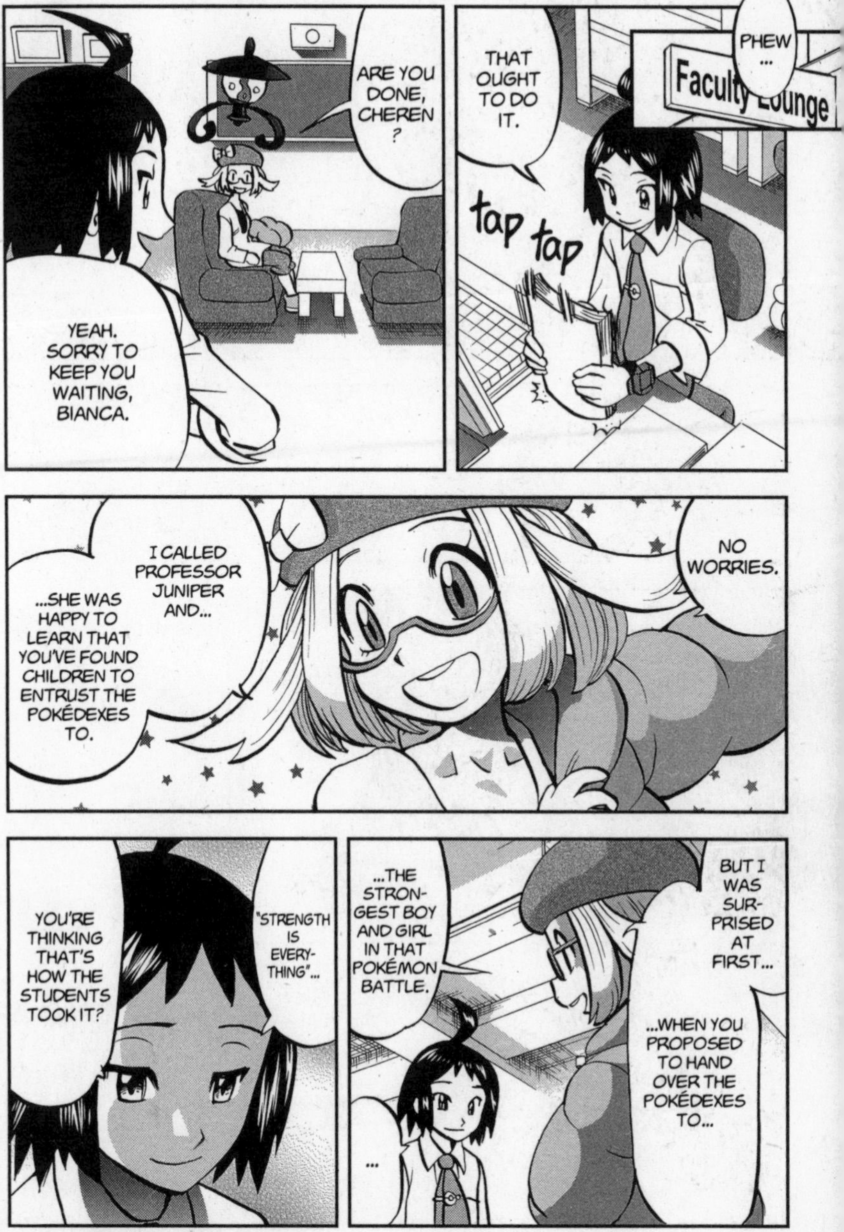
Faculty Lounge
PHEW ...
THAT OUGHT TO DO IT.
tap tap
ARE YOU DONE, CHEREN?
YEAH. SORRY TO KEEP YOU WAITING, BIANCA.
NO WORRIES.
I CALLED PROFESSOR JUNIPER AND...
...SHE WAS HAPPY TO LEARN THAT YOU'VE FOUND CHILDREN TO ENTRUST THE POKÉDEXES TO.
BUT I WAS SURPRISED AT FIRST...
...WHEN YOU PROPOSED TO HAND OVER THE POKÉDEXES TO...
...THE STRONGEST BOY AND GIRL IN THAT POKÉMON BATTLE.
...
"STRENGTH IS EVERYTHING"...
YOU'RE THINKING THAT'S HOW THE STUDENTS TOOK IT?

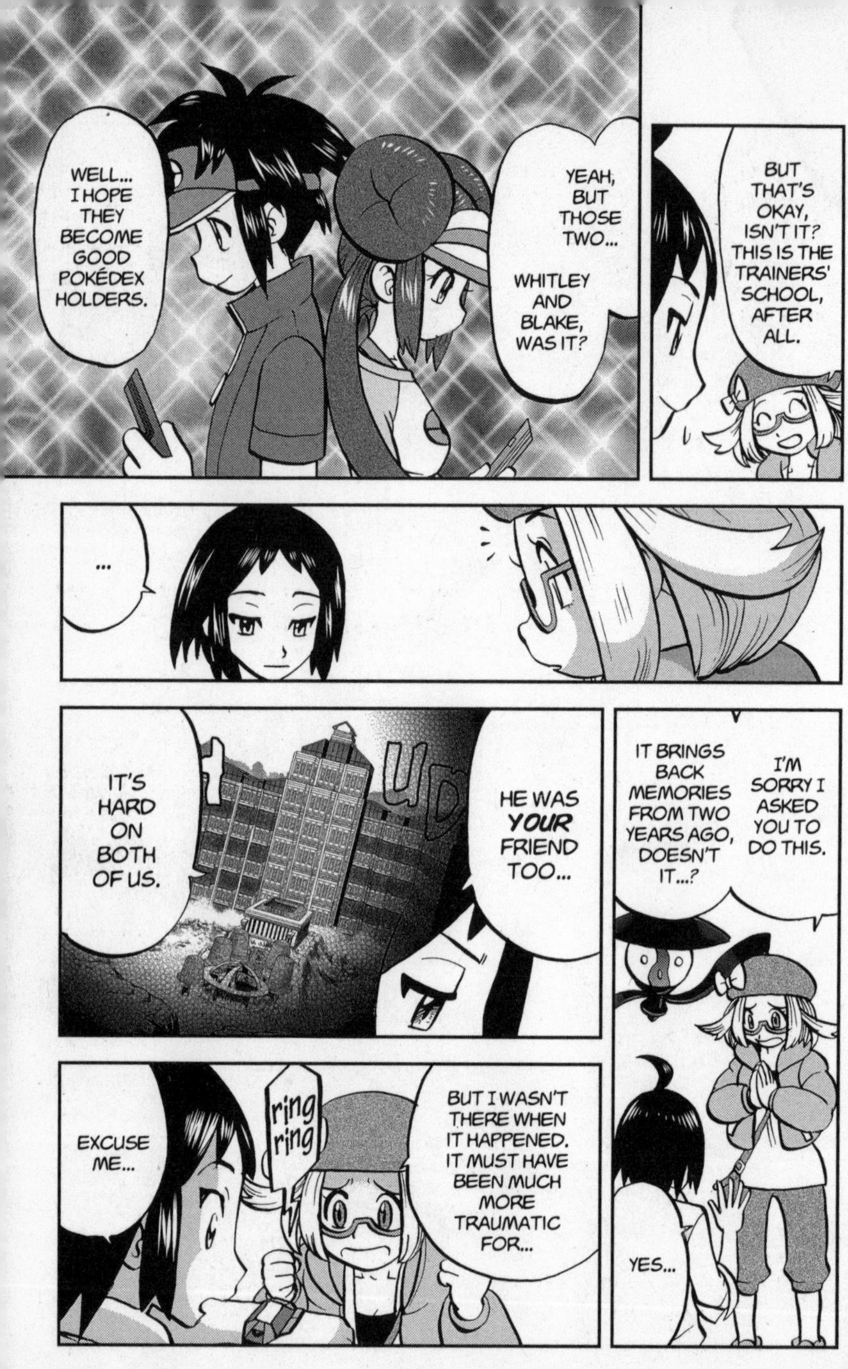

BUT THAT'S OKAY, ISN'T IT? THIS IS THE TRAINERS' SCHOOL, AFTER ALL.
YEAH, BUT THOSE TWO...
WHITLEY AND BLAKE, WAS IT?
WELL... I HOPE THEY BECOME GOOD POKÉDEX HOLDERS.
...
I'M SORRY I ASKED YOU TO DO THIS.
IT BRINGS BACK MEMORIES FROM TWO YEARS AGO, DOESN'T IT...?
YES...
HE WAS ***YOUR*** FRIEND TOO...
IT'S HARD ON BOTH OF US.
BUT I WASN'T THERE WHEN IT HAPPENED. IT MUST HAVE BEEN MUCH MORE TRAUMATIC FOR...
ring ring
EXCUSE ME...

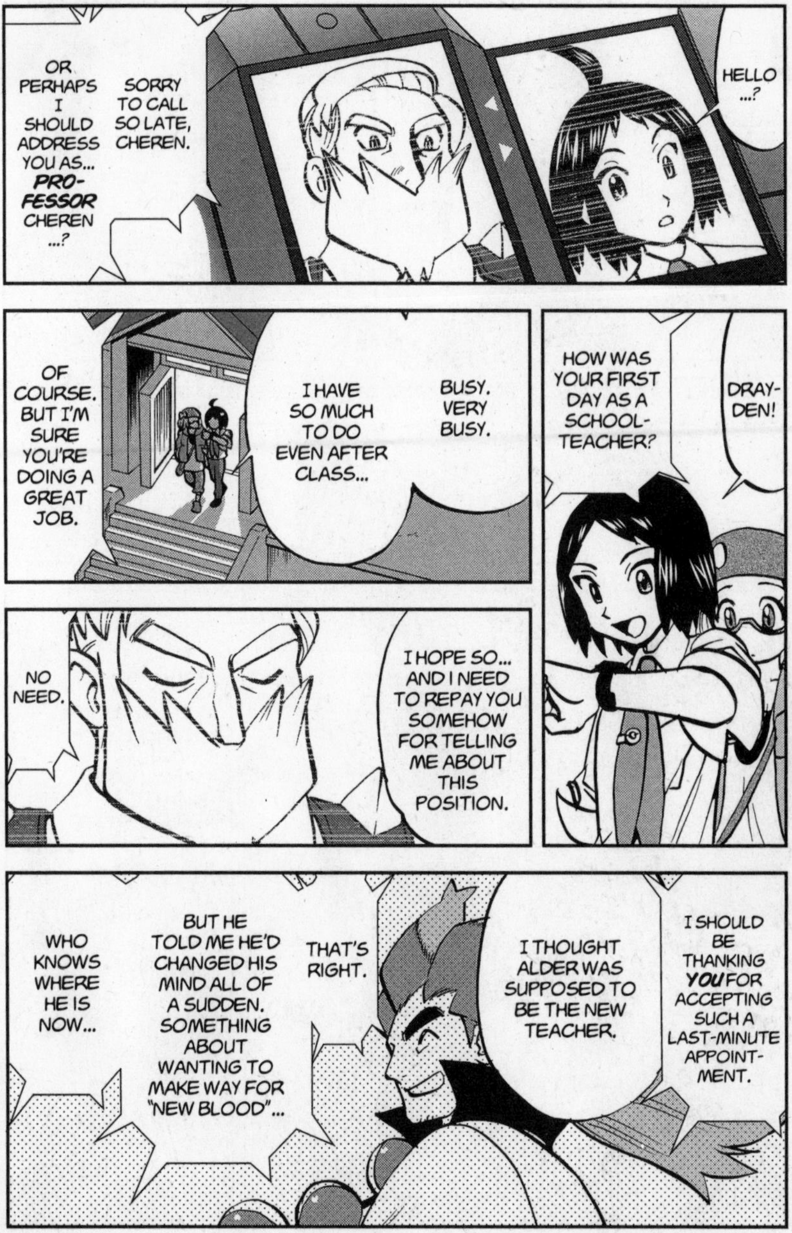
HELLO ...?
SORRY TO CALL SO LATE, CHEREN.
OR PERHAPS I SHOULD ADDRESS YOU AS... **PROFESSOR** CHEREN ...?
DRAYDEN!
HOW WAS YOUR FIRST DAY AS A SCHOOLTEACHER?
BUSY. VERY BUSY.
I HAVE SO MUCH TO DO EVEN AFTER CLASS...
OF COURSE. BUT I'M SURE YOU'RE DOING A GREAT JOB.
I HOPE SO... AND I NEED TO REPAY YOU SOMEHOW FOR TELLING ME ABOUT THIS POSITION.
NO NEED.
I SHOULD BE THANKING **YOU** FOR ACCEPTING SUCH A LAST-MINUTE APPOINTMENT.
I THOUGHT ALDER WAS SUPPOSED TO BE THE NEW TEACHER.
THAT'S RIGHT.
BUT HE TOLD ME HE'D CHANGED HIS MIND ALL OF A SUDDEN. SOMETHING ABOUT WANTING TO MAKE WAY FOR "NEW BLOOD"...
WHO KNOWS WHERE HE IS NOW...

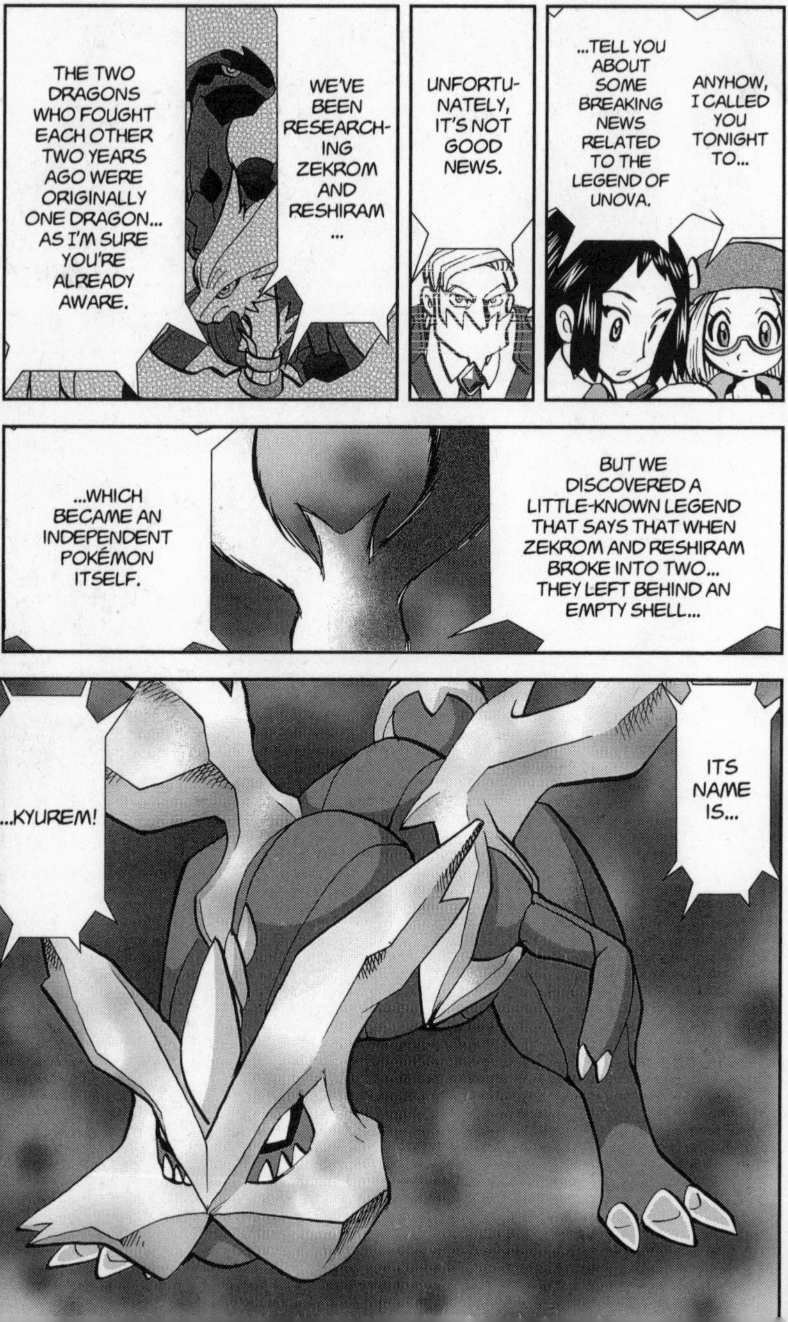
ANYHOW, I CALLED YOU TONIGHT TO...
...TELL YOU ABOUT SOME BREAKING NEWS RELATED TO THE LEGEND OF UNOVA.
UNFORTUNATELY, IT'S NOT GOOD NEWS.
WE'VE BEEN RESEARCHING ZEKROM AND RESHIRAM...
THE TWO DRAGONS WHO FOUGHT EACH OTHER TWO YEARS AGO WERE ORIGINALLY ONE DRAGON... AS I'M SURE YOU'RE ALREADY AWARE.
BUT WE DISCOVERED A LITTLE-KNOWN LEGEND THAT SAYS THAT WHEN ZEKROM AND RESHIRAM BROKE INTO TWO... THEY LEFT BEHIND AN EMPTY SHELL...
...WHICH BECAME AN INDEPENDENT POKÉMON ITSELF.
ITS NAME IS...
...KYUREM!

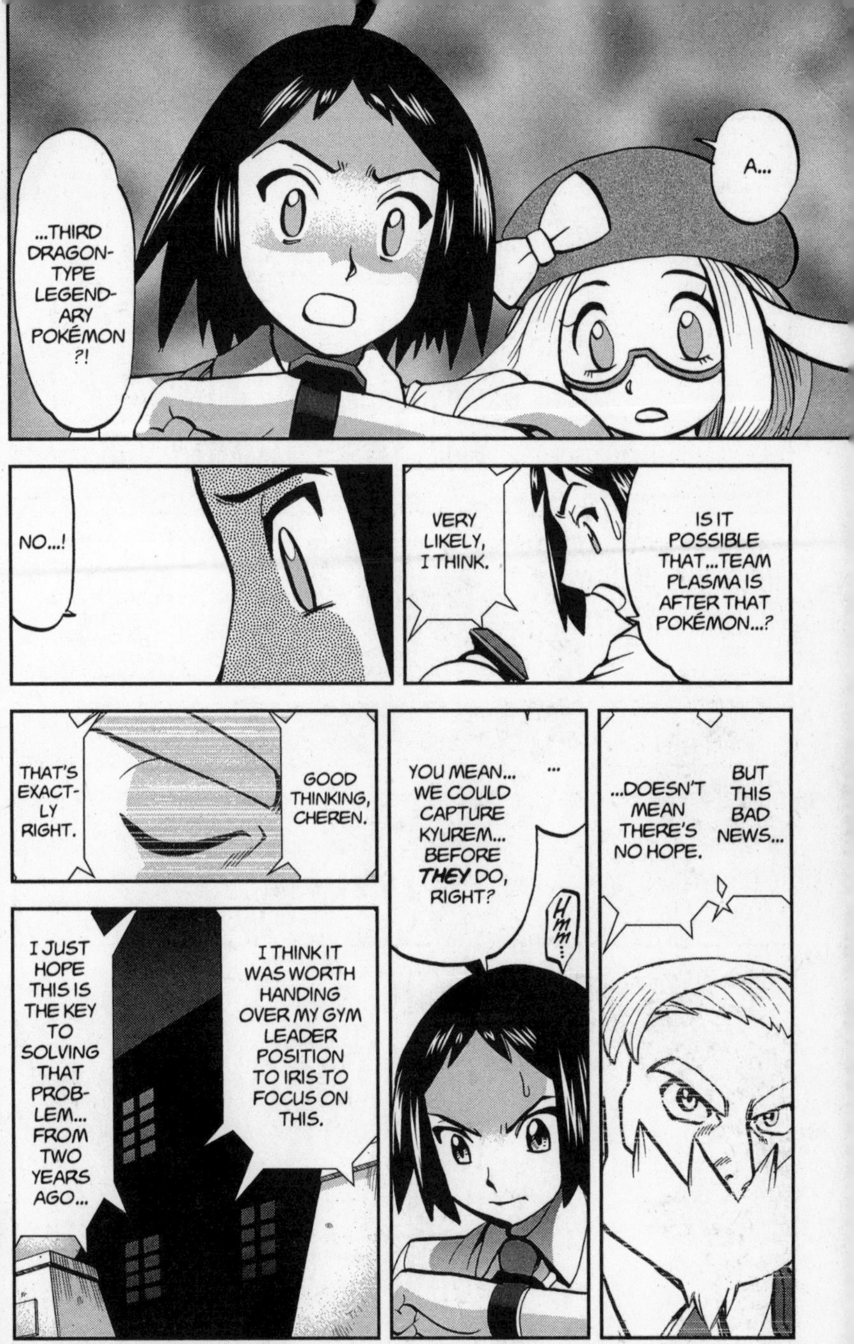
A...
...THIRD DRAGON-TYPE LEGENDARY POKÉMON?!
IS IT POSSIBLE THAT...TEAM PLASMA IS AFTER THAT POKÉMON...?
VERY LIKELY, I THINK.
NO...!
BUT THIS BAD NEWS...
...DOESN'T MEAN THERE'S NO HOPE.
...
YOU MEAN... WE COULD CAPTURE KYUREM... BEFORE THEY DO, RIGHT?
Hmm...
GOOD THINKING, CHEREN.
THAT'S EXACTLY RIGHT.
I THINK IT WAS WORTH HANDING OVER MY GYM LEADER POSITION TO IRIS TO FOCUS ON THIS.
I JUST HOPE THIS IS THE KEY TO SOLVING THAT PROBLEM... FROM TWO YEARS AGO...

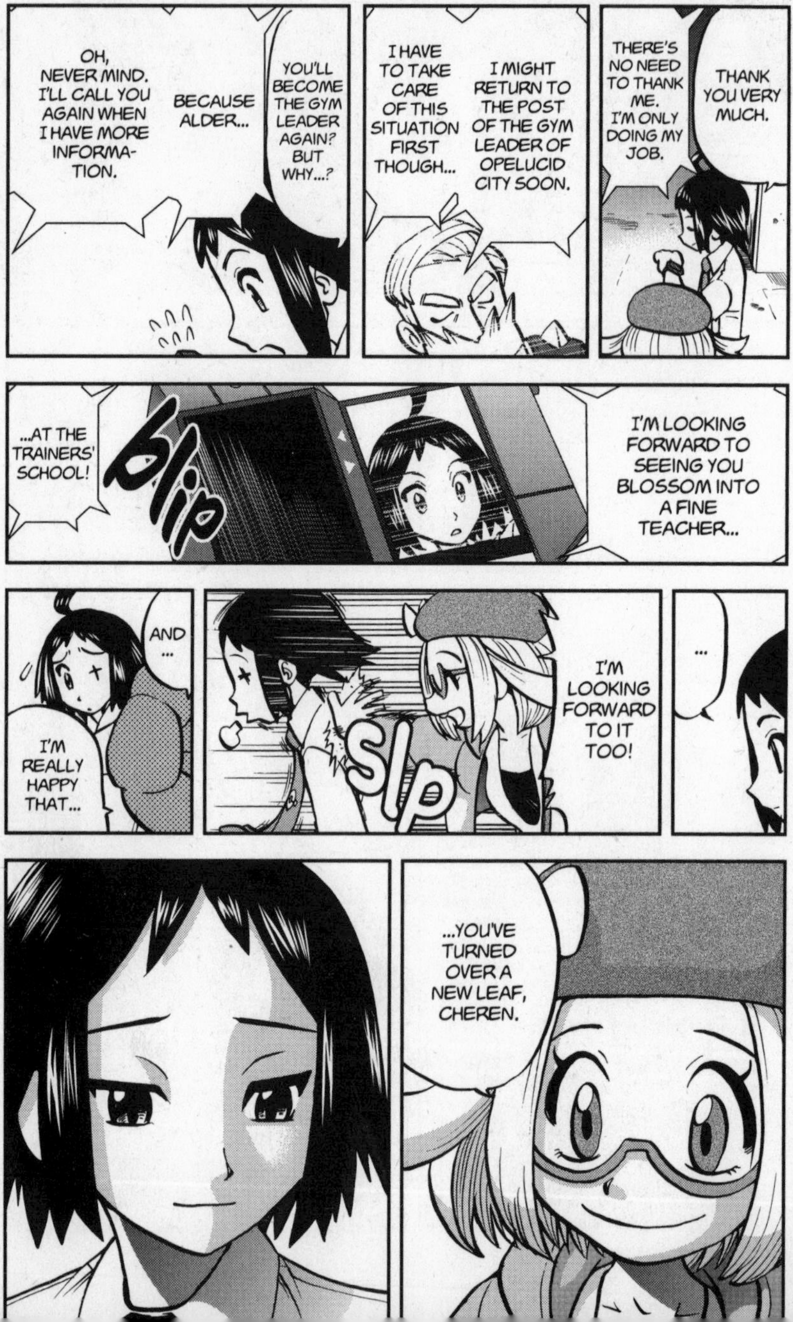
THANK YOU VERY MUCH.
THERE'S NO NEED TO THANK ME. I'M ONLY DOING MY JOB.
I MIGHT RETURN TO THE POST OF THE GYM LEADER OF OPELUCID CITY SOON.
I HAVE TO TAKE CARE OF THIS SITUATION FIRST THOUGH...
YOU'LL BECOME THE GYM LEADER AGAIN? BUT WHY...?
BECAUSE ALDER...
OH, NEVER MIND. I'LL CALL YOU AGAIN WHEN I HAVE MORE INFORMATION.
I'M LOOKING FORWARD TO SEEING YOU BLOSSOM INTO A FINE TEACHER...
blip
...AT THE TRAINERS' SCHOOL!
...
I'M LOOKING FORWARD TO IT TOO!
Slp
AND...
I'M REALLY HAPPY THAT...
...YOU'VE TURNED OVER A NEW LEAF, CHEREN.

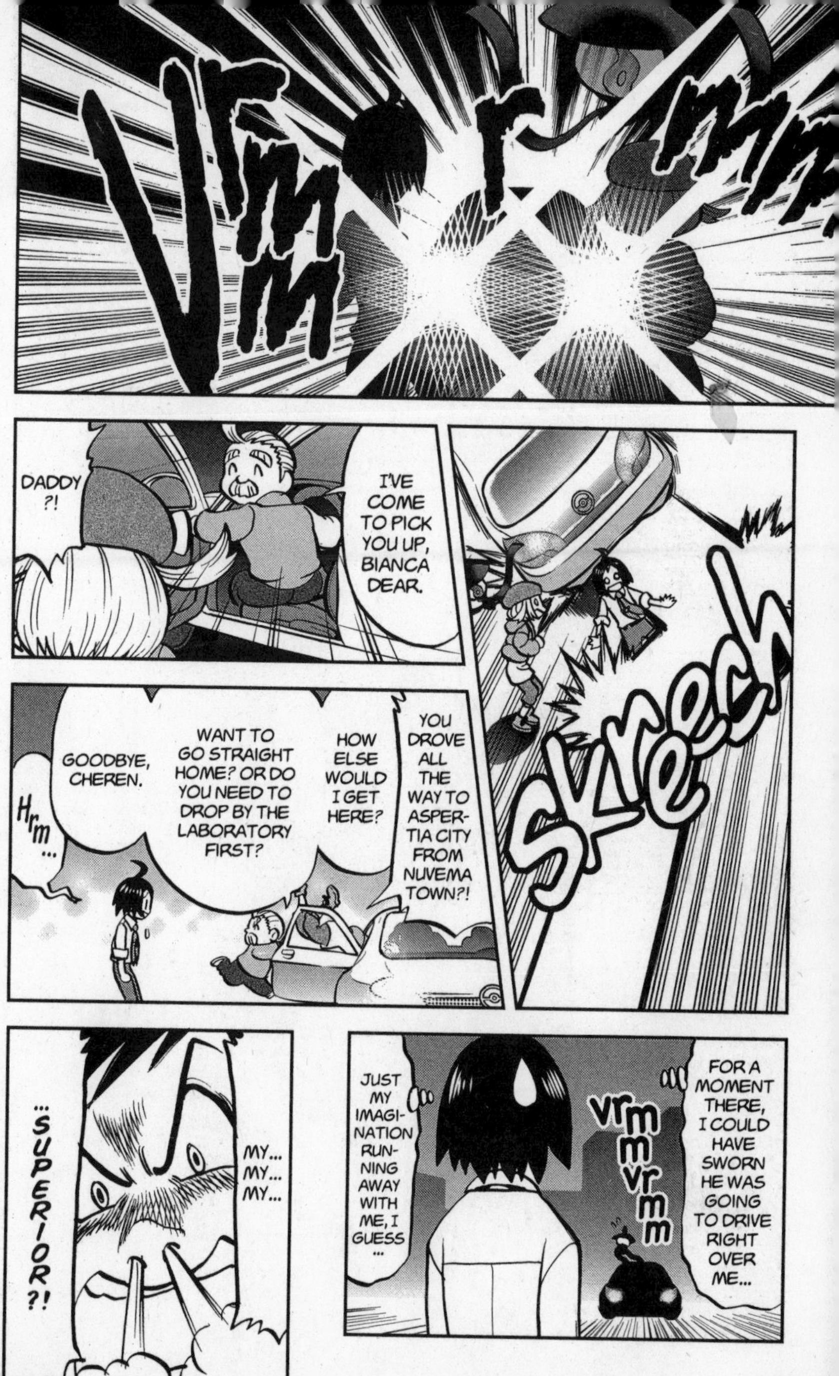
Skreech
I'VE COME TO PICK YOU UP, BIANCA DEAR.
DADDY?!
YOU DROVE ALL THE WAY TO ASPERTIA CITY FROM NUVEMA TOWN?!
HOW ELSE WOULD I GET HERE?
WANT TO GO STRAIGHT HOME? OR DO YOU NEED TO DROP BY THE LABORATORY FIRST?
GOODBYE, CHEREN.
Hrm...
FOR A MOMENT THERE, I COULD HAVE SWORN HE WAS GOING TO DRIVE RIGHT OVER ME...
vrmm vrmm
JUST MY IMAGINATION RUNNING AWAY WITH ME, I GUESS...
MY... MY... MY...
...SUPERIOR?!

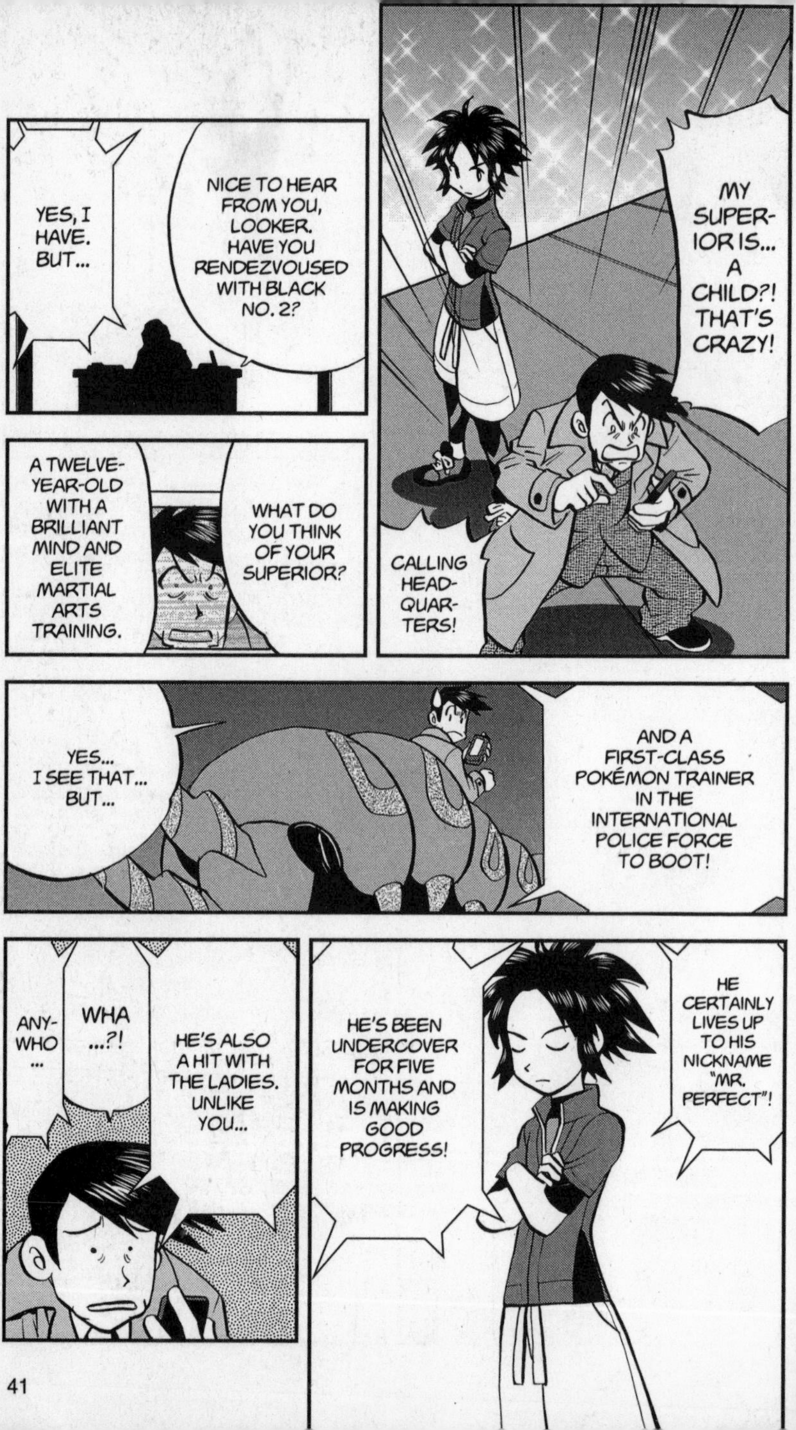
MY SUPERIOR IS... A CHILD?! THAT'S CRAZY!
CALLING HEADQUARTERS!
NICE TO HEAR FROM YOU, LOOKER. HAVE YOU RENDEZVOUSED WITH BLACK NO. 2?
YES, I HAVE. BUT...
WHAT DO YOU THINK OF YOUR SUPERIOR?
A TWELVE-YEAR-OLD WITH A BRILLIANT MIND AND ELITE MARTIAL ARTS TRAINING.
AND A FIRST-CLASS POKÉMON TRAINER IN THE INTERNATIONAL POLICE FORCE TO BOOT!
YES... I SEE THAT... BUT...
HE CERTAINLY LIVES UP TO HIS NICKNAME "MR. PERFECT"!
HE'S BEEN UNDERCOVER FOR FIVE MONTHS AND IS MAKING GOOD PROGRESS!
HE'S ALSO A HIT WITH THE LADIES. UNLIKE YOU...
WHA...?!
ANYWHO...

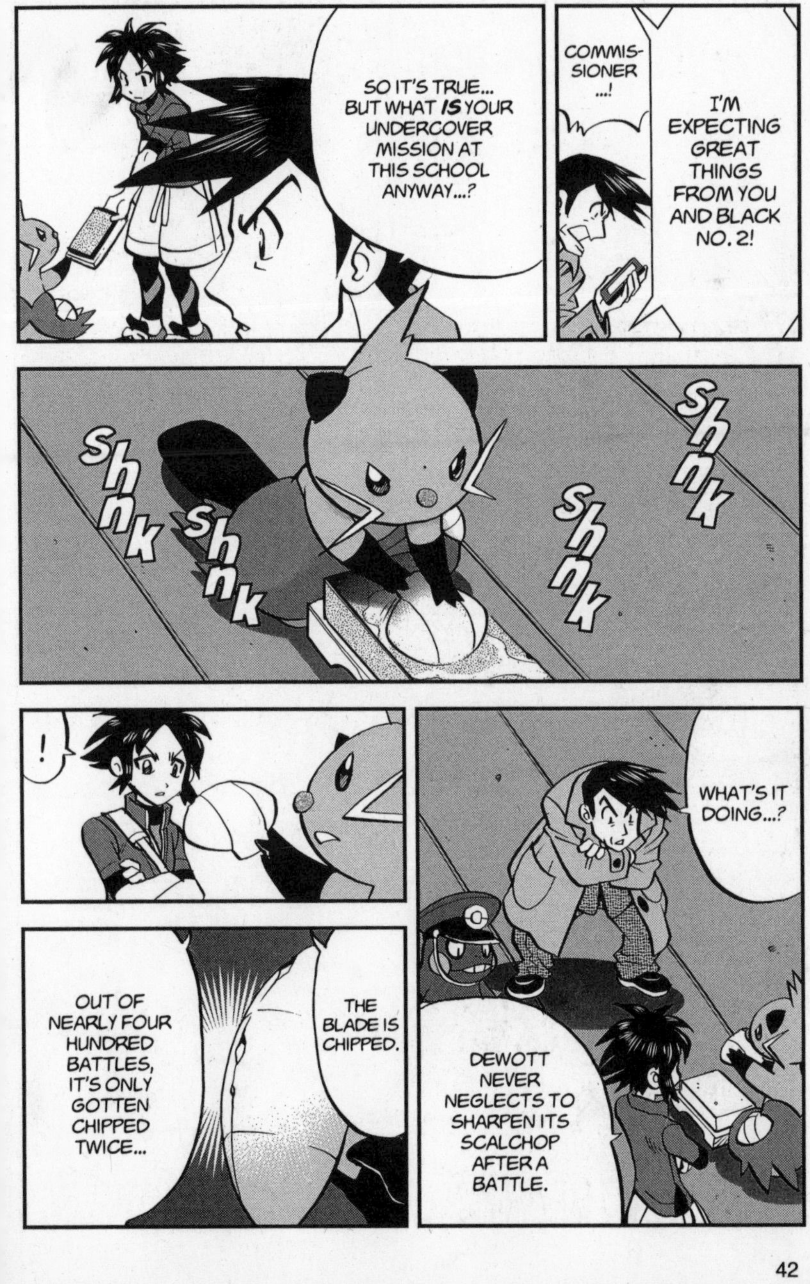
COMMIS-SIONER ...!
I'M EXPECTING GREAT THINGS FROM YOU AND BLACK NO. 2!
SO IT'S TRUE... BUT WHAT **IS** YOUR UNDERCOVER MISSION AT THIS SCHOOL ANYWAY...?
Shnk
Shnk
Shnk
Shnk
WHAT'S IT DOING...?
DEWOTT NEVER NEGLECTS TO SHARPEN ITS SCALCHOP AFTER A BATTLE.
!
THE BLADE IS CHIPPED.
OUT OF NEARLY FOUR HUNDRED BATTLES, IT'S ONLY GOTTEN CHIPPED TWICE...

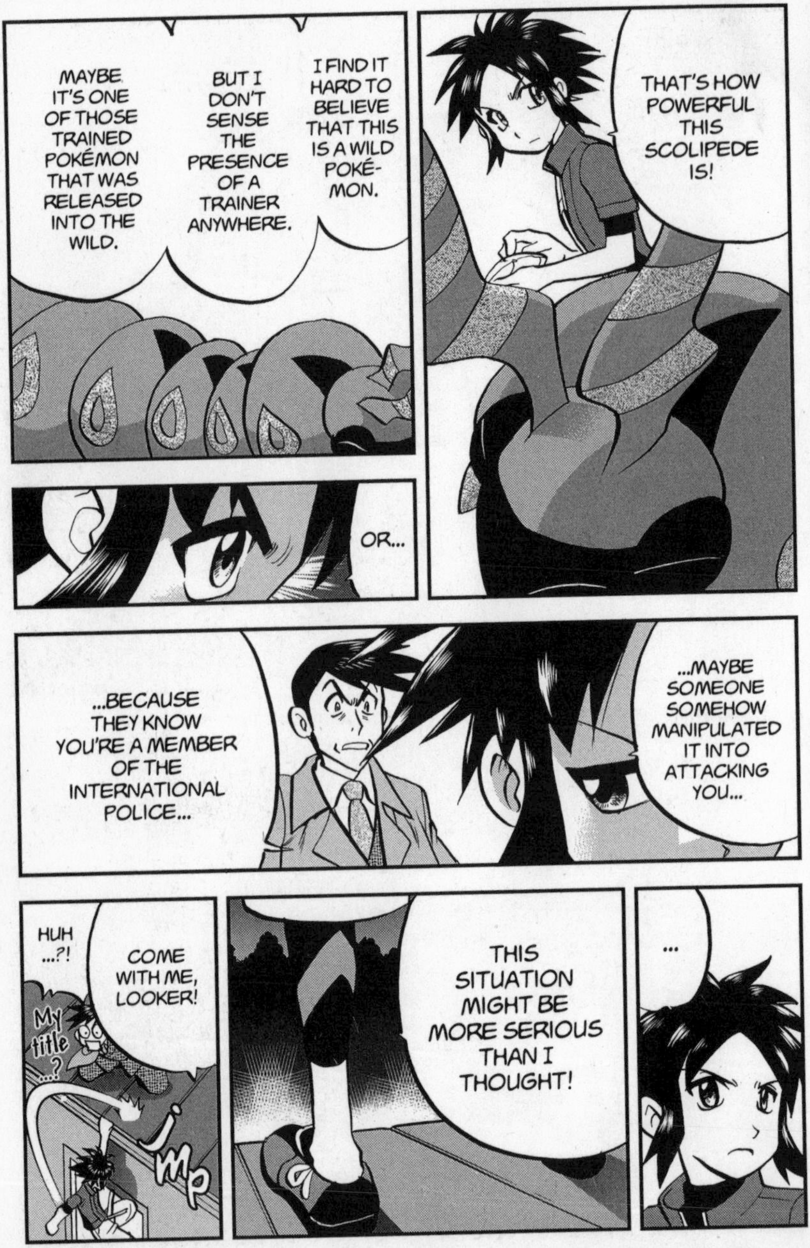
THAT'S HOW POWERFUL THIS SCOLIPEDE IS!
I FIND IT HARD TO BELIEVE THAT THIS IS A WILD POKÉ-MON.
BUT I DON'T SENSE THE PRESENCE OF A TRAINER ANYWHERE.
MAYBE IT'S ONE OF THOSE TRAINED POKÉMON THAT WAS RELEASED INTO THE WILD.
OR...
...MAYBE SOMEONE SOMEHOW MANIPULATED IT INTO ATTACKING YOU...
...BECAUSE THEY KNOW YOU'RE A MEMBER OF THE INTERNATIONAL POLICE...
...
THIS SITUATION MIGHT BE MORE SERIOUS THAN I THOUGHT!
COME WITH ME, LOOKER!
HUH ...?!
My title ...?

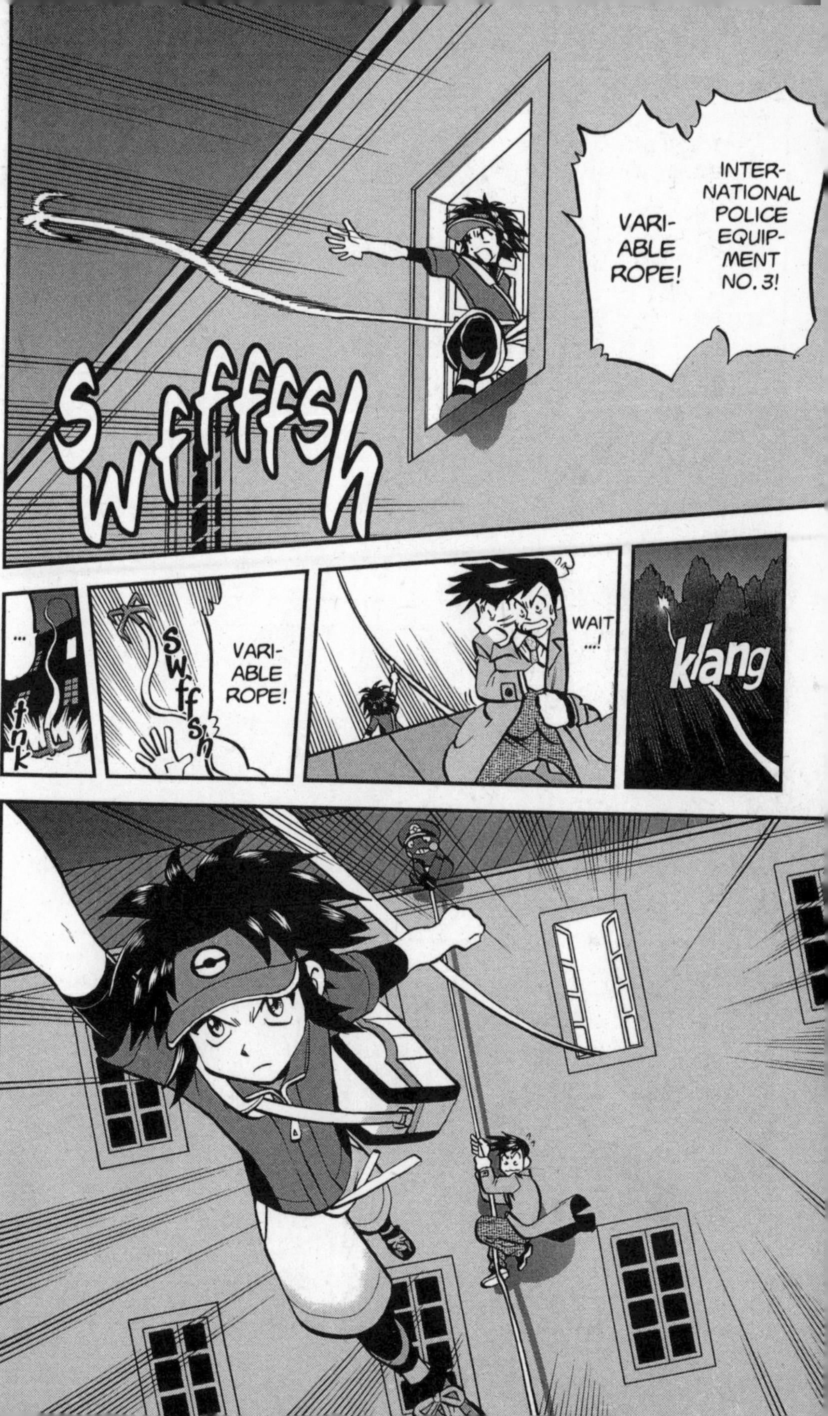

INTER-NATIONAL POLICE EQUIP-MENT NO. 3!
VARI-ABLE ROPE!
swfffsh
klang
WAIT...!
VARI-ABLE ROPE!
swffsh
...
tink

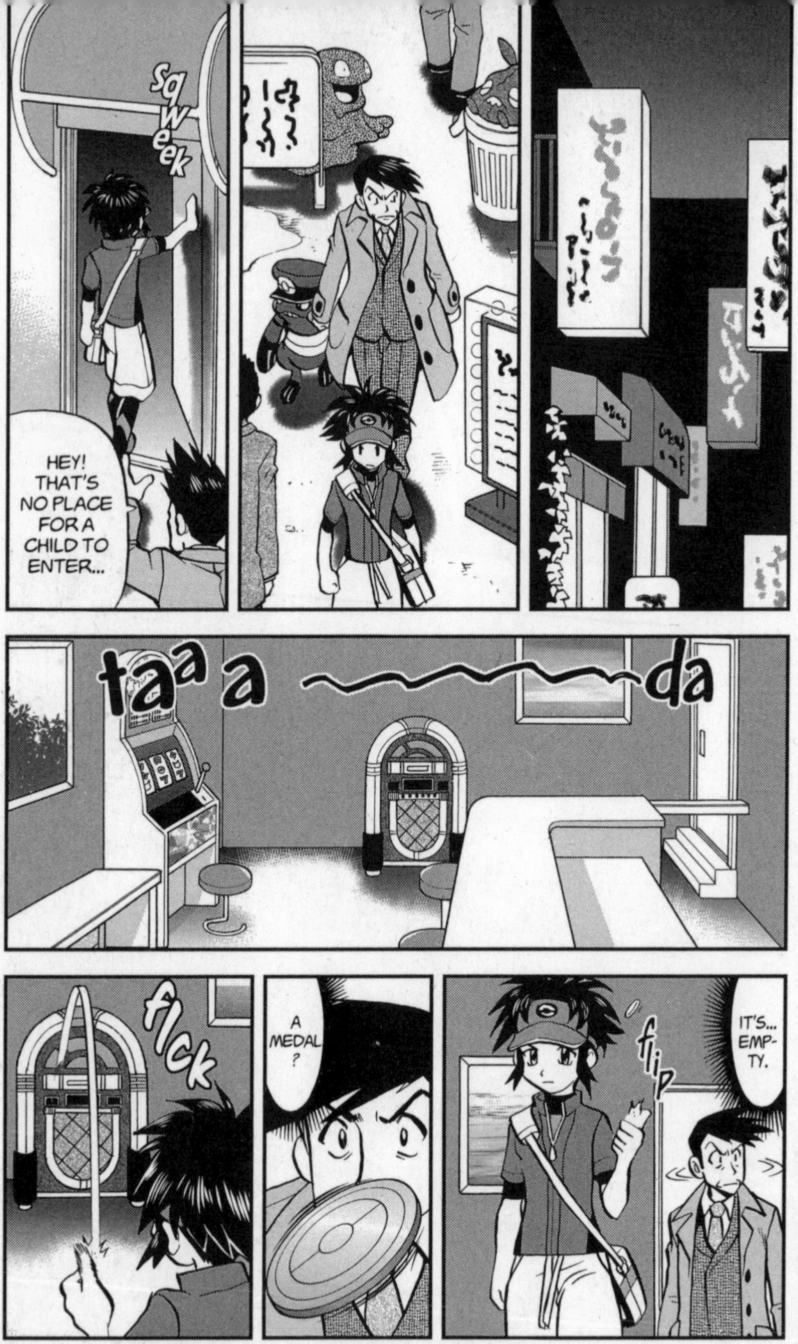
sqweeek
HEY! THAT'S NO PLACE FOR A CHILD TO ENTER...
taaa a ~~~ da
flip
IT'S... EMP-TY.
A MEDAL?
flick

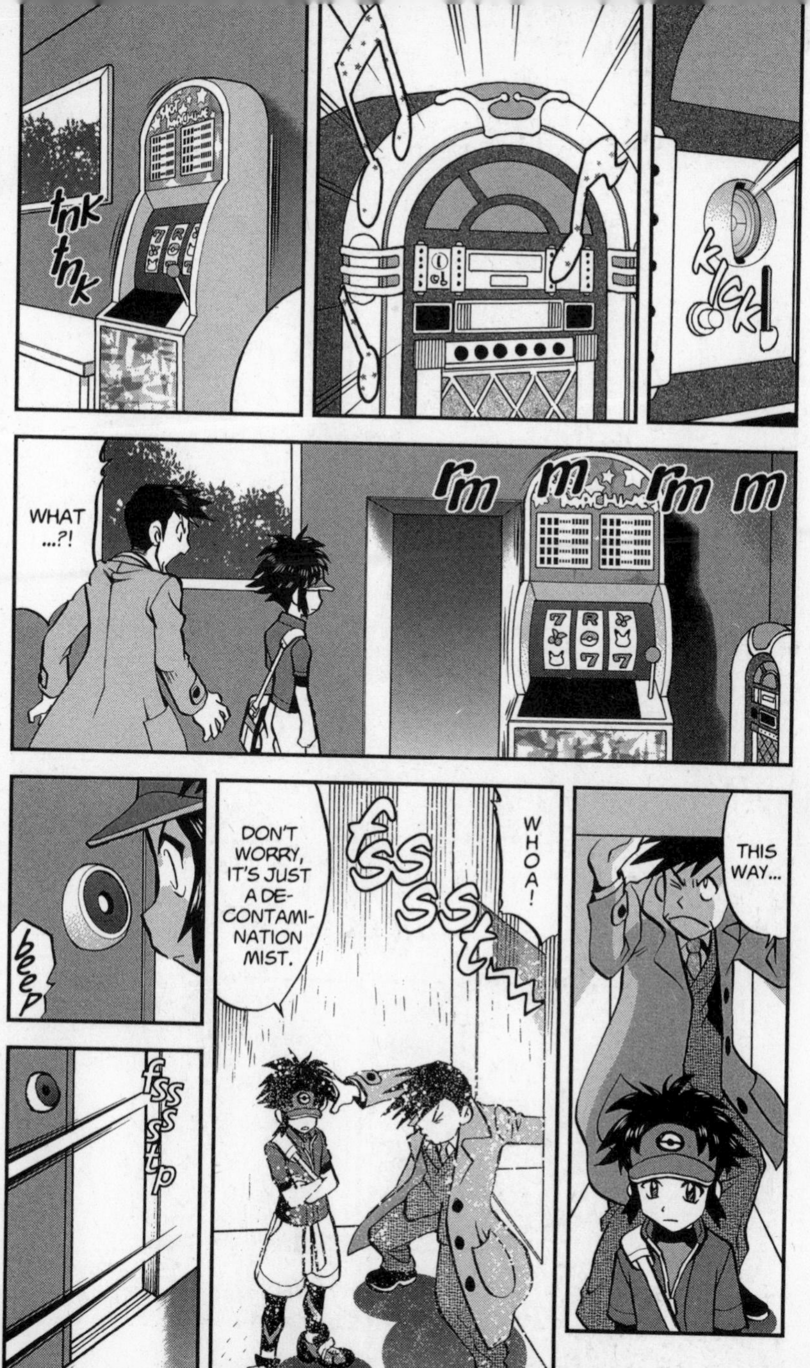
kick
tnk tnk
rm m rm m
WHAT ...?!
THIS WAY...
WHOA!
fsssst
DON'T WORRY, IT'S JUST A DE-CONTAMINATION MIST.
beep
fsssstp

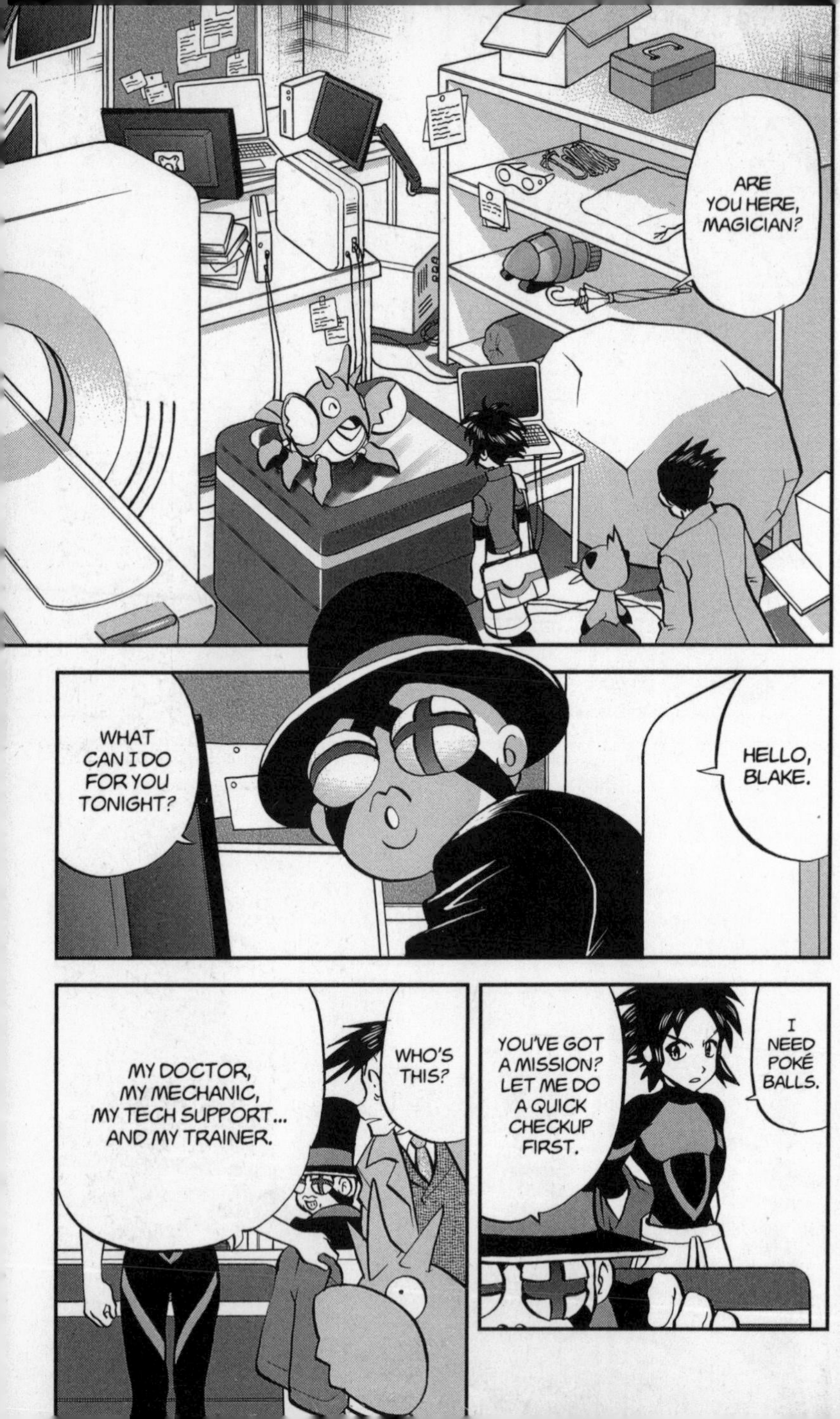
ARE YOU HERE, MAGICIAN?
HELLO, BLAKE.
WHAT CAN I DO FOR YOU TONIGHT?
I NEED POKÉ BALLS.
YOU'VE GOT A MISSION? LET ME DO A QUICK CHECKUP FIRST.
WHO'S THIS?
MY DOCTOR, MY MECHANIC, MY TECH SUPPORT... AND MY TRAINER.

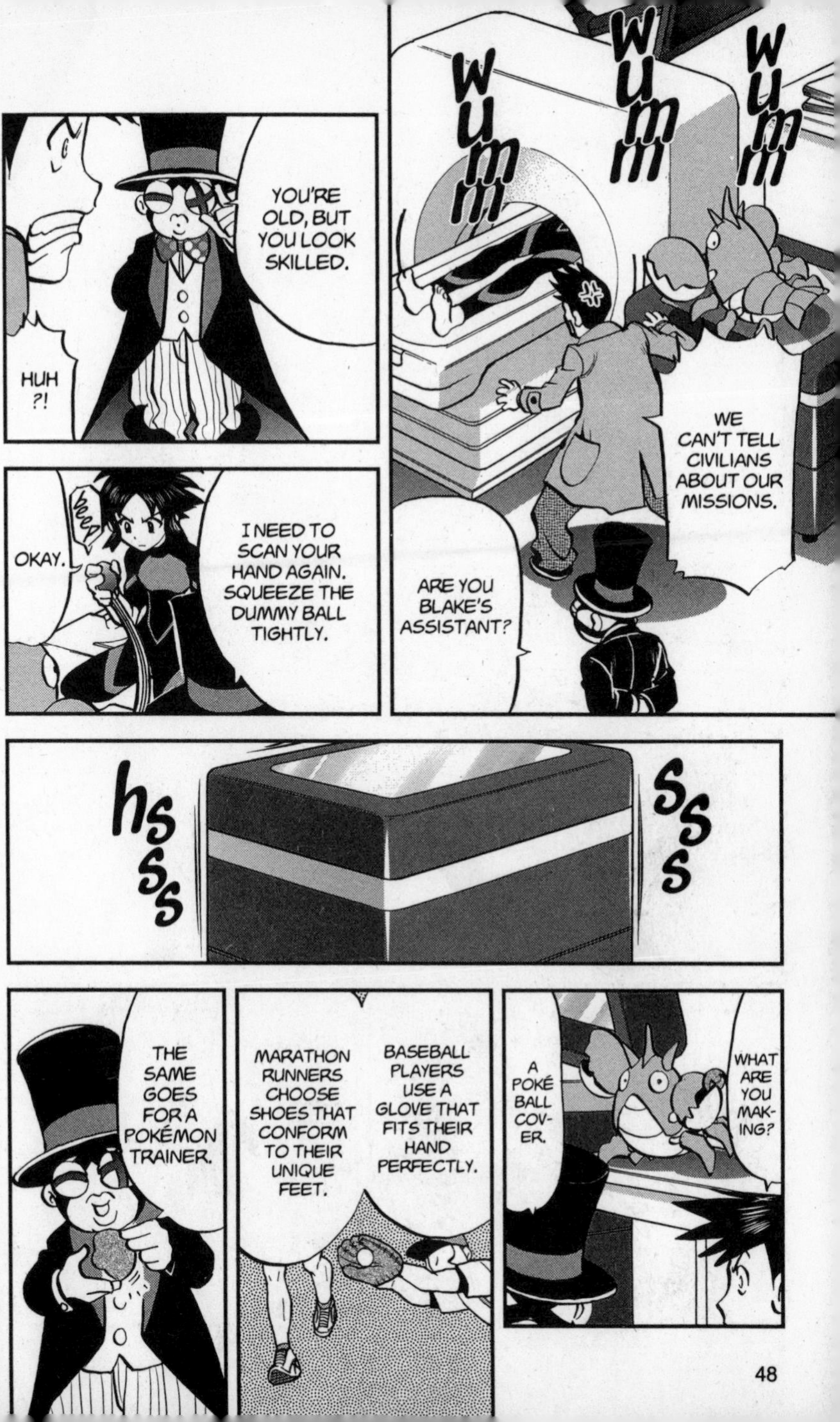

wumm
wumm
wumm
WE CAN'T TELL CIVILIANS ABOUT OUR MISSIONS.
ARE YOU BLAKE'S ASSISTANT?
YOU'RE OLD, BUT YOU LOOK SKILLED.
HUH ?!
I NEED TO SCAN YOUR HAND AGAIN. SQUEEZE THE DUMMY BALL TIGHTLY.
beep
OKAY.
hsss
sss
WHAT ARE YOU MAK-ING?
A POKÉ BALL COV-ER.
BASEBALL PLAYERS USE A GLOVE THAT FITS THEIR HAND PERFECTLY.
MARATHON RUNNERS CHOOSE SHOES THAT CONFORM TO THEIR UNIQUE FEET.
THE SAME GOES FOR A POKÉMON TRAINER.

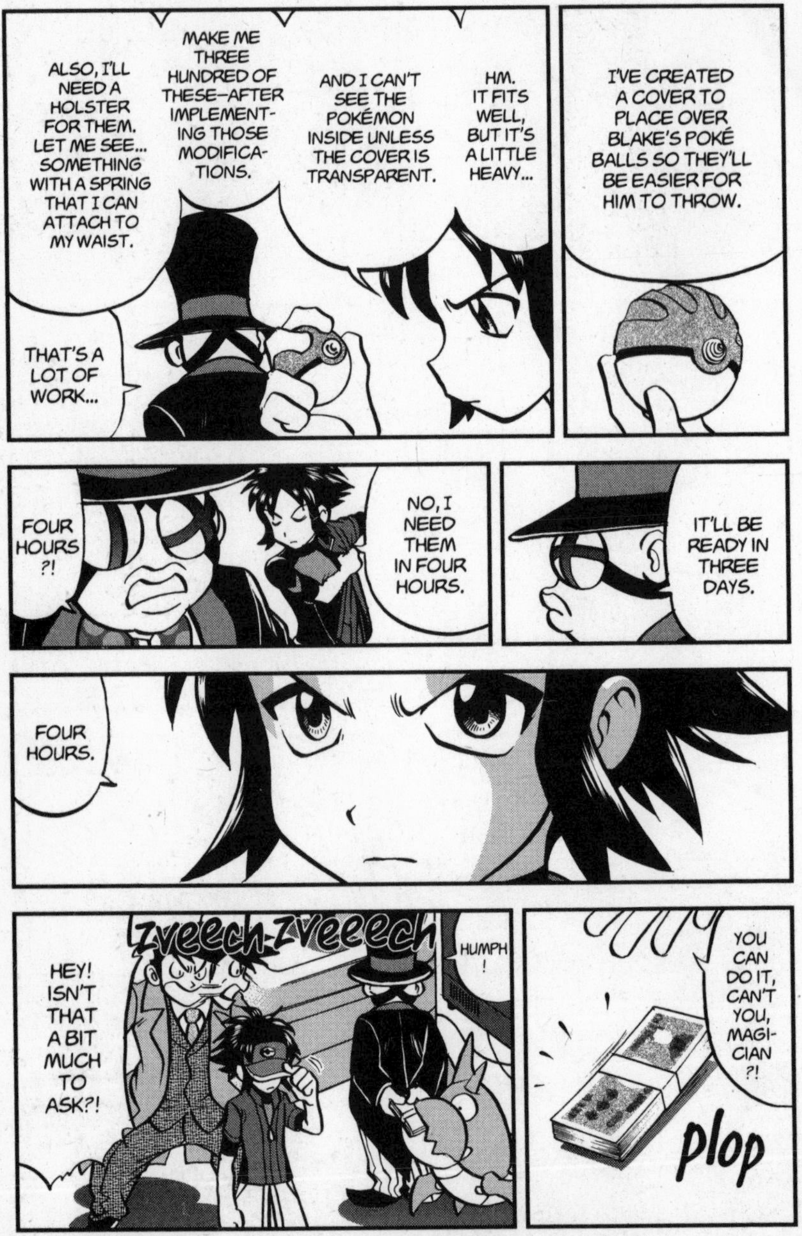
I'VE CREATED A COVER TO PLACE OVER BLAKE'S POKÉ BALLS SO THEY'LL BE EASIER FOR HIM TO THROW.
HM. IT FITS WELL, BUT IT'S A LITTLE HEAVY...
AND I CAN'T SEE THE POKÉMON INSIDE UNLESS THE COVER IS TRANSPARENT.
MAKE ME THREE HUNDRED OF THESE—AFTER IMPLEMENTING THOSE MODIFICATIONS.
ALSO, I'LL NEED A HOLSTER FOR THEM. LET ME SEE... SOMETHING WITH A SPRING THAT I CAN ATTACH TO MY WAIST.
THAT'S A LOT OF WORK...
IT'LL BE READY IN THREE DAYS.
NO, I NEED THEM IN FOUR HOURS.
FOUR HOURS?!
FOUR HOURS.
YOU CAN DO IT, CAN'T YOU, MAGICIAN?!
plop
HUMPH!
Zveech-zveeech
HEY! ISN'T THAT A BIT MUCH TO ASK?!

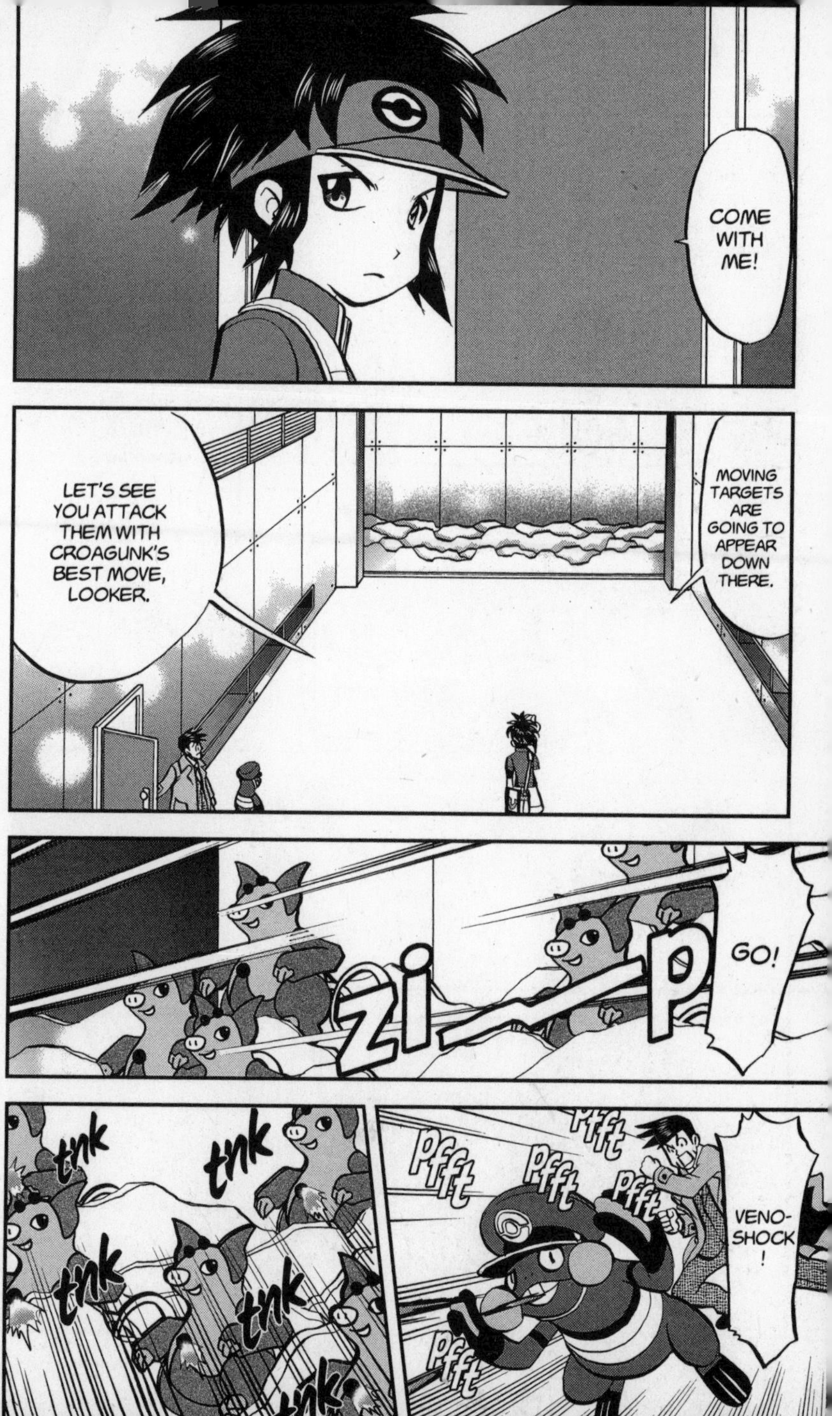
COME WITH ME!
MOVING TARGETS ARE GOING TO APPEAR DOWN THERE.
LET'S SEE YOU ATTACK THEM WITH CROAGUNK'S BEST MOVE, LOOKER.
GO!
zi—p
VENO-SHOCK!
pfft
pfft
pfft
pfft
pfft
pfft
tnk
tnk
tnk
tnk
tnk

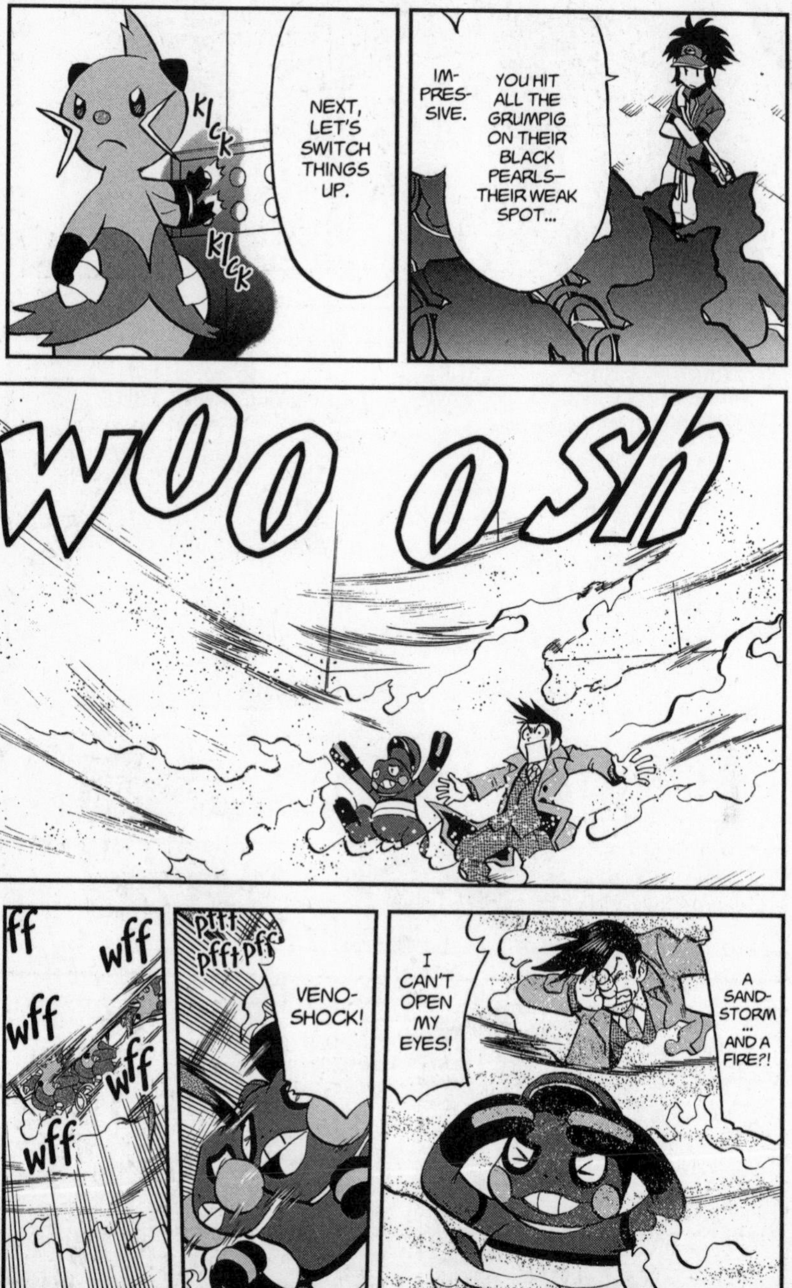

IM-PRES-SIVE.
YOU HIT ALL THE GRUMPIG ON THEIR BLACK PEARLS— THEIR WEAK SPOT...
NEXT, LET'S SWITCH THINGS UP.
KLICK
KLICK
WOOOSH
A SAND-STORM ... AND A FIRE?!
I CAN'T OPEN MY EYES!
pfft pfft pff
VENO-SHOCK!
ff
wff
wff
wff
wff

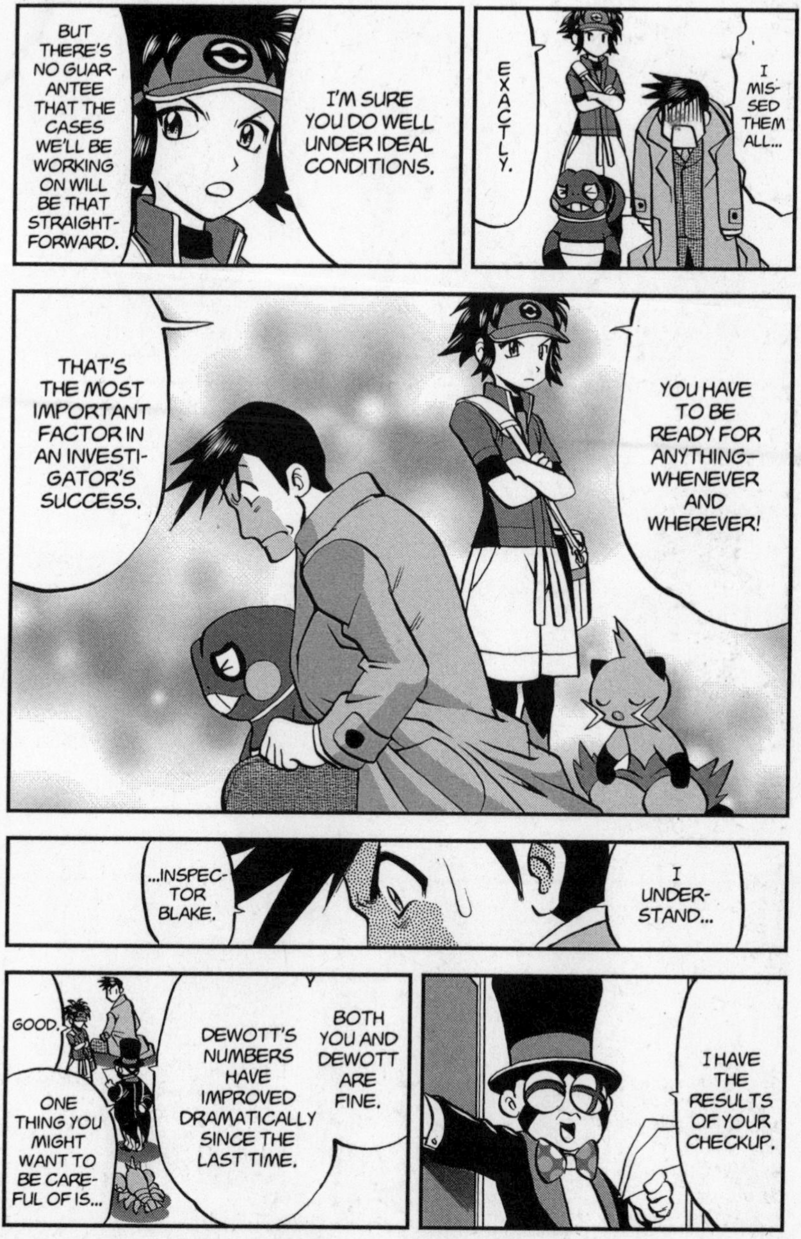
I MISSED THEM ALL...
EXACTLY.
I'M SURE YOU DO WELL UNDER IDEAL CONDITIONS.
BUT THERE'S NO GUARANTEE THAT THE CASES WE'LL BE WORKING ON WILL BE THAT STRAIGHTFORWARD.
YOU HAVE TO BE READY FOR ANYTHING—WHENEVER AND WHEREVER!
THAT'S THE MOST IMPORTANT FACTOR IN AN INVESTIGATOR'S SUCCESS.
I UNDERSTAND...
...INSPECTOR BLAKE.
I HAVE THE RESULTS OF YOUR CHECKUP.
BOTH YOU AND DEWOTT ARE FINE.
DEWOTT'S NUMBERS HAVE IMPROVED DRAMATICALLY SINCE THE LAST TIME.
GOOD.
ONE THING YOU MIGHT WANT TO BE CAREFUL OF IS...

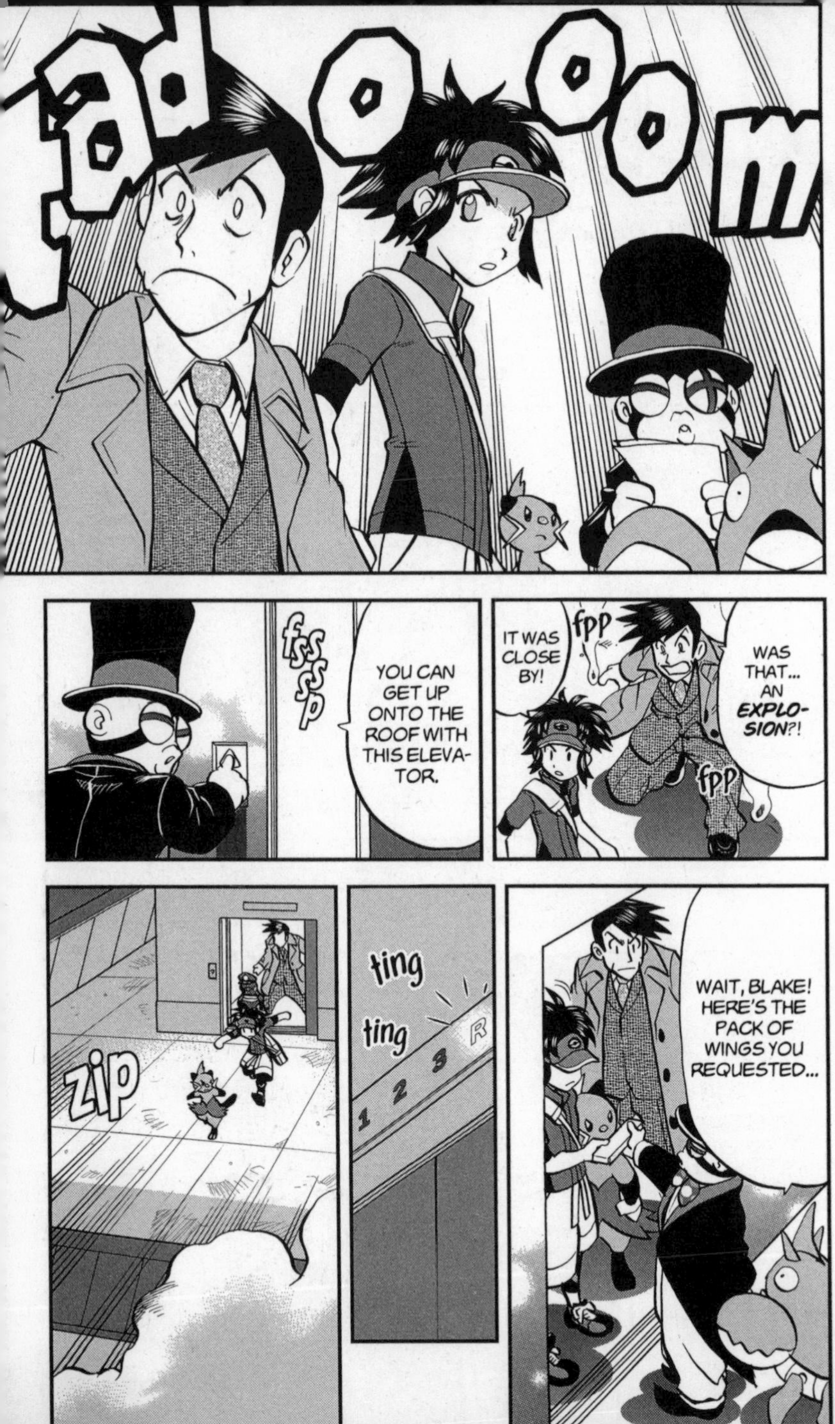
ad-o-o-oom
WAS THAT... AN ***EXPLOSION***?!
fpp
IT WAS CLOSE BY!
fpp
YOU CAN GET UP ONTO THE ROOF WITH THIS ELEVATOR.
fsssp
WAIT, BLAKE! HERE'S THE PACK OF WINGS YOU REQUESTED...
ting
ting
1 2 3 R
zip

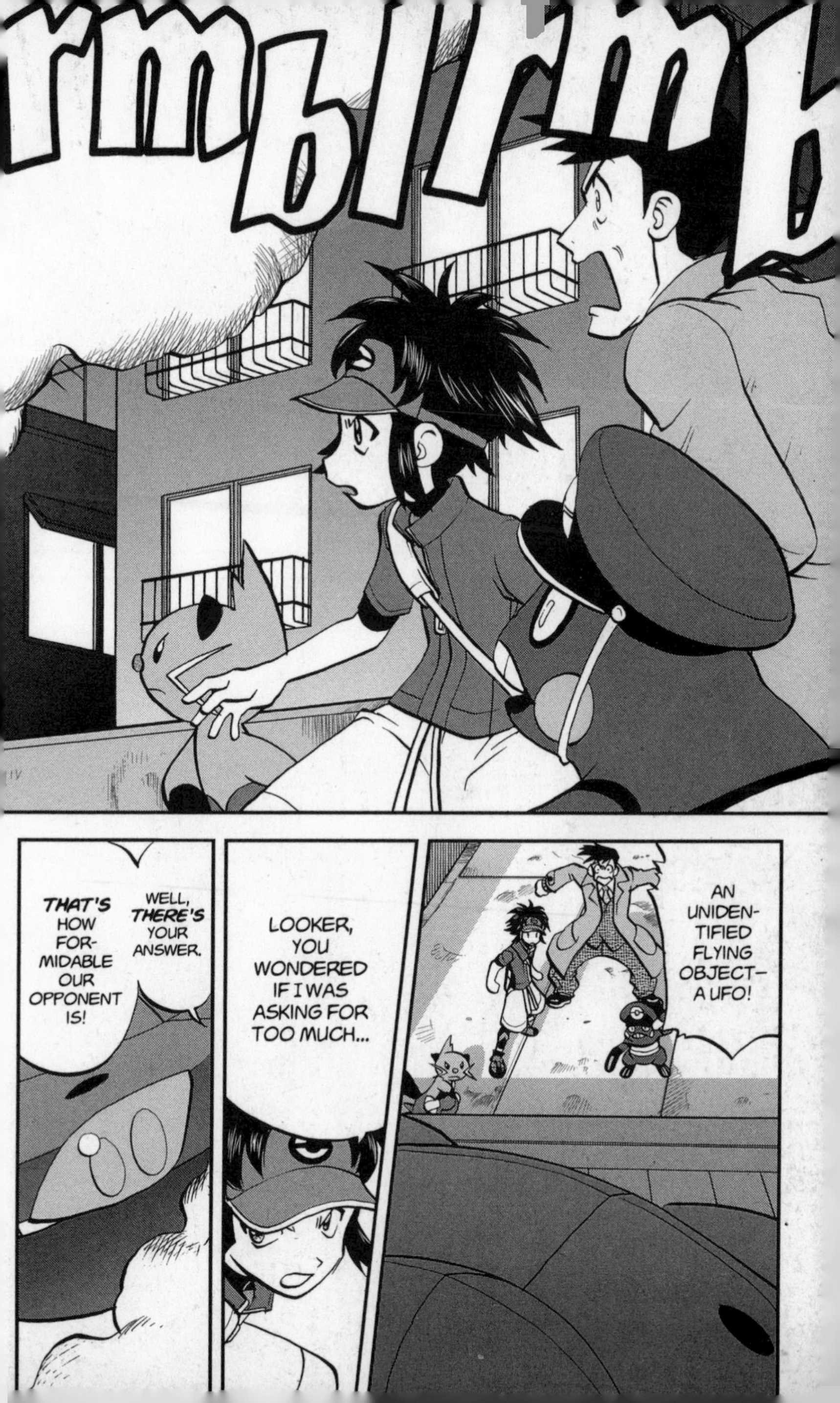
RMBLRMB
AN UNIDEN-TIFIED FLYING OBJECT— A UFO!
LOOKER, YOU WONDERED IF I WAS ASKING FOR TOO MUCH...
WELL, **THERE'S** YOUR ANSWER.
THAT'S HOW FOR-MIDABLE OUR OPPONENT IS!

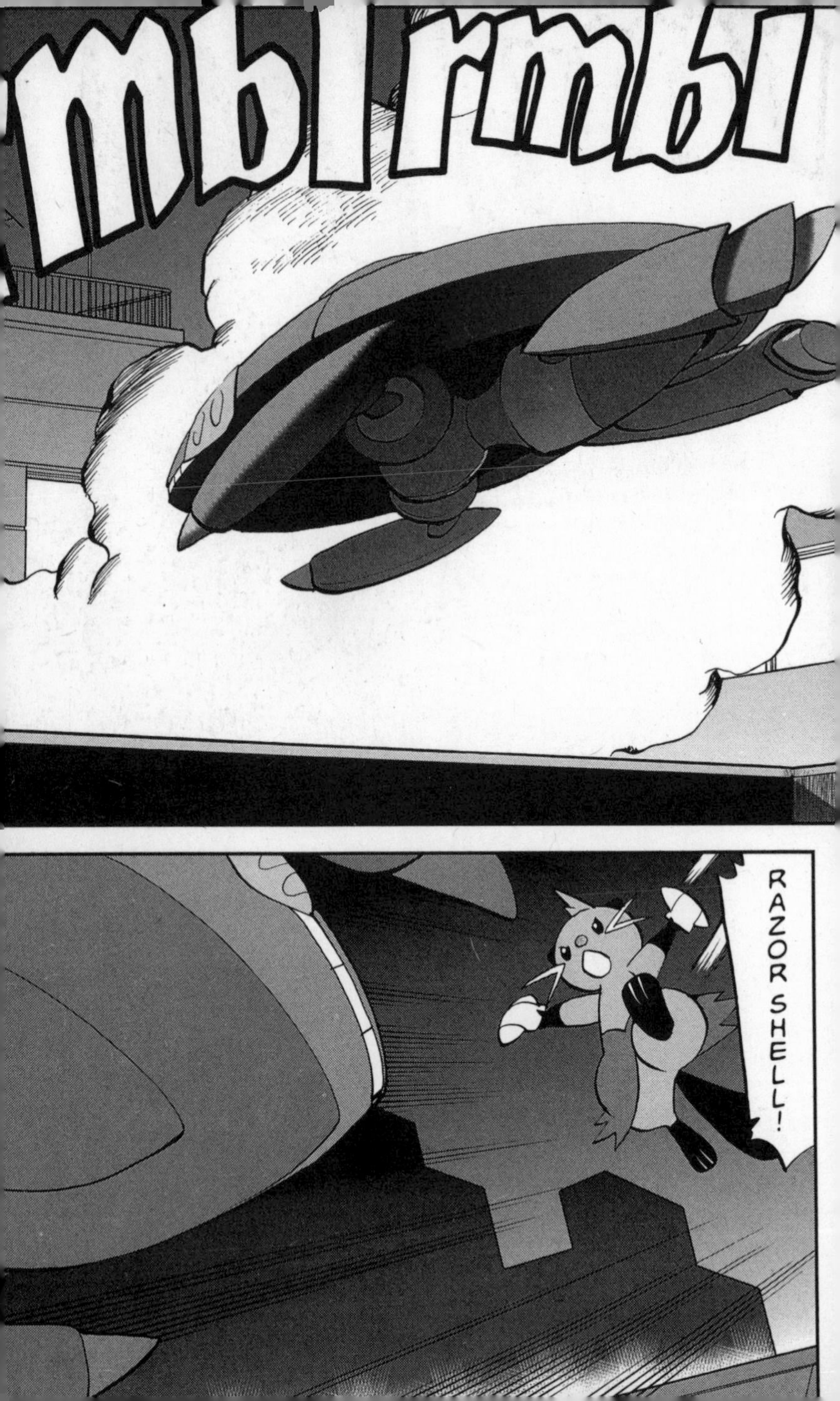
MBL RMBL
RAZOR SHELL!

Character Profile

BLAKE

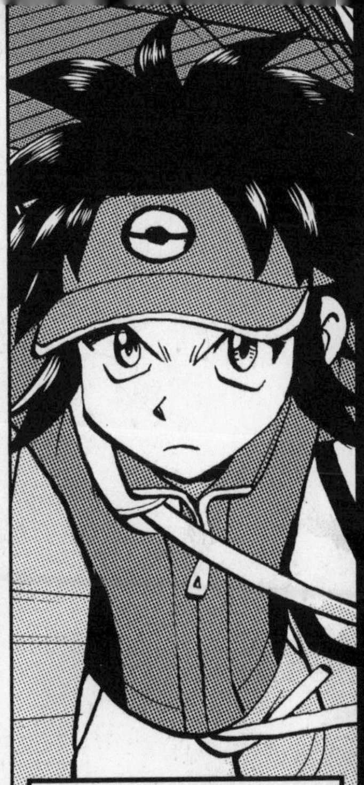

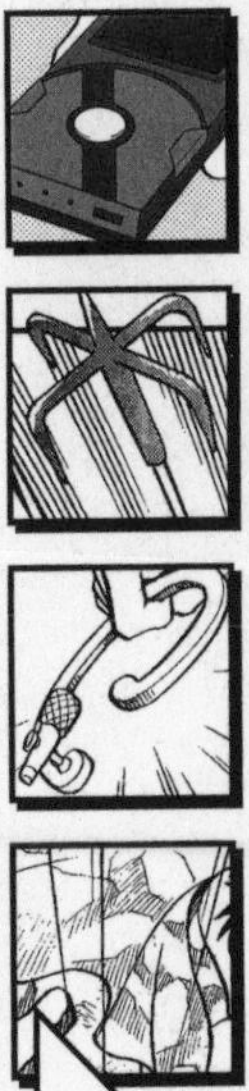

- Job: International Police Investigator
- Rank: Inspector
- Code name: Black No. 2
- Age: 12 years old
- Birthday: May 4
- Constellation: Bouffalant
- Hometown: Unknown
- Family: Unknown

BLAKE

A young junior officer, an Inspector in the International Police. Although he's only 12 years old, he has managed to acquire all the skills he needs to become a police investigator and quickly rose to his current rank in a few short years. He is intelligent and has mastered a special art… Plus he's a first-class Pokémon Trainer skilled at battles as well as Pokémon captures. All this has earned him the nickname "Mr. Perfect."

Blake is a tough self-starter who is "ready for anything—whenever and wherever." He spares no expense to stay at the top of his game, paying a personal manager to take care of both his equipment and his health. Having gone undercover in the Unova Region, his mission is to resolve the current conflict with Team Plasma.

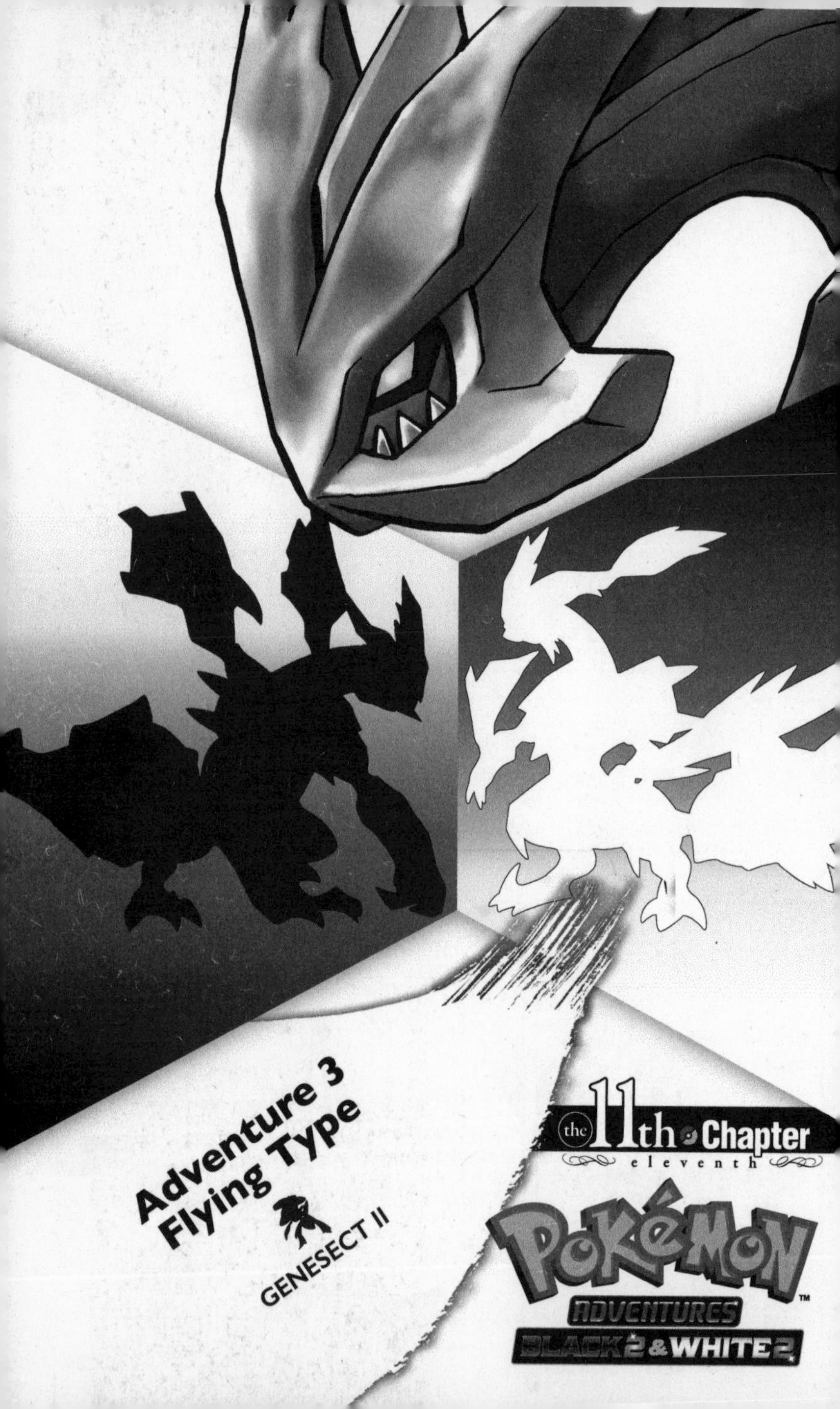

Adventure 3
Flying Type
GENESECT II
the 11th Chapter
eleventh
POKÉMON™
ADVENTURES
BLACK 2 & WHITE 2

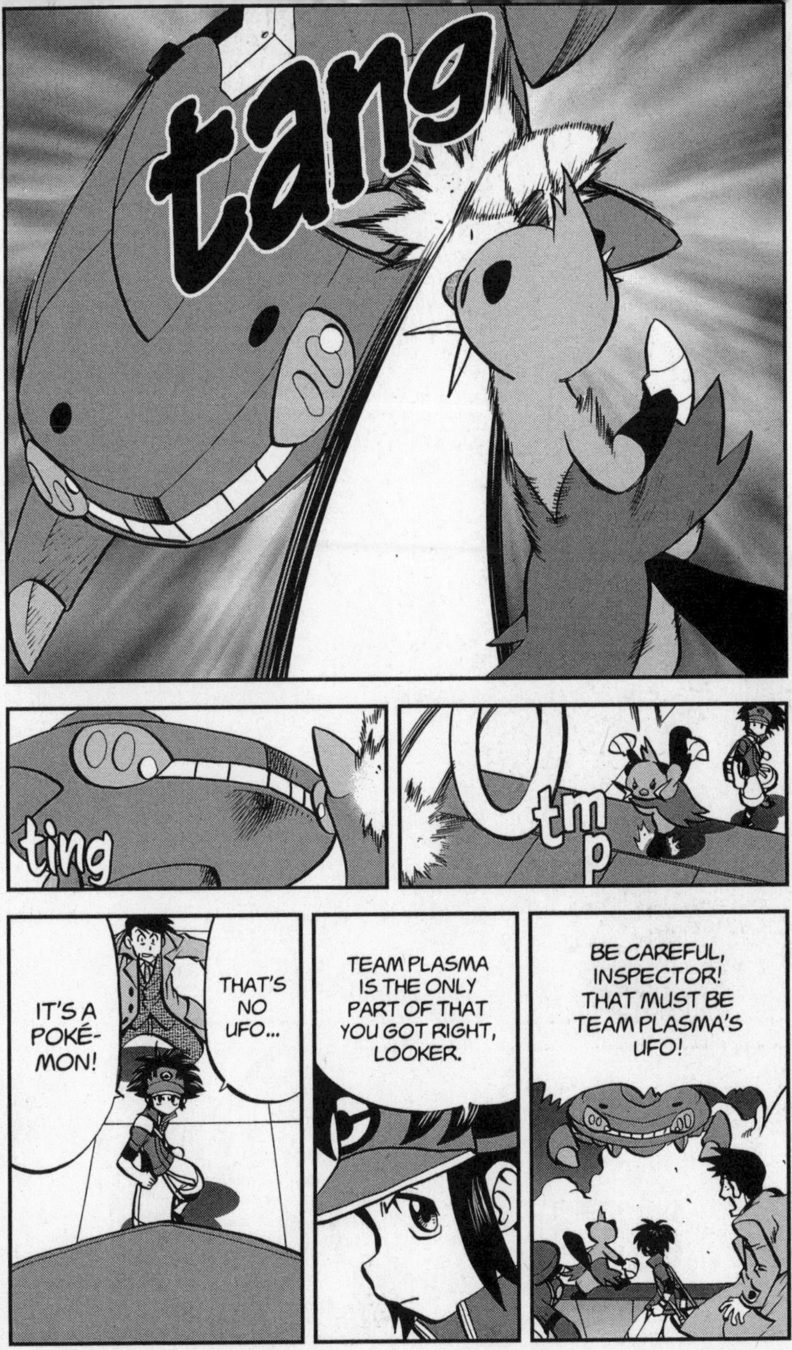
tang
tmp
ting
BE CAREFUL, INSPECTOR! THAT MUST BE TEAM PLASMA'S UFO!
TEAM PLASMA IS THE ONLY PART OF THAT YOU GOT RIGHT, LOOKER.
THAT'S NO UFO...
IT'S A POKÉ-MON!

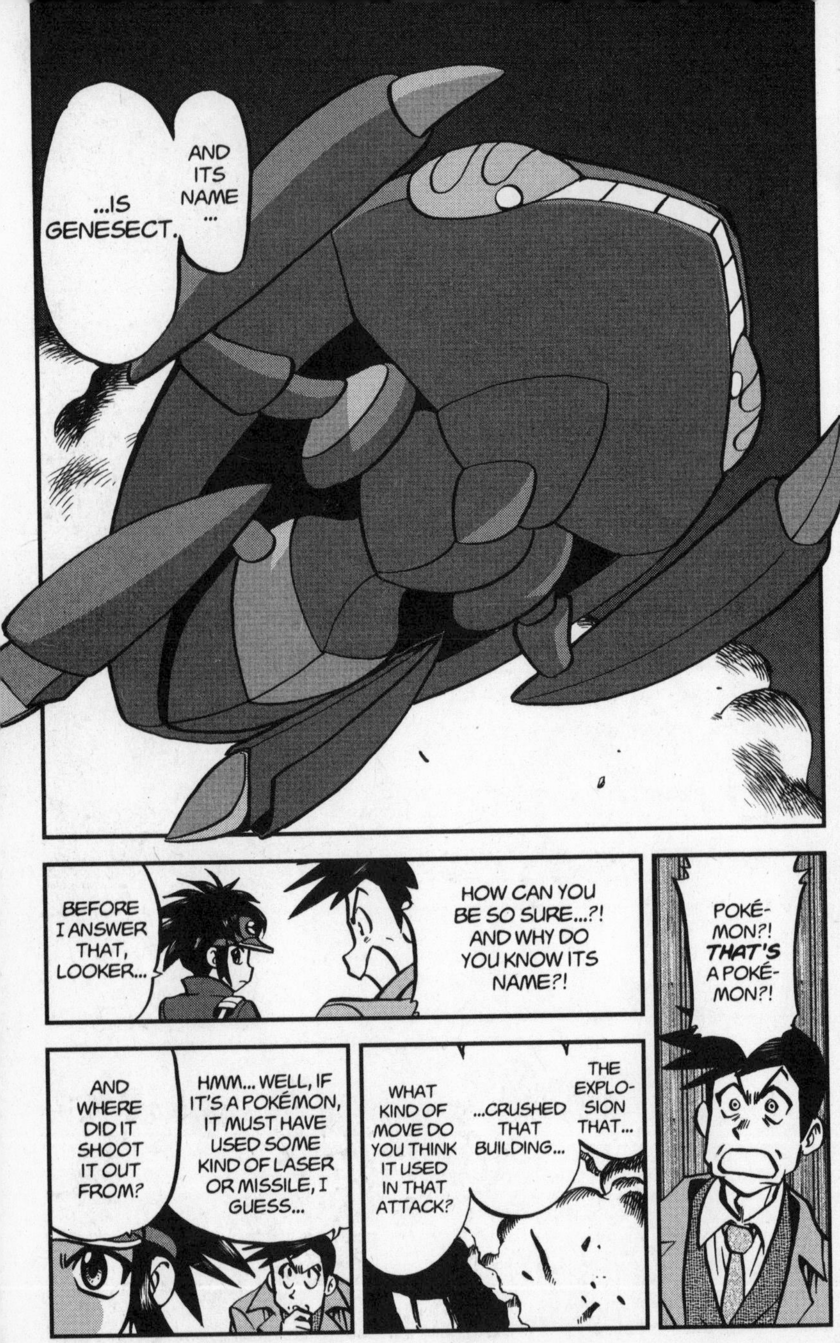
AND ITS NAME ...
...IS GENESECT.
POKÉ-MON?! THAT'S A POKÉ-MON?!
HOW CAN YOU BE SO SURE...?! AND WHY DO YOU KNOW ITS NAME?!
BEFORE I ANSWER THAT, LOOKER...
THE EXPLO-SION THAT...
...CRUSHED THAT BUILDING...
WHAT KIND OF MOVE DO YOU THINK IT USED IN THAT ATTACK?
HMM... WELL, IF IT'S A POKÉMON, IT MUST HAVE USED SOME KIND OF LASER OR MISSILE, I GUESS...
AND WHERE DID IT SHOOT IT OUT FROM?

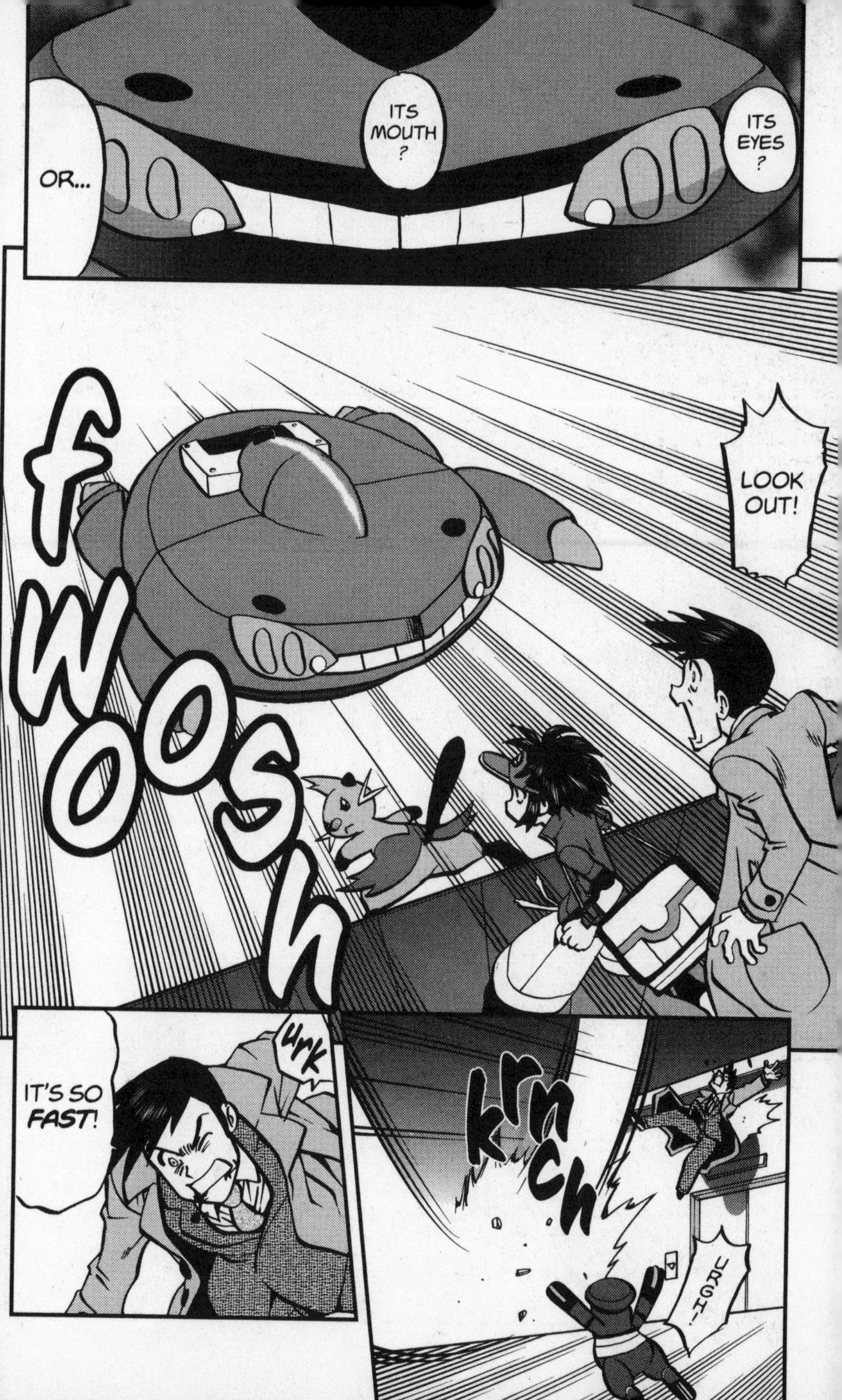
ITS EYES?
ITS MOUTH?
OR...
LOOK OUT!
fwoosh
krnch
URGH!
urk
IT'S SO FAST!

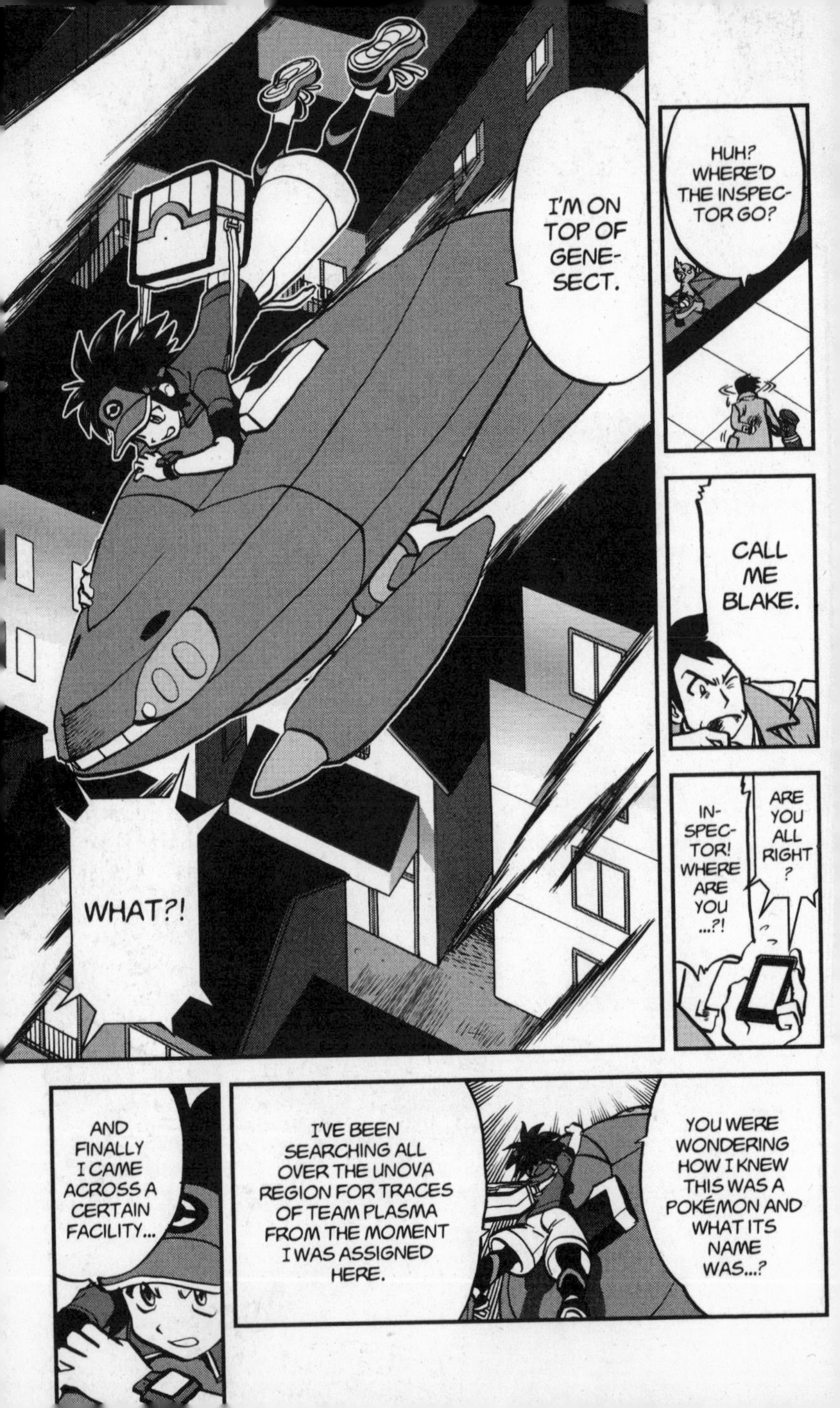
HUH? WHERE'D THE INSPECTOR GO?
CALL ME BLAKE.
ARE YOU ALL RIGHT?
INSPECTOR! WHERE ARE YOU ...?!
I'M ON TOP OF GENESECT.
WHAT?!
YOU WERE WONDERING HOW I KNEW THIS WAS A POKÉMON AND WHAT ITS NAME WAS...?
I'VE BEEN SEARCHING ALL OVER THE UNOVA REGION FOR TRACES OF TEAM PLASMA FROM THE MOMENT I WAS ASSIGNED HERE.
AND FINALLY I CAME ACROSS A CERTAIN FACILITY...

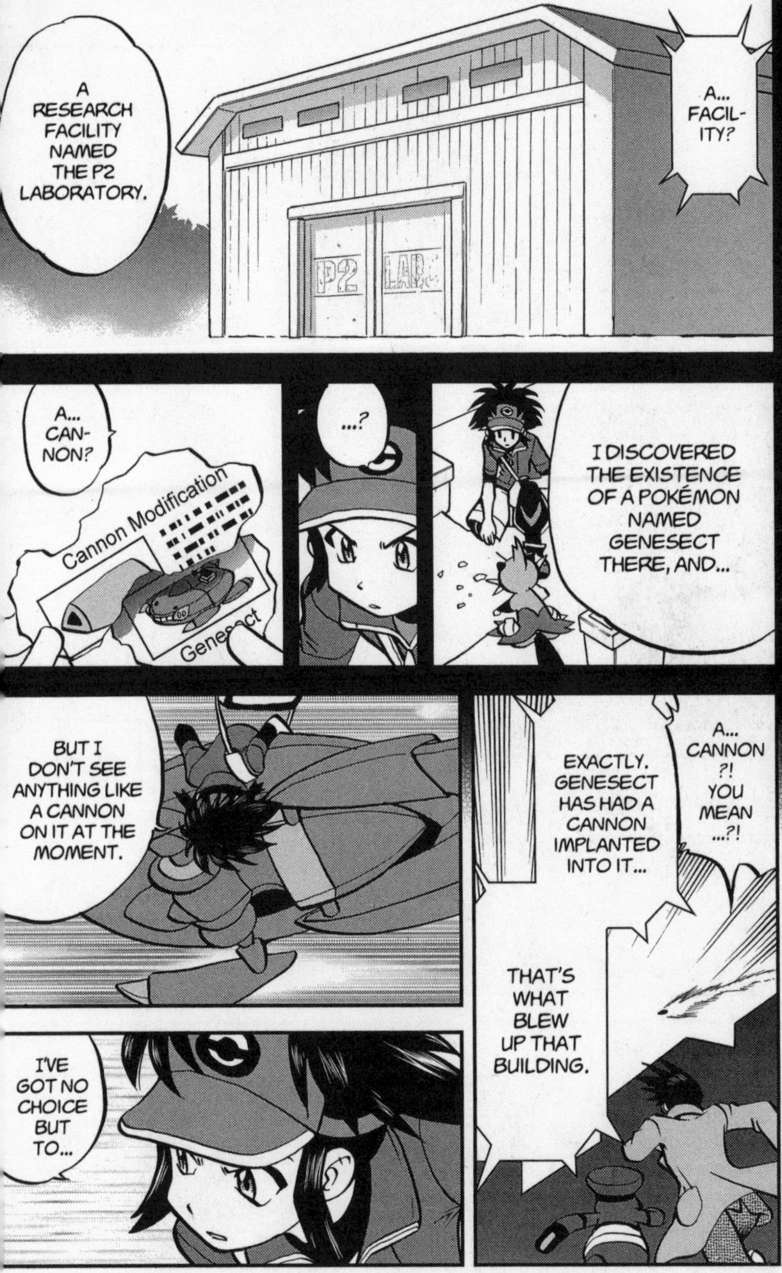
A... FACIL-ITY?
A RESEARCH FACILITY NAMED THE P2 LABORATORY.
I DISCOVERED THE EXISTENCE OF A POKÉMON NAMED GENESECT THERE, AND...
...?
A... CAN-NON?
Cannon Modification
Genesect
A... CANNON ?! YOU MEAN ...?!
EXACTLY. GENESECT HAS HAD A CANNON IMPLANTED INTO IT...
THAT'S WHAT BLEW UP THAT BUILDING.
BUT I DON'T SEE ANYTHING LIKE A CANNON ON IT AT THE MOMENT.
I'VE GOT NO CHOICE BUT TO...

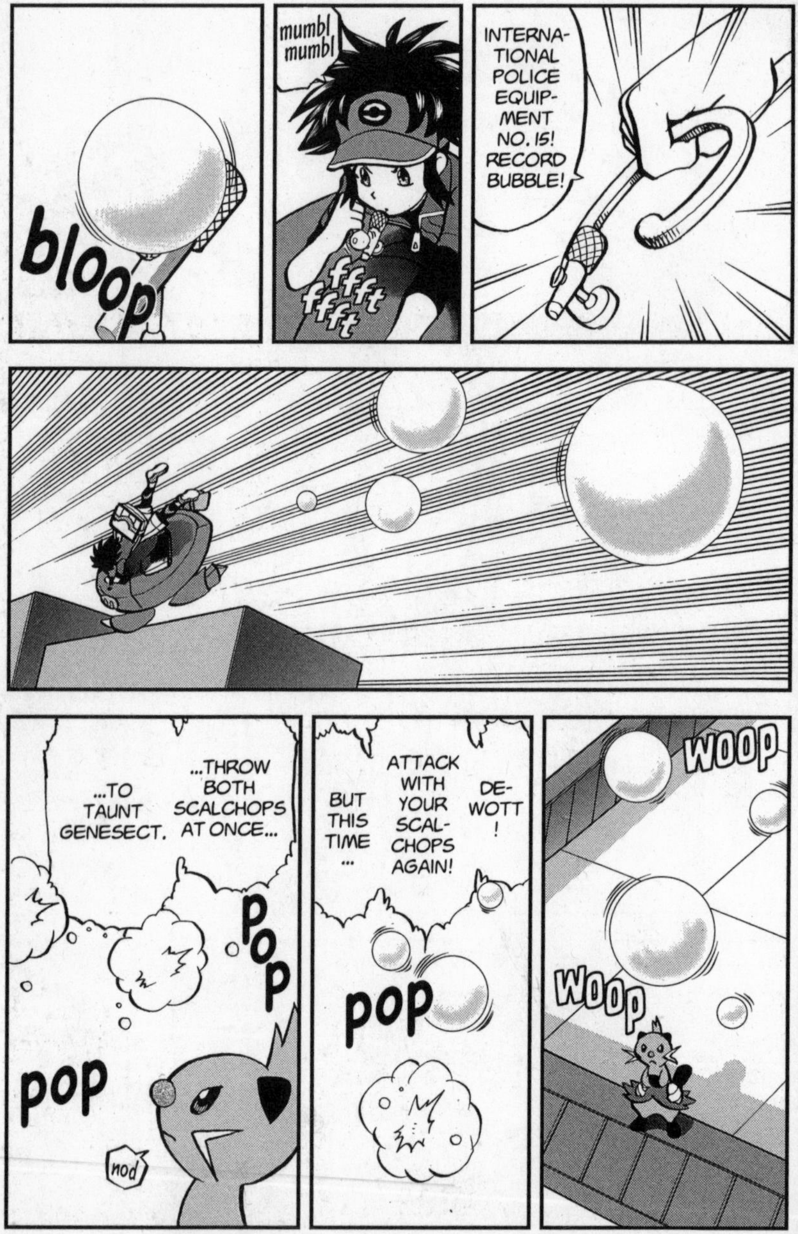
INTERNATIONAL POLICE EQUIPMENT NO. 15! RECORD BUBBLE!
mumbl mumbl
ffft ffft
bloop
WOOP
WOOP
DEWOTT!
ATTACK WITH YOUR SCALCHOPS AGAIN!
BUT THIS TIME...
pop
...THROW BOTH SCALCHOPS AT ONCE...
...TO TAUNT GENESECT.
pop
pop
nod

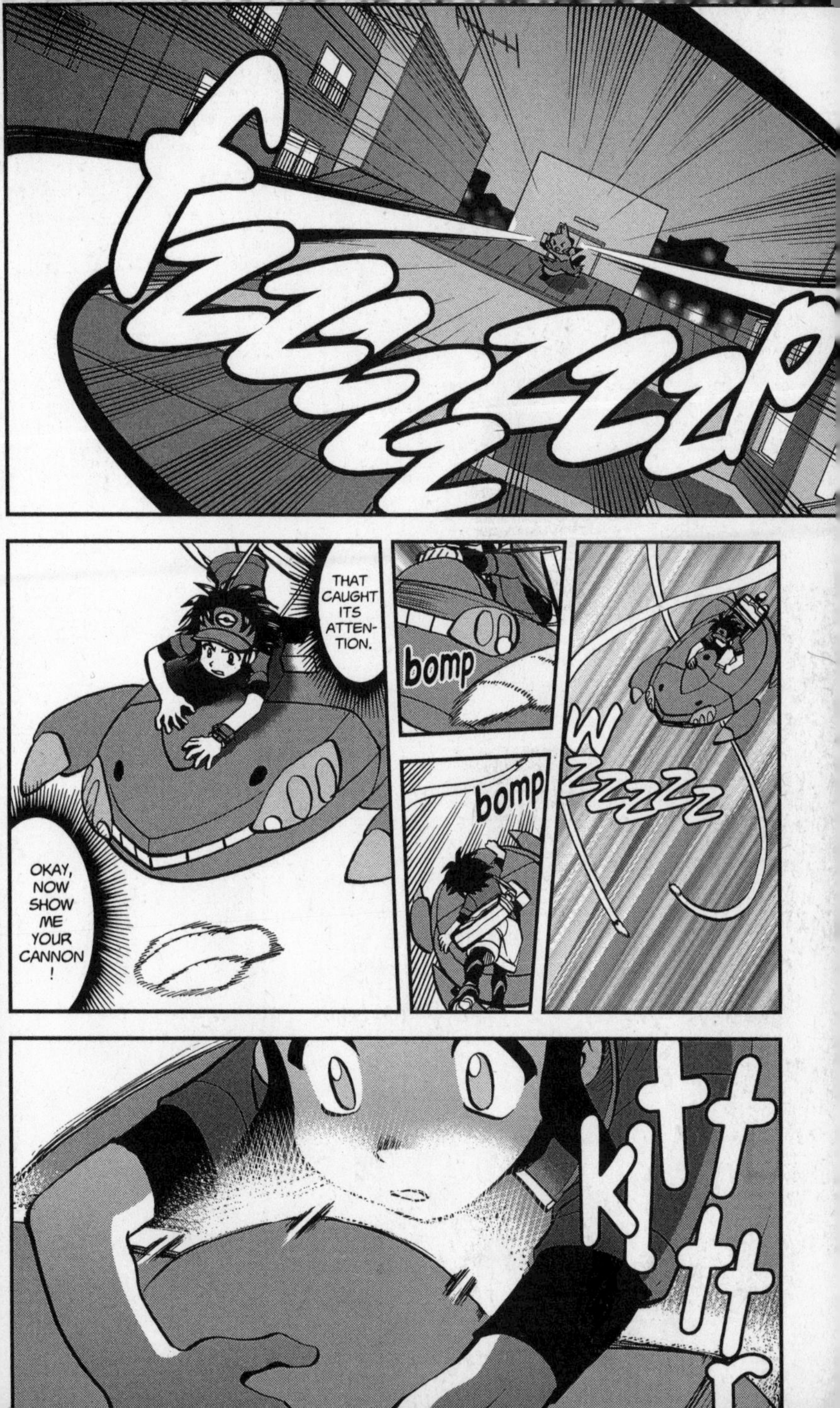
bomp
bomp
THAT CAUGHT ITS ATTEN-TION.
OKAY, NOW SHOW ME YOUR CANNON!

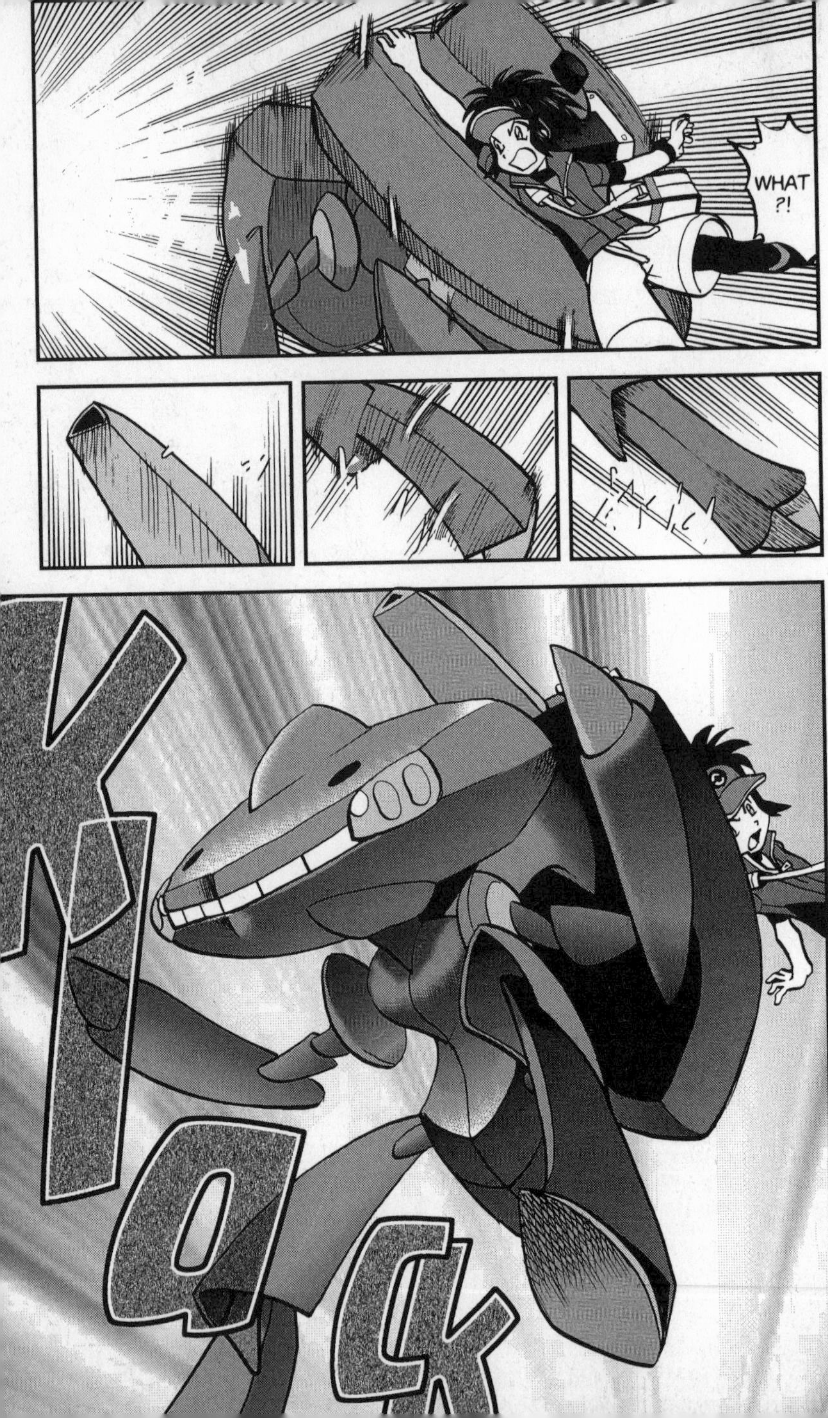
WHAT ?!

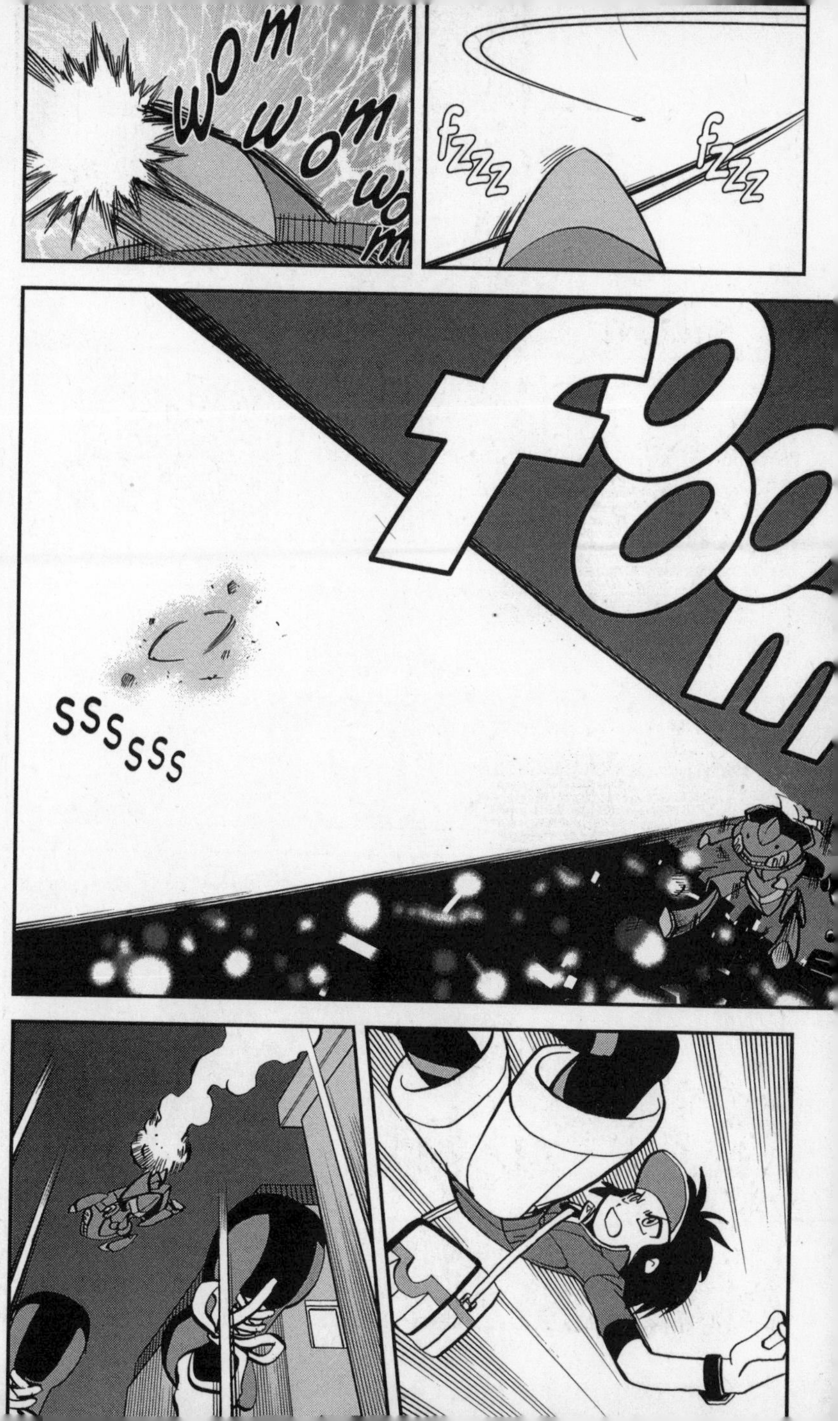
fzzz
fzzz
wom
wom
wom
fooom
ssssss

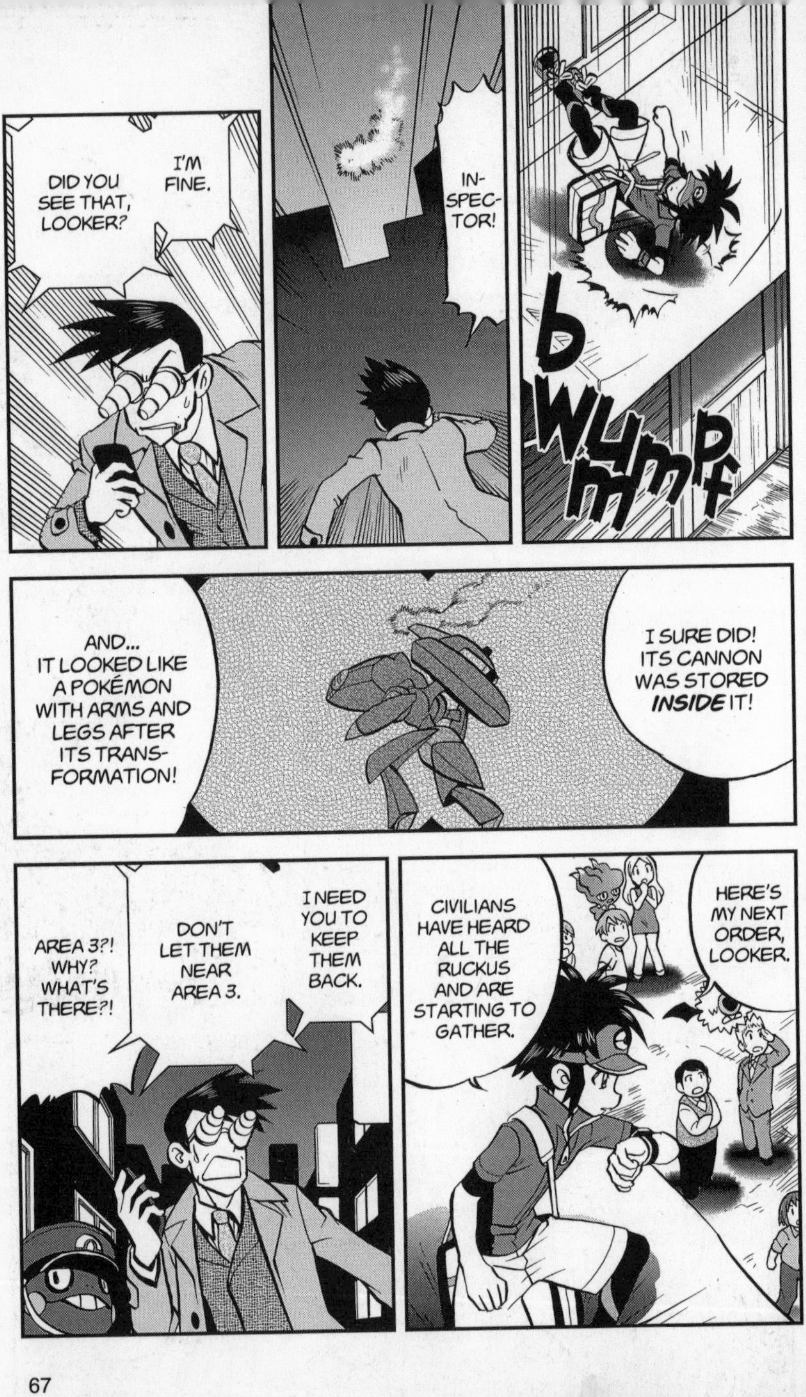
bWHUMPF
IN-SPEC-TOR!
I'M FINE.
DID YOU SEE THAT, LOOKER?
I SURE DID! ITS CANNON WAS STORED INSIDE IT!
AND... IT LOOKED LIKE A POKÉMON WITH ARMS AND LEGS AFTER ITS TRANS-FORMATION!
HERE'S MY NEXT ORDER, LOOKER.
CIVILIANS HAVE HEARD ALL THE RUCKUS AND ARE STARTING TO GATHER.
I NEED YOU TO KEEP THEM BACK.
DON'T LET THEM NEAR AREA 3.
AREA 3?! WHY? WHAT'S THERE?!

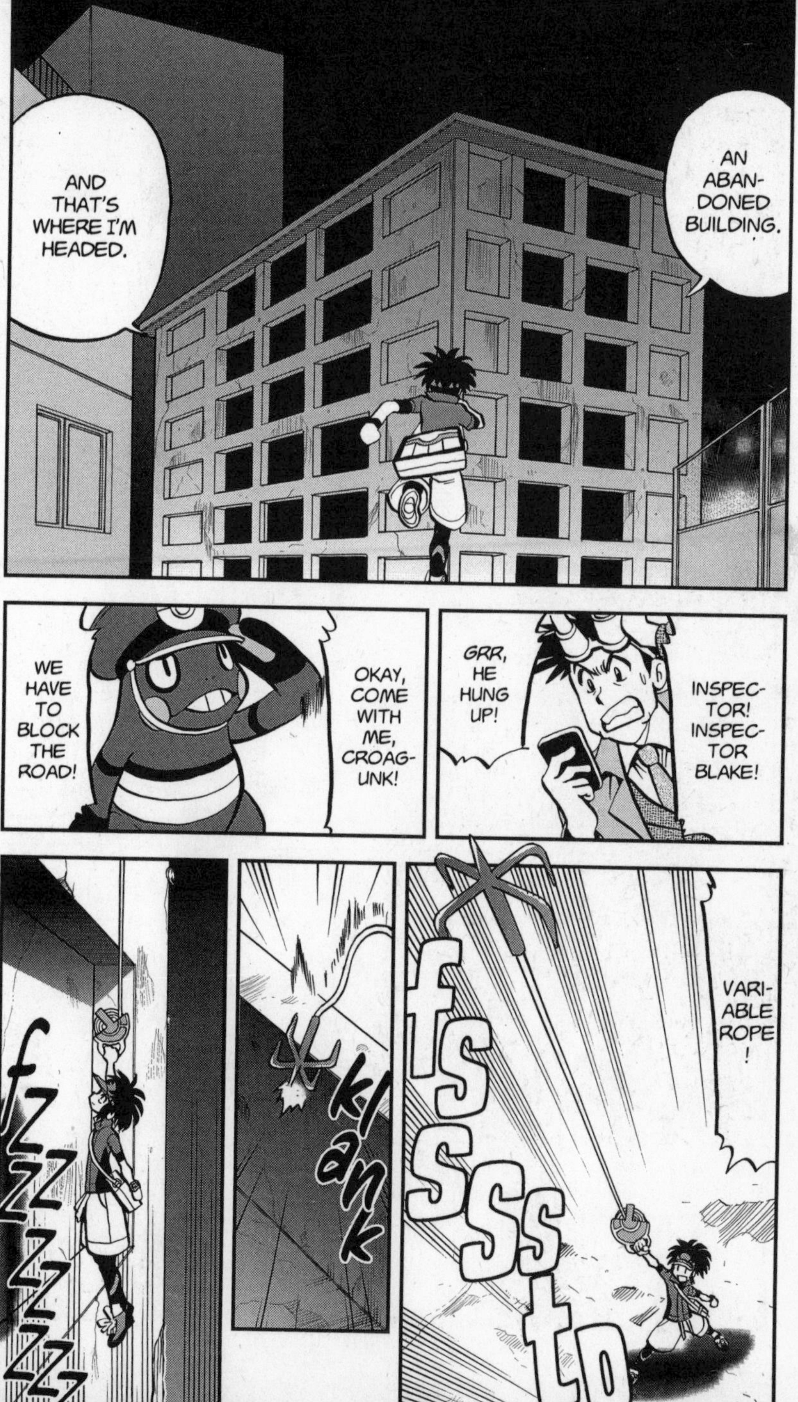
AN ABAN-DONED BUILDING.
AND THAT'S WHERE I'M HEADED.
INSPEC-TOR! INSPEC-TOR BLAKE!
GRR, HE HUNG UP!
OKAY, COME WITH ME, CROAG-UNK!
WE HAVE TO BLOCK THE ROAD!
VARI-ABLE ROPE!
fsSSSsto
klank
fZZZZZZZ

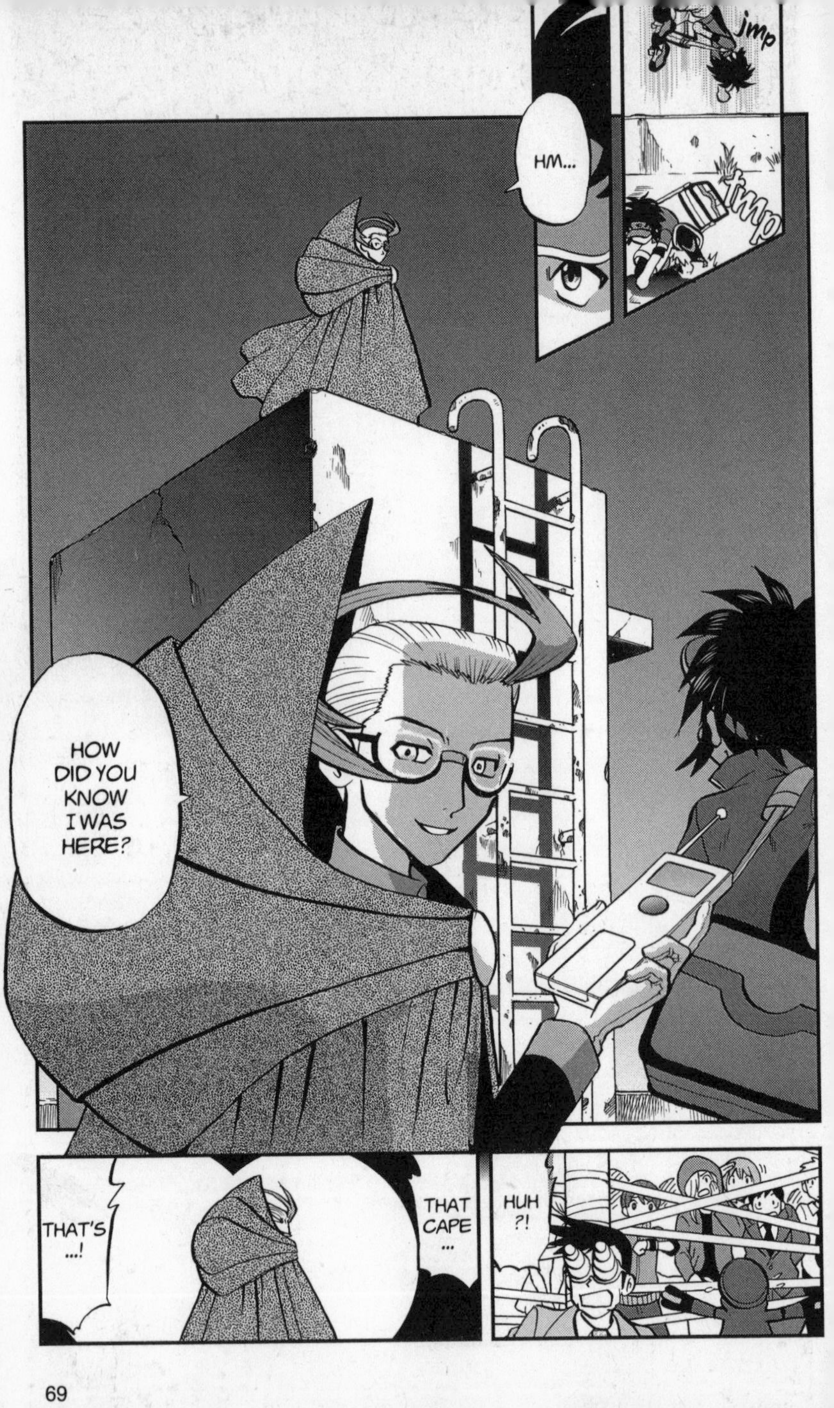
jmp
tmp
HM...
HOW DID YOU KNOW I WAS HERE?
HUH ?!
THAT CAPE ...
THAT'S ...!

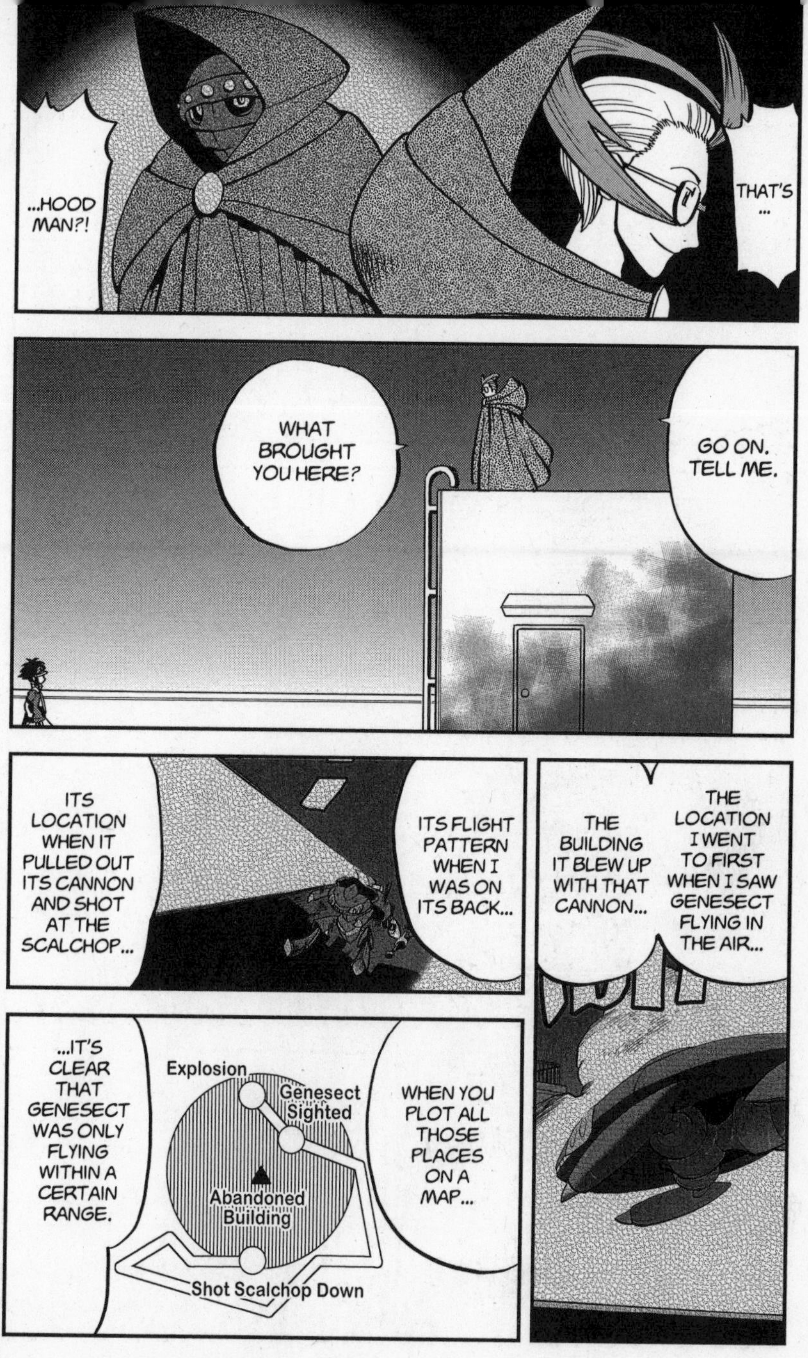
THAT'S ...
...HOOD MAN?!
GO ON. TELL ME.
WHAT BROUGHT YOU HERE?
THE LOCATION I WENT TO FIRST WHEN I SAW GENESECT FLYING IN THE AIR...
THE BUILDING IT BLEW UP WITH THAT CANNON...
ITS FLIGHT PATTERN WHEN I WAS ON ITS BACK...
ITS LOCATION WHEN IT PULLED OUT ITS CANNON AND SHOT AT THE SCALCHOP...
WHEN YOU PLOT ALL THOSE PLACES ON A MAP...
Explosion
Genesect Sighted
Abandoned Building
Shot Scalchop Down
...IT'S CLEAR THAT GENESECT WAS ONLY FLYING WITHIN A CERTAIN RANGE.

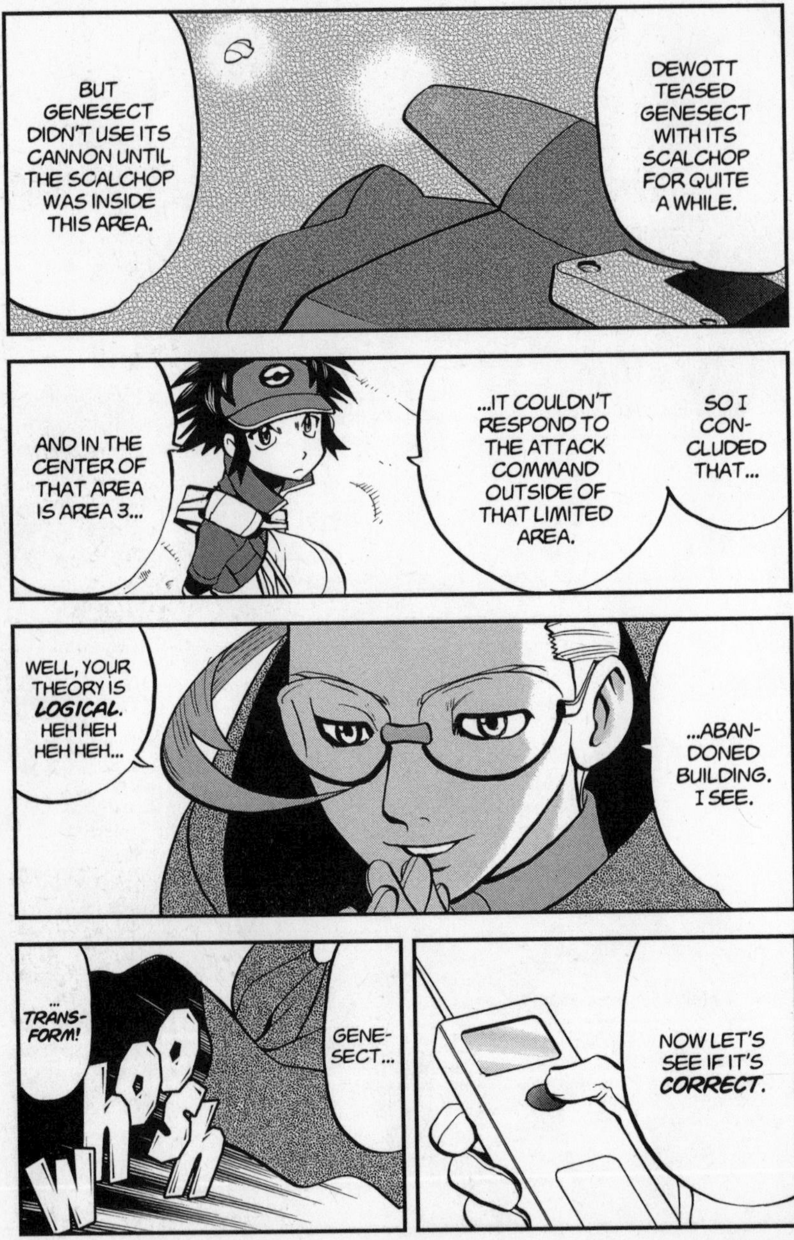
DEWOTT TEASED GENESECT WITH ITS SCALCHOP FOR QUITE A WHILE.
BUT GENESECT DIDN'T USE ITS CANNON UNTIL THE SCALCHOP WAS INSIDE THIS AREA.
SO I CONCLUDED THAT...
...IT COULDN'T RESPOND TO THE ATTACK COMMAND OUTSIDE OF THAT LIMITED AREA.
AND IN THE CENTER OF THAT AREA IS AREA 3...
...ABANDONED BUILDING. I SEE.
WELL, YOUR THEORY IS ***LOGICAL***. HEH HEH HEH HEH...
NOW LET'S SEE IF IT'S ***CORRECT***.
GENESECT...
...*TRANSFORM!*
WHOOSH

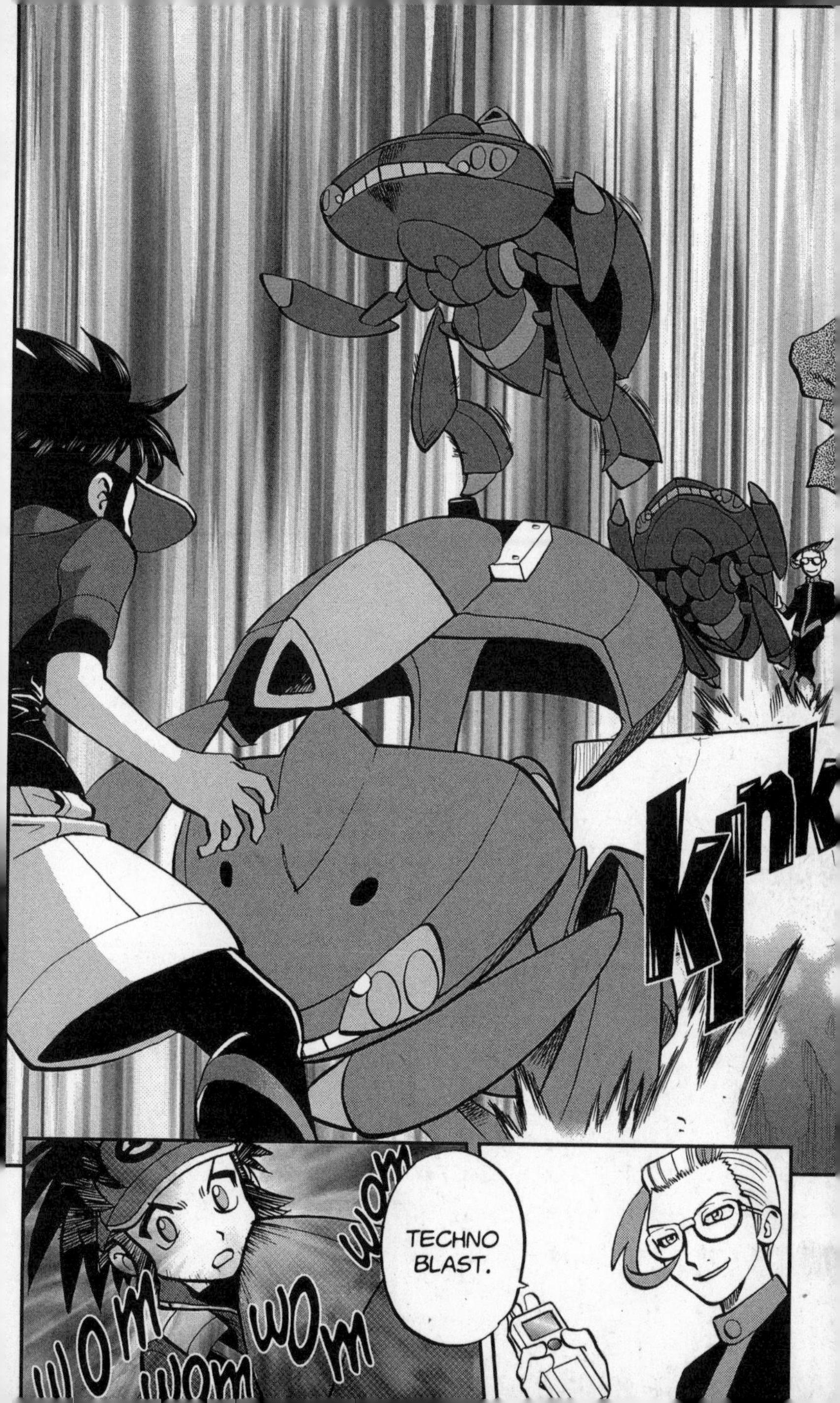
KINK
TECHNO BLAST.
WOM WOM
WOM WOM
WOM WOM

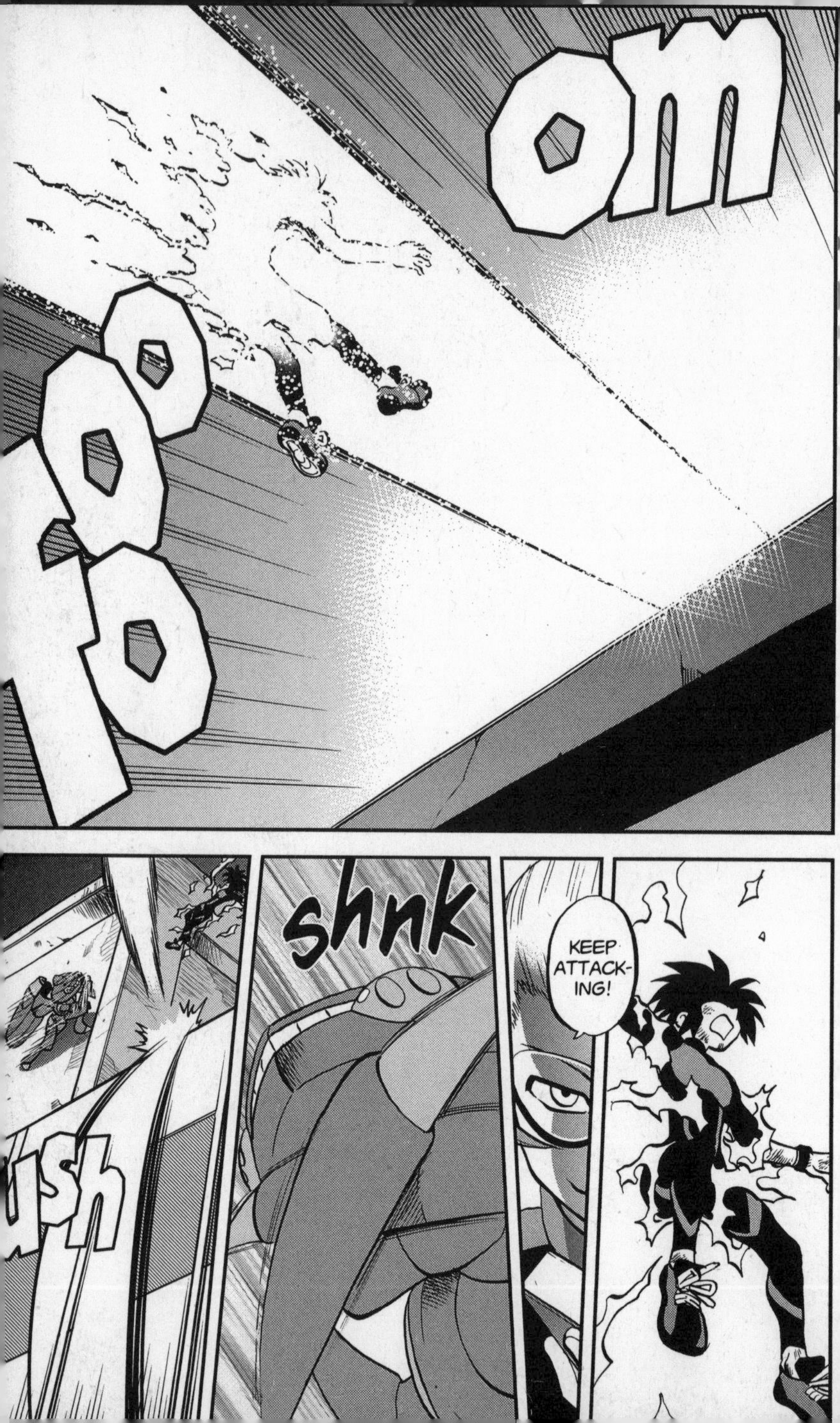
KEEP ATTACK-ING!
shnk

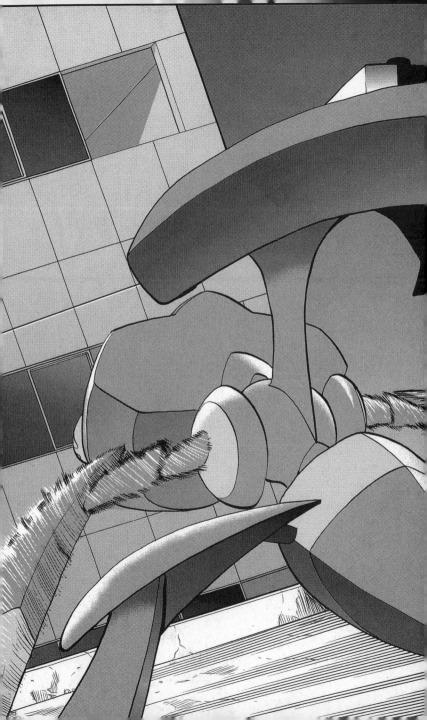

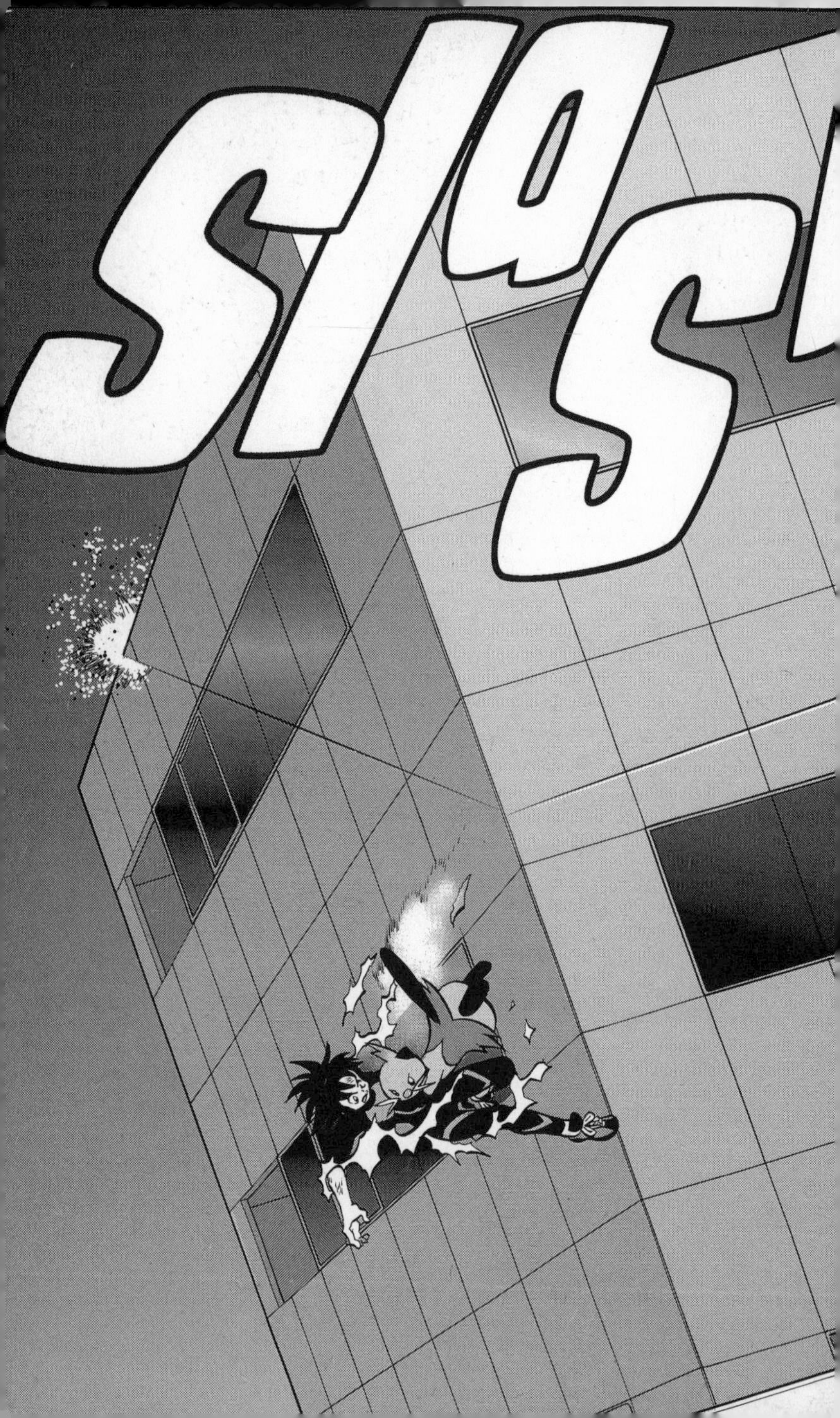
Sla
S

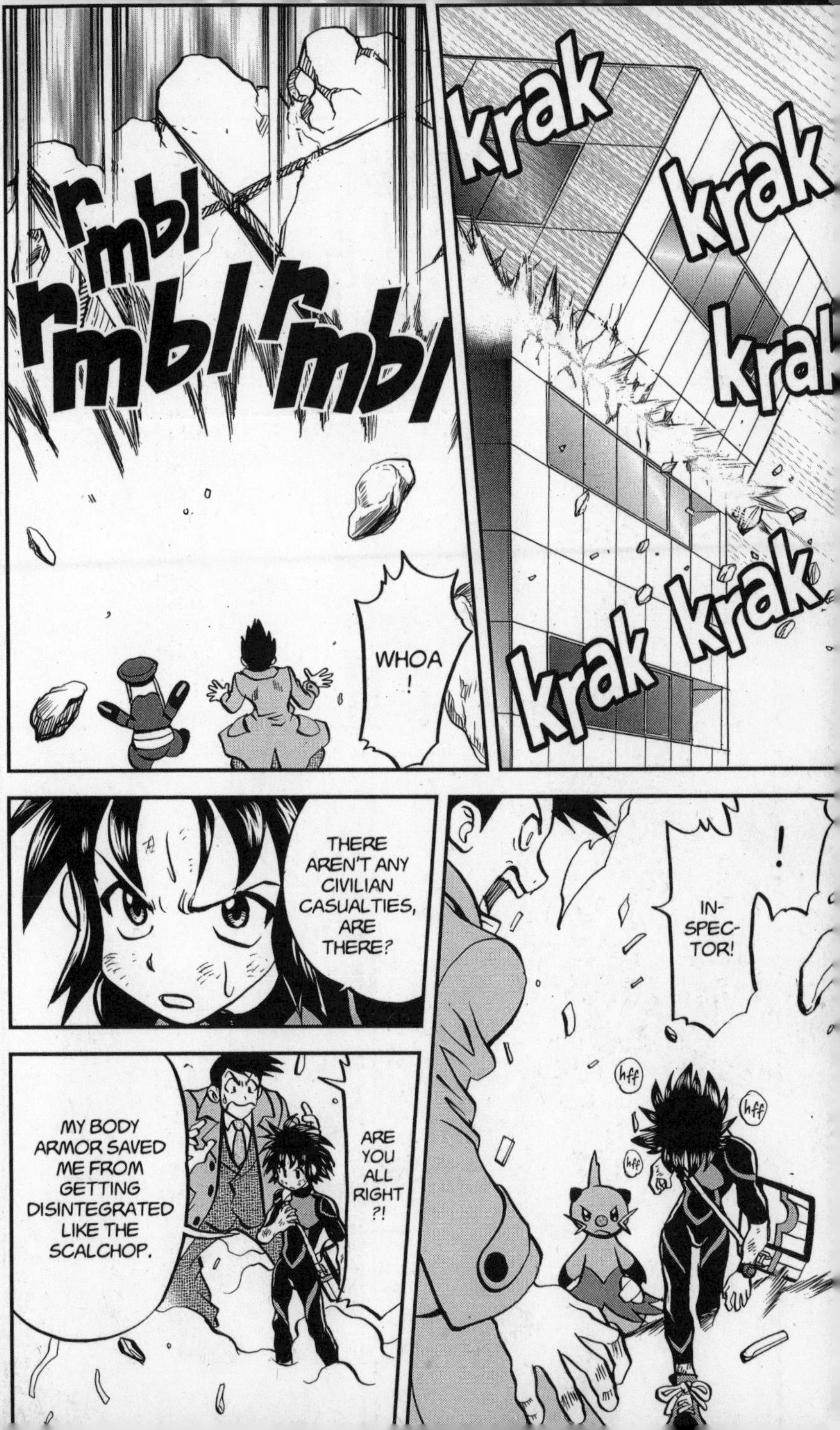
krak
krak
krak
krak krak
rmbl
rmbl rmbl rmbl
WHOA!
!
INSPECTOR!
hff
hff
hff
THERE AREN'T ANY CIVILIAN CASUALTIES, ARE THERE?
ARE YOU ALL RIGHT?!
MY BODY ARMOR SAVED ME FROM GETTING DISINTEGRATED LIKE THE SCALCHOP.

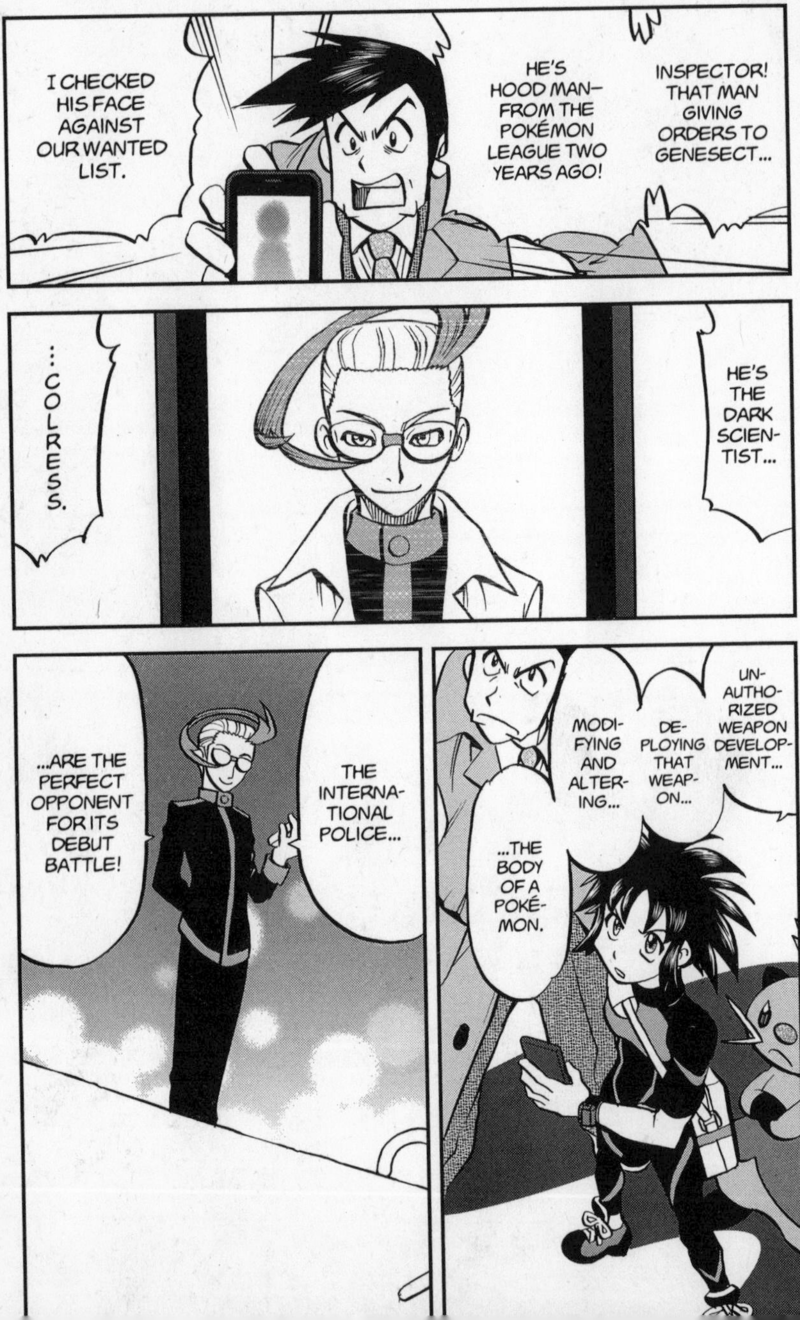
INSPECTOR! THAT MAN GIVING ORDERS TO GENESECT...
HE'S HOOD MAN—FROM THE POKÉMON LEAGUE TWO YEARS AGO!
I CHECKED HIS FACE AGAINST OUR WANTED LIST.
HE'S THE DARK SCIENTIST...
...COLRESS.
UNAUTHORIZED WEAPON DEVELOPMENT...
DEPLOYING THAT WEAPON...
MODIFYING AND ALTERING...
...THE BODY OF A POKÉMON.
THE INTERNATIONAL POLICE...
...ARE THE PERFECT OPPONENT FOR ITS DEBUT BATTLE!

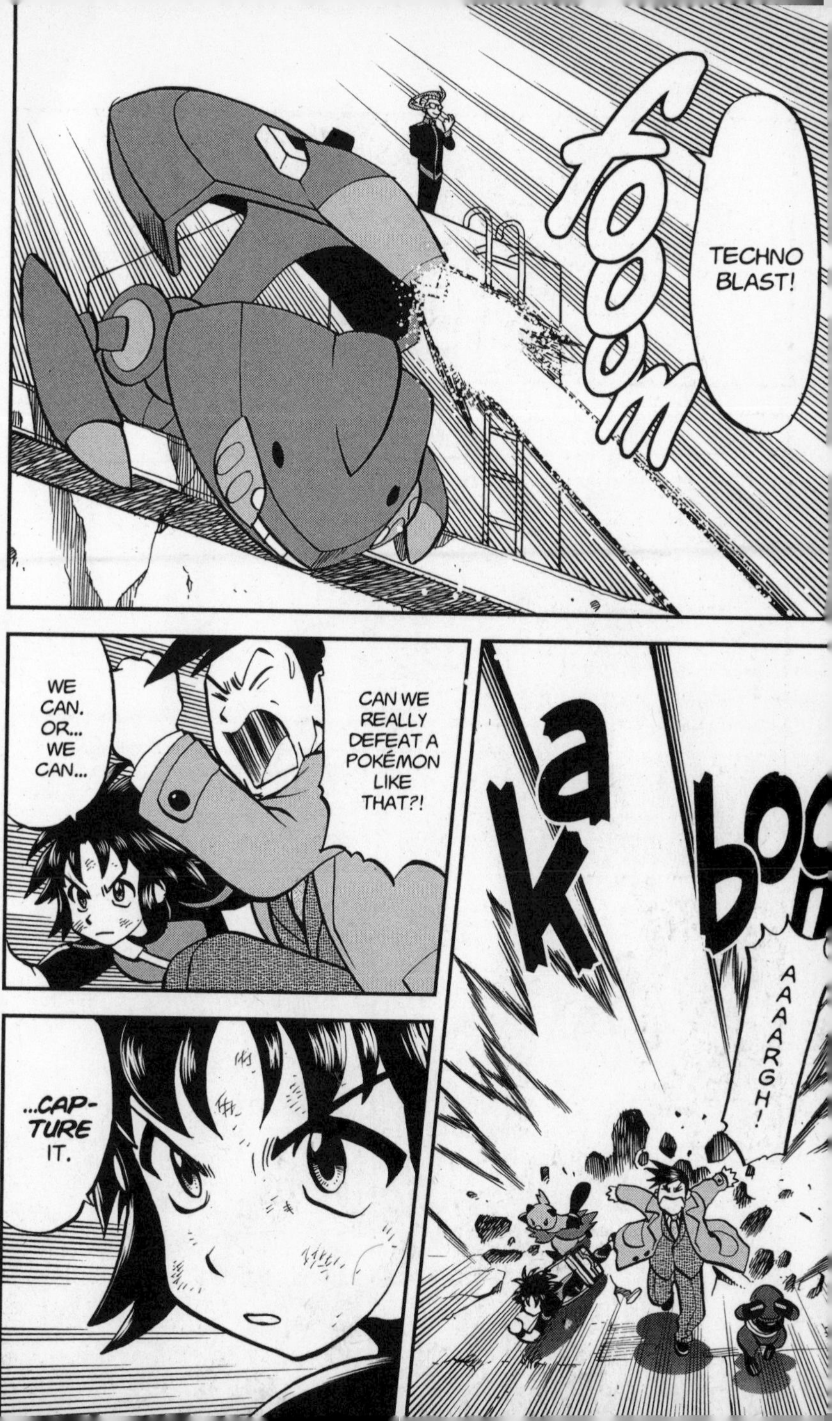
TECHNO BLAST!
FOOOOM
KABOOM
AAAARGH!
CAN WE REALLY DEFEAT A POKÉMON LIKE THAT?!
WE CAN. OR... WE CAN...
...CAPTURE IT.

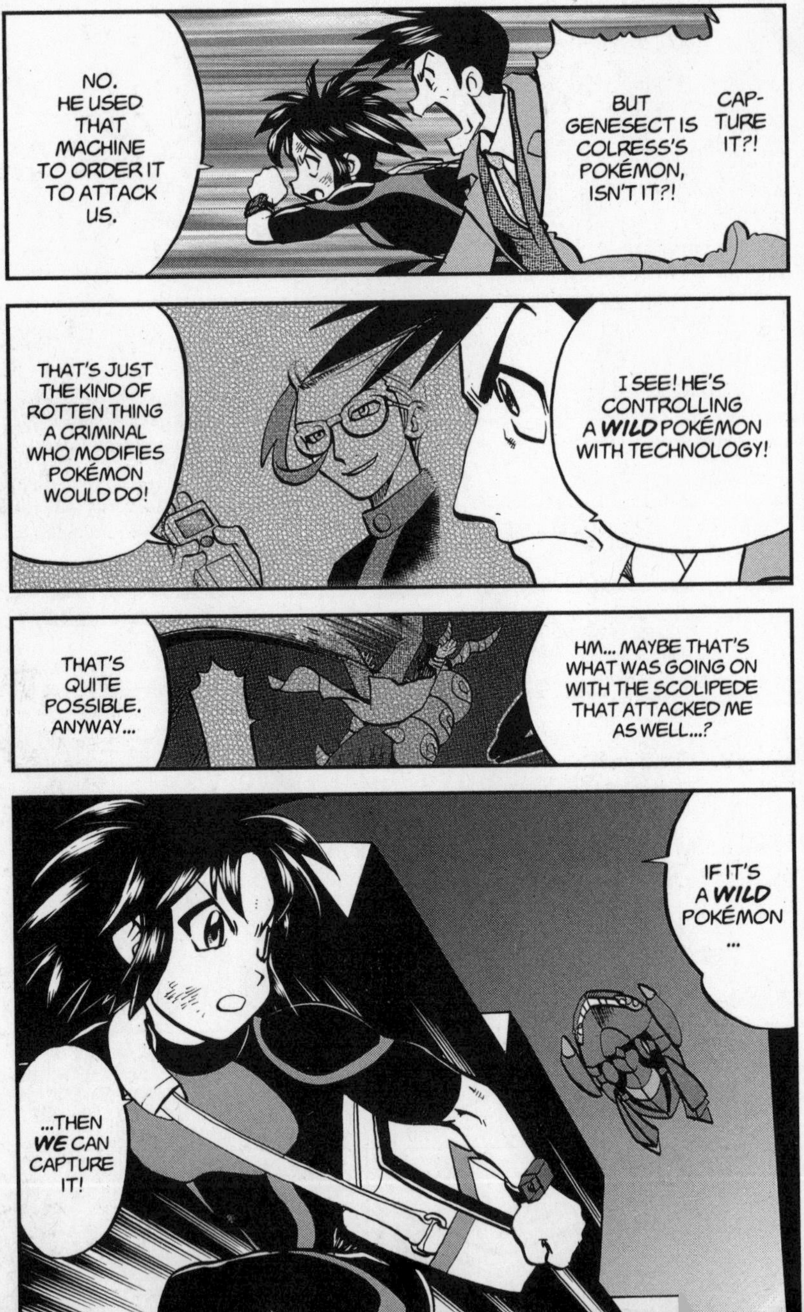
CAP-TURE IT?!
BUT GENESECT IS COLRESS'S POKÉMON, ISN'T IT?!
NO. HE USED THAT MACHINE TO ORDER IT TO ATTACK US.
I SEE! HE'S CONTROLLING A ***WILD*** POKÉMON WITH TECHNOLOGY!
THAT'S JUST THE KIND OF ROTTEN THING A CRIMINAL WHO MODIFIES POKÉMON WOULD DO!
HM... MAYBE THAT'S WHAT WAS GOING ON WITH THE SCOLIPEDE THAT ATTACKED ME AS WELL...?
THAT'S QUITE POSSIBLE. ANYWAY...
IF IT'S A ***WILD*** POKÉMON ...
...THEN ***WE*** CAN CAPTURE IT!

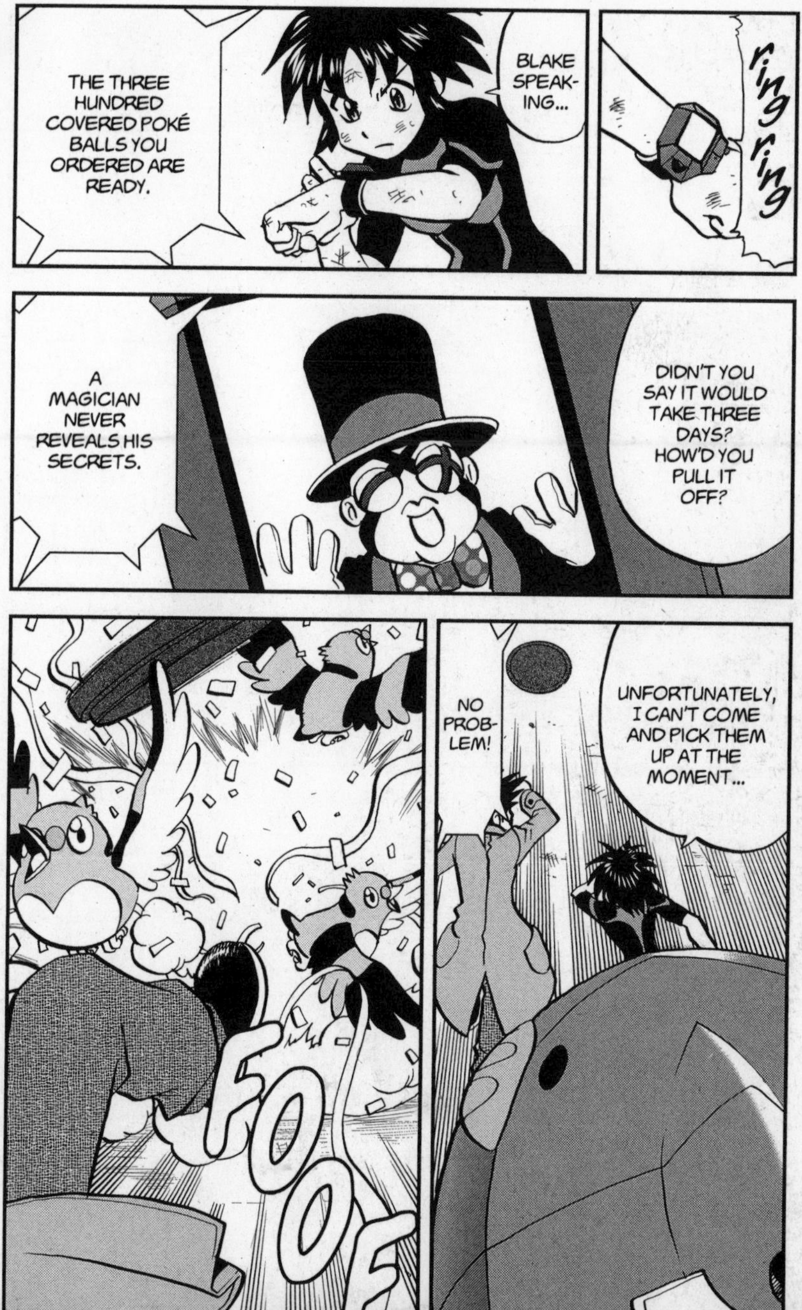
ring ring
BLAKE SPEAK-ING...
THE THREE HUNDRED COVERED POKÉ BALLS YOU ORDERED ARE READY.
DIDN'T YOU SAY IT WOULD TAKE THREE DAYS? HOW'D YOU PULL IT OFF?
A MAGICIAN NEVER REVEALS HIS SECRETS.
UNFORTUNATELY, I CAN'T COME AND PICK THEM UP AT THE MOMENT...
NO PROB-LEM!
FOOF

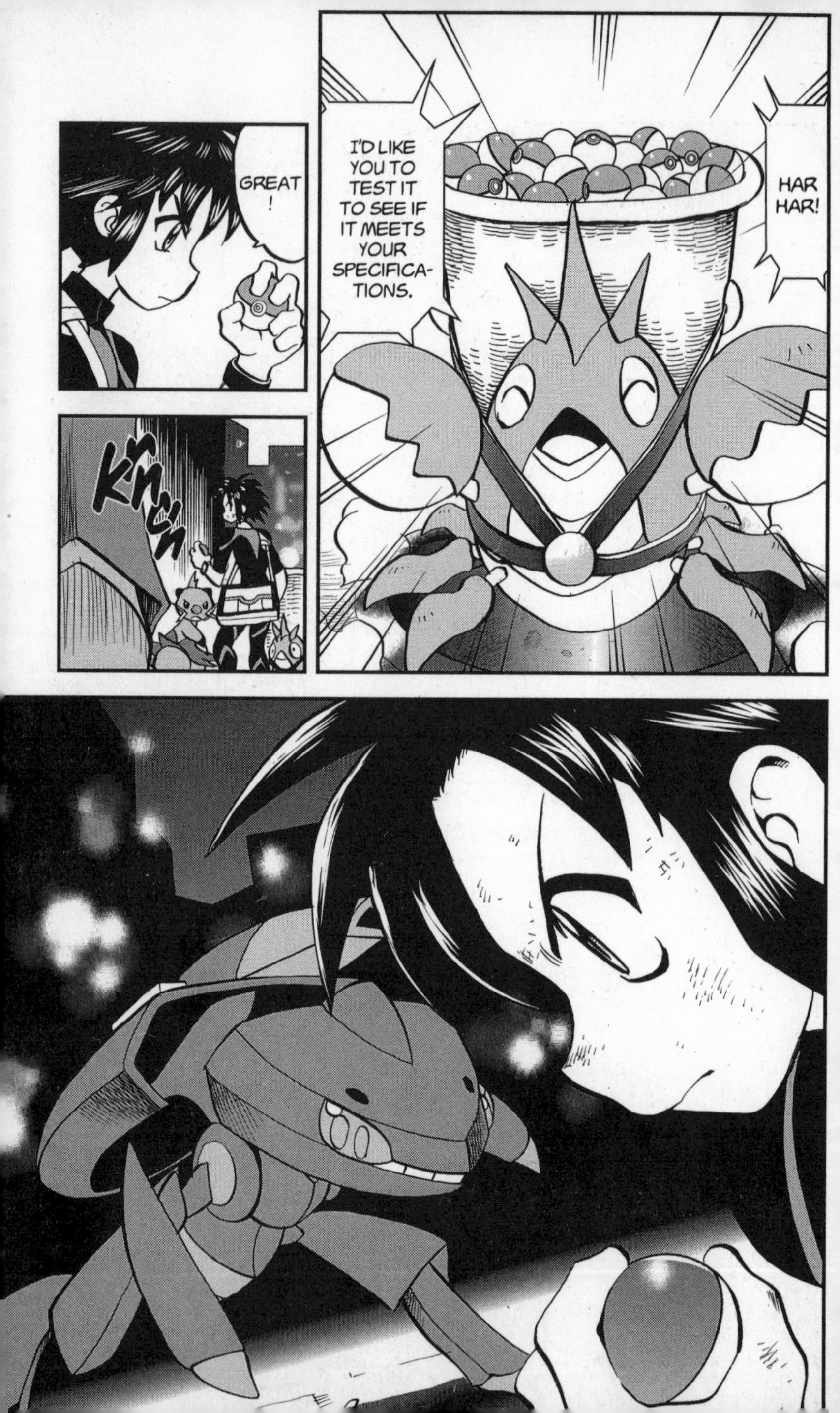
HAR HAR!
I'D LIKE YOU TO TEST IT TO SEE IF IT MEETS YOUR SPECIFICATIONS.
GREAT!
Krnch

Officially Approved by the Pokémon Association The Pokémon Trainers' School

Trainers' School Prospectus

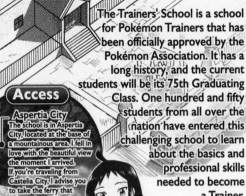

The Trainers' School is a school for Pokémon Trainers that has been officially approved by the Pokémon Association. It has a long history, and the current students will be its 75th Graduating Class. One hundred and fifty students from all over the nation have entered this challenging school to learn about the basics and professional skills needed to become a Trainer.

Access

Aspertia City
The school is in Aspertia City, located at the base of a mountainous area. I fell in love with the beautiful view the moment I arrived. If you're traveling from Castelia City, I advise you to take the ferry that departs from Virbank City.

New Teacher:
Mr. Cheren

Timetable

	Monday	Tuesday	Wednesday	Th
1st Period 9:30–10:30	■ **Type Advantage Studies** (Teacher: Cheren) Class 401	■ **Status Condition Studies** (Teacher: Otoha) Laboratory	■ **Berry Studies** (Teacher: Carl) School Field	
2nd Period 10:40–11:40	■ **Ability Studies** (Teacher: Kisoda) Class 501	■ **Battle Training** (Teacher: Cheren) Gymnasium	■ **Ball Studies** (Teacher: Kurt) Class 301	
3rd Period 11:50–12:50	■ **Weather Studies** (Teacher: Cheren) Class 401	■ **Habitat Studies** (Teacher: Kera) Class 202	■ **Form Studies** (Teacher: Komodo) Class 302	

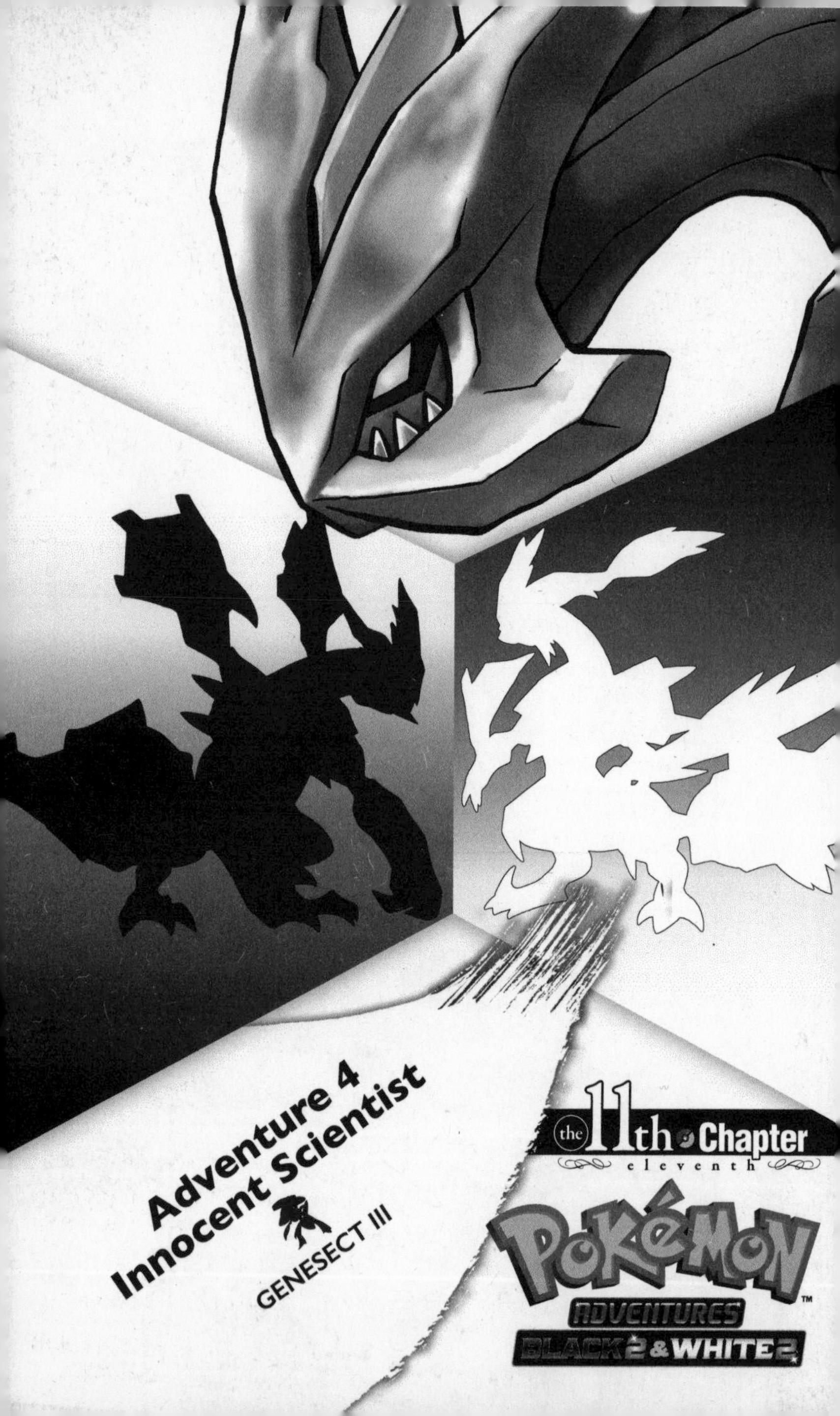
Adventure 4
Innocent Scientist
GENESECT III
the 11th Chapter
eleventh
POKÉMON
ADVENTURES
BLACK 2 & WHITE 2

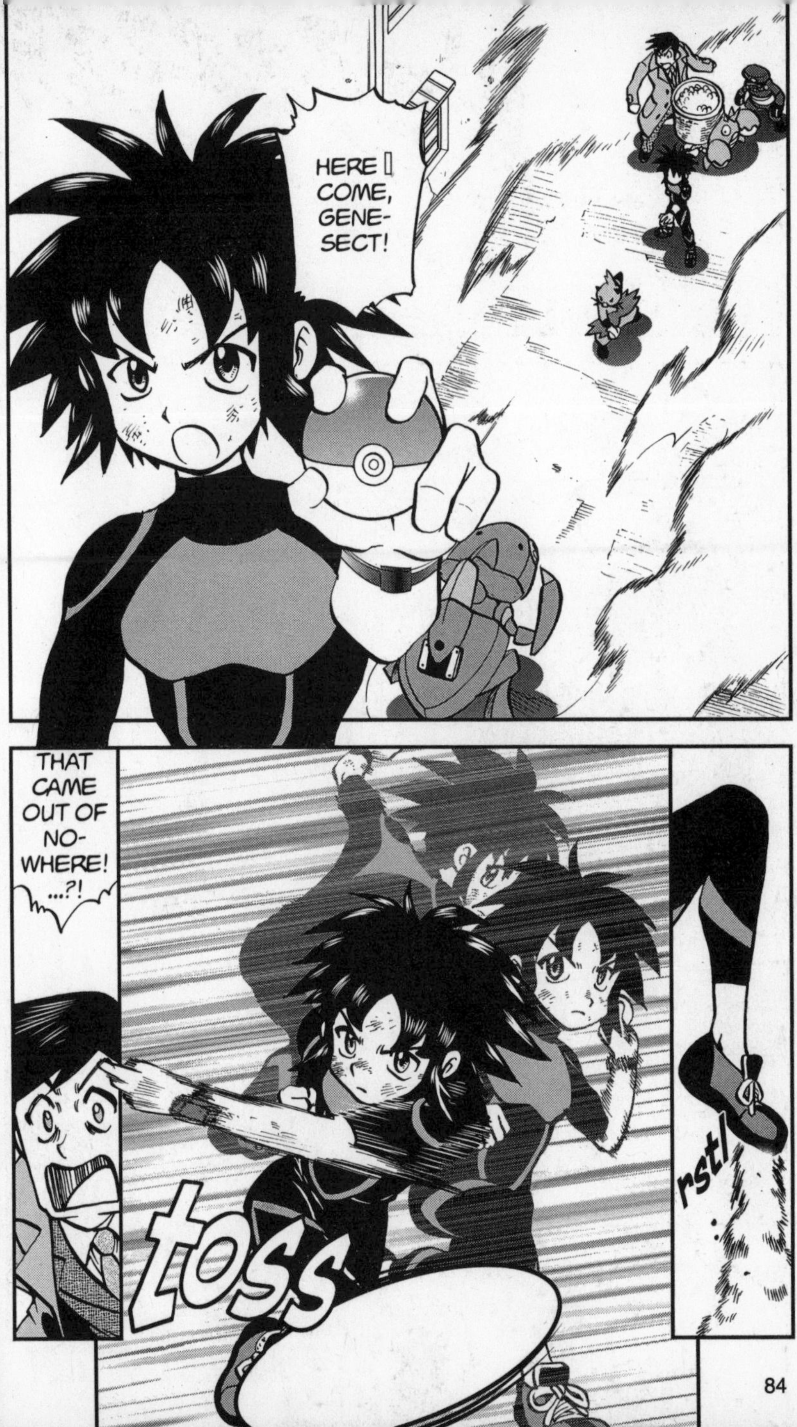
HERE I COME, GENE-SECT!
THAT CAME OUT OF NO-WHERE! ...?!
rstl
toss

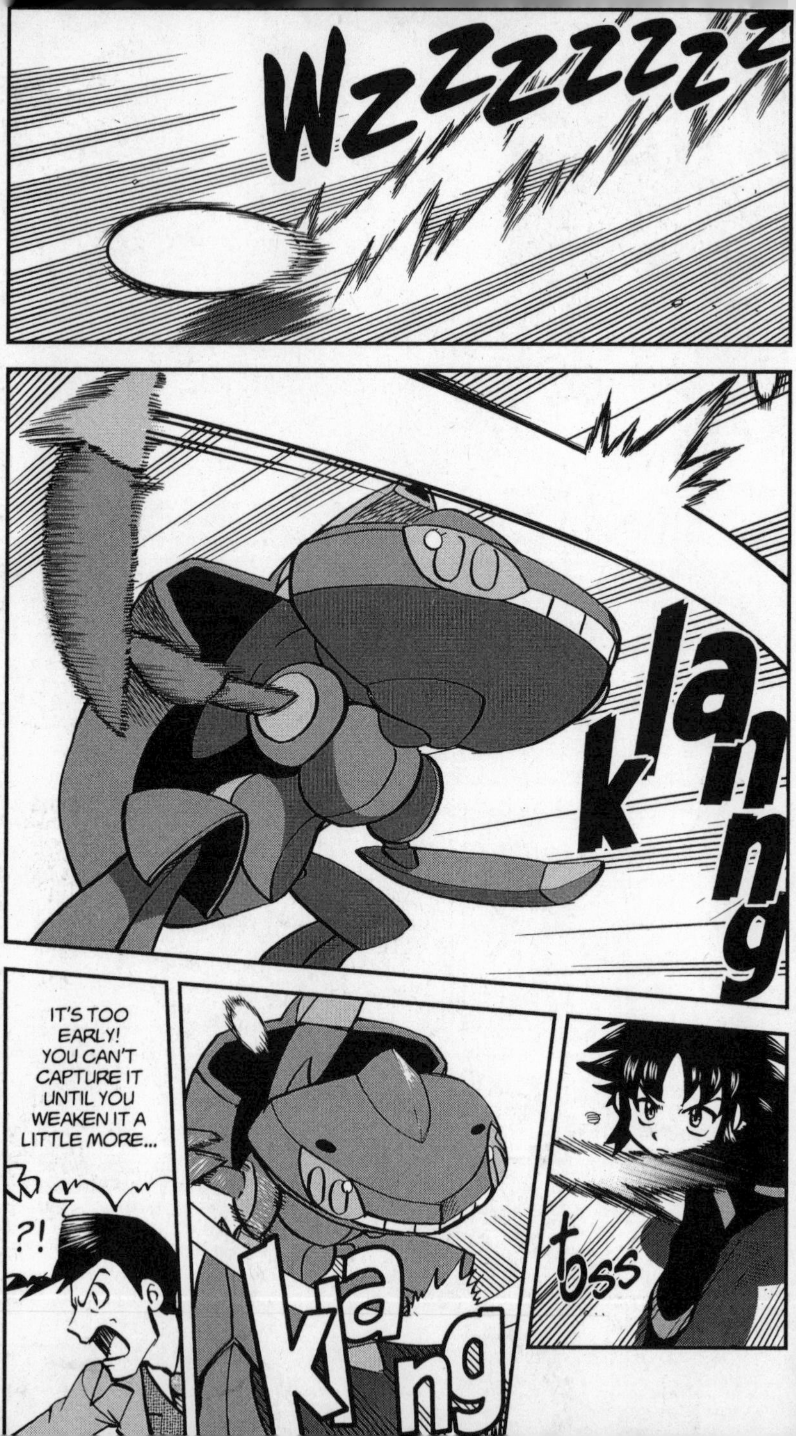
WZZZZZZZ
KLANG
TOSS
KLANG
IT'S TOO EARLY! YOU CAN'T CAPTURE IT UNTIL YOU WEAKEN IT A LITTLE MORE...
?!

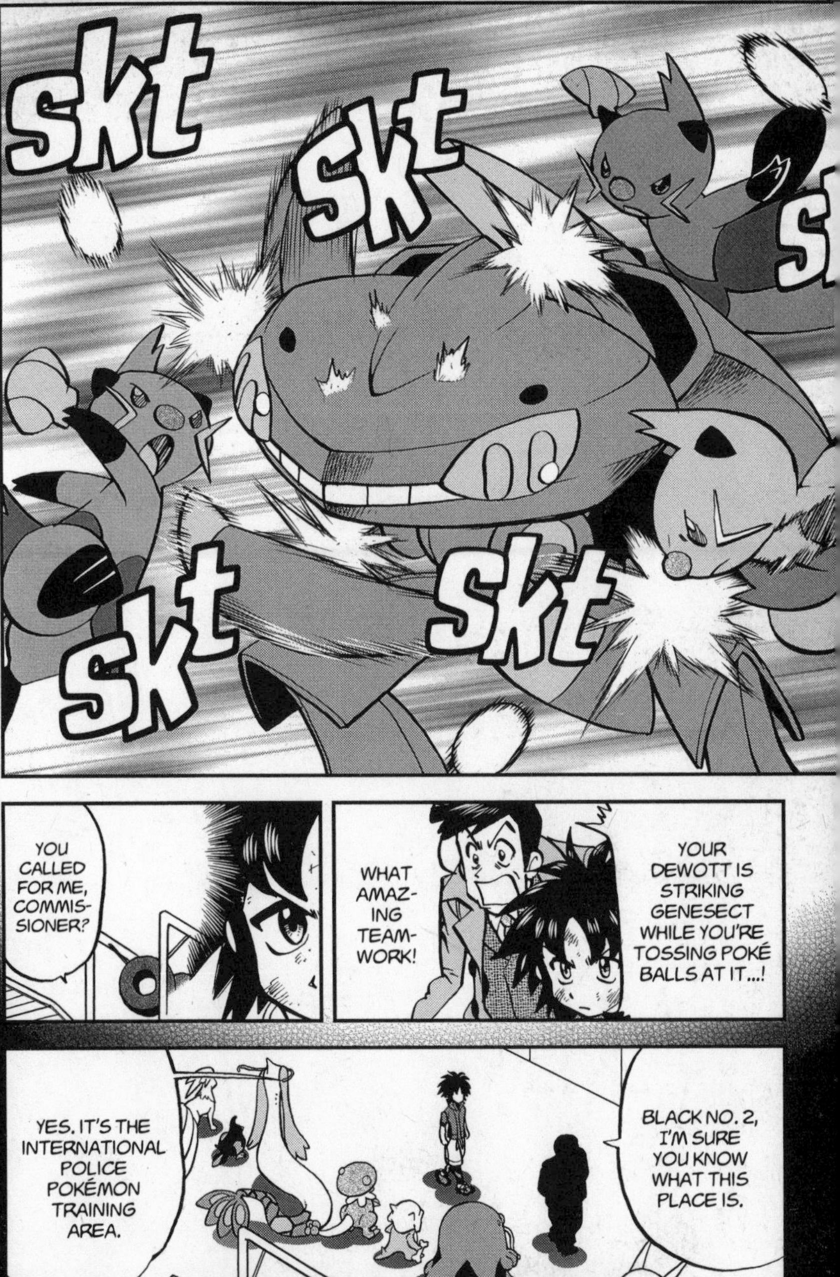
skt
skt
skt
skt
YOUR DEWOTT IS STRIKING GENESECT WHILE YOU'RE TOSSING POKÉ BALLS AT IT...!
WHAT AMAZING TEAMWORK!
YOU CALLED FOR ME, COMMISSIONER?
BLACK NO. 2, I'M SURE YOU KNOW WHAT THIS PLACE IS.
YES. IT'S THE INTERNATIONAL POLICE POKÉMON TRAINING AREA.

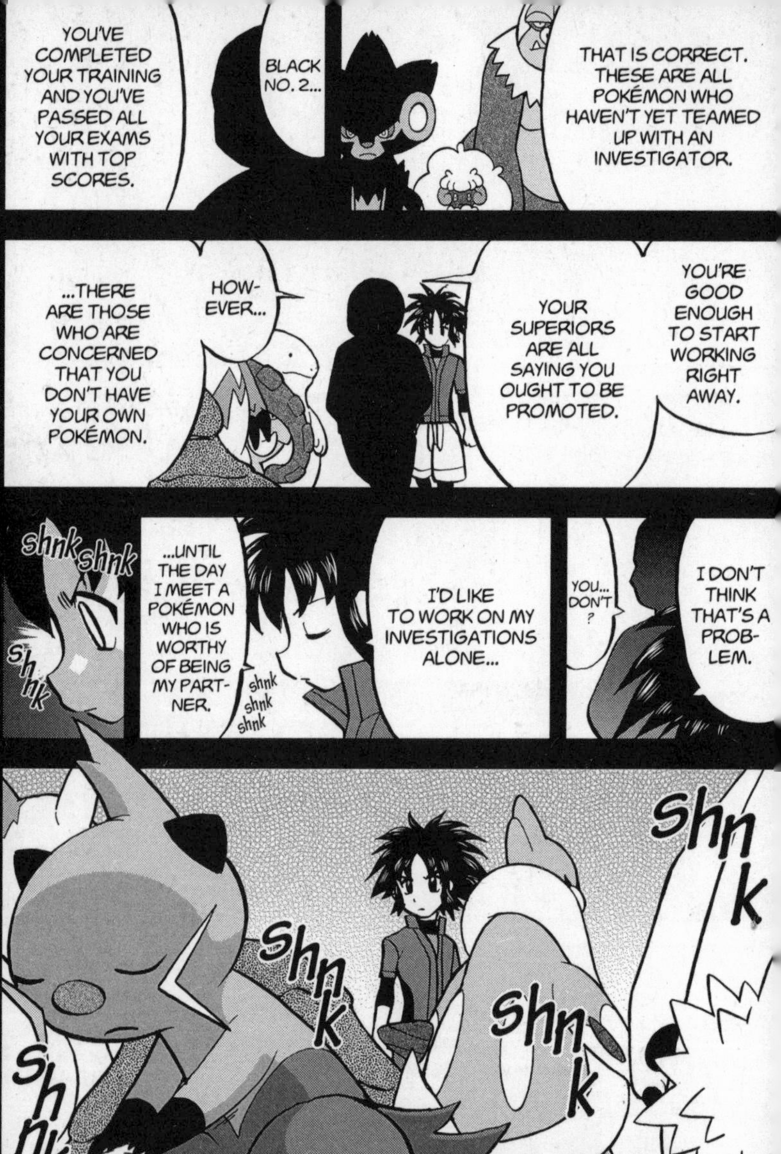
THAT IS CORRECT. THESE ARE ALL POKÉMON WHO HAVEN'T YET TEAMED UP WITH AN INVESTIGATOR.
BLACK NO. 2...
YOU'VE COMPLETED YOUR TRAINING AND YOU'VE PASSED ALL YOUR EXAMS WITH TOP SCORES.
YOU'RE GOOD ENOUGH TO START WORKING RIGHT AWAY.
YOUR SUPERIORS ARE ALL SAYING YOU OUGHT TO BE PROMOTED.
HOW-EVER...
...THERE ARE THOSE WHO ARE CONCERNED THAT YOU DON'T HAVE YOUR OWN POKÉMON.
I DON'T THINK THAT'S A PROB-LEM.
YOU... DON'T ?
I'D LIKE TO WORK ON MY INVESTIGATIONS ALONE...
...UNTIL THE DAY I MEET A POKÉMON WHO IS WORTHY OF BEING MY PART-NER.
shnk shnk shnk
shnk shnk
shnk
Shnk
Shnk
Shnk
Shnk

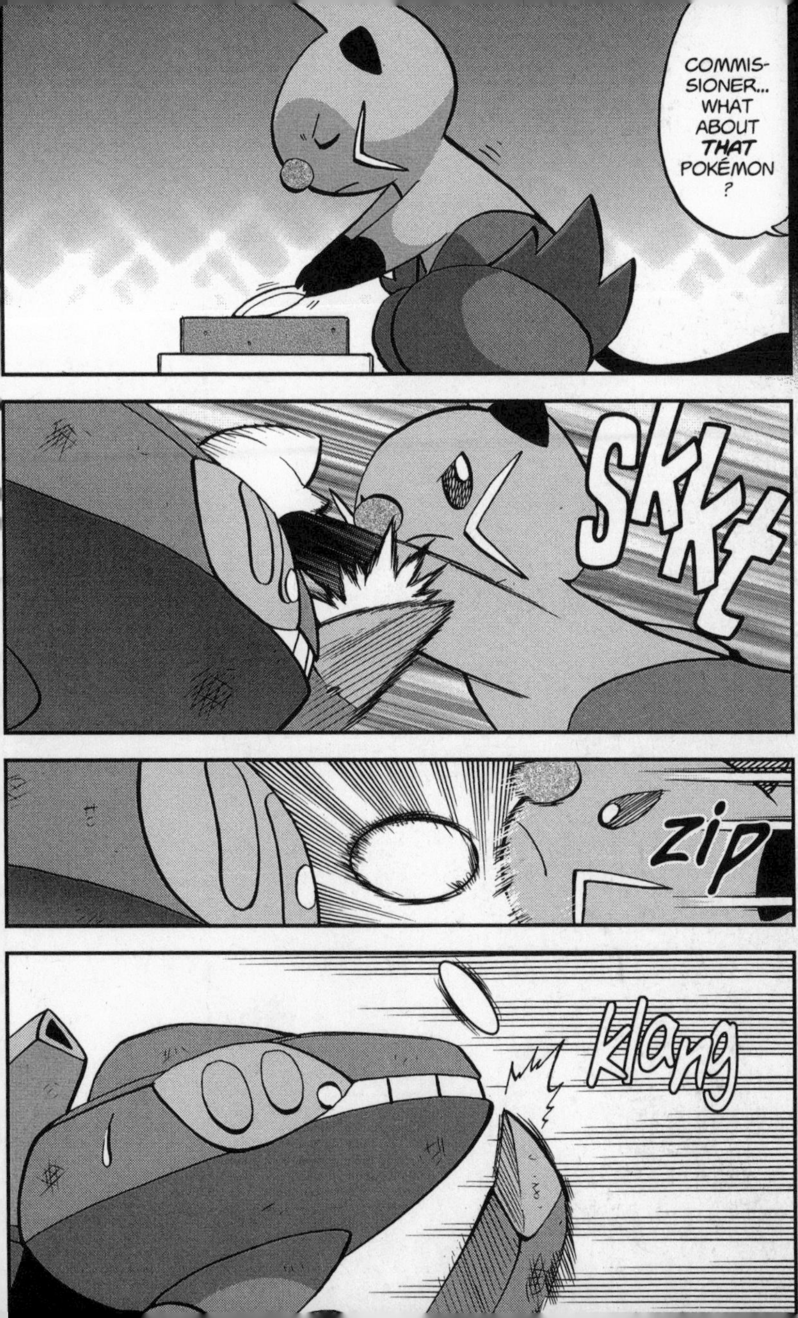
COMMISSIONER... WHAT ABOUT THAT POKÉMON?
SKKT
ZIP
KLANG

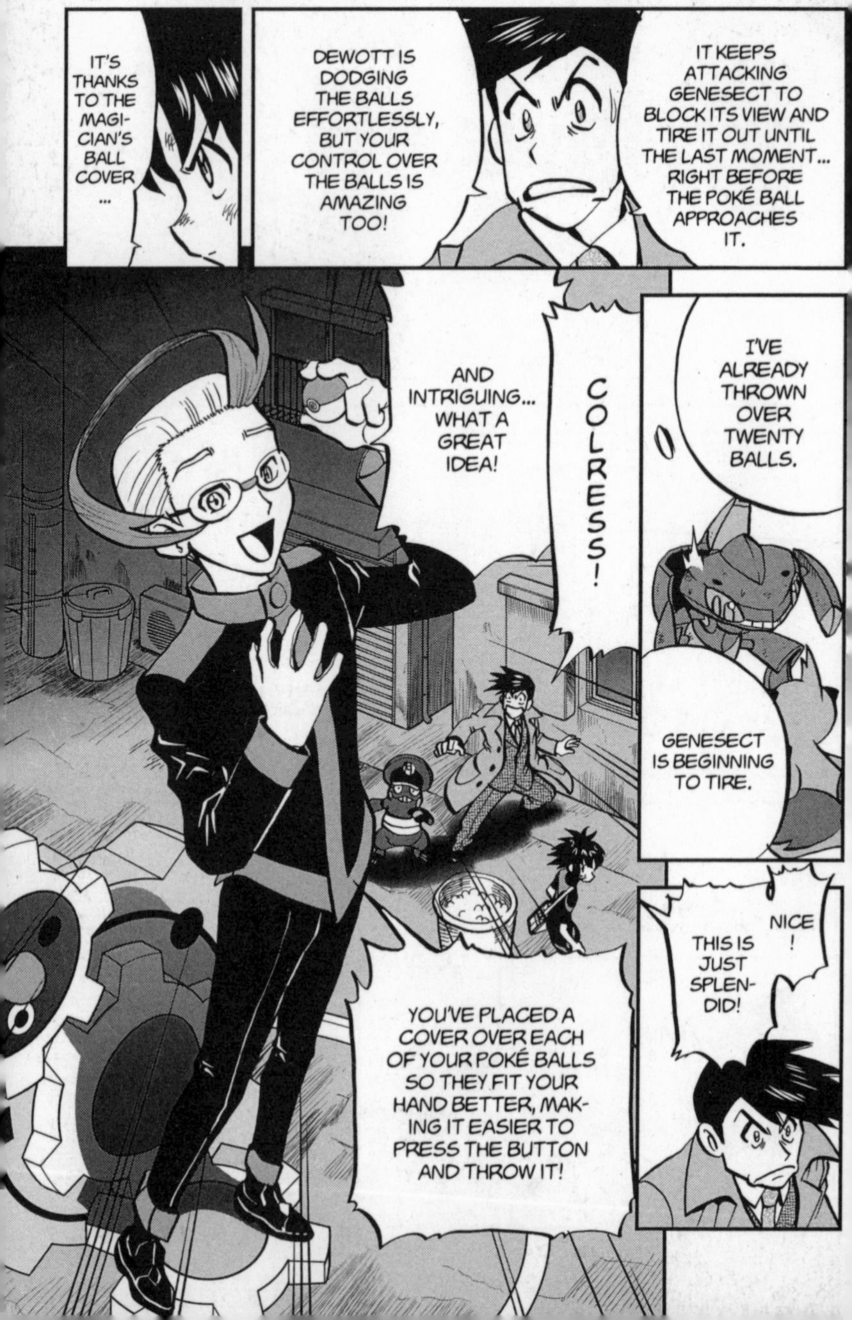
IT KEEPS ATTACKING GENESECT TO BLOCK ITS VIEW AND TIRE IT OUT UNTIL THE LAST MOMENT... RIGHT BEFORE THE POKÉ BALL APPROACHES IT.
DEWOTT IS DODGING THE BALLS EFFORTLESSLY, BUT YOUR CONTROL OVER THE BALLS IS AMAZING TOO!
IT'S THANKS TO THE MAGICIAN'S BALL COVER...
I'VE ALREADY THROWN OVER TWENTY BALLS.
GENESECT IS BEGINNING TO TIRE.
NICE!
THIS IS JUST SPLENDID!
COLRESS!
AND INTRIGUING... WHAT A GREAT IDEA!
YOU'VE PLACED A COVER OVER EACH OF YOUR POKÉ BALLS SO THEY FIT YOUR HAND BETTER, MAKING IT EASIER TO PRESS THE BUTTON AND THROW IT!

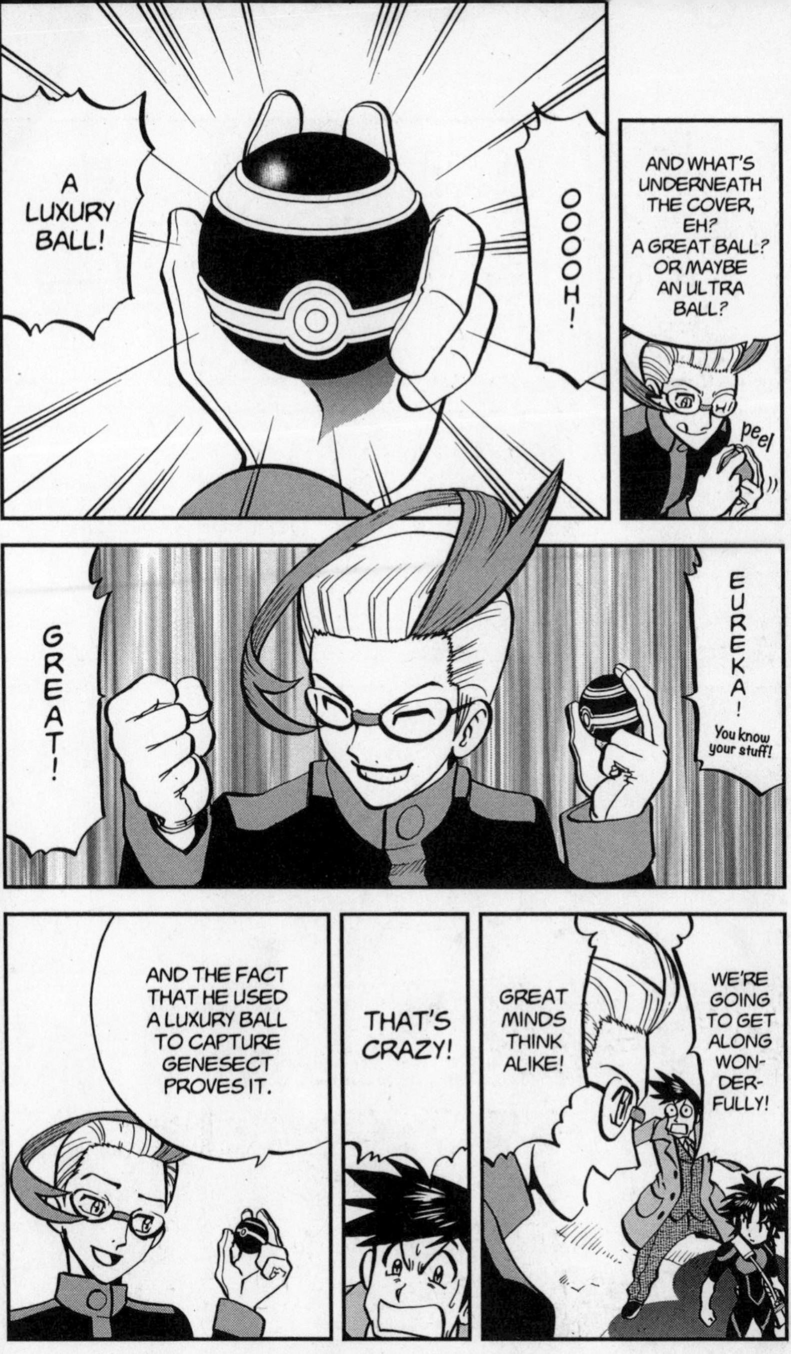

AND WHAT'S UNDERNEATH THE COVER, EH? A GREAT BALL? OR MAYBE AN ULTRA BALL?
peel
OOOOH!
A LUXURY BALL!
EUREKA!
You know your stuff!
GREAT!
WE'RE GOING TO GET ALONG WON-DER-FULLY!
GREAT MINDS THINK ALIKE!
THAT'S CRAZY!
AND THE FACT THAT HE USED A LUXURY BALL TO CAPTURE GENESECT PROVES IT.

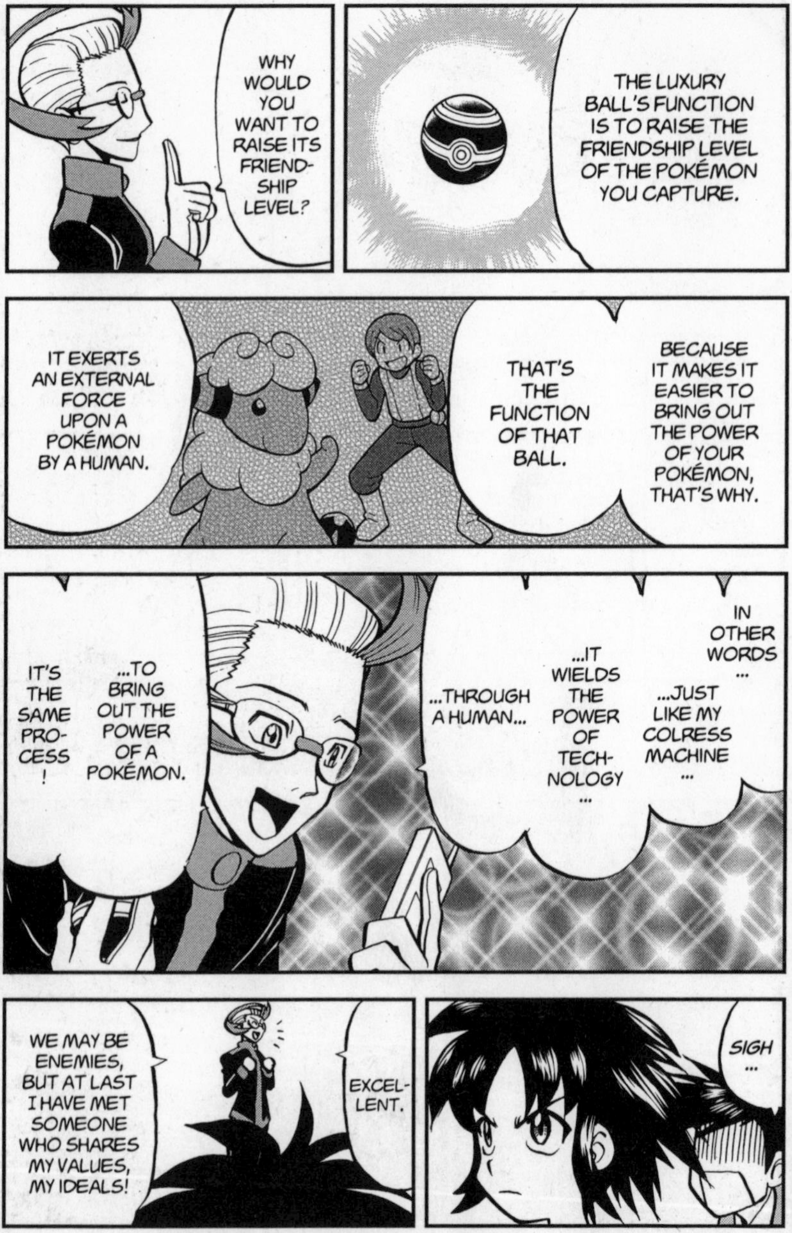
THE LUXURY BALL'S FUNCTION IS TO RAISE THE FRIENDSHIP LEVEL OF THE POKÉMON YOU CAPTURE.
WHY WOULD YOU WANT TO RAISE ITS FRIENDSHIP LEVEL?
BECAUSE IT MAKES IT EASIER TO BRING OUT THE POWER OF YOUR POKÉMON, THAT'S WHY.
THAT'S THE FUNCTION OF THAT BALL.
IT EXERTS AN EXTERNAL FORCE UPON A POKÉMON BY A HUMAN.
IN OTHER WORDS...
...JUST LIKE MY COLRESS MACHINE...
...IT WIELDS THE POWER OF TECHNOLOGY...
...THROUGH A HUMAN...
...TO BRING OUT THE POWER OF A POKÉMON.
IT'S THE SAME PROCESS!
SIGH...
EXCELLENT.
WE MAY BE ENEMIES, BUT AT LAST I HAVE MET SOMEONE WHO SHARES MY VALUES, MY IDEALS!

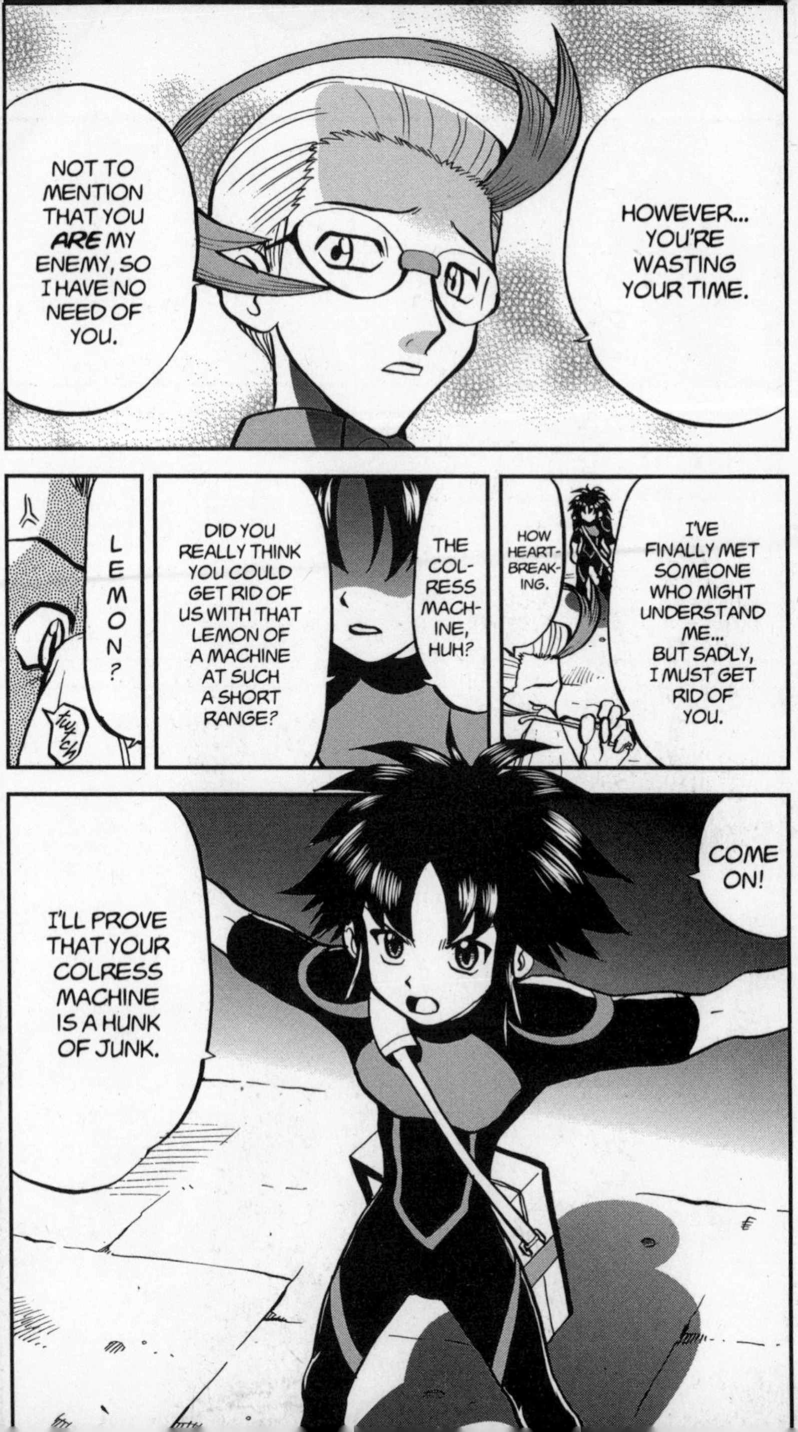
HOWEVER... YOU'RE WASTING YOUR TIME.
NOT TO MENTION THAT YOU ARE MY ENEMY, SO I HAVE NO NEED OF YOU.
I'VE FINALLY MET SOMEONE WHO MIGHT UNDERSTAND ME... BUT SADLY, I MUST GET RID OF YOU.
HOW HEART-BREAKING.
THE COLRESS MACHINE, HUH?
DID YOU REALLY THINK YOU COULD GET RID OF US WITH THAT LEMON OF A MACHINE AT SUCH A SHORT RANGE?
LEMON?
twitch
COME ON!
I'LL PROVE THAT YOUR COLRESS MACHINE IS A HUNK OF JUNK.

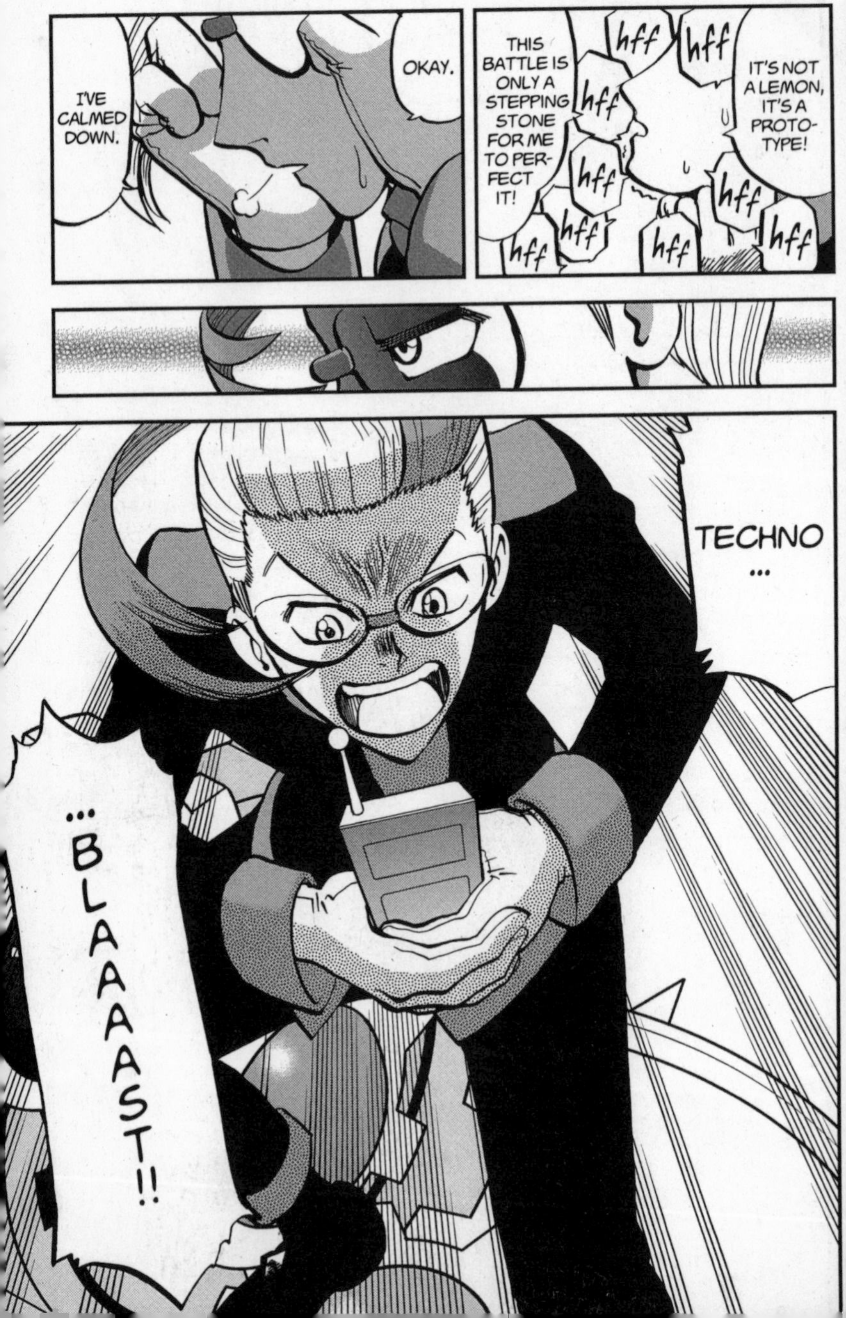
hff hff
IT'S NOT A LEMON, IT'S A PROTOTYPE!
hff hff hff hff hff hff hff hff
THIS BATTLE IS ONLY A STEPPING STONE FOR ME TO PERFECT IT!
OKAY.
I'VE CALMED DOWN.
TECHNO...
...BLAAAAST!!

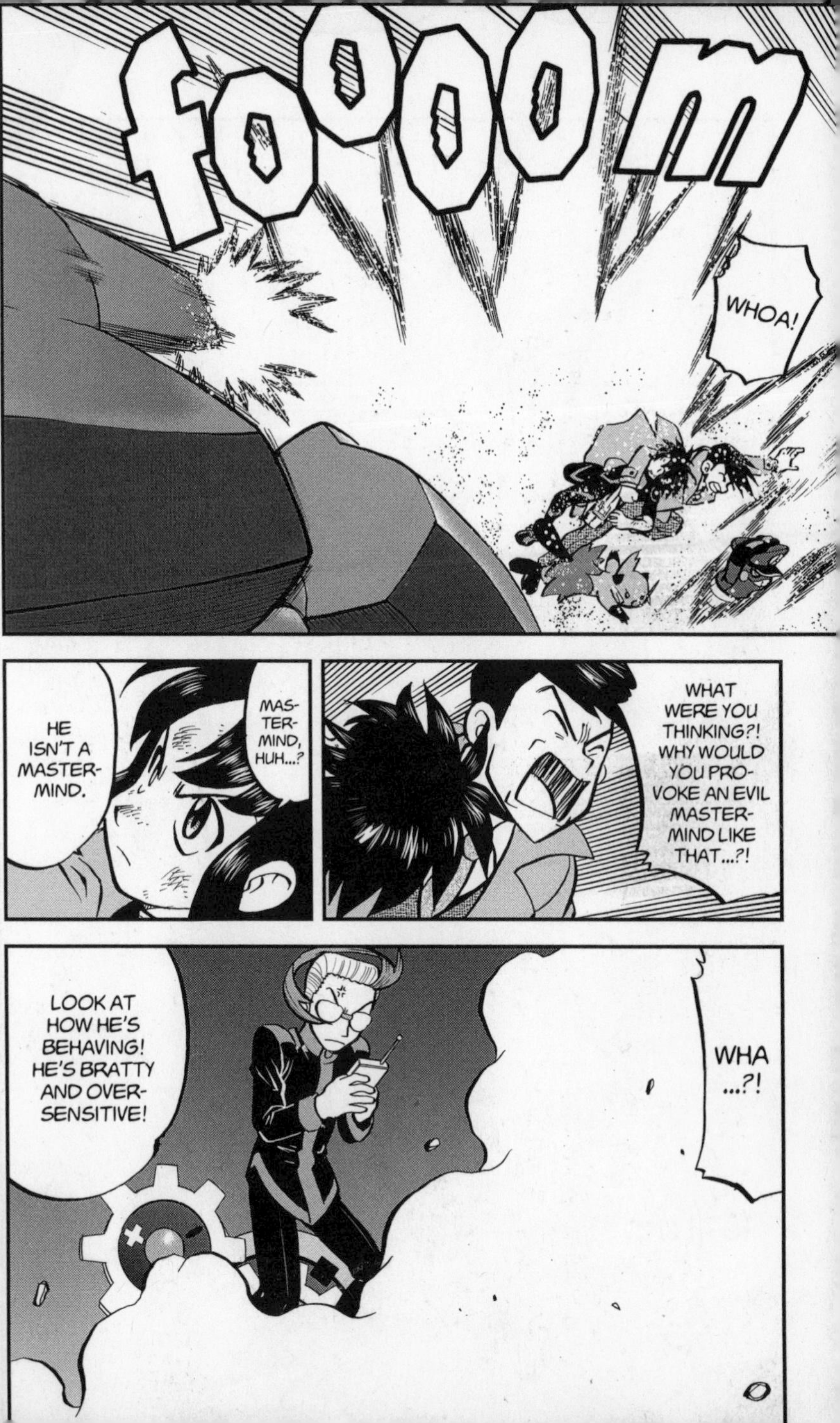
fooom
WHOA!
WHAT WERE YOU THINKING?! WHY WOULD YOU PRO-VOKE AN EVIL MASTER-MIND LIKE THAT...?!
MAS-TER-MIND, HUH...?
HE ISN'T A MASTER-MIND.
WHA ...?!
LOOK AT HOW HE'S BEHAVING! HE'S BRATTY AND OVER-SENSITIVE!

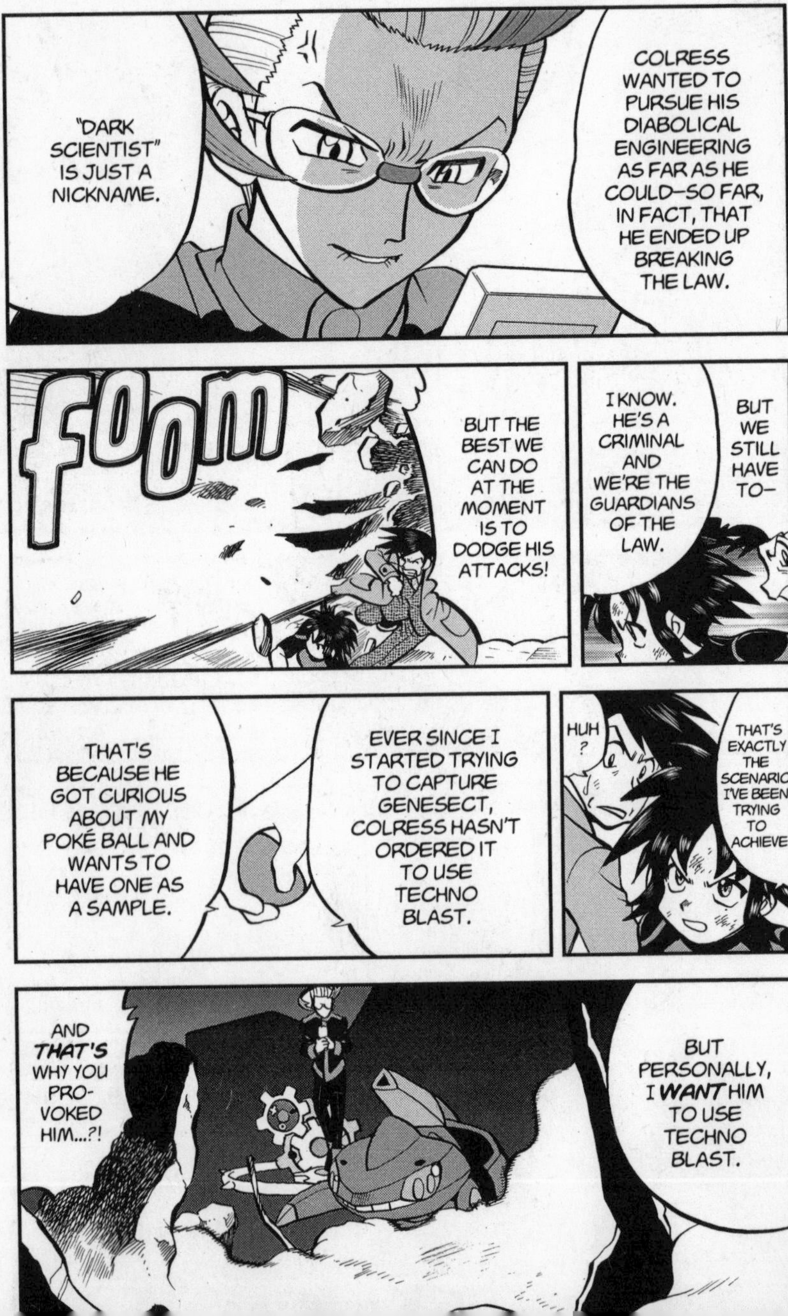
COLRESS WANTED TO PURSUE HIS DIABOLICAL ENGINEERING AS FAR AS HE COULD—SO FAR, IN FACT, THAT HE ENDED UP BREAKING THE LAW.
"DARK SCIENTIST" IS JUST A NICKNAME.
BUT WE STILL HAVE TO—
I KNOW. HE'S A CRIMINAL AND WE'RE THE GUARDIANS OF THE LAW.
BUT THE BEST WE CAN DO AT THE MOMENT IS TO DODGE HIS ATTACKS!
FOOM
THAT'S EXACTLY THE SCENARIO I'VE BEEN TRYING TO ACHIEVE.
HUH?
EVER SINCE I STARTED TRYING TO CAPTURE GENESECT, COLRESS HASN'T ORDERED IT TO USE TECHNO BLAST.
THAT'S BECAUSE HE GOT CURIOUS ABOUT MY POKÉ BALL AND WANTS TO HAVE ONE AS A SAMPLE.
BUT PERSONALLY, I *WANT* HIM TO USE TECHNO BLAST.
AND *THAT'S* WHY YOU PRO-VOKED HIM...?!

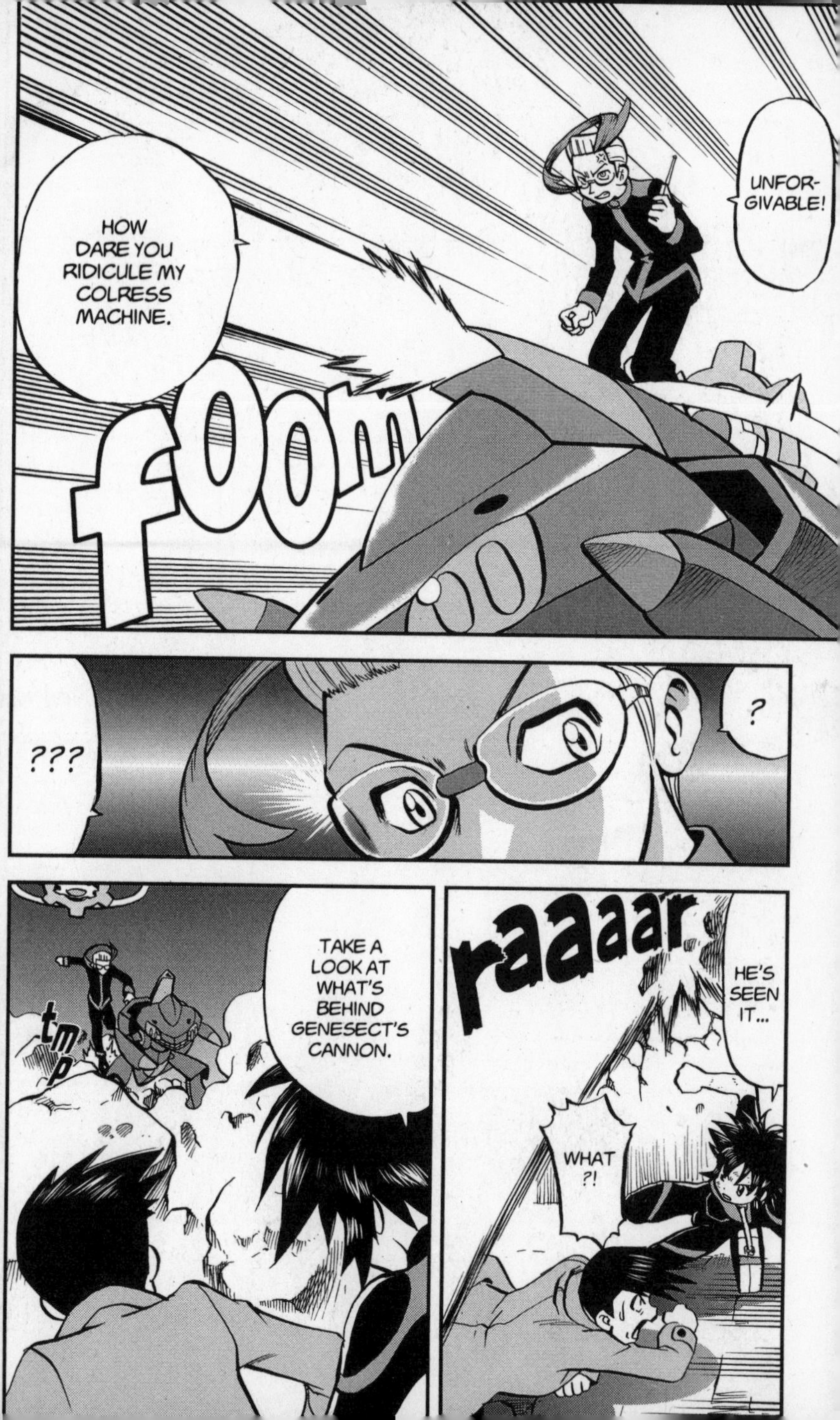
UNFORGIVABLE!
HOW DARE YOU RIDICULE MY COLRESS MACHINE.
fOOm
?
???
raaaar
HE'S SEEN IT...
WHAT ?!
TAKE A LOOK AT WHAT'S BEHIND GENESECT'S CANNON.
tmp

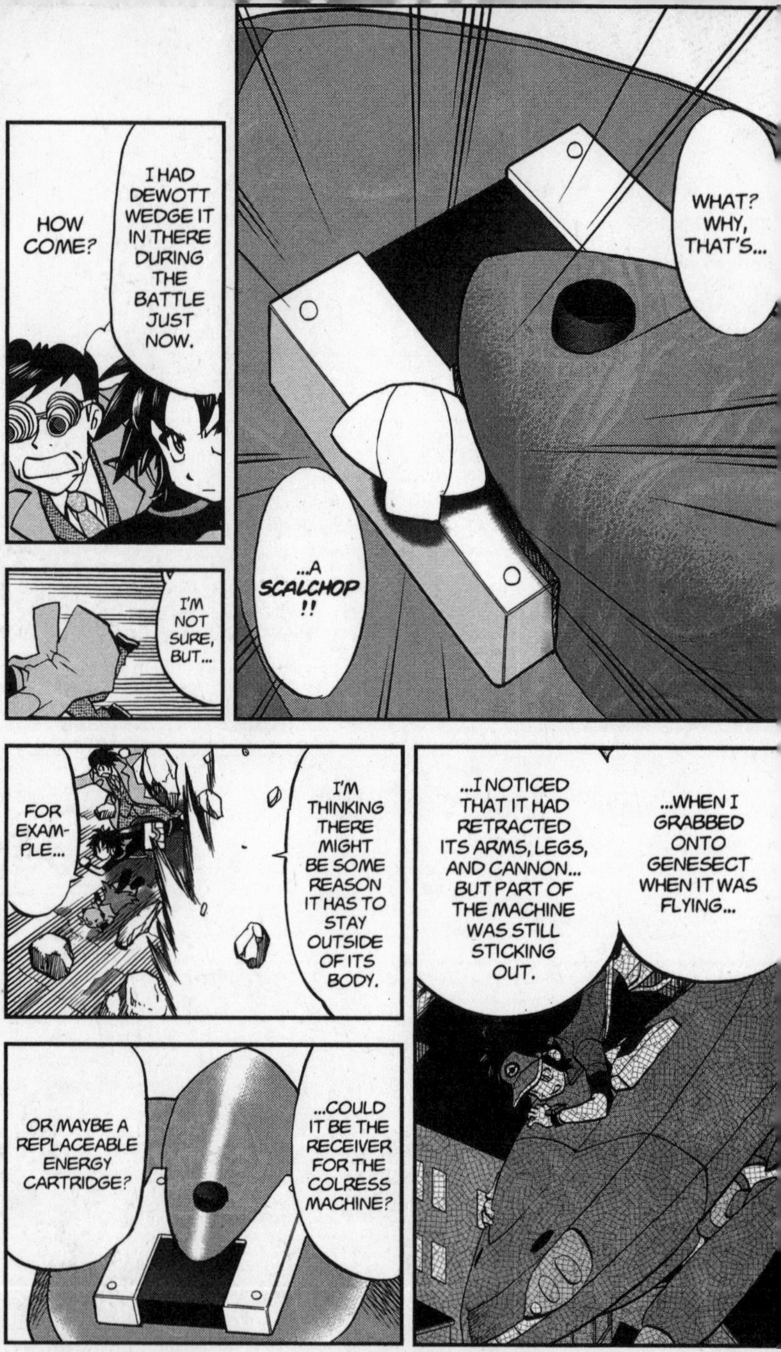
WHAT? WHY, THAT'S...
...A SCALCHOP!!
I HAD DEWOTT WEDGE IT IN THERE DURING THE BATTLE JUST NOW.
HOW COME?
I'M NOT SURE, BUT...
...WHEN I GRABBED ONTO GENESECT WHEN IT WAS FLYING...
...I NOTICED THAT IT HAD RETRACTED ITS ARMS, LEGS, AND CANNON... BUT PART OF THE MACHINE WAS STILL STICKING OUT.
I'M THINKING THERE MIGHT BE SOME REASON IT HAS TO STAY OUTSIDE OF ITS BODY.
FOR EXAMPLE...
...COULD IT BE THE RECEIVER FOR THE COLRESS MACHINE?
OR MAYBE A REPLACEABLE ENERGY CARTRIDGE?

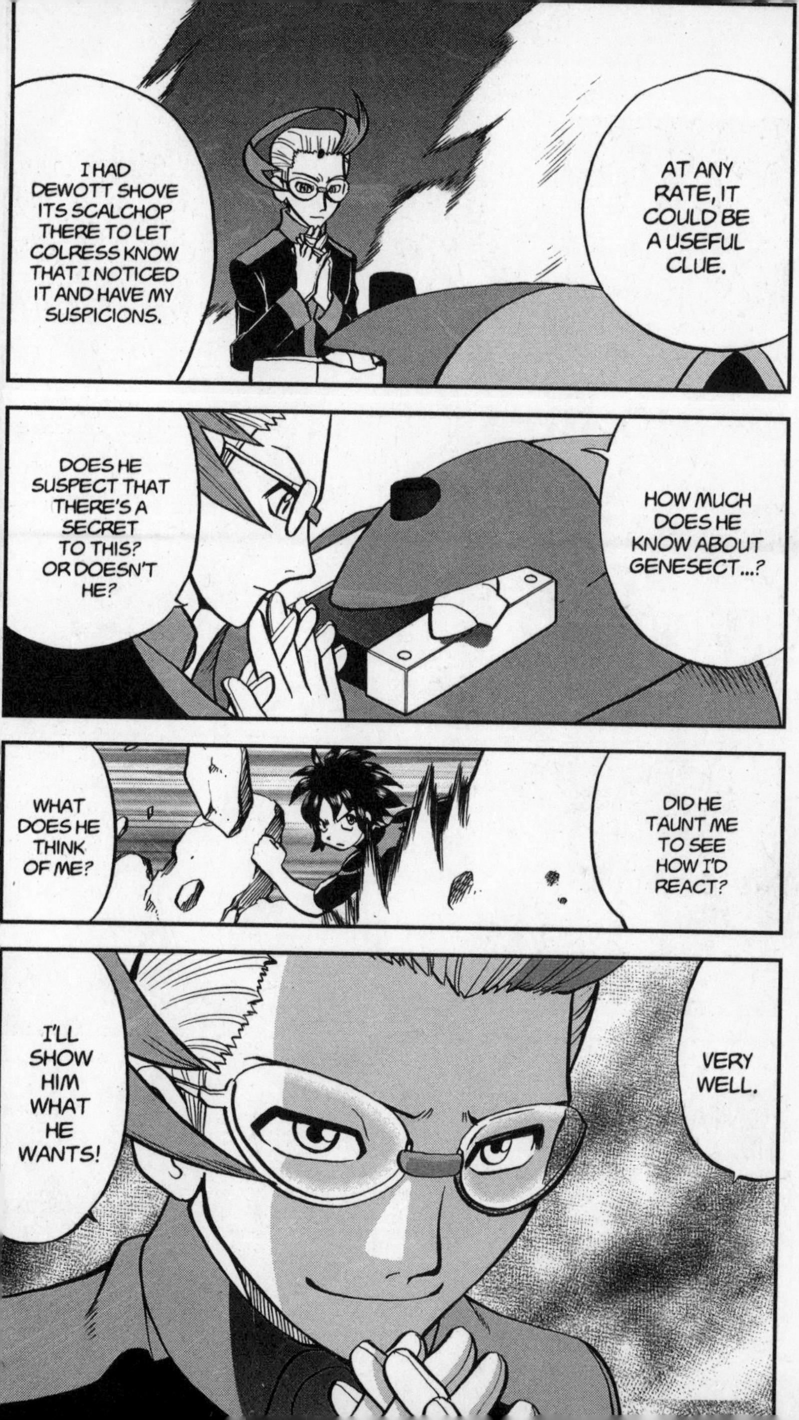
AT ANY RATE, IT COULD BE A USEFUL CLUE.
I HAD DEWOTT SHOVE ITS SCALCHOP THERE TO LET COLRESS KNOW THAT I NOTICED IT AND HAVE MY SUSPICIONS.
HOW MUCH DOES HE KNOW ABOUT GENESECT...?
DOES HE SUSPECT THAT THERE'S A SECRET TO THIS? OR DOESN'T HE?
DID HE TAUNT ME TO SEE HOW I'D REACT?
WHAT DOES HE THINK OF ME?
VERY WELL.
I'LL SHOW HIM WHAT HE WANTS!

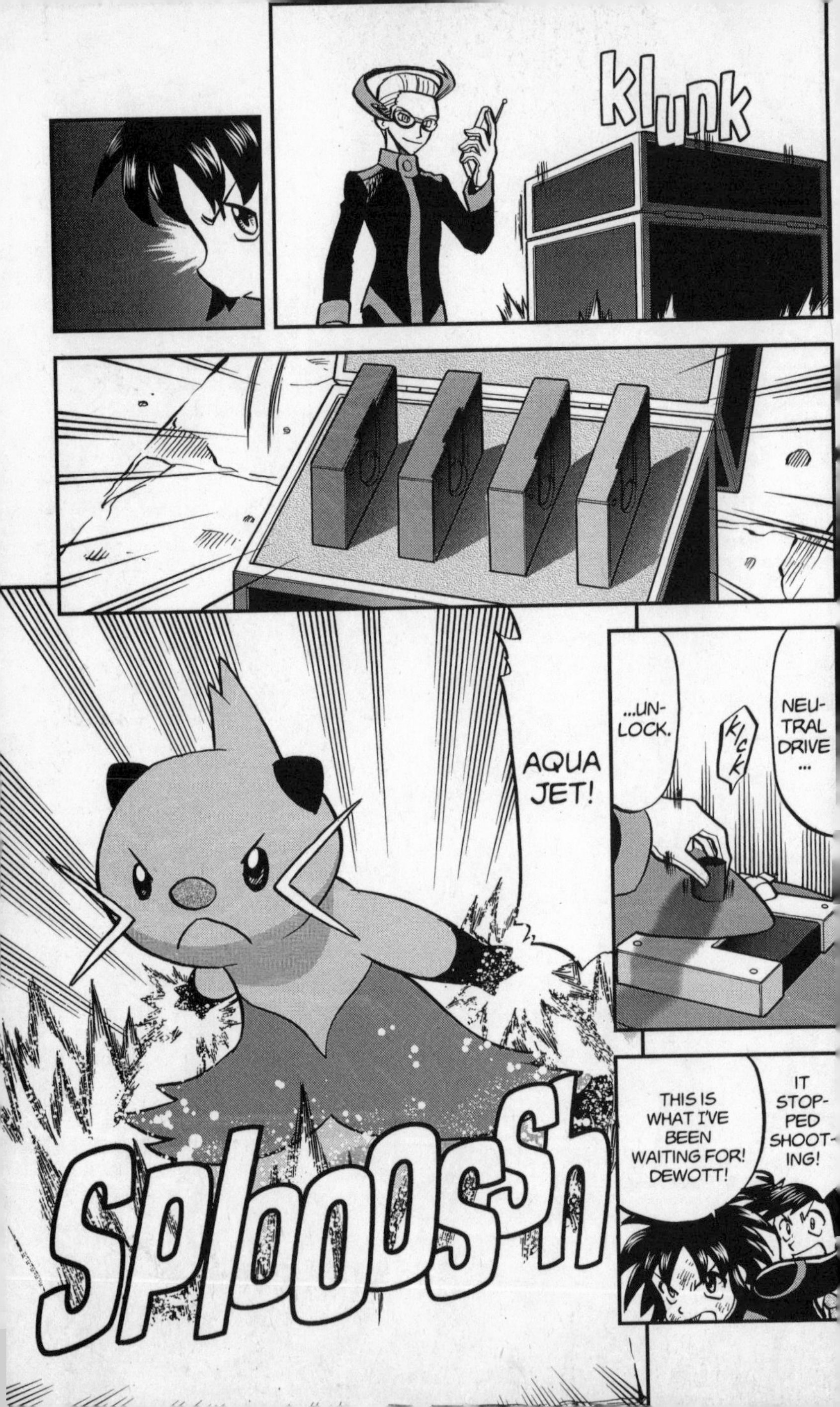
klunk
NEU-
TRAL
DRIVE
...
KICK
...UN-
LOCK.
IT
STOP-
PED
SHOOT-
ING!
THIS IS
WHAT I'VE
BEEN
WAITING FOR!
DEWOTT!
AQUA
JET!
SPLOOOSSH

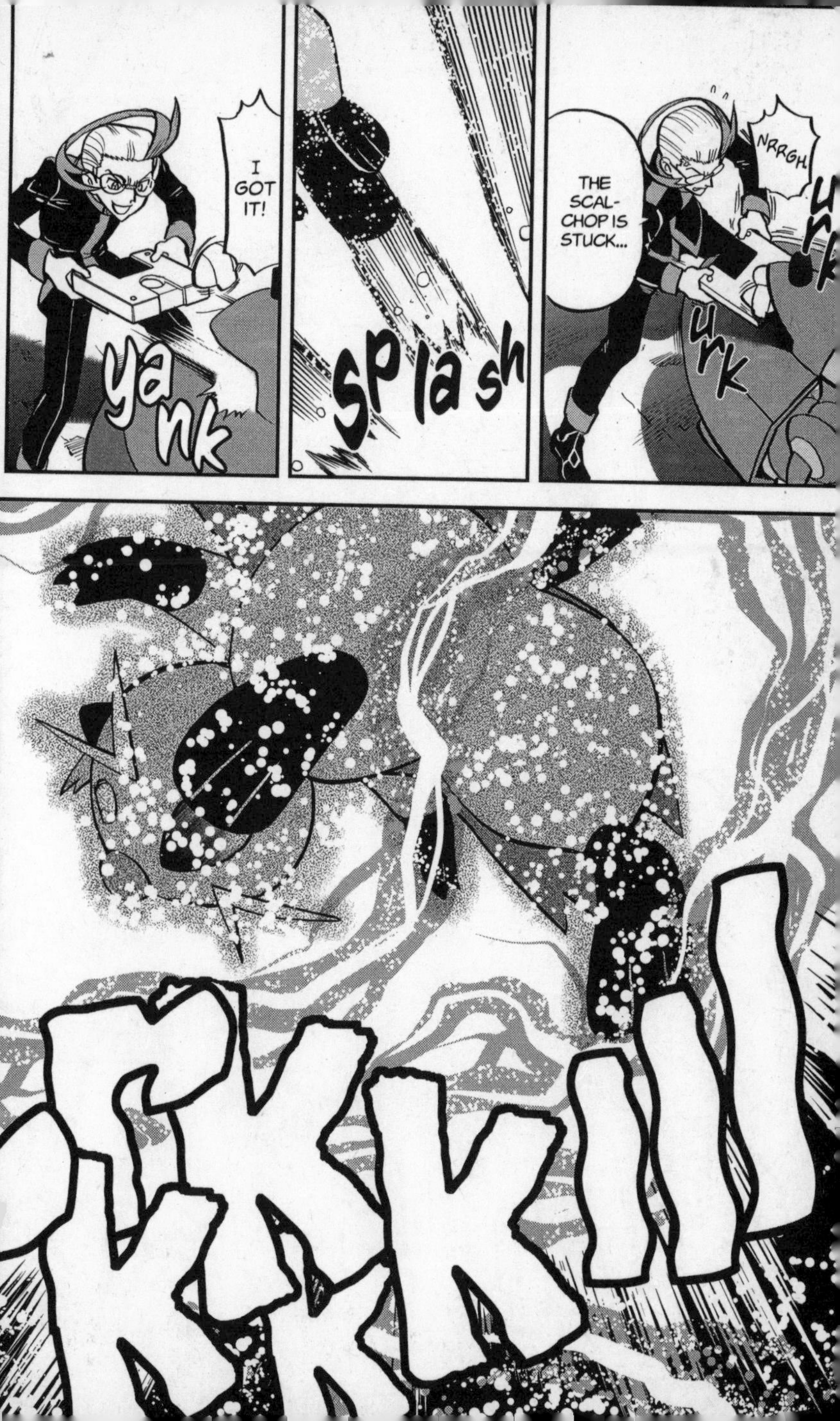
NRRGH!
THE SCAL-CHOP IS STUCK...
urk
urk
splash
I GOT IT!
yank

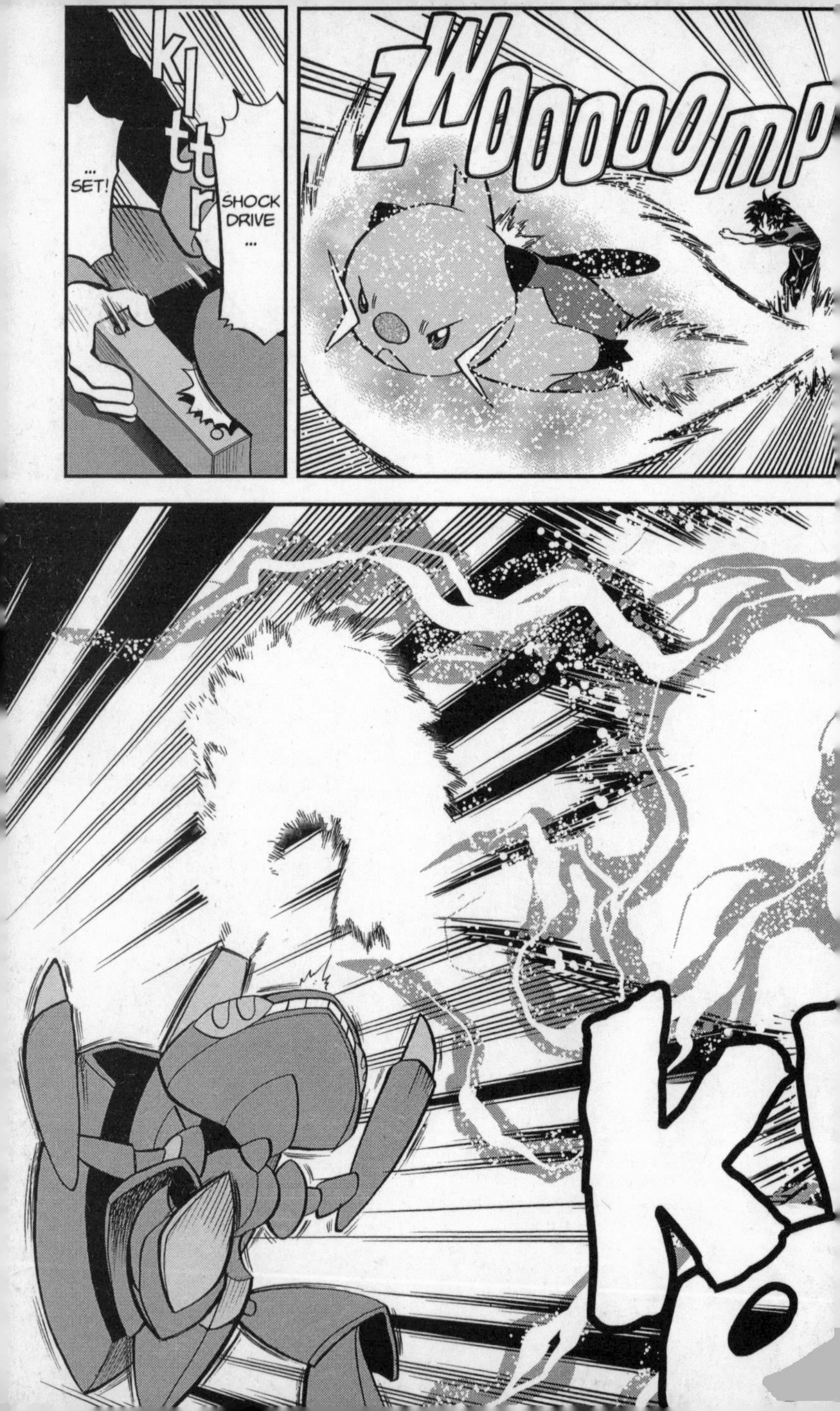
ZWOOOOOMP
klttr
SHOCK DRIVE ...
... SET!
K!

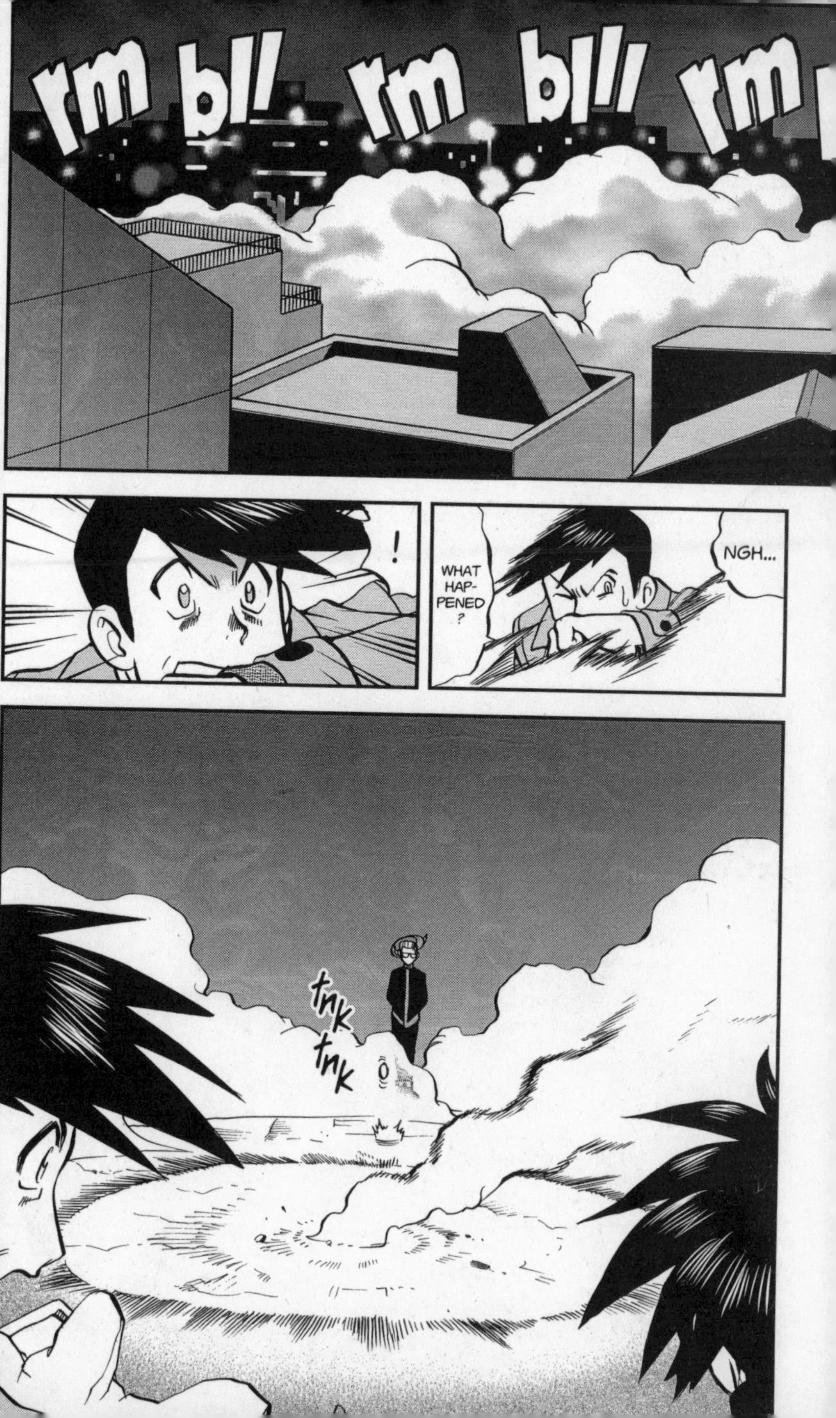
rm bl! rm bl!! rm
NGH...
WHAT HAP-PENED?
!
tnk tnk

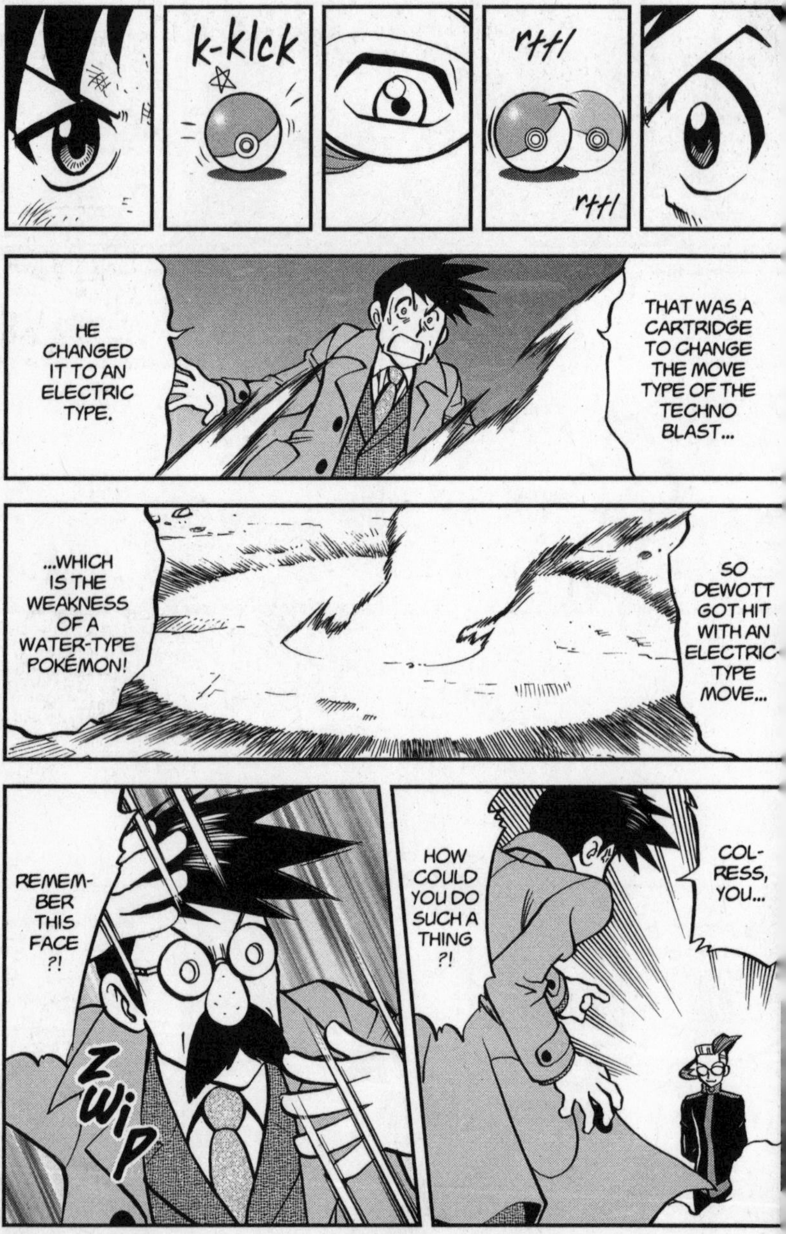
rttl
rttl
k-klck
THAT WAS A CARTRIDGE TO CHANGE THE MOVE TYPE OF THE TECHNO BLAST...
HE CHANGED IT TO AN ELECTRIC TYPE.
SO DEWOTT GOT HIT WITH AN ELECTRIC-TYPE MOVE...
...WHICH IS THE WEAKNESS OF A WATER-TYPE POKÉMON!
COL-RESS, YOU...
HOW COULD YOU DO SUCH A THING ?!
REMEM-BER THIS FACE ?!
ZWIP

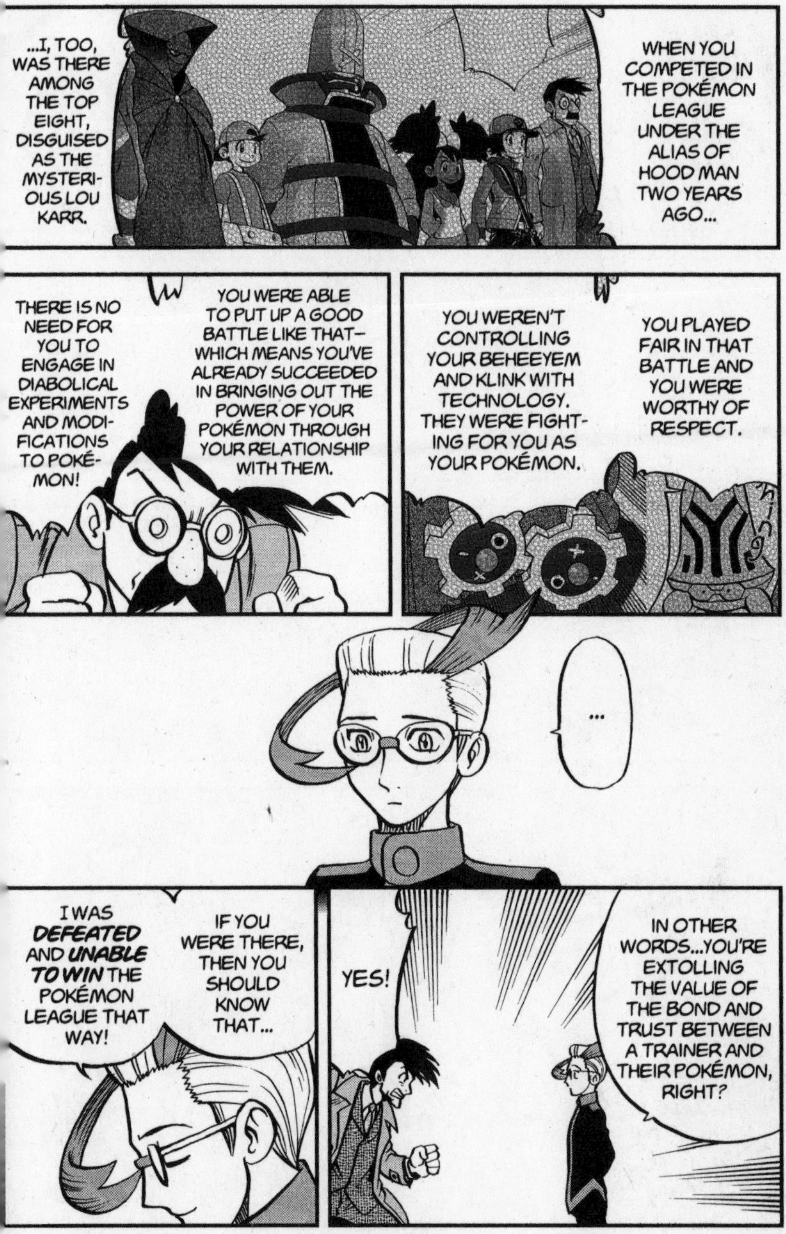
WHEN YOU COMPETED IN THE POKÉMON LEAGUE UNDER THE ALIAS OF HOOD MAN TWO YEARS AGO...
...I, TOO, WAS THERE AMONG THE TOP EIGHT, DISGUISED AS THE MYSTERIOUS LOU KARR.
YOU PLAYED FAIR IN THAT BATTLE AND YOU WERE WORTHY OF RESPECT.
YOU WEREN'T CONTROLLING YOUR BEHEEYEM AND KLINK WITH TECHNOLOGY. THEY WERE FIGHTING FOR YOU AS YOUR POKÉMON.
YOU WERE ABLE TO PUT UP A GOOD BATTLE LIKE THAT—WHICH MEANS YOU'VE ALREADY SUCCEEDED IN BRINGING OUT THE POWER OF YOUR POKÉMON THROUGH YOUR RELATIONSHIP WITH THEM.
THERE IS NO NEED FOR YOU TO ENGAGE IN DIABOLICAL EXPERIMENTS AND MODIFICATIONS TO POKÉMON!
...
IN OTHER WORDS...YOU'RE EXTOLLING THE VALUE OF THE BOND AND TRUST BETWEEN A TRAINER AND THEIR POKÉMON, RIGHT?
YES!
IF YOU WERE THERE, THEN YOU SHOULD KNOW THAT...
I WAS ***DEFEATED*** AND ***UNABLE TO WIN*** THE POKÉMON LEAGUE THAT WAY!

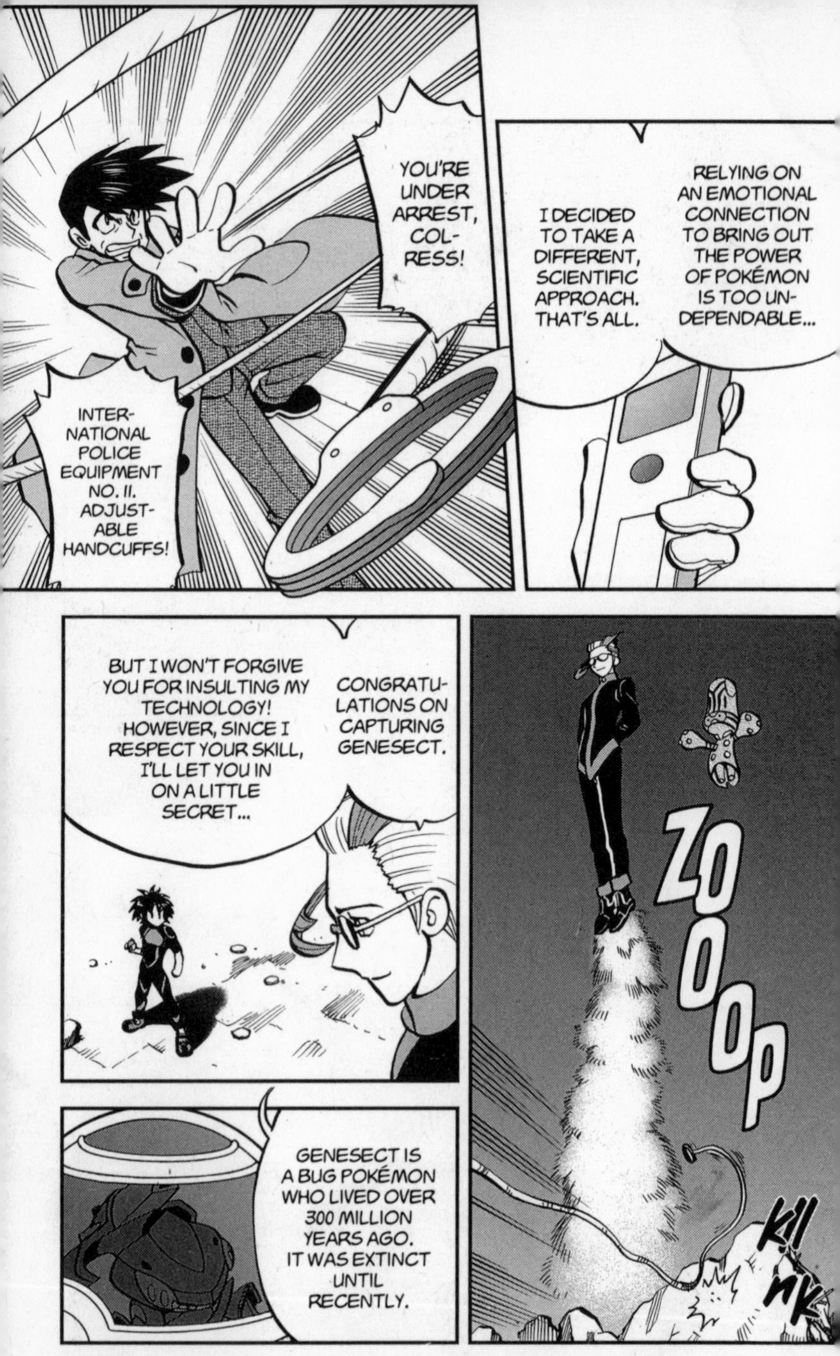
RELYING ON AN EMOTIONAL CONNECTION TO BRING OUT THE POWER OF POKÉMON IS TOO UN-DEPENDABLE...
I DECIDED TO TAKE A DIFFERENT, SCIENTIFIC APPROACH. THAT'S ALL.
YOU'RE UNDER ARREST, COL-RESS!
INTER-NATIONAL POLICE EQUIPMENT NO. II. ADJUST-ABLE HANDCUFFS!
ZOOOP
KLINK
CONGRATU-LATIONS ON CAPTURING GENESECT.
BUT I WON'T FORGIVE YOU FOR INSULTING MY TECHNOLOGY! HOWEVER, SINCE I RESPECT YOUR SKILL, I'LL LET YOU IN ON A LITTLE SECRET...
GENESECT IS A BUG POKÉMON WHO LIVED OVER 300 MILLION YEARS AGO. IT WAS EXTINCT UNTIL RECENTLY.

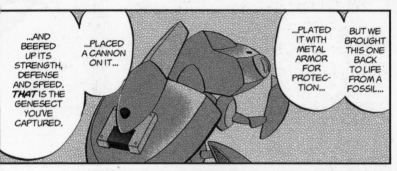

BUT WE BROUGHT THIS ONE BACK TO LIFE FROM A FOSSIL...
...PLATED IT WITH METAL ARMOR FOR PROTEC-TION...
...PLACED A CANNON ON IT...
...AND BEEFED UP ITS STRENGTH, DEFENSE AND SPEED. **THAT** IS THE GENESECT YOU'VE CAPTURED.
IN ADDITION, WE DEVELOPED **DRIVES** THAT CAN CHANGE THE **TYPE** OF ITS TECHNO BLAST.
SHOCK DRIVE FOR FIGHTING AN ELECTRIC TYPE, BURN DRIVE FOR FIRE TYPE, CHILL DRIVE FOR ICE TYPE AND DOUSE DRIVE FOR WATER TYPE.
THIS GENESECT IS INVINCIBLE IN POKÉMON BATTLES...
...OR SO I THOUGHT. UNFORTUNATELY, IT TURNED OUT TO BE A BIT **TOO** STRONG.
TEAM PLASMA'S ENGINEERS WERE UNABLE TO CAPTURE IT WITH THEIR POKÉ BALL...
...AND IT WAS UNCONTROLLABLE. THAT'S WHY WE DECIDED TO USE MY MACHINE TO CONTROL IT.
BUT **YOU** MAN-AGED TO CAP-TURE IT...!
MAY I HAVE THE HONOR OF LEARNING YOUR NAME?

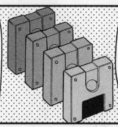

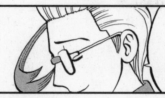

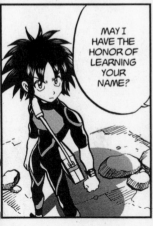

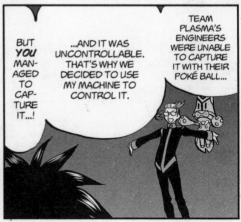

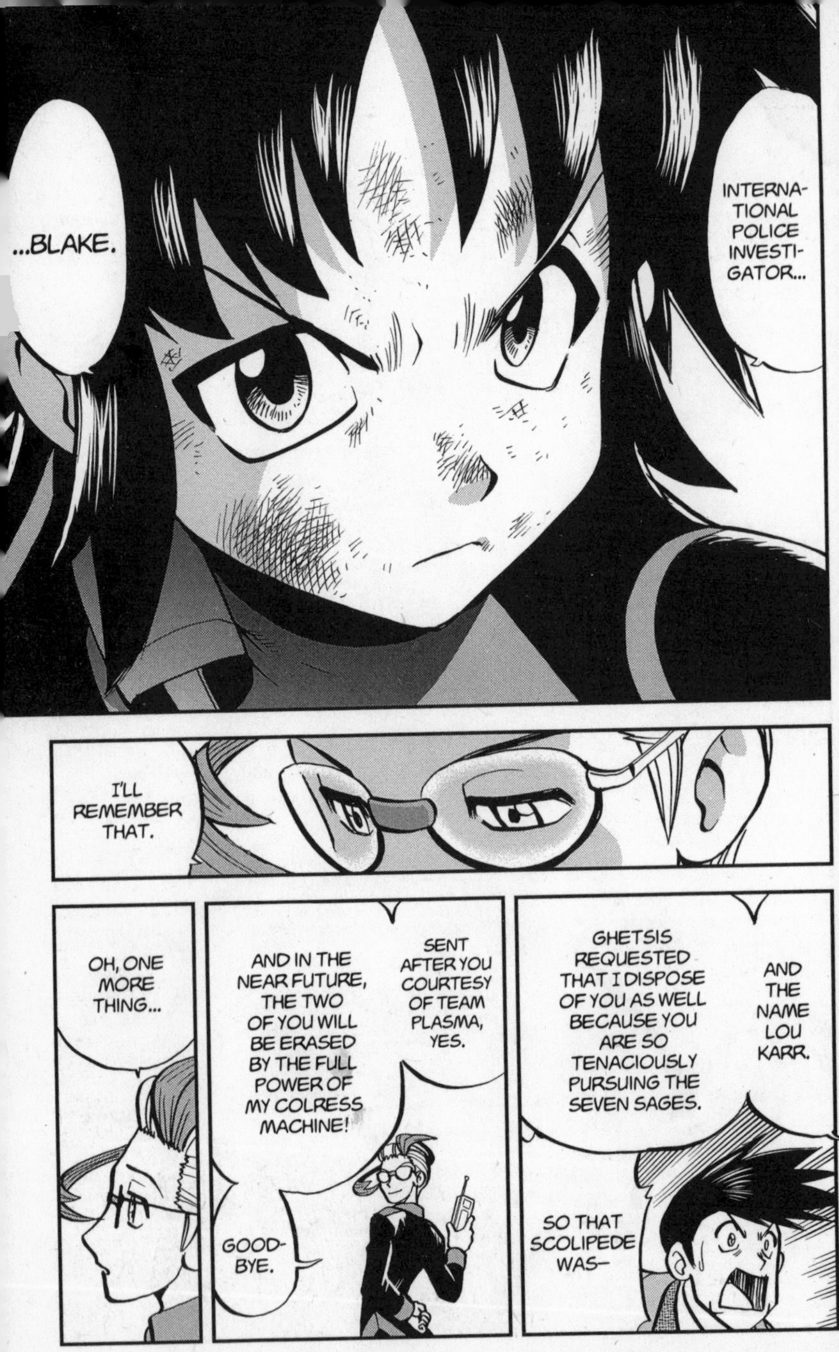
INTERNATIONAL POLICE INVESTIGATOR...
...BLAKE.
I'LL REMEMBER THAT.
AND THE NAME LOU KARR.
GHETSIS REQUESTED THAT I DISPOSE OF YOU AS WELL BECAUSE YOU ARE SO TENACIOUSLY PURSUING THE SEVEN SAGES.
SO THAT SCOLIPEDE WAS—
SENT AFTER YOU COURTESY OF TEAM PLASMA, YES.
AND IN THE NEAR FUTURE, THE TWO OF YOU WILL BE ERASED BY THE FULL POWER OF MY COLRESS MACHINE!
GOOD-BYE.
OH, ONE MORE THING...

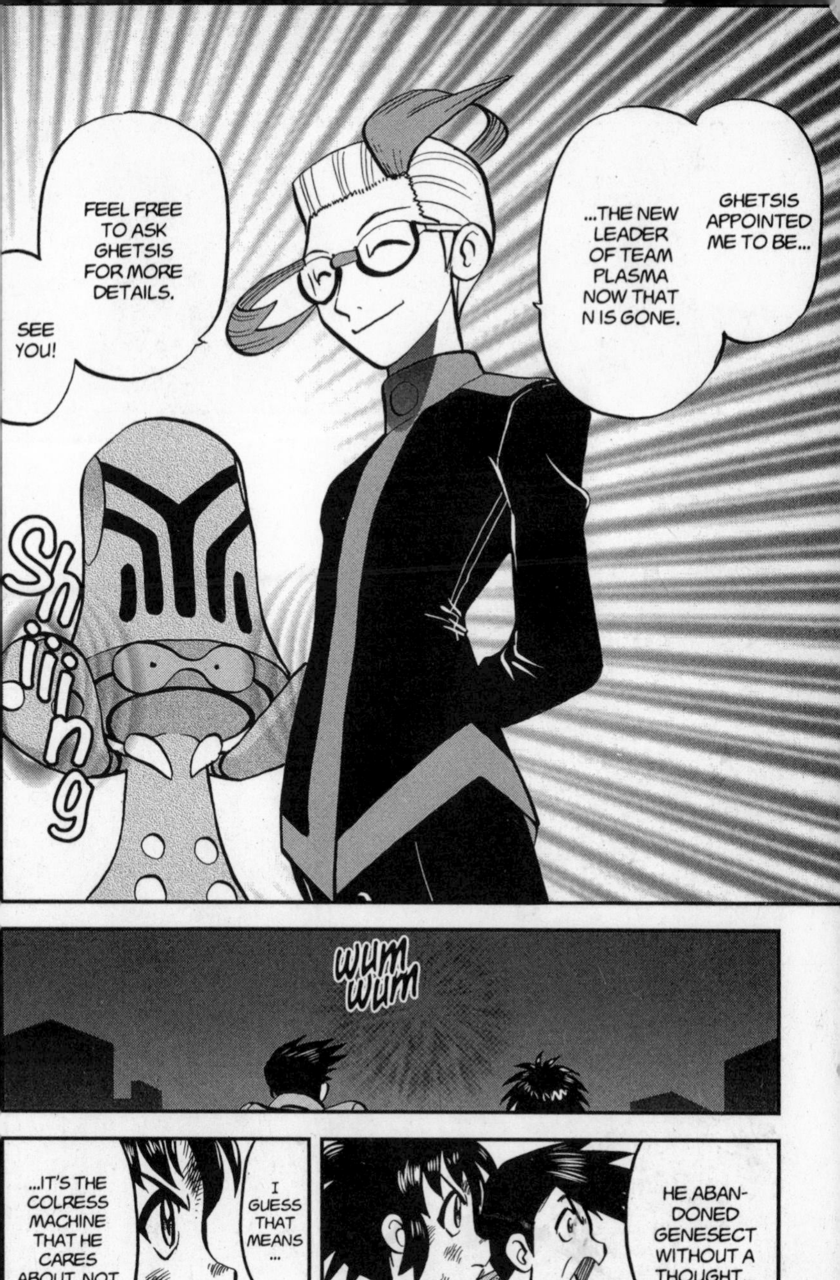
GHETSIS APPOINTED ME TO BE...
...THE NEW LEADER OF TEAM PLASMA NOW THAT N IS GONE.
FEEL FREE TO ASK GHETSIS FOR MORE DETAILS.
SEE YOU!
Shiiing
wum wum
HE ABAN-DONED GENESECT WITHOUT A THOUGHT...
I GUESS THAT MEANS...
...IT'S THE COLRESS MACHINE THAT HE CARES ABOUT, NOT POKÉMON.

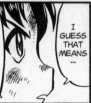

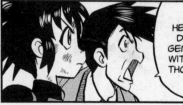

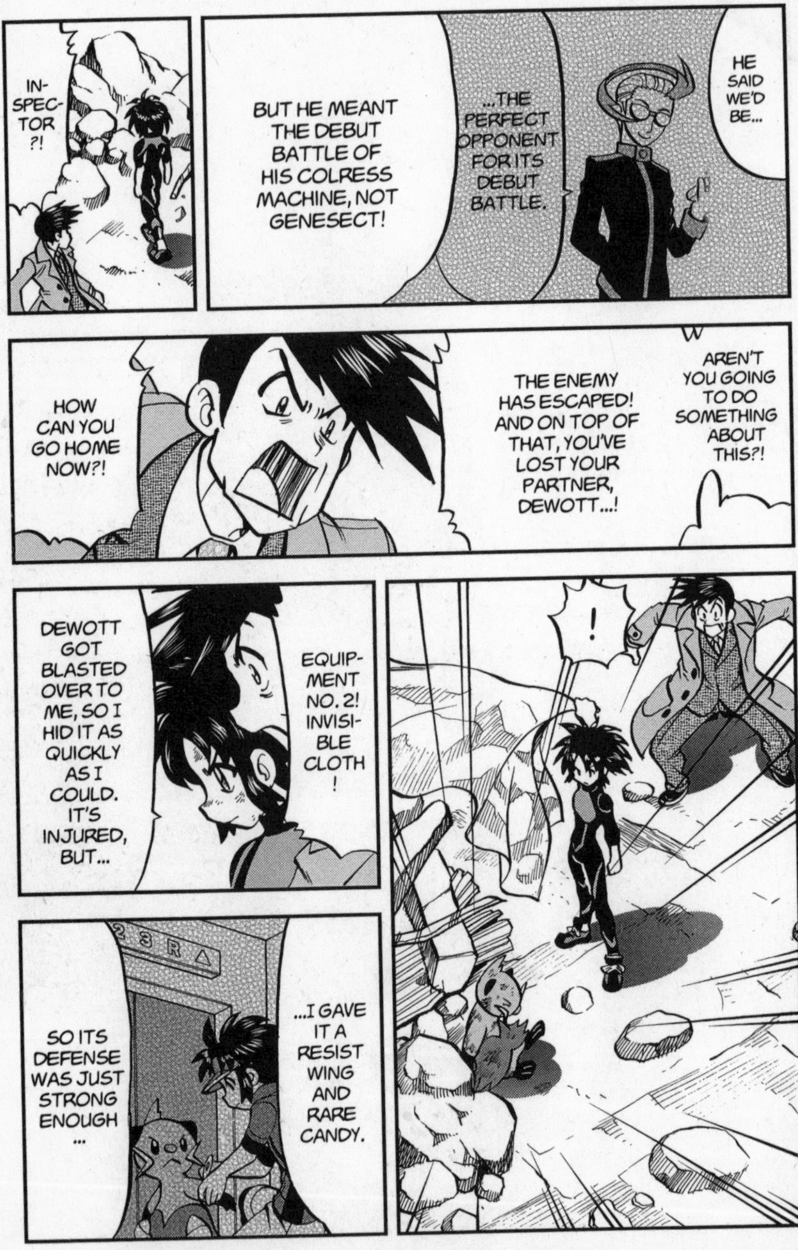
HE SAID WE'D BE...
...THE PERFECT OPPONENT FOR ITS DEBUT BATTLE.
BUT HE MEANT THE DEBUT BATTLE OF HIS COLRESS MACHINE, NOT GENESECT!
IN-SPECTOR?!
AREN'T YOU GOING TO DO SOMETHING ABOUT THIS?!
THE ENEMY HAS ESCAPED! AND ON TOP OF THAT, YOU'VE LOST YOUR PARTNER, DEWOTT...!
HOW CAN YOU GO HOME NOW?!
!
EQUIPMENT NO. 2! INVISIBLE CLOTH!
DEWOTT GOT BLASTED OVER TO ME, SO I HID IT AS QUICKLY AS I COULD. IT'S INJURED, BUT...
...I GAVE IT A RESIST WING AND RARE CANDY.
SO ITS DEFENSE WAS JUST STRONG ENOUGH...

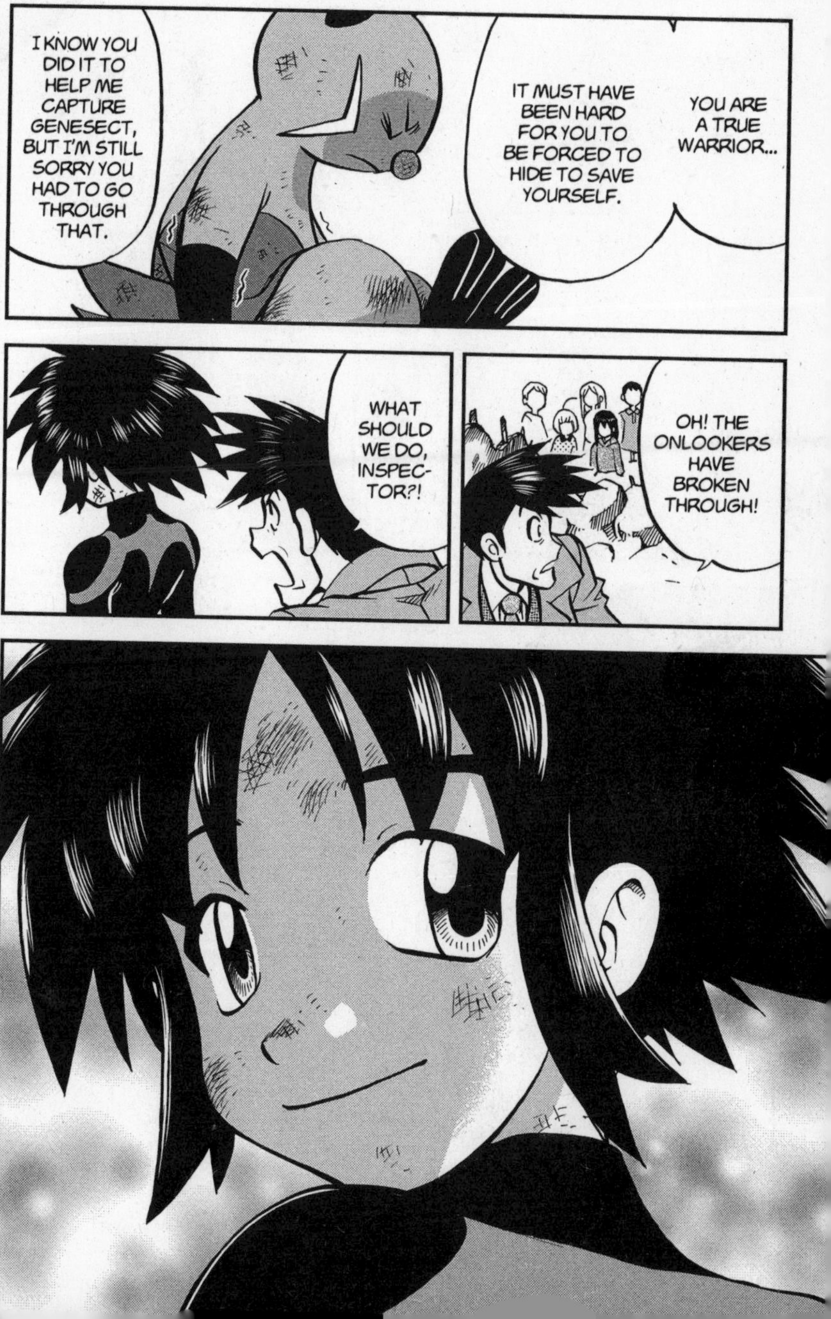
YOU ARE A TRUE WARRIOR...
IT MUST HAVE BEEN HARD FOR YOU TO BE FORCED TO HIDE TO SAVE YOURSELF.
I KNOW YOU DID IT TO HELP ME CAPTURE GENESECT, BUT I'M STILL SORRY YOU HAD TO GO THROUGH THAT.
OH! THE ONLOOKERS HAVE BROKEN THROUGH!
WHAT SHOULD WE DO, INSPECTOR?!

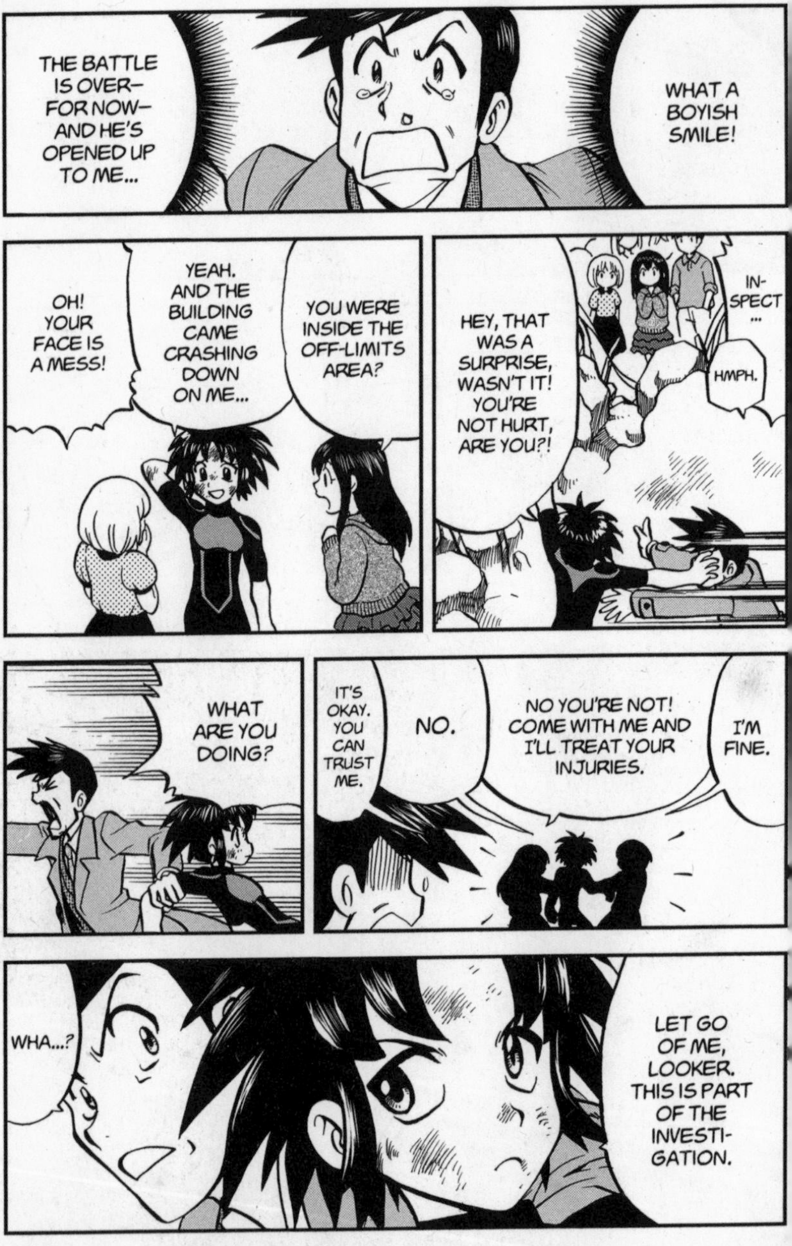
WHAT A BOYISH SMILE!
THE BATTLE IS OVER—FOR NOW—AND HE'S OPENED UP TO ME...
IN-SPECT...
HMPH.
HEY, THAT WAS A SURPRISE, WASN'T IT! YOU'RE NOT HURT, ARE YOU?!
YOU WERE INSIDE THE OFF-LIMITS AREA?
YEAH. AND THE BUILDING CAME CRASHING DOWN ON ME...
OH! YOUR FACE IS A MESS!
I'M FINE.
NO YOU'RE NOT! COME WITH ME AND I'LL TREAT YOUR INJURIES.
NO.
IT'S OKAY. YOU CAN TRUST ME.
WHAT ARE YOU DOING?
LET GO OF ME, LOOKER. THIS IS PART OF THE INVESTIGATION.
WHA...?

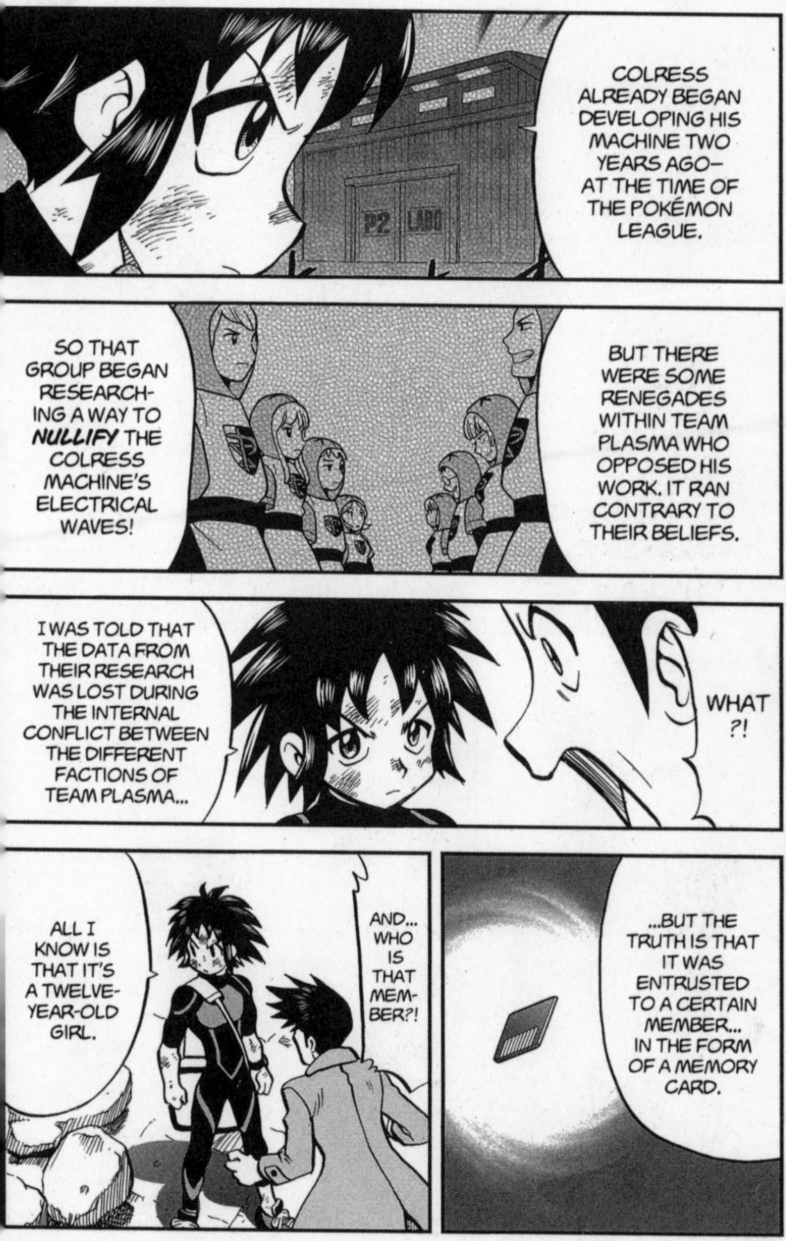
COLRESS ALREADY BEGAN DEVELOPING HIS MACHINE TWO YEARS AGO—AT THE TIME OF THE POKÉMON LEAGUE.
P2 LABO
BUT THERE WERE SOME RENEGADES WITHIN TEAM PLASMA WHO OPPOSED HIS WORK. IT RAN CONTRARY TO THEIR BELIEFS.
SO THAT GROUP BEGAN RESEARCH-ING A WAY TO ***NULLIFY*** THE COLRESS MACHINE'S ELECTRICAL WAVES!
WHAT?!
I WAS TOLD THAT THE DATA FROM THEIR RESEARCH WAS LOST DURING THE INTERNAL CONFLICT BETWEEN THE DIFFERENT FACTIONS OF TEAM PLASMA...
...BUT THE TRUTH IS THAT IT WAS ENTRUSTED TO A CERTAIN MEMBER... IN THE FORM OF A MEMORY CARD.
AND... WHO IS THAT MEM-BER?!
ALL I KNOW IS THAT IT'S A TWELVE-YEAR-OLD GIRL.

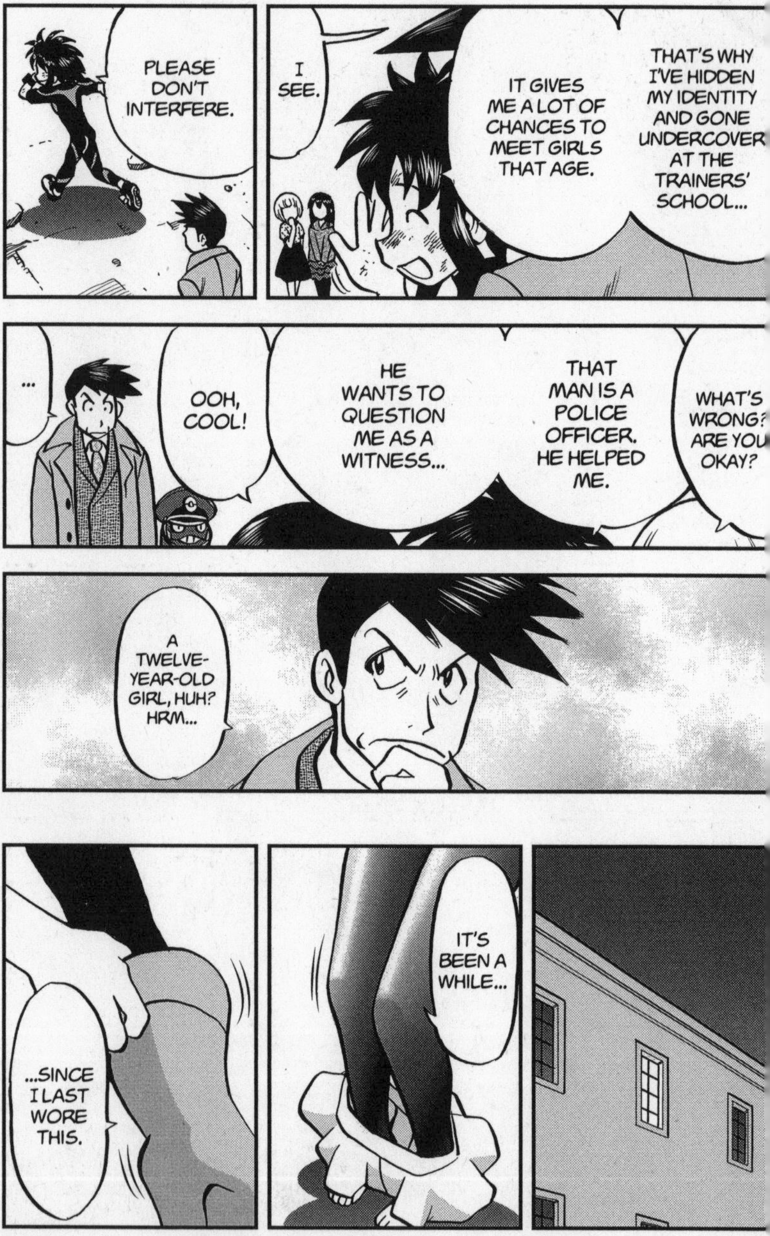
THAT'S WHY I'VE HIDDEN MY IDENTITY AND GONE UNDERCOVER AT THE TRAINERS' SCHOOL...
IT GIVES ME A LOT OF CHANCES TO MEET GIRLS THAT AGE.
I SEE.
PLEASE DON'T INTERFERE.
WHAT'S WRONG? ARE YOU OKAY?
THAT MAN IS A POLICE OFFICER. HE HELPED ME.
HE WANTS TO QUESTION ME AS A WITNESS...
OOH, COOL!
...
A TWELVE-YEAR-OLD GIRL, HUH? HRM...
IT'S BEEN A WHILE...
...SINCE I LAST WORE THIS.

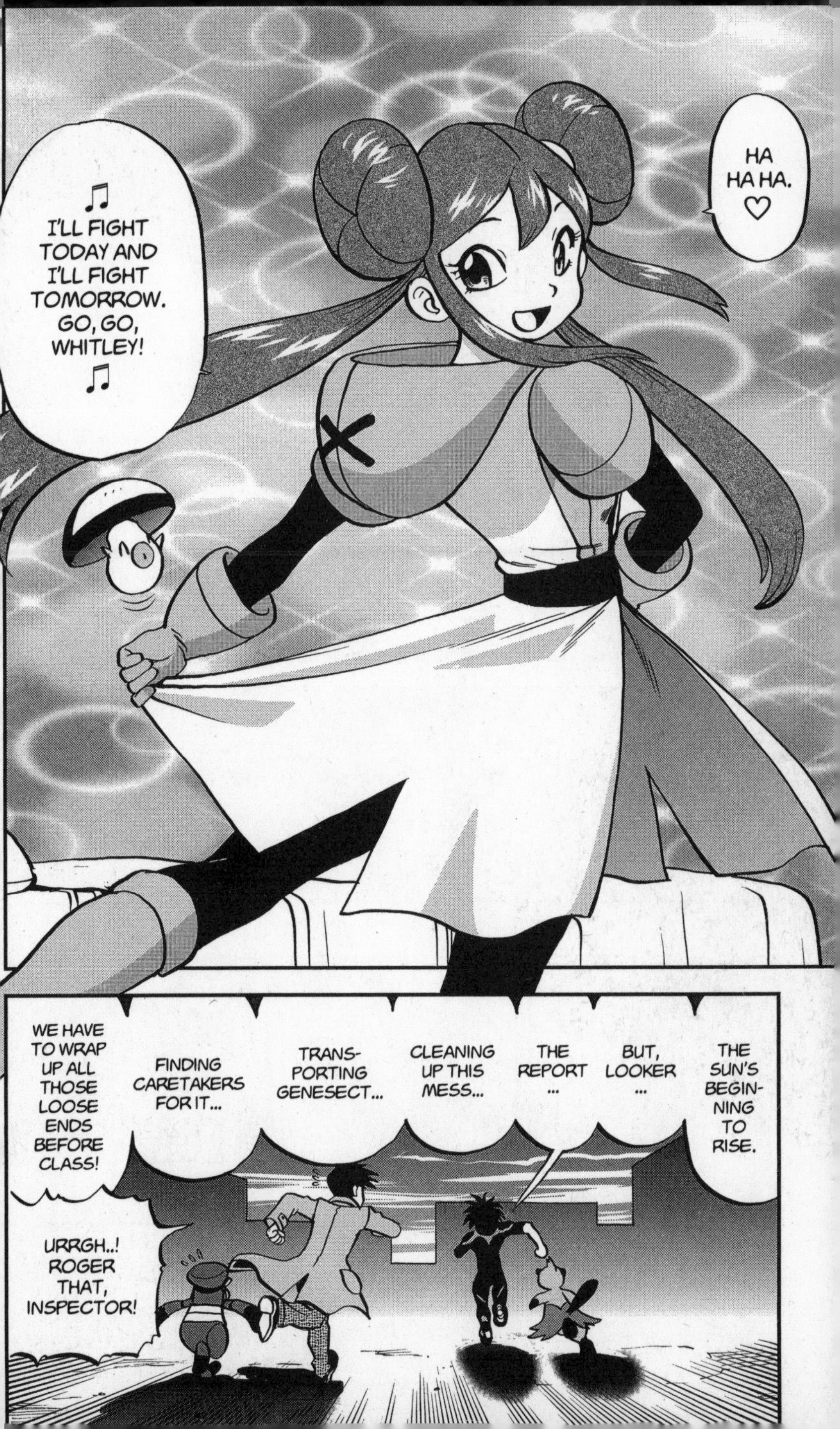
HA HA HA. ♡
♫ I'LL FIGHT TODAY AND I'LL FIGHT TOMORROW. GO, GO, WHITLEY! ♫
THE SUN'S BEGINNING TO RISE.
BUT, LOOKER...
THE REPORT...
CLEANING UP THIS MESS...
TRANSPORTING GENESECT...
FINDING CARETAKERS FOR IT...
WE HAVE TO WRAP UP ALL THOSE LOOSE ENDS BEFORE CLASS!
URRGH..! ROGER THAT, INSPECTOR!

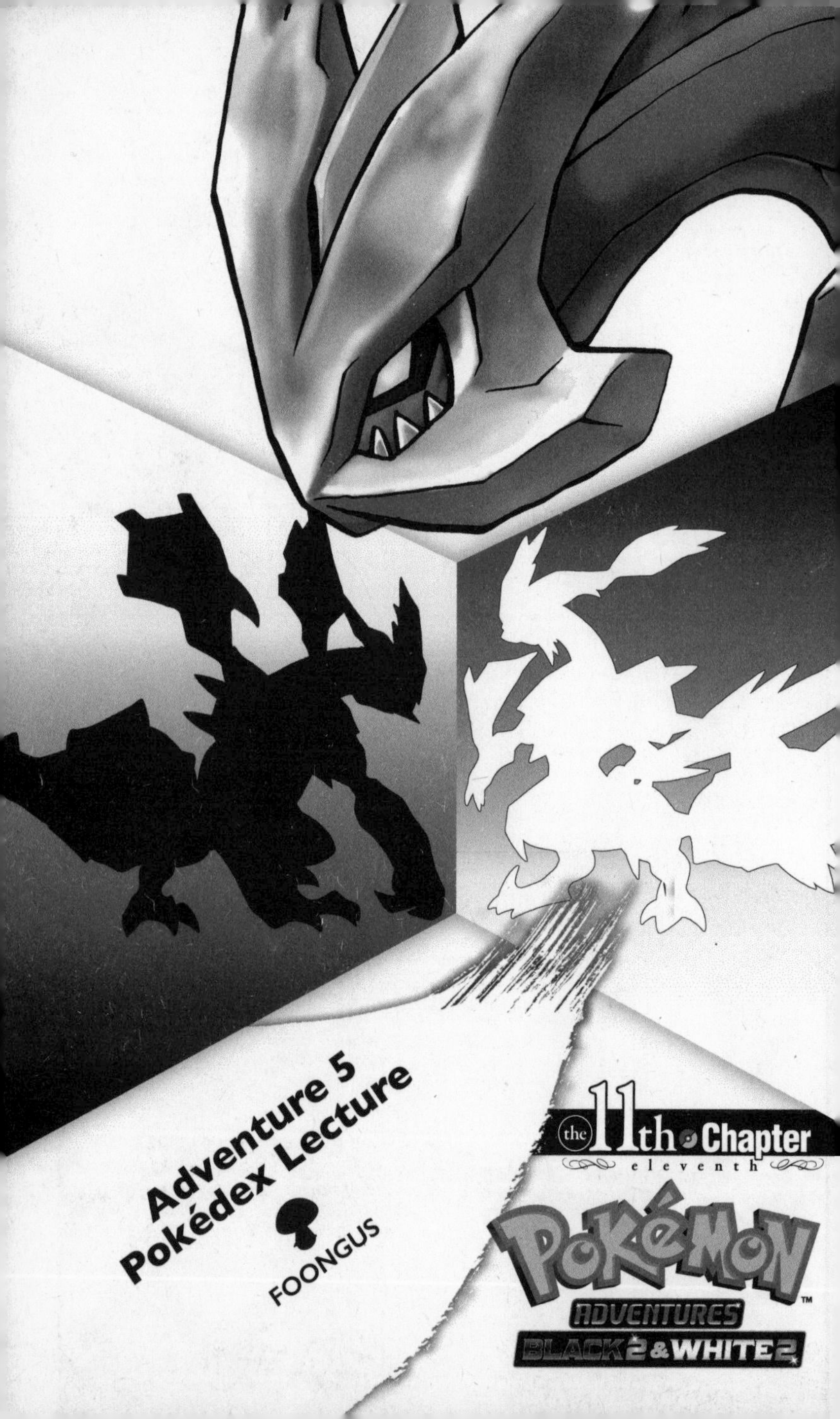
Adventure 5
Pokédex Lecture
FOONGUS
the 11th Chapter
eleventh
POKÉMON
ADVENTURES
BLACK 2 & WHITE 2

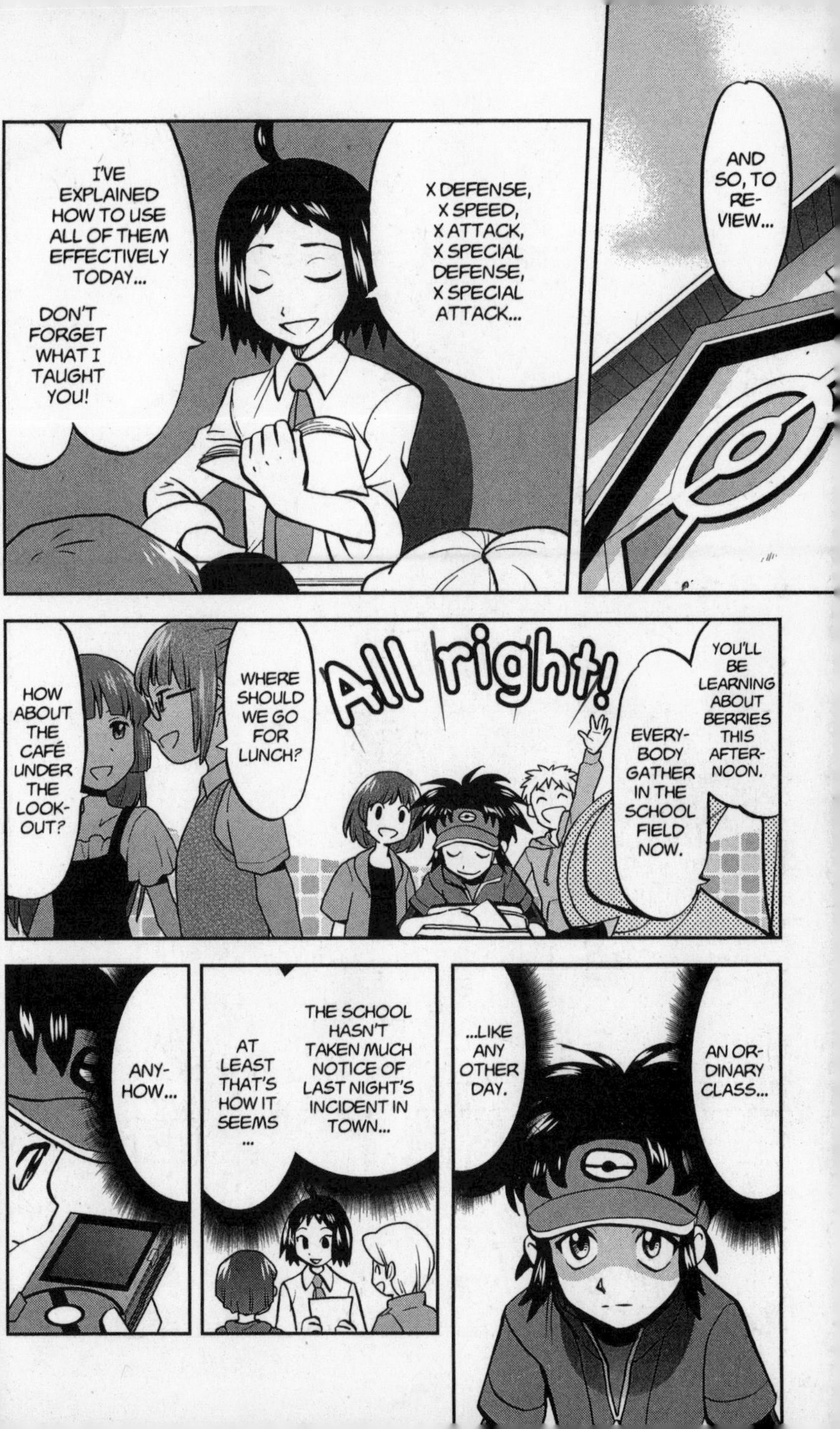
AND SO, TO REVIEW...
X DEFENSE, X SPEED, X ATTACK, X SPECIAL DEFENSE, X SPECIAL ATTACK...
I'VE EXPLAINED HOW TO USE ALL OF THEM EFFECTIVELY TODAY...
DON'T FORGET WHAT I TAUGHT YOU!
YOU'LL BE LEARNING ABOUT BERRIES THIS AFTERNOON.
EVERYBODY GATHER IN THE SCHOOL FIELD NOW.
All right!
WHERE SHOULD WE GO FOR LUNCH?
HOW ABOUT THE CAFÉ UNDER THE LOOKOUT?
AN ORDINARY CLASS...
...LIKE ANY OTHER DAY.
THE SCHOOL HASN'T TAKEN MUCH NOTICE OF LAST NIGHT'S INCIDENT IN TOWN...
AT LEAST THAT'S HOW IT SEEMS...
ANYHOW...

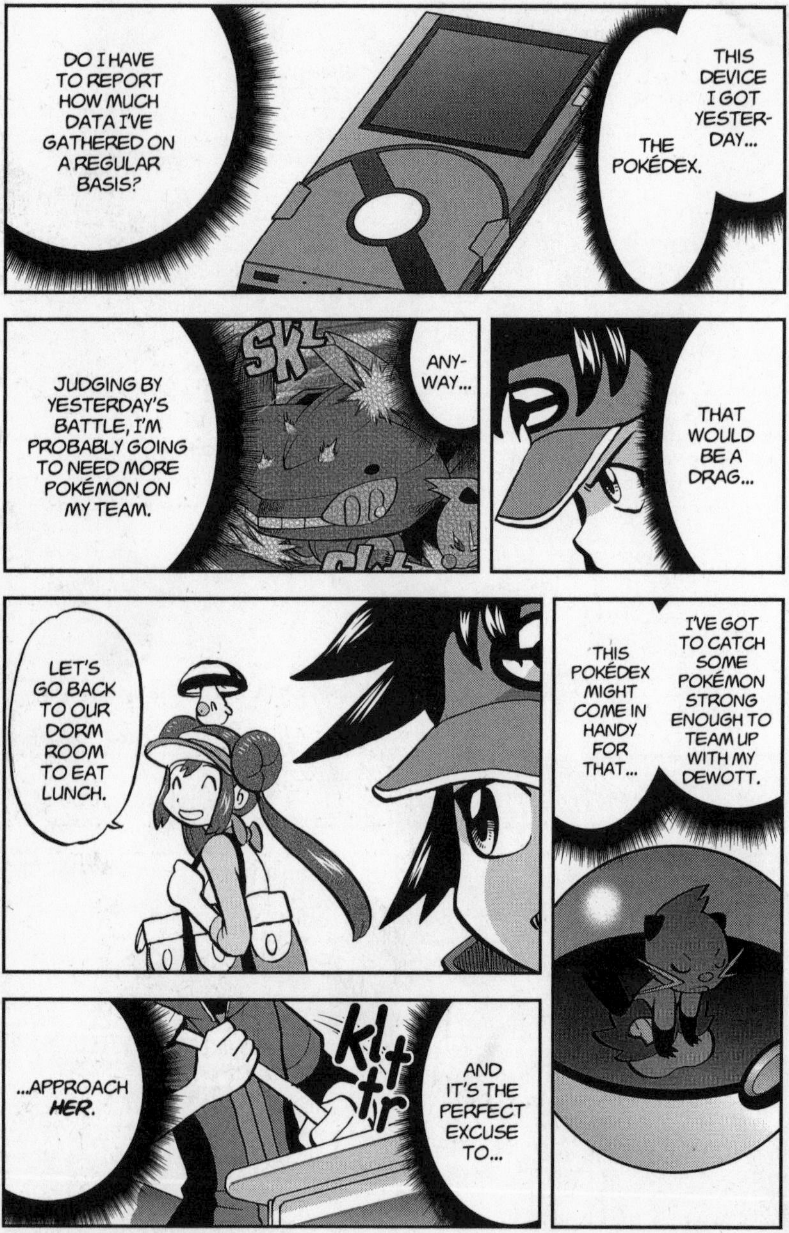
THIS DEVICE I GOT YESTER-DAY...
THE POKÉDEX.
DO I HAVE TO REPORT HOW MUCH DATA I'VE GATHERED ON A REGULAR BASIS?
THAT WOULD BE A DRAG...
ANY-WAY...
SKL
JUDGING BY YESTERDAY'S BATTLE, I'M PROBABLY GOING TO NEED MORE POKÉMON ON MY TEAM.
I'VE GOT TO CATCH SOME POKÉMON STRONG ENOUGH TO TEAM UP WITH MY DEWOTT.
THIS POKÉDEX MIGHT COME IN HANDY FOR THAT...
LET'S GO BACK TO OUR DORM ROOM TO EAT LUNCH.
AND IT'S THE PERFECT EXCUSE TO...
klt tr
...APPROACH ***HER***.

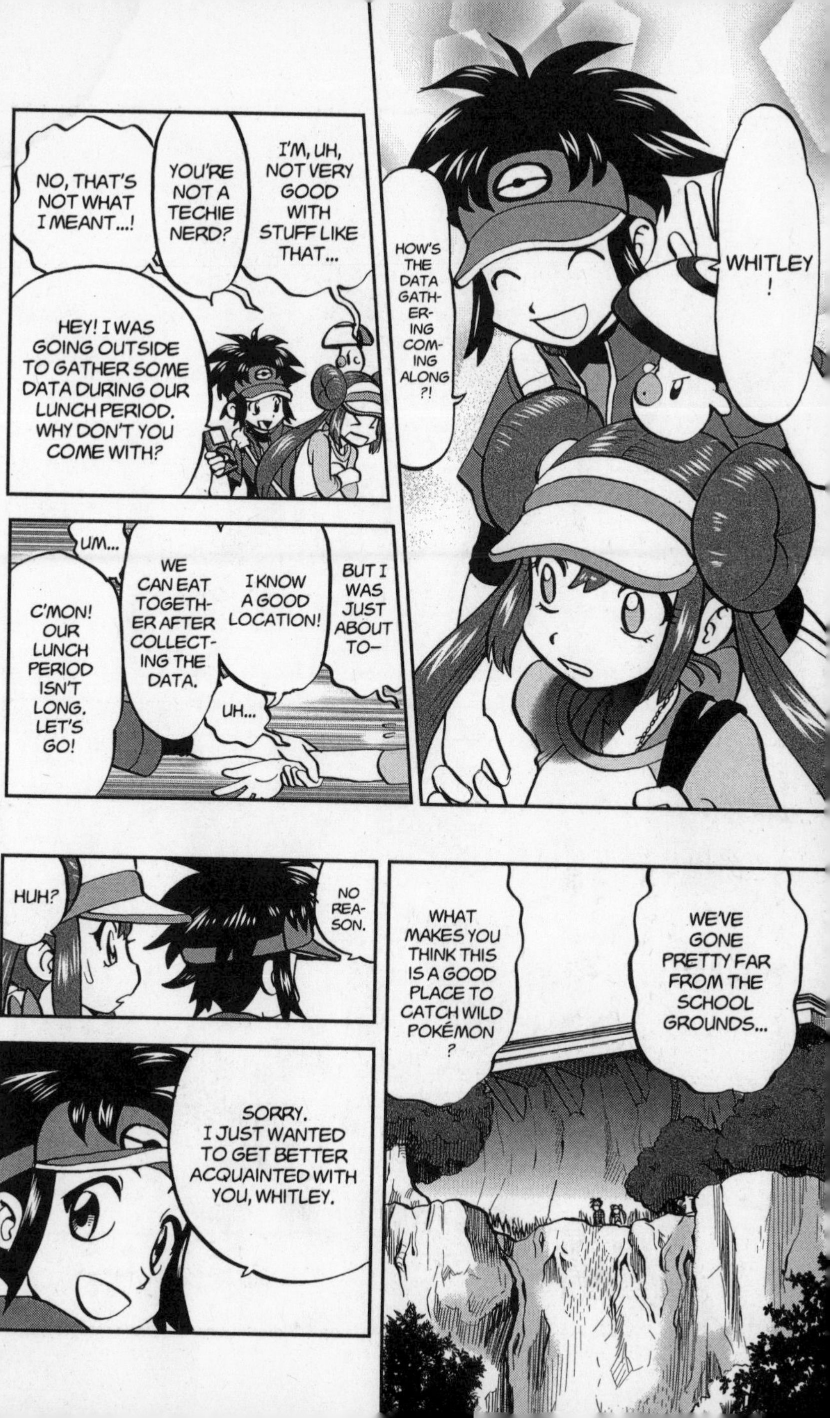
WHITLEY!
HOW'S THE DATA GATHERING COMING ALONG?!
I'M, UH, NOT VERY GOOD WITH STUFF LIKE THAT...
YOU'RE NOT A TECHIE NERD?
NO, THAT'S NOT WHAT I MEANT...!
HEY! I WAS GOING OUTSIDE TO GATHER SOME DATA DURING OUR LUNCH PERIOD. WHY DON'T YOU COME WITH?
BUT I WAS JUST ABOUT TO-
I KNOW A GOOD LOCATION!
WE CAN EAT TOGETHER AFTER COLLECTING THE DATA.
UM...
C'MON! OUR LUNCH PERIOD ISN'T LONG. LET'S GO!
UH...
WE'VE GONE PRETTY FAR FROM THE SCHOOL GROUNDS...
WHAT MAKES YOU THINK THIS IS A GOOD PLACE TO CATCH WILD POKÉMON?
NO REASON.
HUH?
SORRY. I JUST WANTED TO GET BETTER ACQUAINTED WITH YOU, WHITLEY.

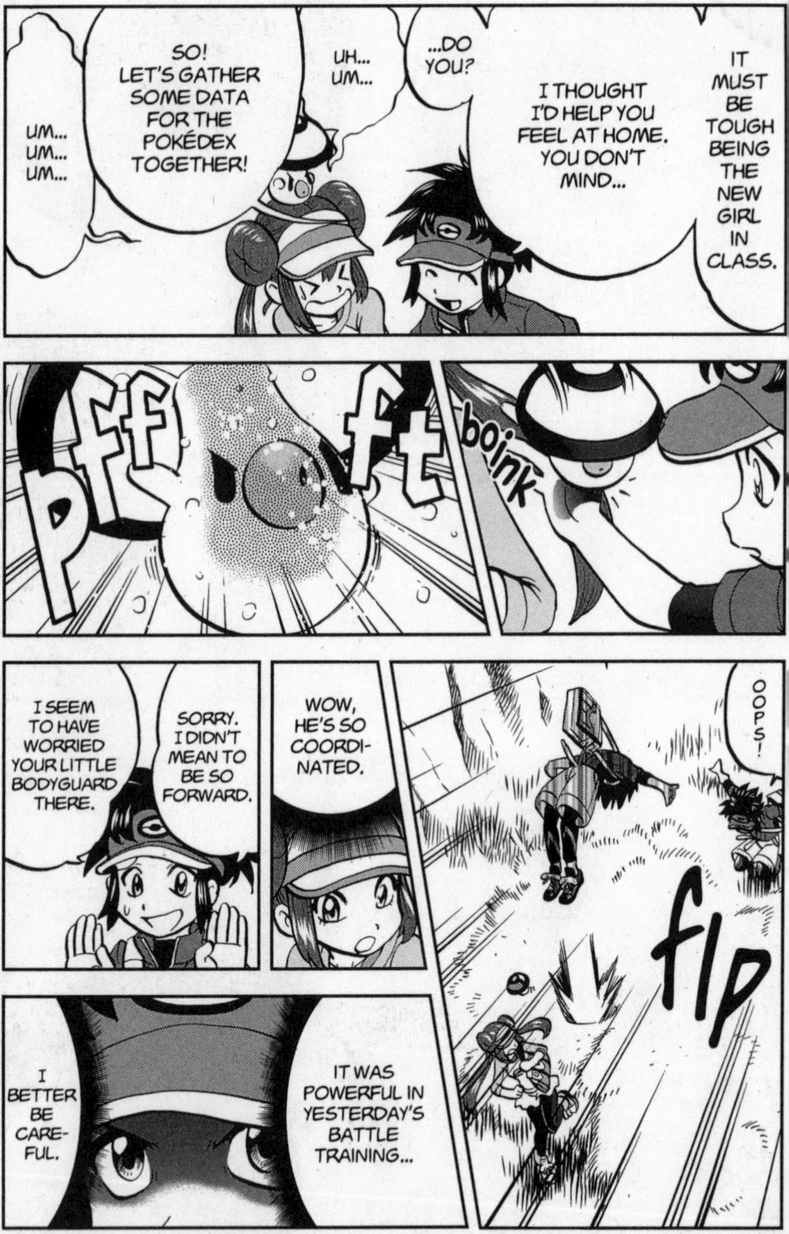
IT MUST BE TOUGH BEING THE NEW GIRL IN CLASS.
I THOUGHT I'D HELP YOU FEEL AT HOME. YOU DON'T MIND...
...DO YOU?
UH... UM...
SO! LET'S GATHER SOME DATA FOR THE POKÉDEX TOGETHER!
UM... UM... UM...
boink
pff ft
OOPS!
flp
WOW, HE'S SO COORDINATED.
SORRY. I DIDN'T MEAN TO BE SO FORWARD.
I SEEM TO HAVE WORRIED YOUR LITTLE BODYGUARD THERE.
IT WAS POWERFUL IN YESTERDAY'S BATTLE TRAINING...
I BETTER BE CAREFUL.

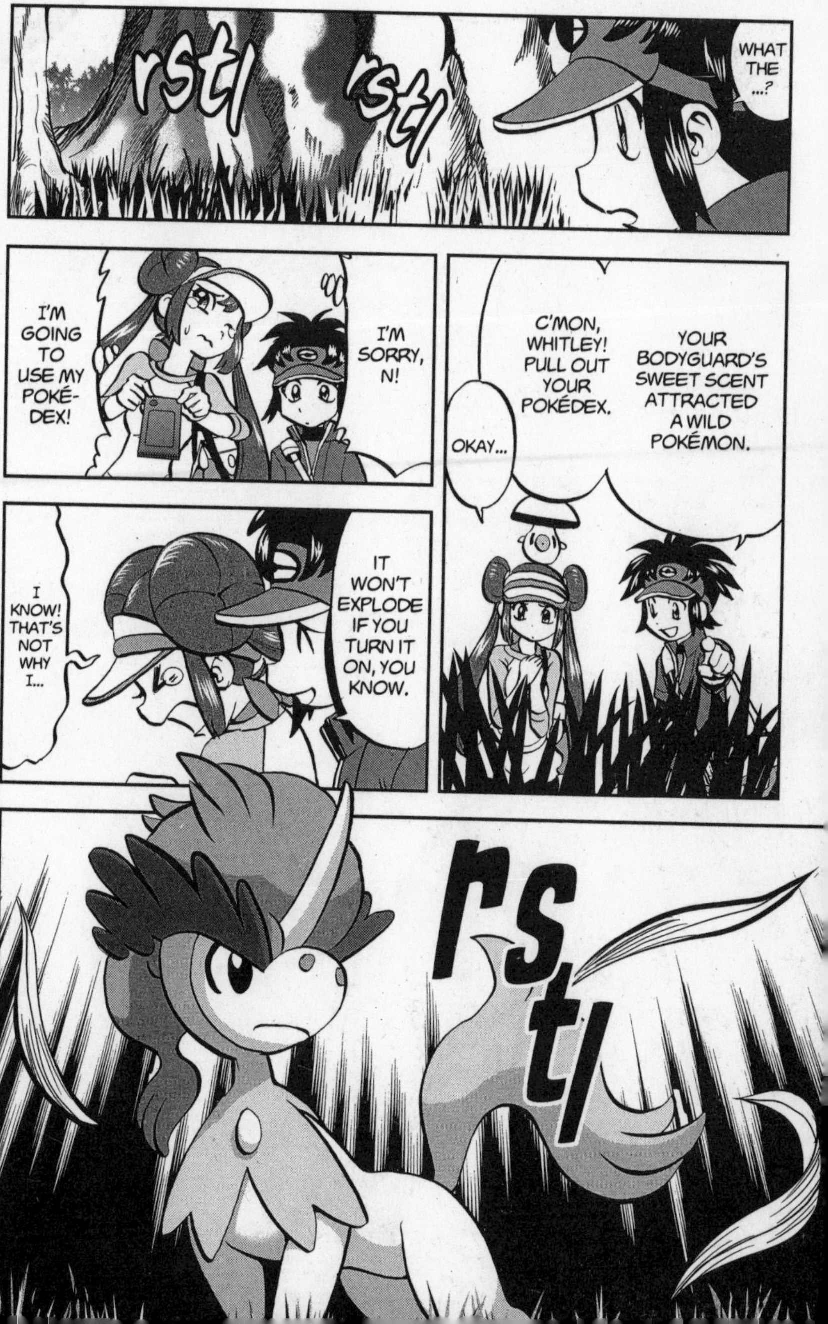
WHAT THE ...?
rstl
rstl
YOUR BODYGUARD'S SWEET SCENT ATTRACTED A WILD POKÉMON.
C'MON, WHITLEY! PULL OUT YOUR POKÉDEX.
OKAY...
I'M SORRY, N!
I'M GOING TO USE MY POKÉ-DEX!
IT WON'T EXPLODE IF YOU TURN IT ON, YOU KNOW.
I KNOW! THAT'S NOT WHY I...
rstl

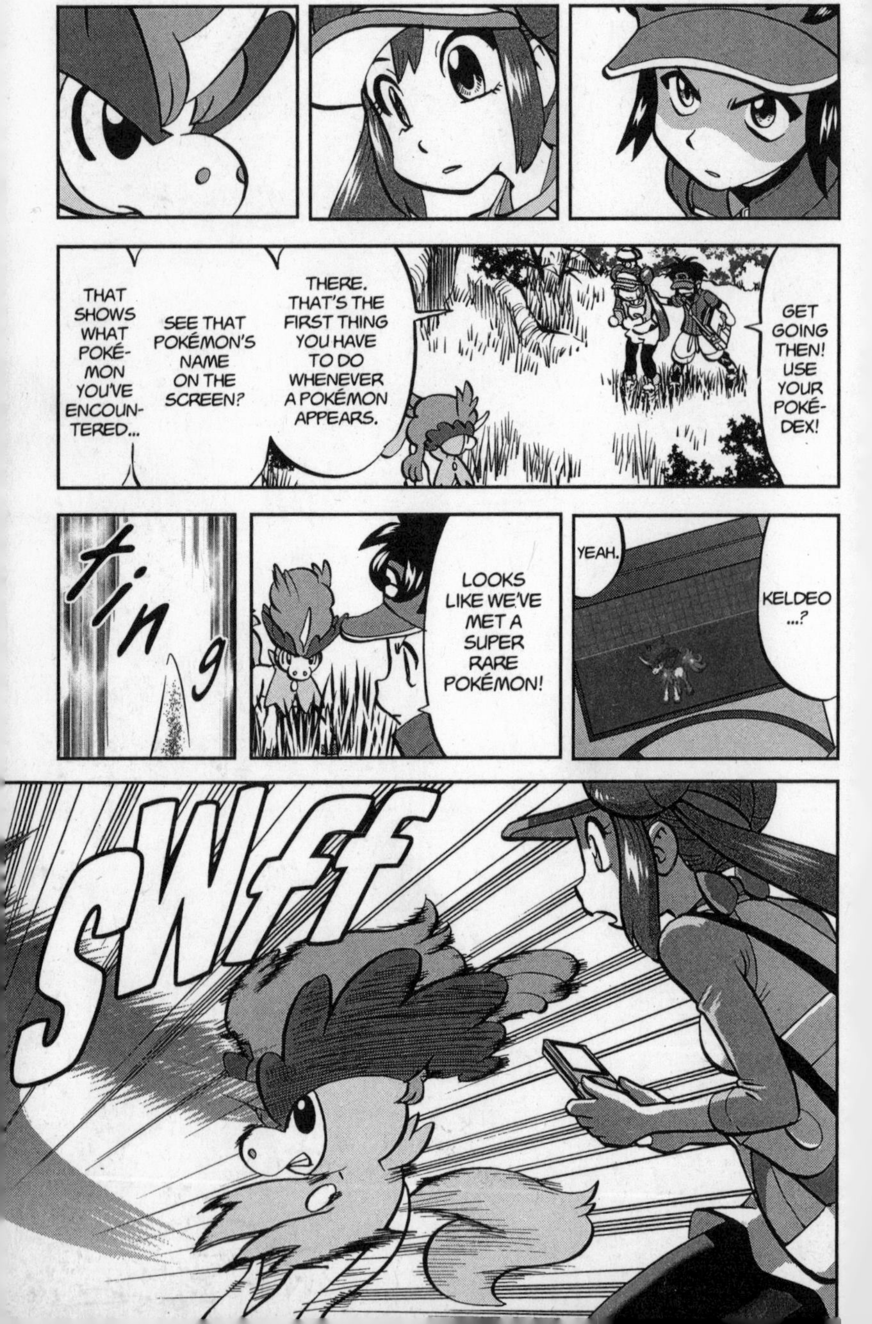
GET GOING THEN! USE YOUR POKÉ-DEX!
THERE. THAT'S THE FIRST THING YOU HAVE TO DO WHENEVER A POKÉMON APPEARS.
SEE THAT POKÉMON'S NAME ON THE SCREEN?
THAT SHOWS WHAT POKÉ-MON YOU'VE ENCOUN-TERED...
KELDEO ...?
YEAH.
LOOKS LIKE WE'VE MET A SUPER RARE POKÉMON!
ting
SWFF

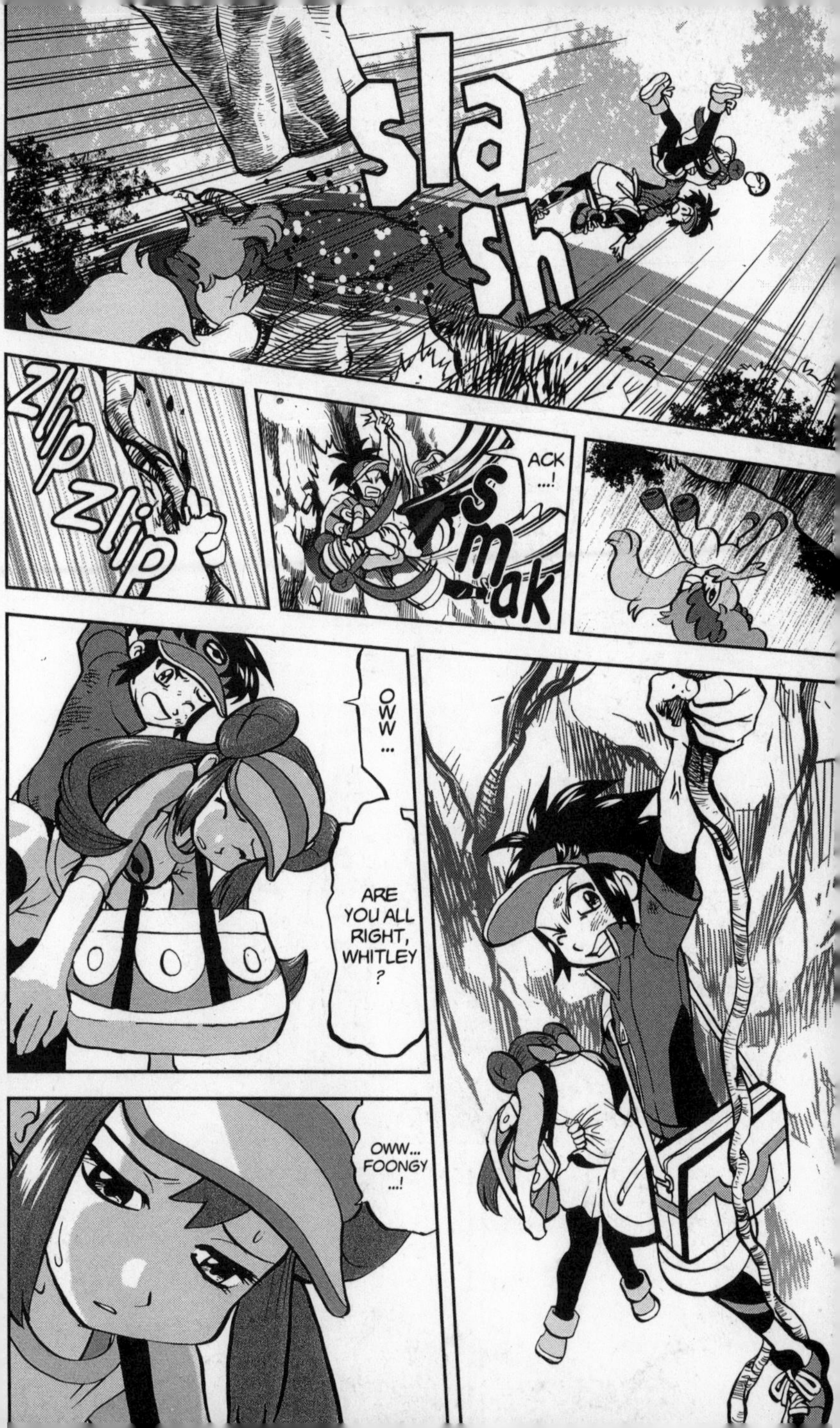
slash
ACK ...!
smak
zlip zlip zlip
OWW ...
ARE YOU ALL RIGHT, WHITLEY?
OWW... FOONGY ...!

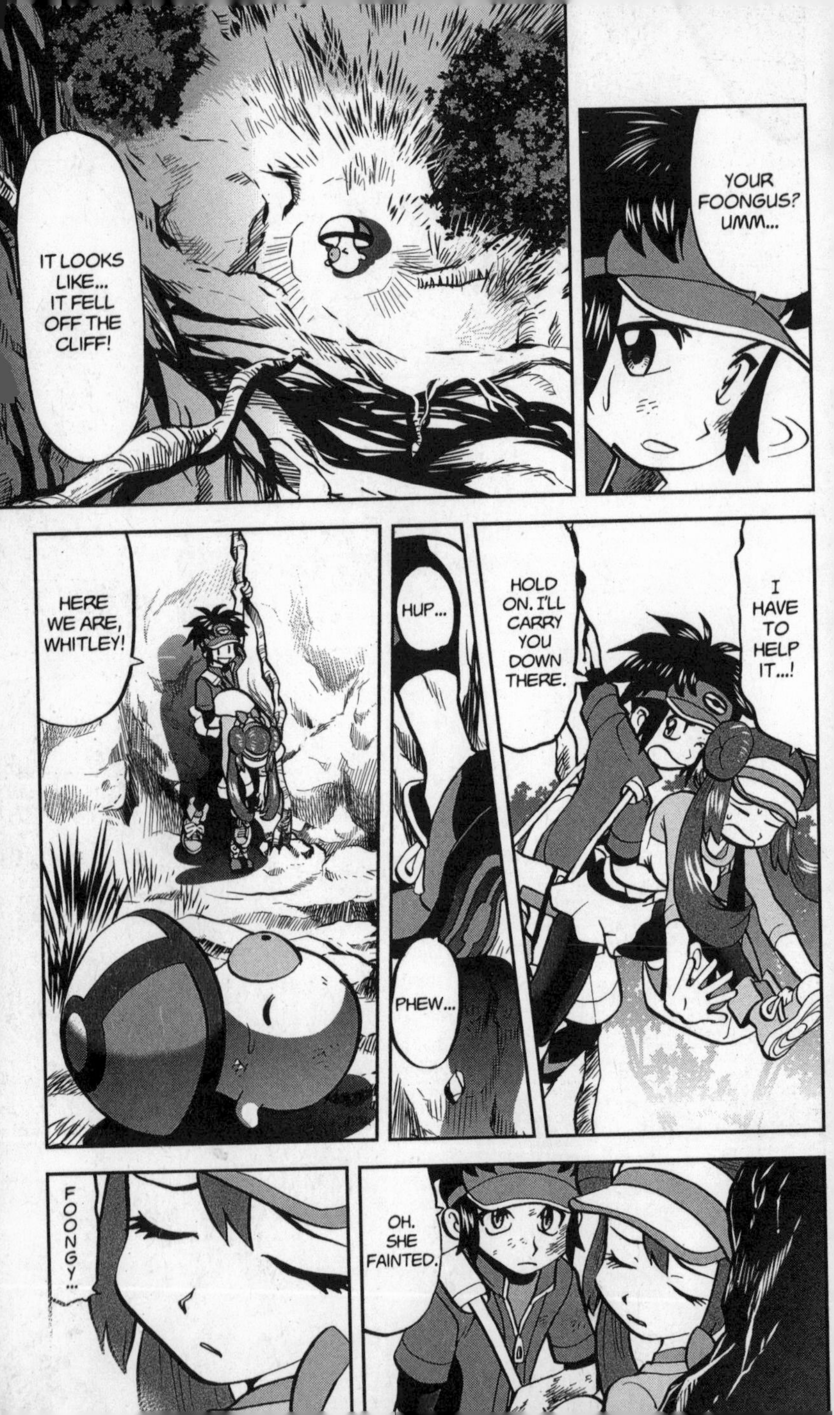
YOUR FOONGUS? UMM...
IT LOOKS LIKE... IT FELL OFF THE CLIFF!
I HAVE TO HELP IT...!
HOLD ON. I'LL CARRY YOU DOWN THERE.
HUP...
PHEW...
HERE WE ARE, WHITLEY!
OH. SHE FAINTED.
FOONGY...

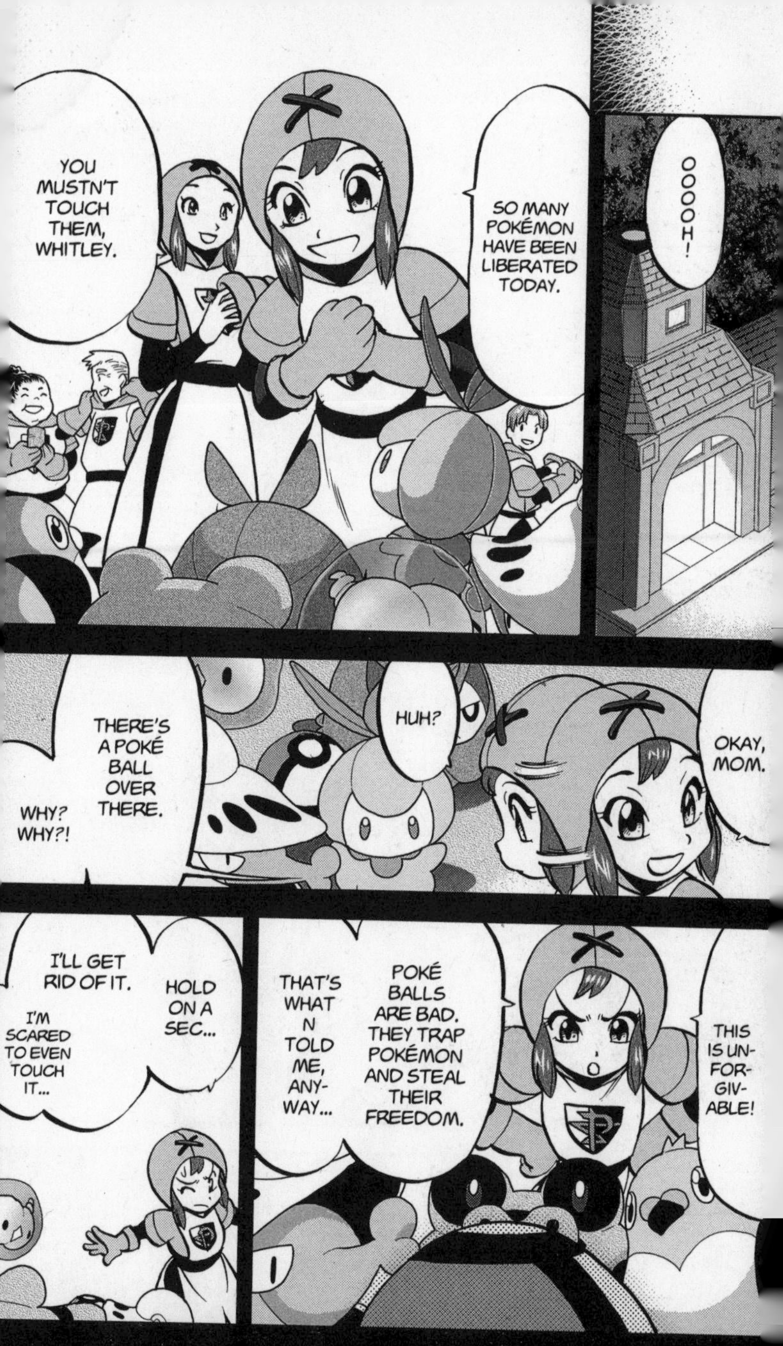
OOOOH!
SO MANY POKÉMON HAVE BEEN LIBERATED TODAY.
YOU MUSTN'T TOUCH THEM, WHITLEY.
OKAY, MOM.
HUH?
THERE'S A POKÉ BALL OVER THERE.
WHY? WHY?!
THIS IS UNFORGIVABLE!
POKÉ BALLS ARE BAD. THEY TRAP POKÉMON AND STEAL THEIR FREEDOM.
THAT'S WHAT N TOLD ME, ANYWAY...
HOLD ON A SEC...
I'LL GET RID OF IT.
I'M SCARED TO EVEN TOUCH IT...

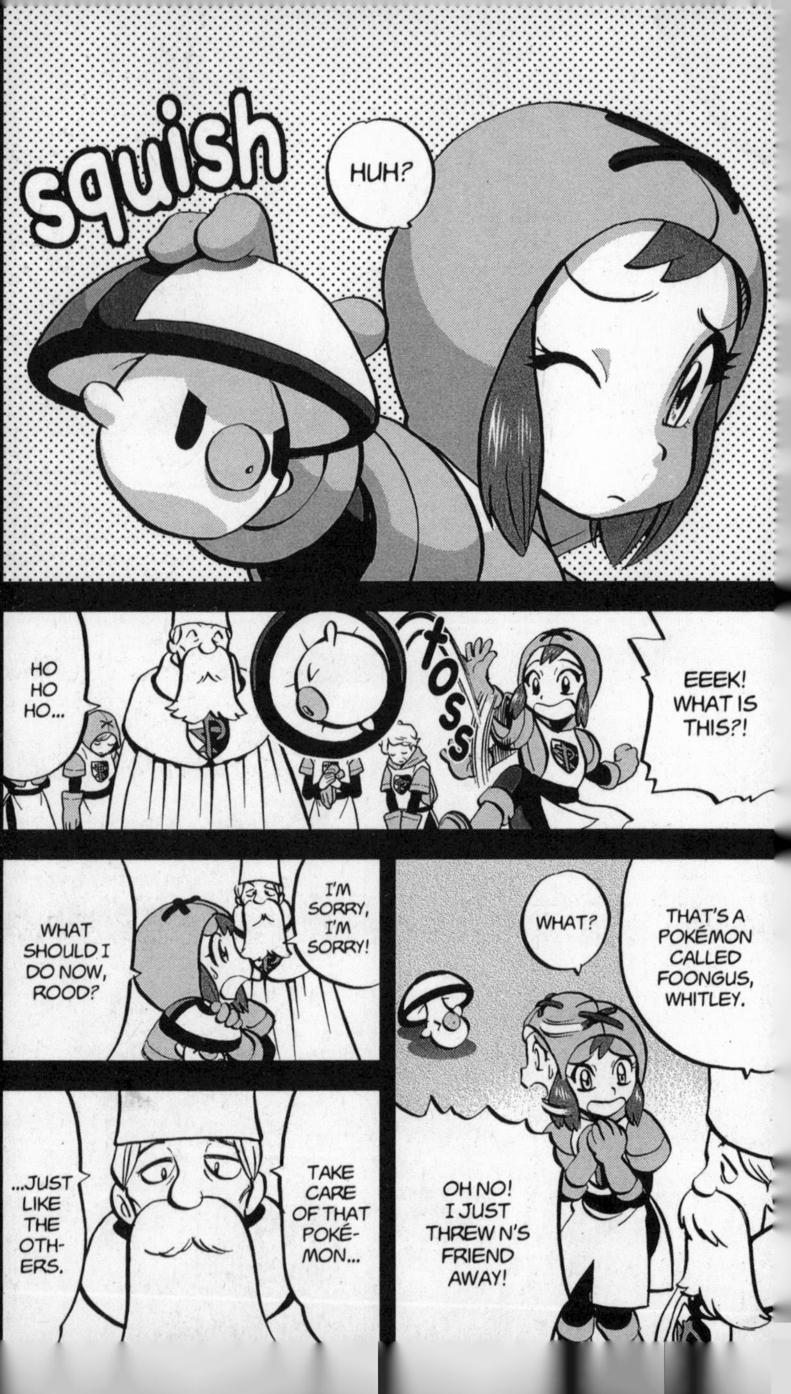
HUH?
squish
EEEK! WHAT IS THIS?!
toss
HO HO HO...
THAT'S A POKÉMON CALLED FOONGUS, WHITLEY.
WHAT?
OH NO! I JUST THREW N'S FRIEND AWAY!
I'M SORRY, I'M SORRY!
WHAT SHOULD I DO NOW, ROOD?
TAKE CARE OF THAT POKÉMON...
...JUST LIKE THE OTHERS.

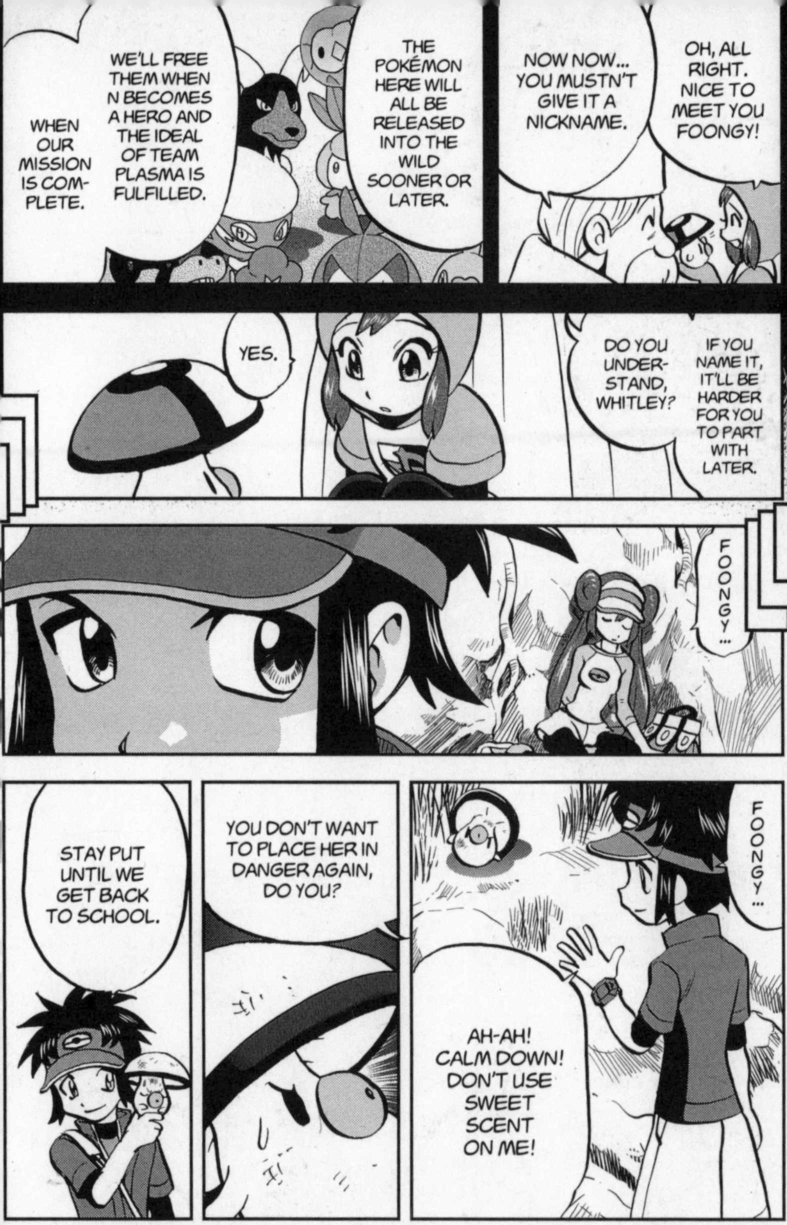
OH, ALL RIGHT. NICE TO MEET YOU FOONGY!
NOW NOW... YOU MUSTN'T GIVE IT A NICKNAME.
THE POKÉMON HERE WILL ALL BE RELEASED INTO THE WILD SOONER OR LATER.
WE'LL FREE THEM WHEN N BECOMES A HERO AND THE IDEAL OF TEAM PLASMA IS FULFILLED.
WHEN OUR MISSION IS COMPLETE.
IF YOU NAME IT, IT'LL BE HARDER FOR YOU TO PART WITH LATER.
DO YOU UNDERSTAND, WHITLEY?
YES.
FOONGY...
FOONGY...
AH-AH! CALM DOWN! DON'T USE SWEET SCENT ON ME!
YOU DON'T WANT TO PLACE HER IN DANGER AGAIN, DO YOU?
STAY PUT UNTIL WE GET BACK TO SCHOOL.

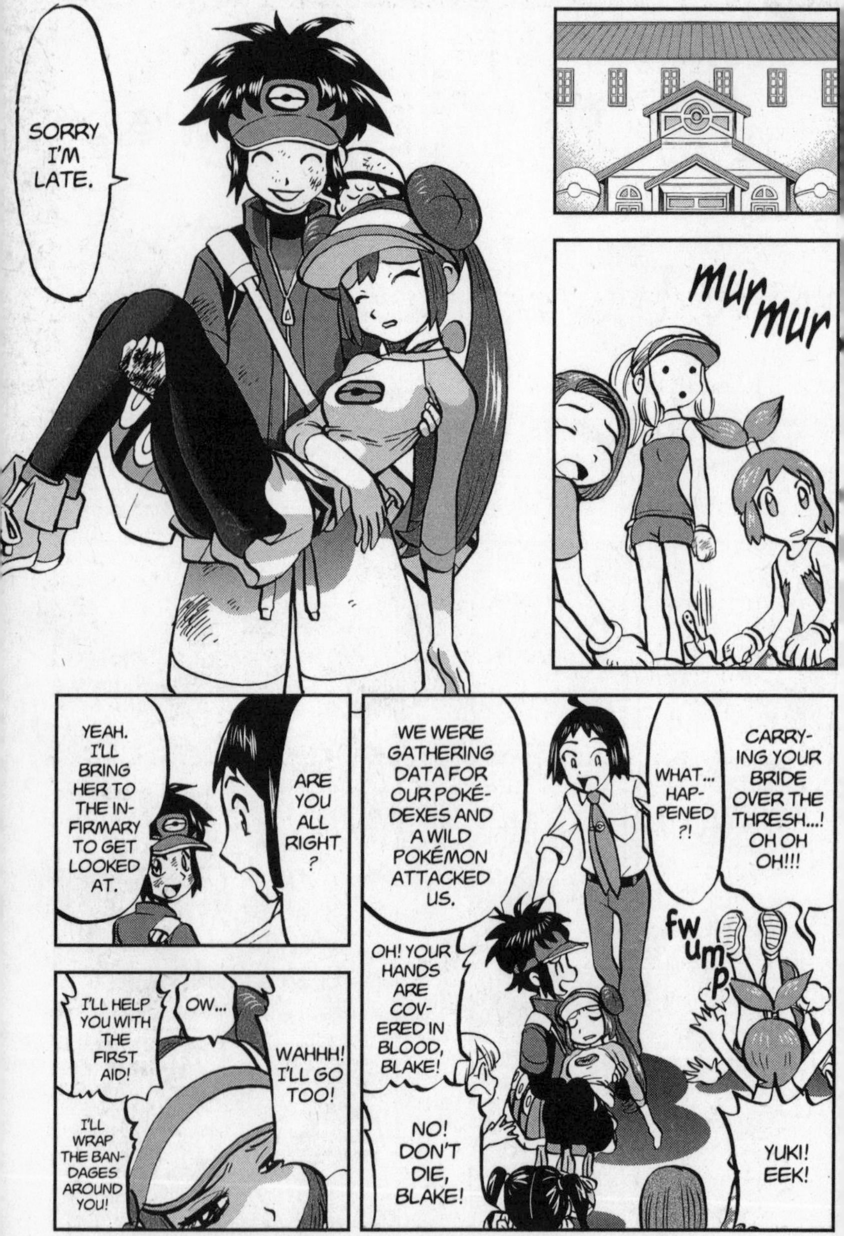
murmur
SORRY I'M LATE.
CARRYING YOUR BRIDE OVER THE THRESH...! OH OH OH!!!
WHAT... HAPPENED?!
WE WERE GATHERING DATA FOR OUR POKÉDEXES AND A WILD POKÉMON ATTACKED US.
fwump
OH! YOUR HANDS ARE COVERED IN BLOOD, BLAKE!
YUKI! EEK!
NO! DON'T DIE, BLAKE!
ARE YOU ALL RIGHT?
YEAH. I'LL BRING HER TO THE INFIRMARY TO GET LOOKED AT.
WAHHH! I'LL GO TOO!
OW...
I'LL HELP YOU WITH THE FIRST AID!
I'LL WRAP THE BANDAGES AROUND YOU!

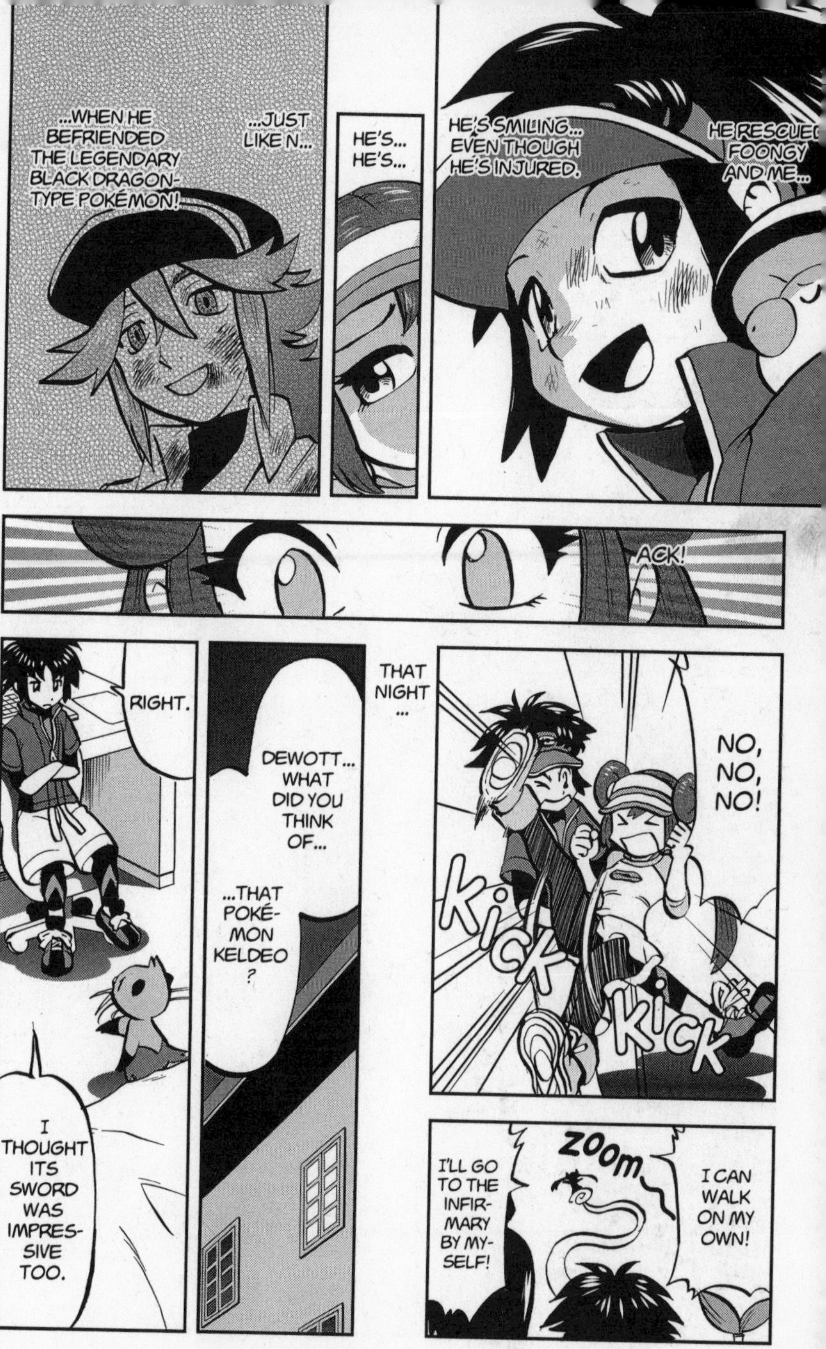
HE RESCUED FOONGY AND ME...
HE'S SMILING... EVEN THOUGH HE'S INJURED.
HE'S... HE'S...
...JUST LIKE N...
...WHEN HE BEFRIENDED THE LEGENDARY BLACK DRAGON-TYPE POKÉMON!
ACK!
NO, NO, NO!
KICK
KICK
I CAN WALK ON MY OWN!
ZOOM
I'LL GO TO THE INFIRMARY BY MYSELF!
THAT NIGHT ...
DEWOTT... WHAT DID YOU THINK OF...
...THAT POKÉMON KELDEO?
RIGHT.
I THOUGHT ITS SWORD WAS IMPRESSIVE TOO.

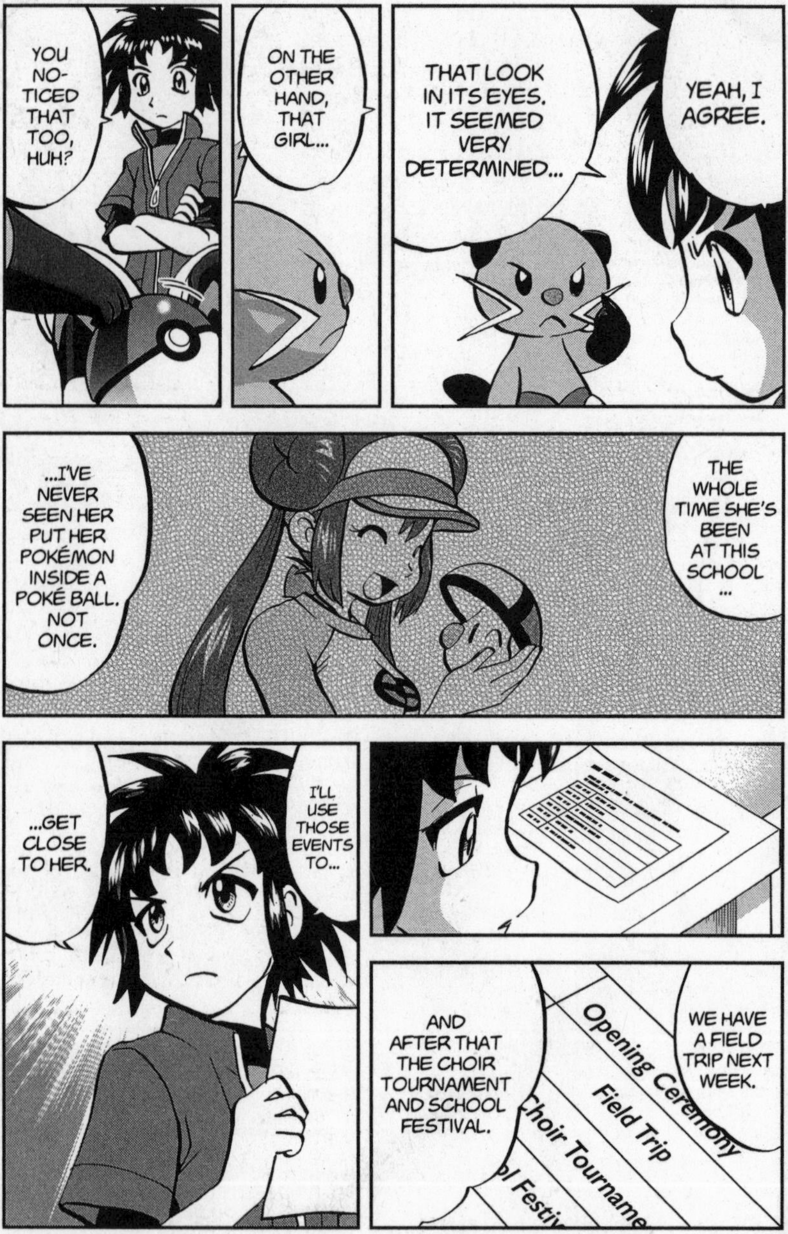
YEAH, I AGREE.
THAT LOOK IN ITS EYES. IT SEEMED VERY DETERMINED...
ON THE OTHER HAND, THAT GIRL...
YOU NO-TICED THAT TOO, HUH?
THE WHOLE TIME SHE'S BEEN AT THIS SCHOOL...
...I'VE NEVER SEEN HER PUT HER POKÉMON INSIDE A POKÉ BALL. NOT ONCE.
WE HAVE A FIELD TRIP NEXT WEEK.
AND AFTER THAT THE CHOIR TOURNAMENT AND SCHOOL FESTIVAL.
Opening Ceremony
Field Trip
I'LL USE THOSE EVENTS TO...
...GET CLOSE TO HER.

Officially Approved by the Pokémon Association
The Pokémon Trainers' School

Trainers' School Prospectus

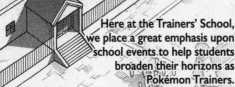

Here at the Trainers' School, we place a great emphasis upon school events to help students broaden their horizons as Pokémon Trainers.
We conduct two field trips a year with the theme, "People Living With Pokémon."
Also, unique school events like the School Festival and Berry Harvest Festival are popular with students as well as the community at large.

School Dorm

Dorms, divided by gender, are provided for non-local students. Students live an independent life at school. We offer the ideal environment for learning and growth.

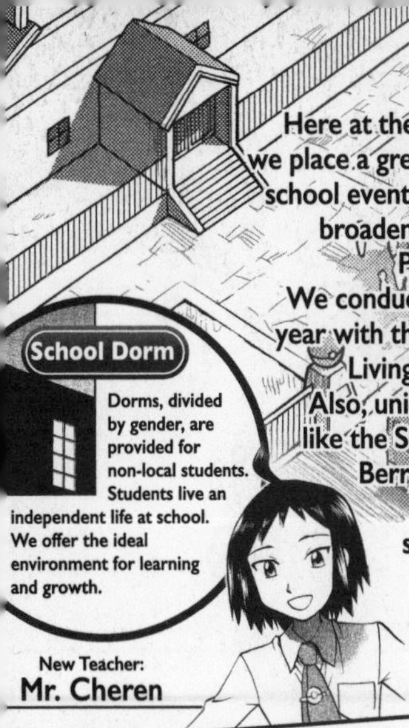

New Teacher:
Mr. Cheren

School Event Schedule

1st Semester

[April]
- School Entrance Ceremony
- Orientation

[June]
- Field Trip 1 Join Avenue

2nd Semester

[September]
- Field Trip 2 Pokéstar Studios

[October]
- Choir Tournament
- School Festival

3rd Semester

[January]
- Berry Harvest Festival
- School Battle Tourname

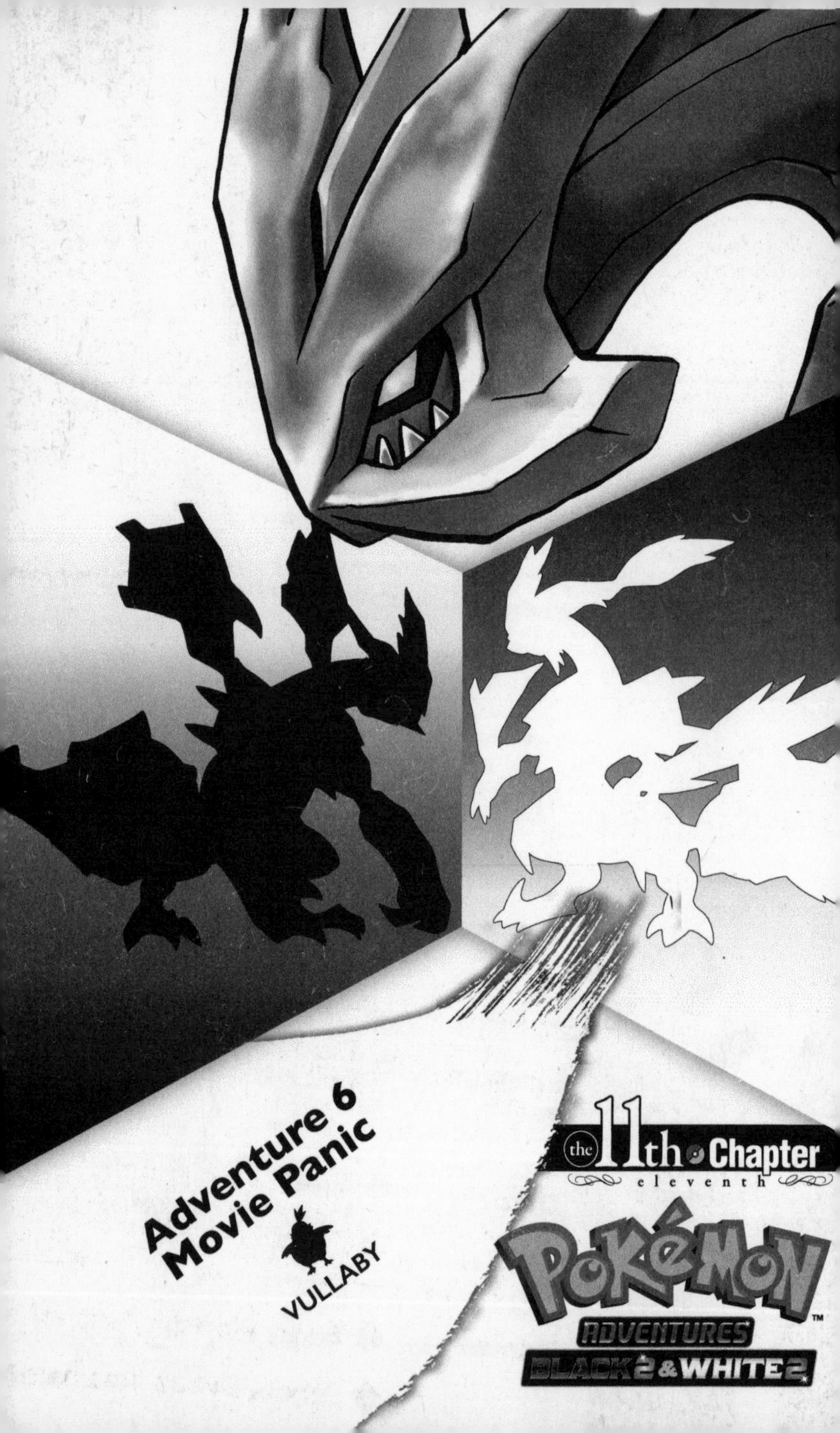
Adventure 6
Movie Panic
VULLABY
the 11th Chapter
eleventh
POKÉMON
ADVENTURES
BLACK 2 & WHITE 2

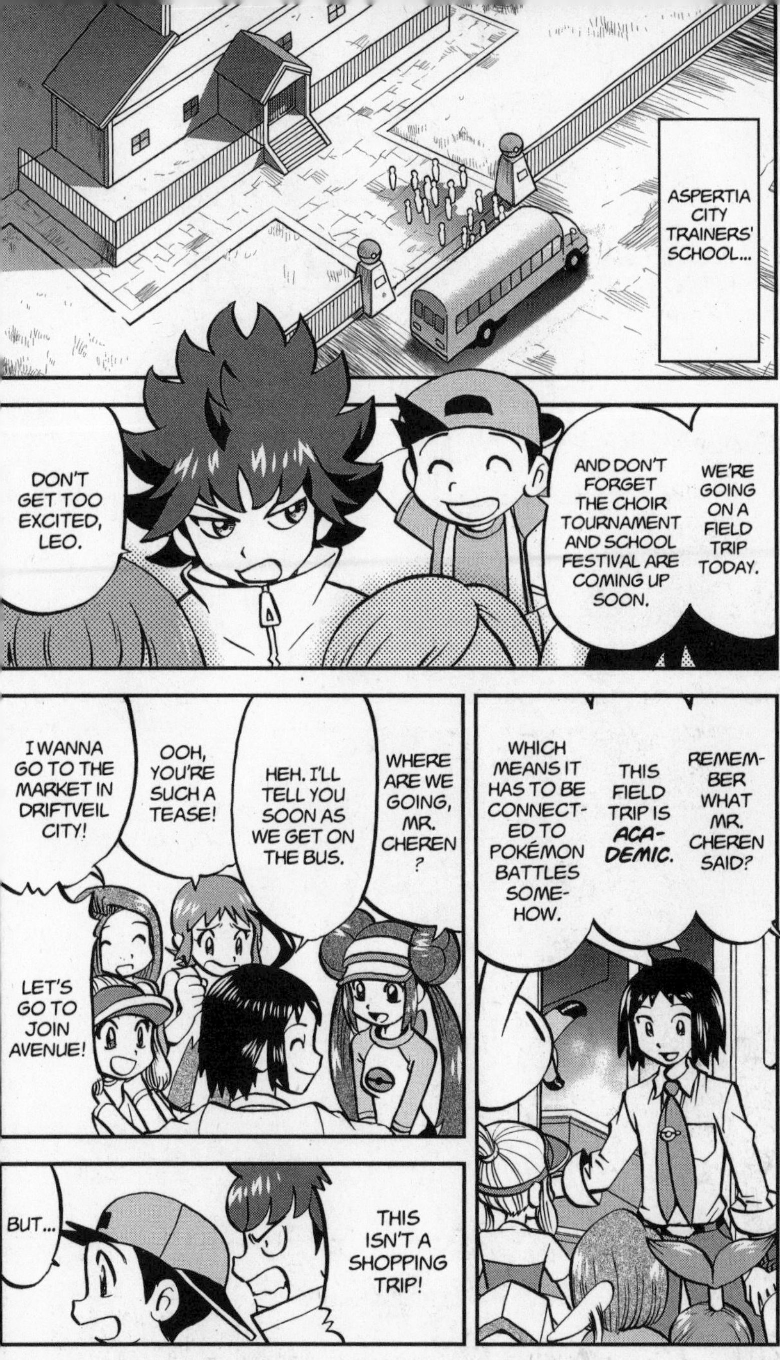
ASPERTIA CITY TRAINERS' SCHOOL...
WE'RE GOING ON A FIELD TRIP TODAY.
AND DON'T FORGET THE CHOIR TOURNAMENT AND SCHOOL FESTIVAL ARE COMING UP SOON.
DON'T GET TOO EXCITED, LEO.
REMEMBER WHAT MR. CHEREN SAID?
THIS FIELD TRIP IS ***ACADEMIC***.
WHICH MEANS IT HAS TO BE CONNECTED TO POKÉMON BATTLES SOMEHOW.
WHERE ARE WE GOING, MR. CHEREN?
HEH. I'LL TELL YOU SOON AS WE GET ON THE BUS.
OOH, YOU'RE SUCH A TEASE!
I WANNA GO TO THE MARKET IN DRIFTVEIL CITY!
LET'S GO TO JOIN AVENUE!
THIS ISN'T A SHOPPING TRIP!
BUT...

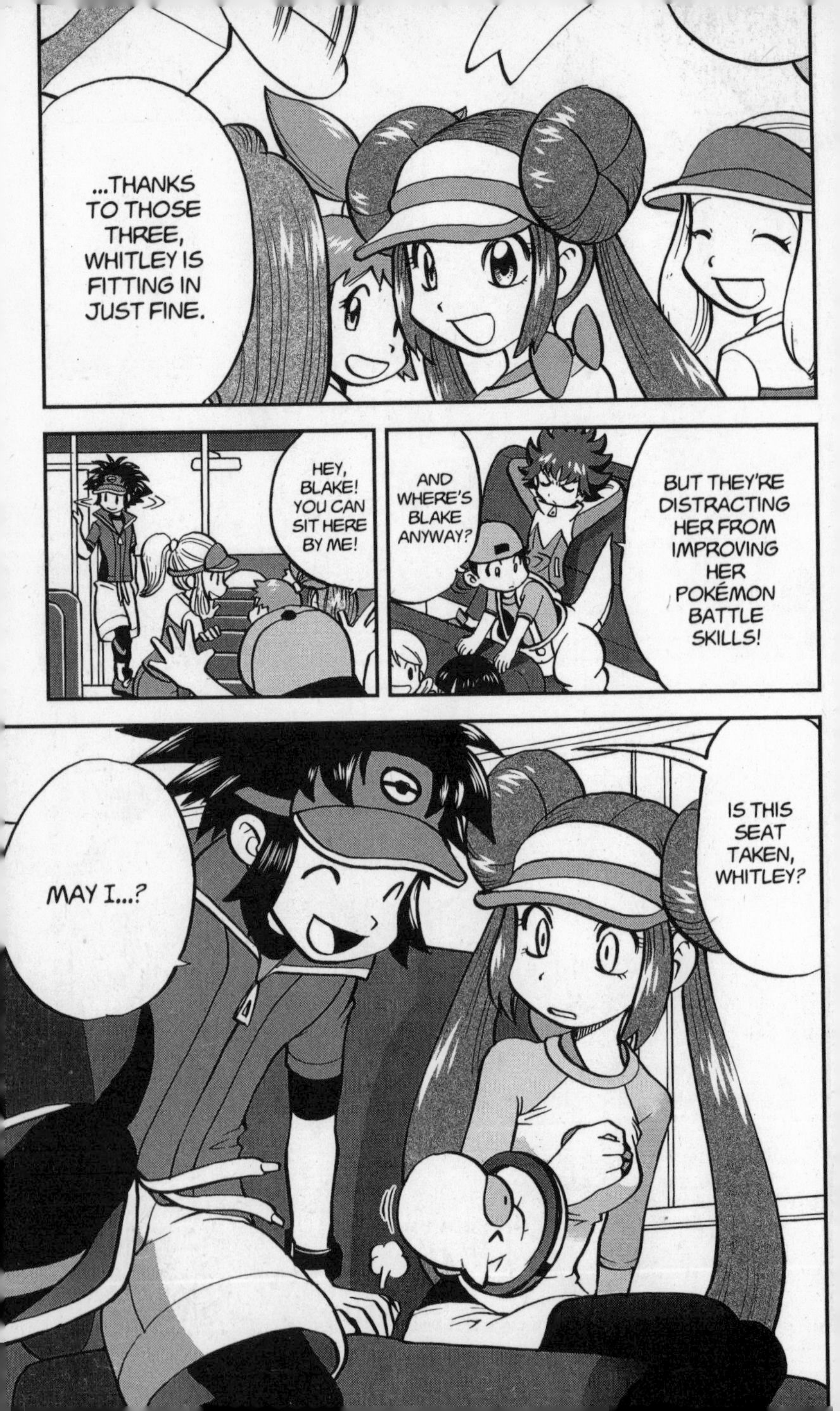
...THANKS TO THOSE THREE, WHITLEY IS FITTING IN JUST FINE.
BUT THEY'RE DISTRACTING HER FROM IMPROVING HER POKÉMON BATTLE SKILLS!
AND WHERE'S BLAKE ANYWAY?
HEY, BLAKE! YOU CAN SIT HERE BY ME!
IS THIS SEAT TAKEN, WHITLEY?
MAY I...?

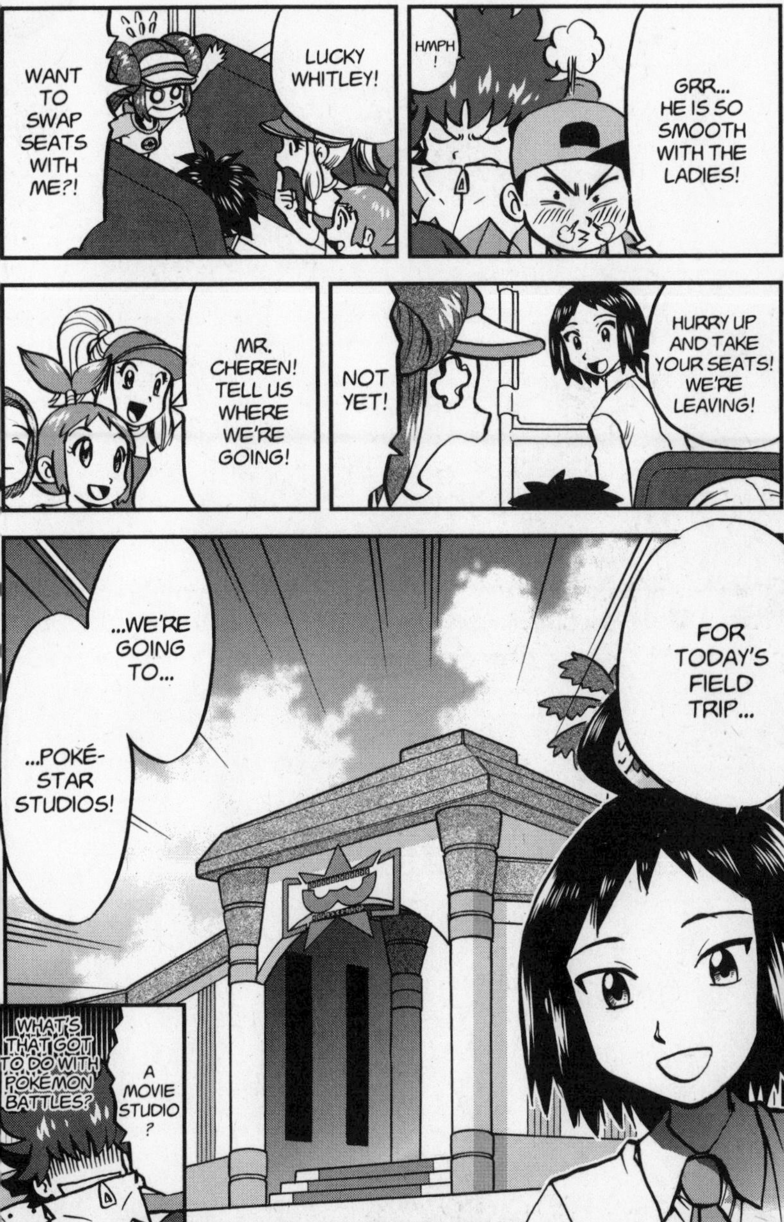
GRR... HE IS SO SMOOTH WITH THE LADIES!
HMPH!
LUCKY WHITLEY!
WANT TO SWAP SEATS WITH ME?!
HURRY UP AND TAKE YOUR SEATS! WE'RE LEAVING!
NOT YET!
MR. CHEREN! TELL US WHERE WE'RE GOING!
FOR TODAY'S FIELD TRIP...
...WE'RE GOING TO...
...POKÉ-STAR STUDIOS!
A MOVIE STUDIO?
WHAT'S THAT GOT TO DO WITH POKÉMON BATTLES?

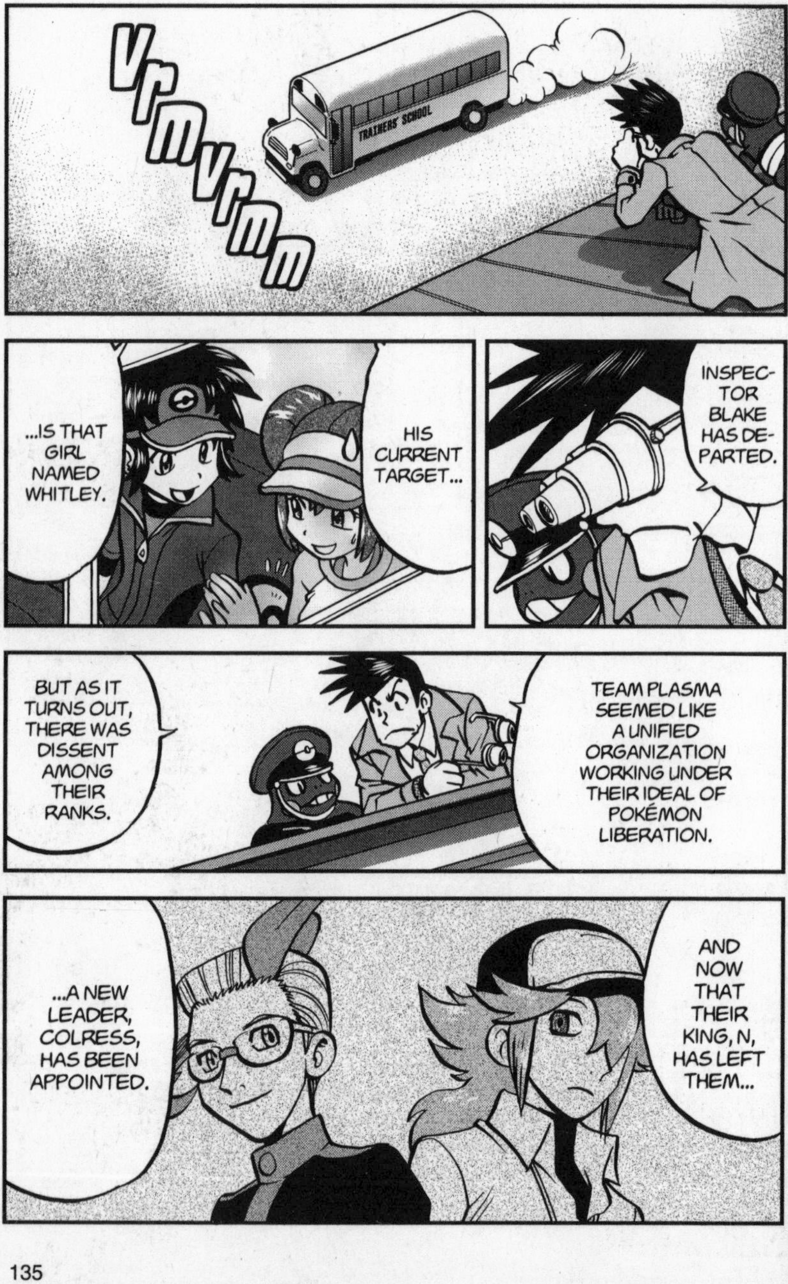
Vrmvrmm
TRAINERS' SCHOOL
INSPECTOR BLAKE HAS DEPARTED.
HIS CURRENT TARGET...
...IS THAT GIRL NAMED WHITLEY.
TEAM PLASMA SEEMED LIKE A UNIFIED ORGANIZATION WORKING UNDER THEIR IDEAL OF POKÉMON LIBERATION.
BUT AS IT TURNS OUT, THERE WAS DISSENT AMONG THEIR RANKS.
AND NOW THAT THEIR KING, N, HAS LEFT THEM...
...A NEW LEADER, COLRESS, HAS BEEN APPOINTED.

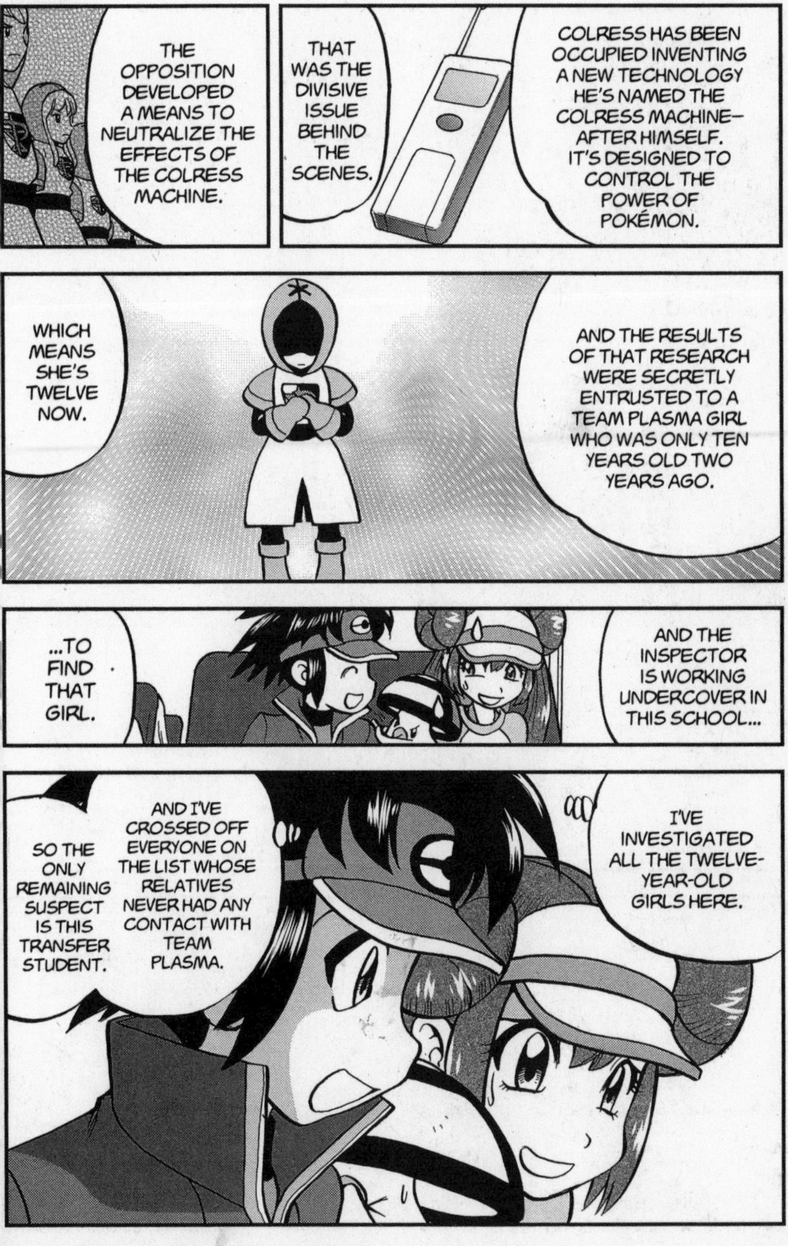
COLRESS HAS BEEN OCCUPIED INVENTING A NEW TECHNOLOGY HE'S NAMED THE COLRESS MACHINE—AFTER HIMSELF. IT'S DESIGNED TO CONTROL THE POWER OF POKÉMON.
THAT WAS THE DIVISIVE ISSUE BEHIND THE SCENES.
THE OPPOSITION DEVELOPED A MEANS TO NEUTRALIZE THE EFFECTS OF THE COLRESS MACHINE.
AND THE RESULTS OF THAT RESEARCH WERE SECRETLY ENTRUSTED TO A TEAM PLASMA GIRL WHO WAS ONLY TEN YEARS OLD TWO YEARS AGO.
WHICH MEANS SHE'S TWELVE NOW.
AND THE INSPECTOR IS WORKING UNDERCOVER IN THIS SCHOOL...
...TO FIND THAT GIRL.
I'VE INVESTIGATED ALL THE TWELVE-YEAR-OLD GIRLS HERE.
AND I'VE CROSSED OFF EVERYONE ON THE LIST WHOSE RELATIVES NEVER HAD ANY CONTACT WITH TEAM PLASMA.
SO THE ONLY REMAINING SUSPECT IS THIS TRANSFER STUDENT.

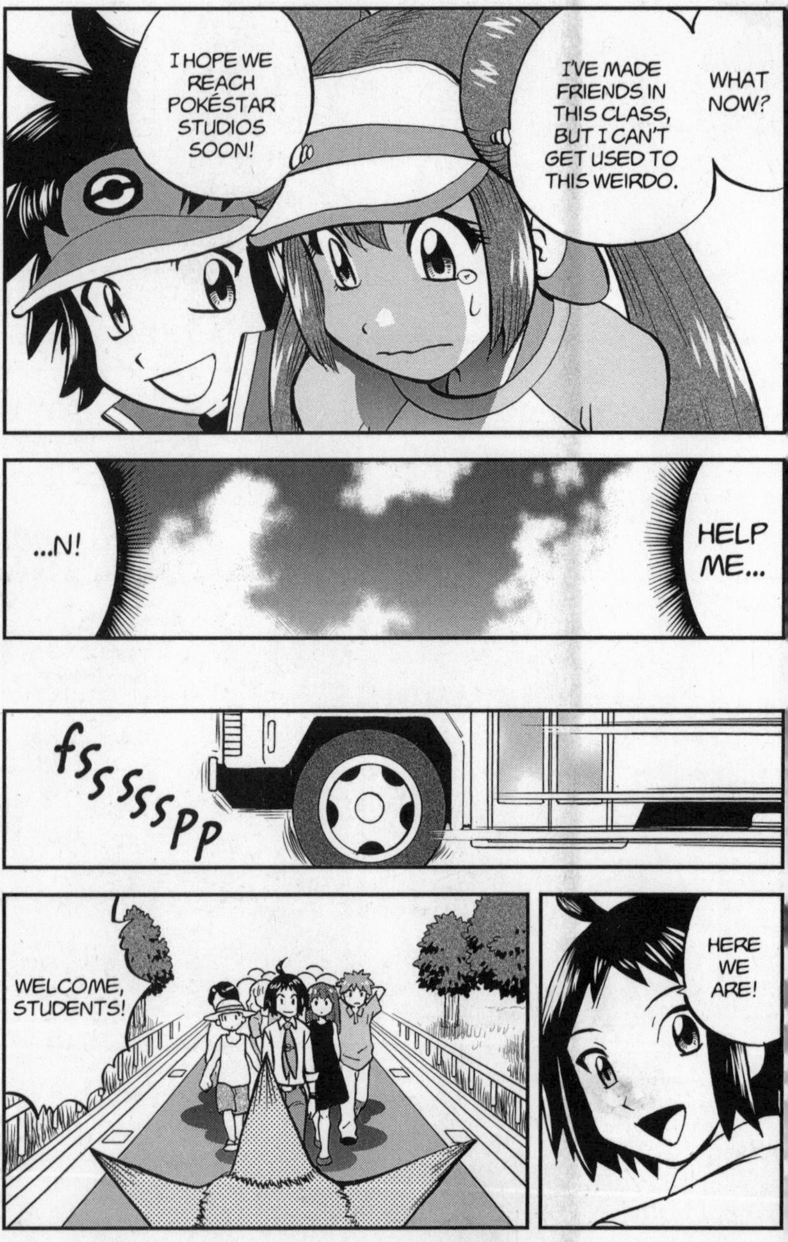
WHAT NOW?
I'VE MADE FRIENDS IN THIS CLASS, BUT I CAN'T GET USED TO THIS WEIRDO.
I HOPE WE REACH POKÉSTAR STUDIOS SOON!
HELP ME...
...N!
fsssssspp
HERE WE ARE!
WELCOME, STUDENTS!

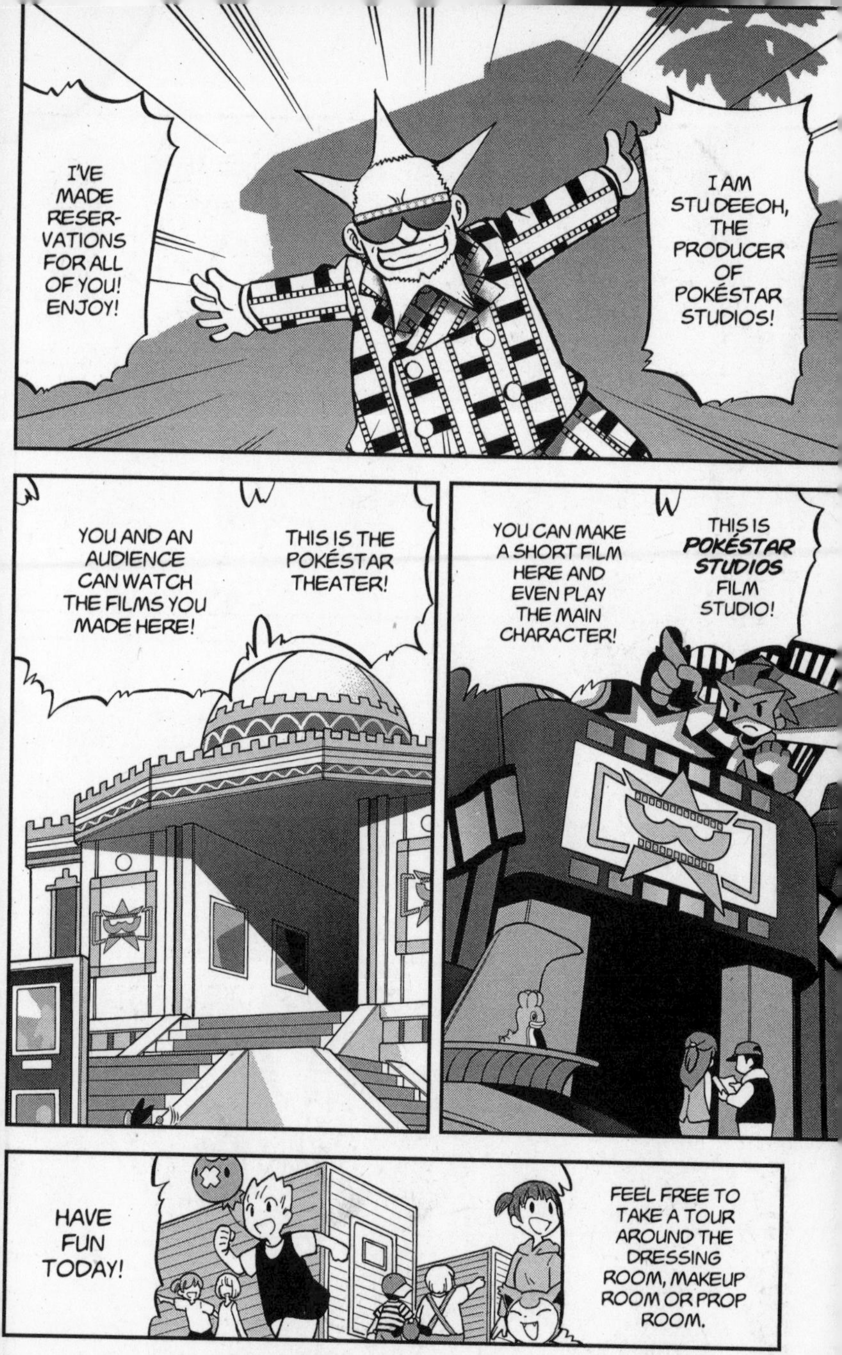
I AM STU DEEOH, THE PRODUCER OF POKÉSTAR STUDIOS!
I'VE MADE RESERVATIONS FOR ALL OF YOU! ENJOY!
THIS IS **POKÉSTAR STUDIOS** FILM STUDIO!
YOU CAN MAKE A SHORT FILM HERE AND EVEN PLAY THE MAIN CHARACTER!
THIS IS THE POKÉSTAR THEATER!
YOU AND AN AUDIENCE CAN WATCH THE FILMS YOU MADE HERE!
FEEL FREE TO TAKE A TOUR AROUND THE DRESSING ROOM, MAKEUP ROOM OR PROP ROOM.
HAVE FUN TODAY!

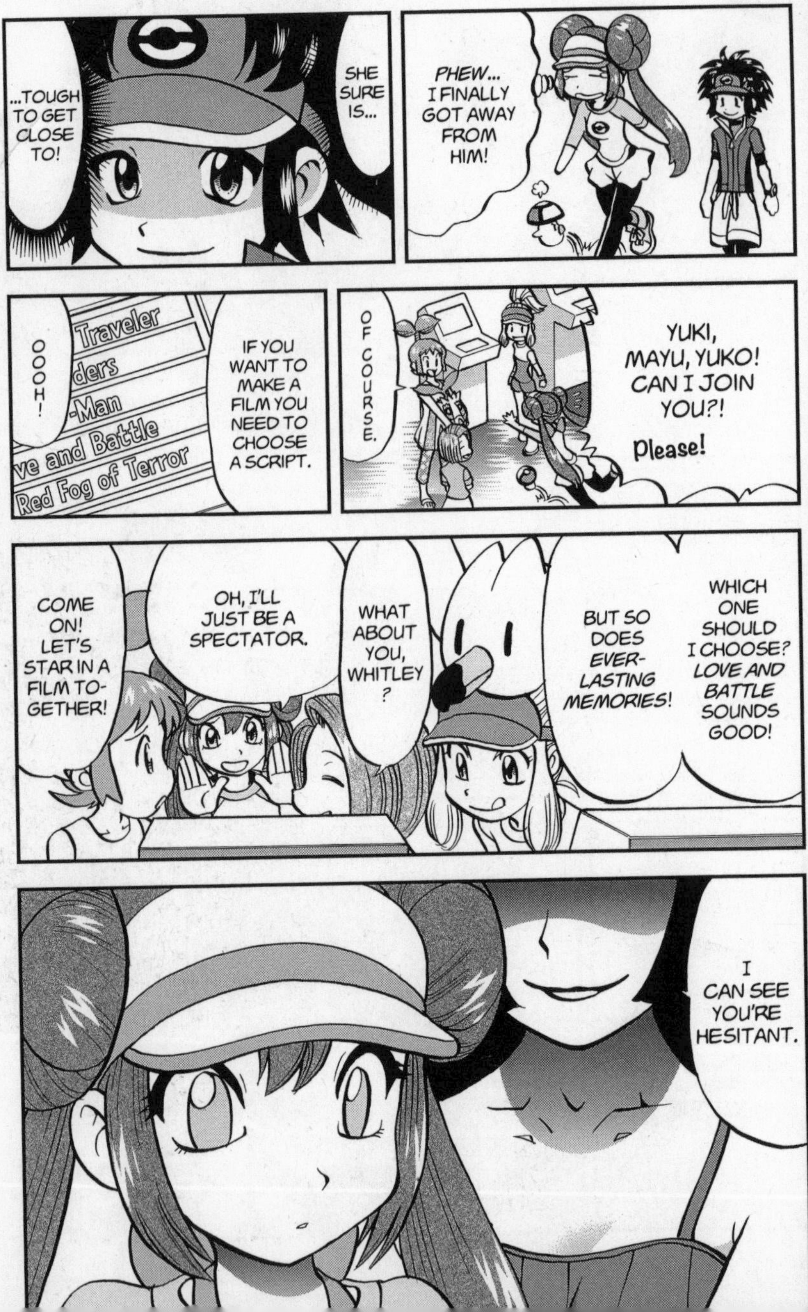
PHEW... I FINALLY GOT AWAY FROM HIM!
SHE SURE IS...
...TOUGH TO GET CLOSE TO!
YUKI, MAYU, YUKO! CAN I JOIN YOU?!
Please!
OF COURSE.
IF YOU WANT TO MAKE A FILM YOU NEED TO CHOOSE A SCRIPT.
OOOH!
Traveler
ders
-Man
ve and Battle
Red Fog of Terror
WHICH ONE SHOULD I CHOOSE? LOVE AND BATTLE SOUNDS GOOD!
BUT SO DOES EVER-LASTING MEMORIES!
WHAT ABOUT YOU, WHITLEY?
OH, I'LL JUST BE A SPECTATOR.
COME ON! LET'S STAR IN A FILM TO-GETHER!
I CAN SEE YOU'RE HESITANT.

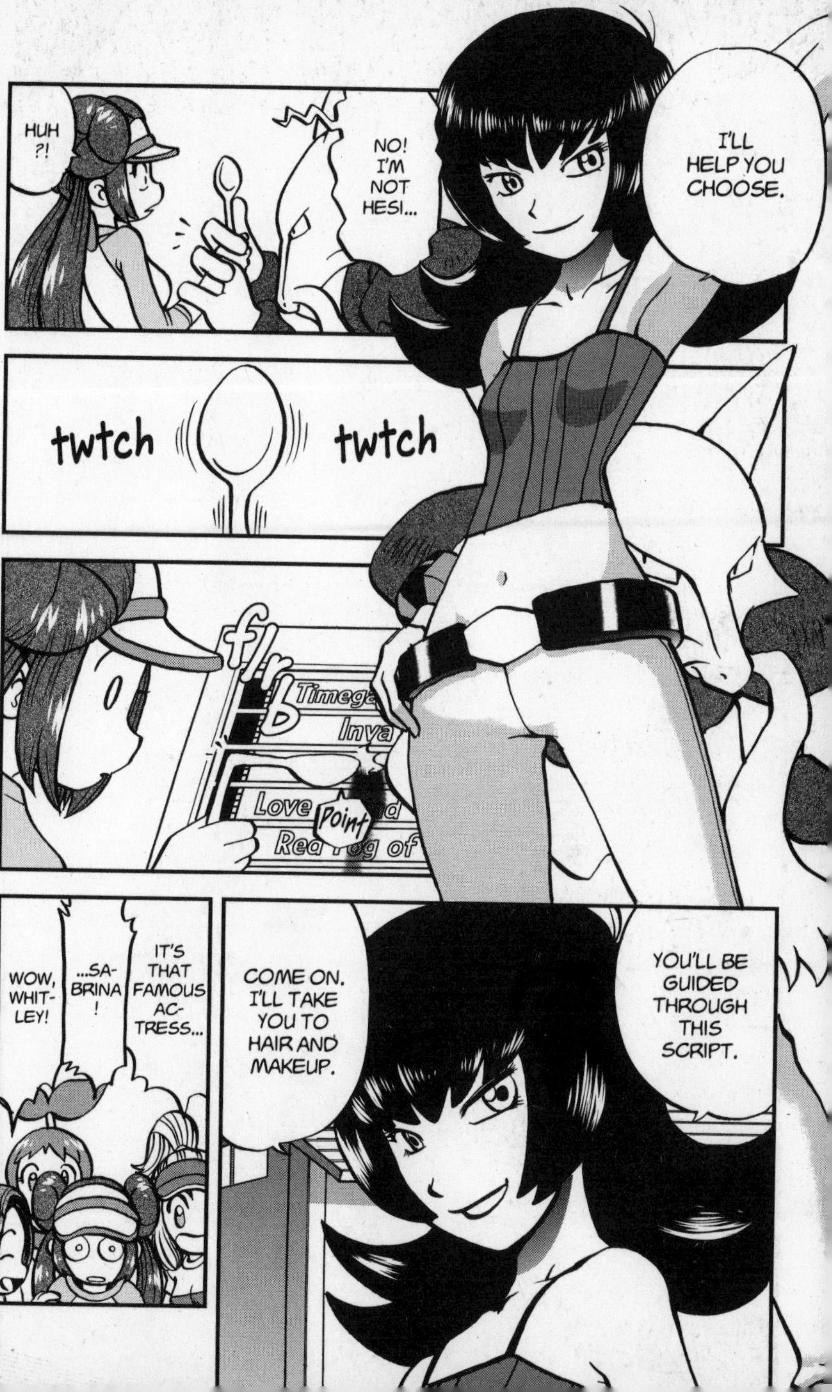
I'LL HELP YOU CHOOSE.
NO! I'M NOT HESI...
HUH ?!
twtch
twtch
Timega
Inva
Point
YOU'LL BE GUIDED THROUGH THIS SCRIPT.
COME ON. I'LL TAKE YOU TO HAIR AND MAKEUP.
IT'S THAT FAMOUS AC-TRESS...
...SA-BRINA!
WOW, WHIT-LEY!

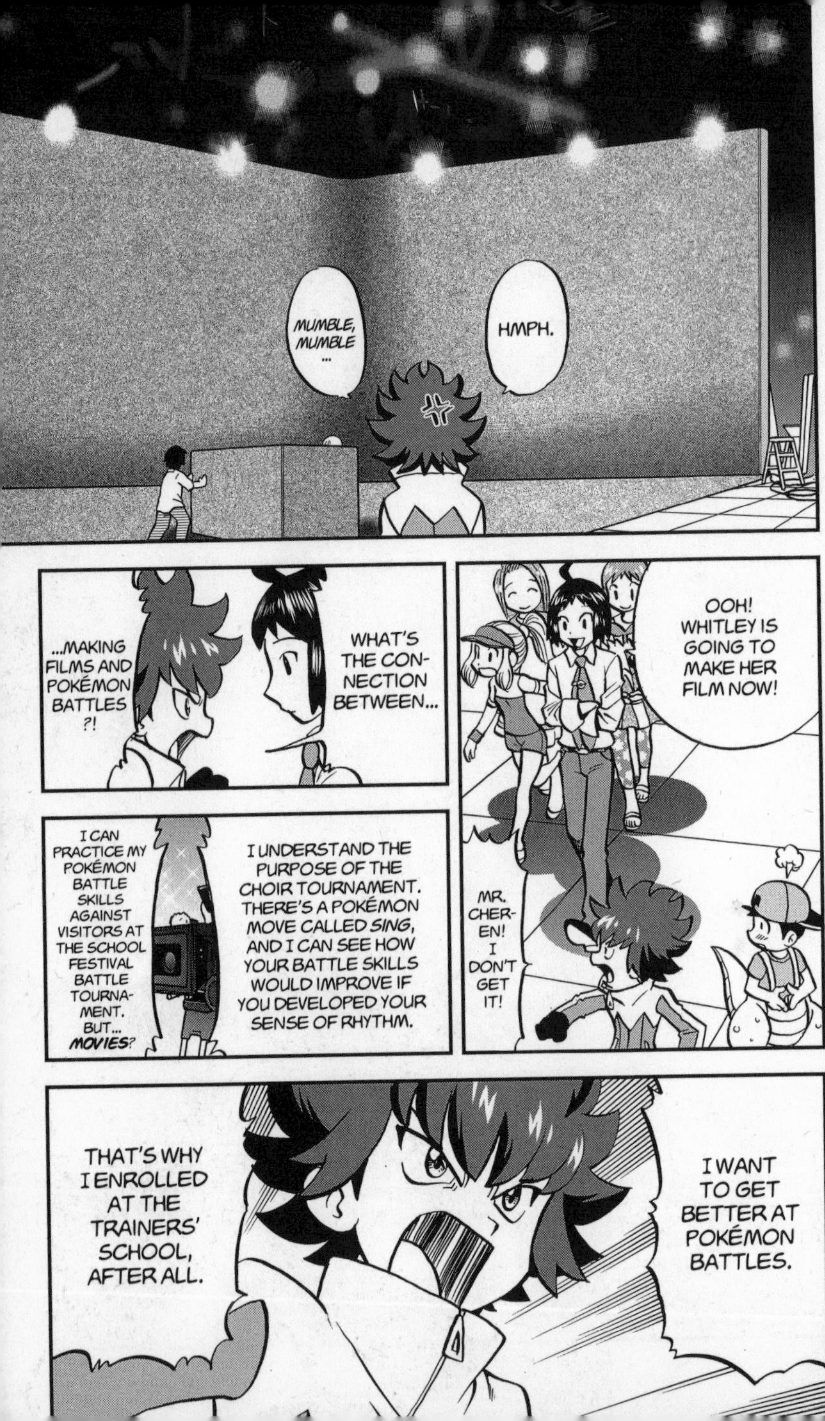
HMPH.
MUMBLE, MUMBLE ...
OOH! WHITLEY IS GOING TO MAKE HER FILM NOW!
MR. CHEREN! I DON'T GET IT!
WHAT'S THE CONNECTION BETWEEN...
...MAKING FILMS AND POKÉMON BATTLES?!
I UNDERSTAND THE PURPOSE OF THE CHOIR TOURNAMENT. THERE'S A POKÉMON MOVE CALLED *SING*, AND I CAN SEE HOW YOUR BATTLE SKILLS WOULD IMPROVE IF YOU DEVELOPED YOUR SENSE OF RHYTHM.
I CAN PRACTICE MY POKÉMON BATTLE SKILLS AGAINST VISITORS AT THE SCHOOL FESTIVAL BATTLE TOURNAMENT. BUT... ***MOVIES***?
I WANT TO GET BETTER AT POKÉMON BATTLES.
THAT'S WHY I ENROLLED AT THE TRAINERS' SCHOOL, AFTER ALL.

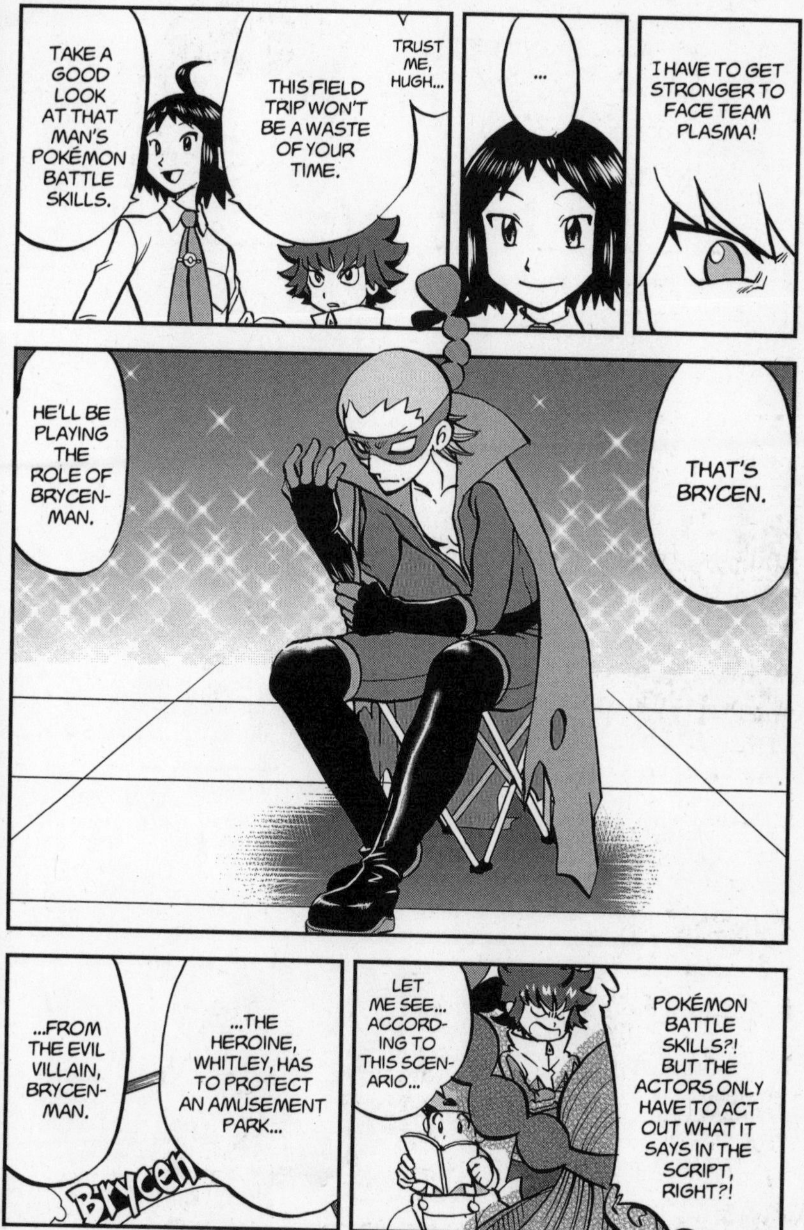
I HAVE TO GET STRONGER TO FACE TEAM PLASMA!
...
TRUST ME, HUGH...
THIS FIELD TRIP WON'T BE A WASTE OF YOUR TIME.
TAKE A GOOD LOOK AT THAT MAN'S POKÉMON BATTLE SKILLS.
THAT'S BRYCEN.
HE'LL BE PLAYING THE ROLE OF BRYCEN-MAN.
POKÉMON BATTLE SKILLS?! BUT THE ACTORS ONLY HAVE TO ACT OUT WHAT IT SAYS IN THE SCRIPT, RIGHT?!
LET ME SEE... ACCORD-ING TO THIS SCEN-ARIO...
...THE HEROINE, WHITLEY, HAS TO PROTECT AN AMUSEMENT PARK...
...FROM THE EVIL VILLAIN, BRYCEN-MAN.
Brycen

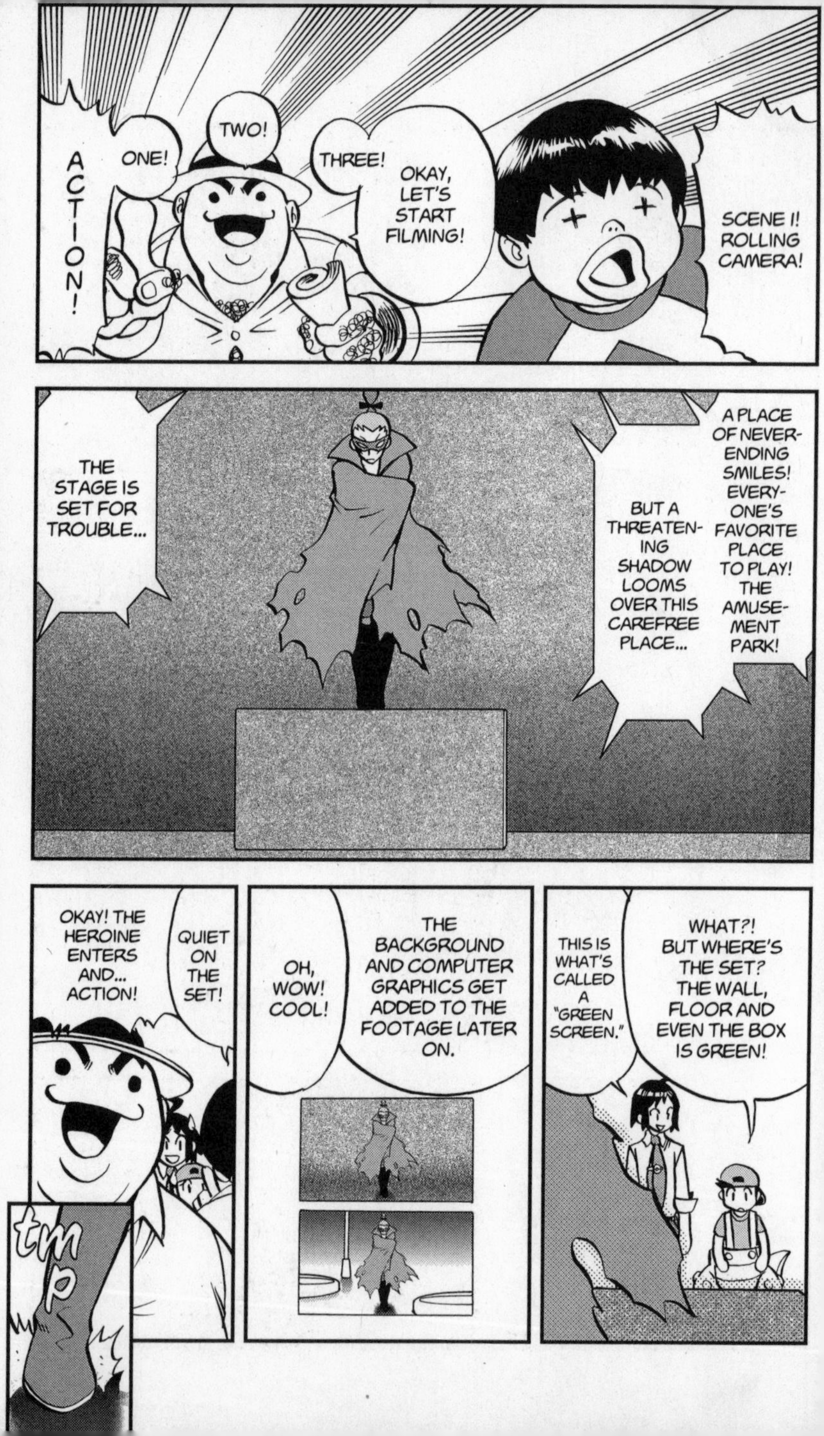
SCENE 1! ROLLING CAMERA!
OKAY, LET'S START FILMING!
THREE!
TWO!
ONE!
ACTION!
A PLACE OF NEVER-ENDING SMILES! EVERYONE'S FAVORITE PLACE TO PLAY! THE AMUSEMENT PARK!
BUT A THREATENING SHADOW LOOMS OVER THIS CAREFREE PLACE...
THE STAGE IS SET FOR TROUBLE...
WHAT?! BUT WHERE'S THE SET? THE WALL, FLOOR AND EVEN THE BOX IS GREEN!
THIS IS WHAT'S CALLED A "GREEN SCREEN."
THE BACKGROUND AND COMPUTER GRAPHICS GET ADDED TO THE FOOTAGE LATER ON.
OH, WOW! COOL!
QUIET ON THE SET!
OKAY! THE HEROINE ENTERS AND... ACTION!
tmp

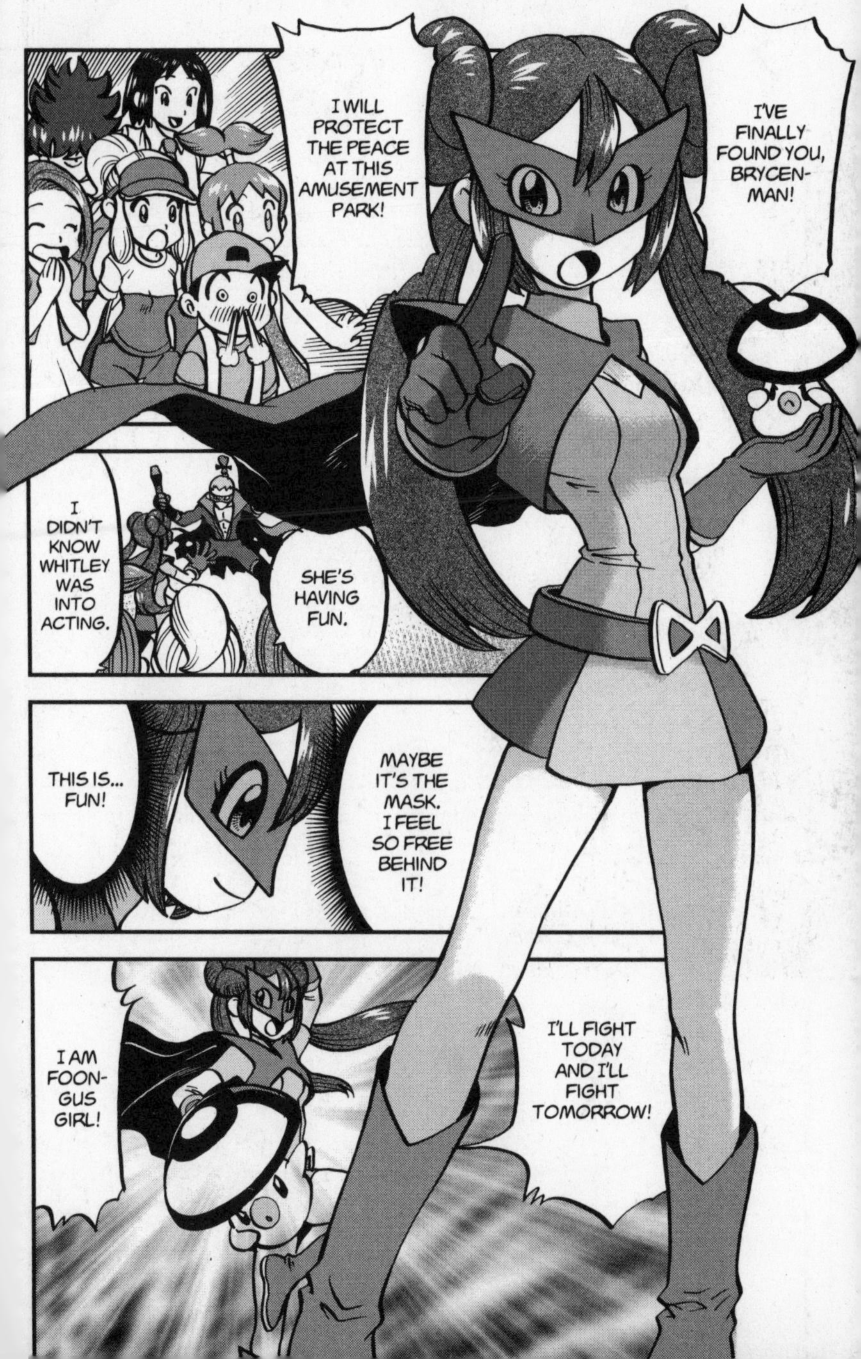
I'VE FINALLY FOUND YOU, BRYCEN-MAN!
I WILL PROTECT THE PEACE AT THIS AMUSEMENT PARK!
SHE'S HAVING FUN.
I DIDN'T KNOW WHITLEY WAS INTO ACTING.
MAYBE IT'S THE MASK. I FEEL SO FREE BEHIND IT!
THIS IS... FUN!
I'LL FIGHT TODAY AND I'LL FIGHT TOMORROW!
I AM FOON-GUS GIRL!

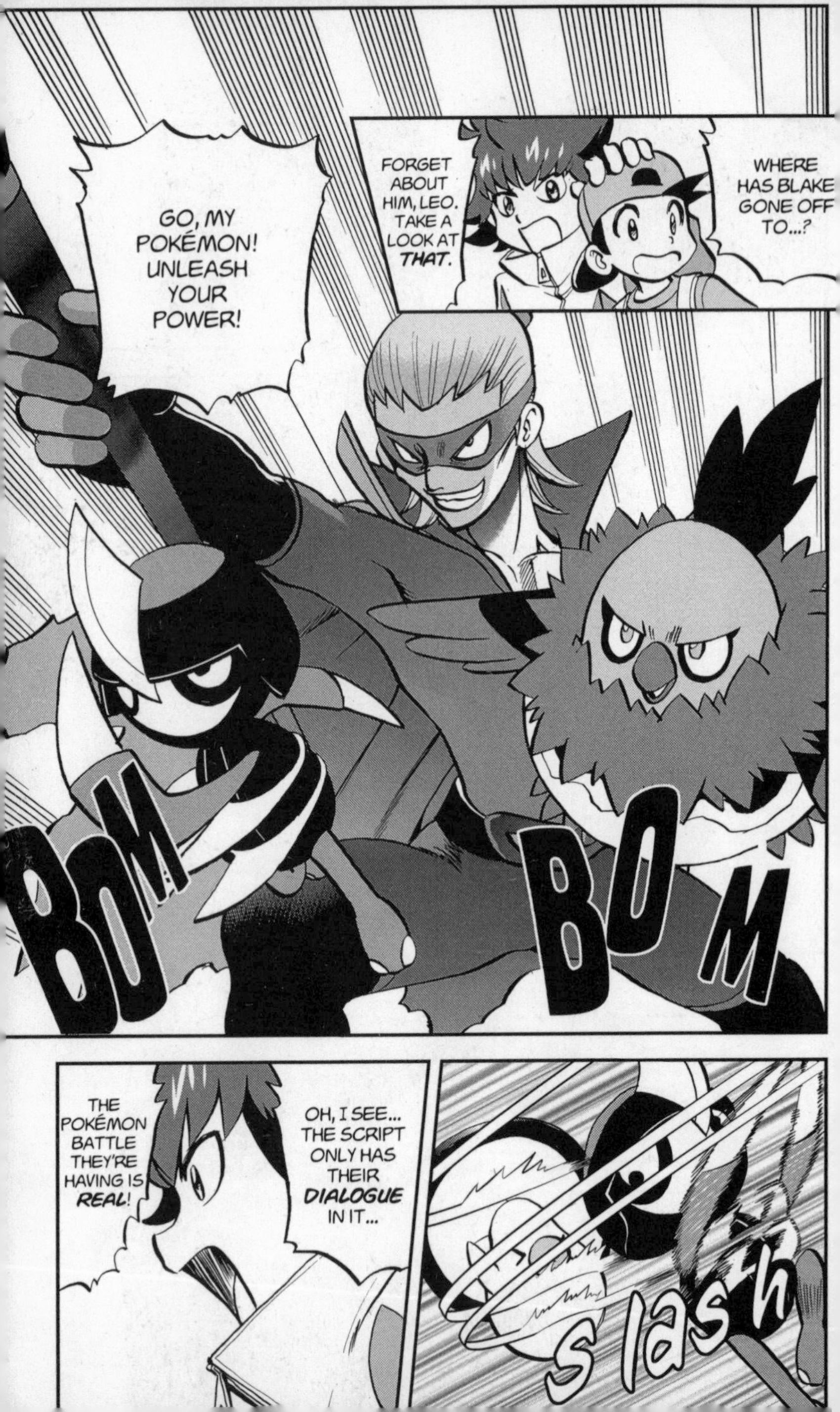
WHERE HAS BLAKE GONE OFF TO...?
FORGET ABOUT HIM, LEO. TAKE A LOOK AT *THAT*.
GO, MY POKÉMON! UNLEASH YOUR POWER!
BOM
BOM
slash
OH, I SEE... THE SCRIPT ONLY HAS THEIR *DIALOGUE* IN IT...
THE POKÉMON BATTLE THEY'RE HAVING IS *REAL*!

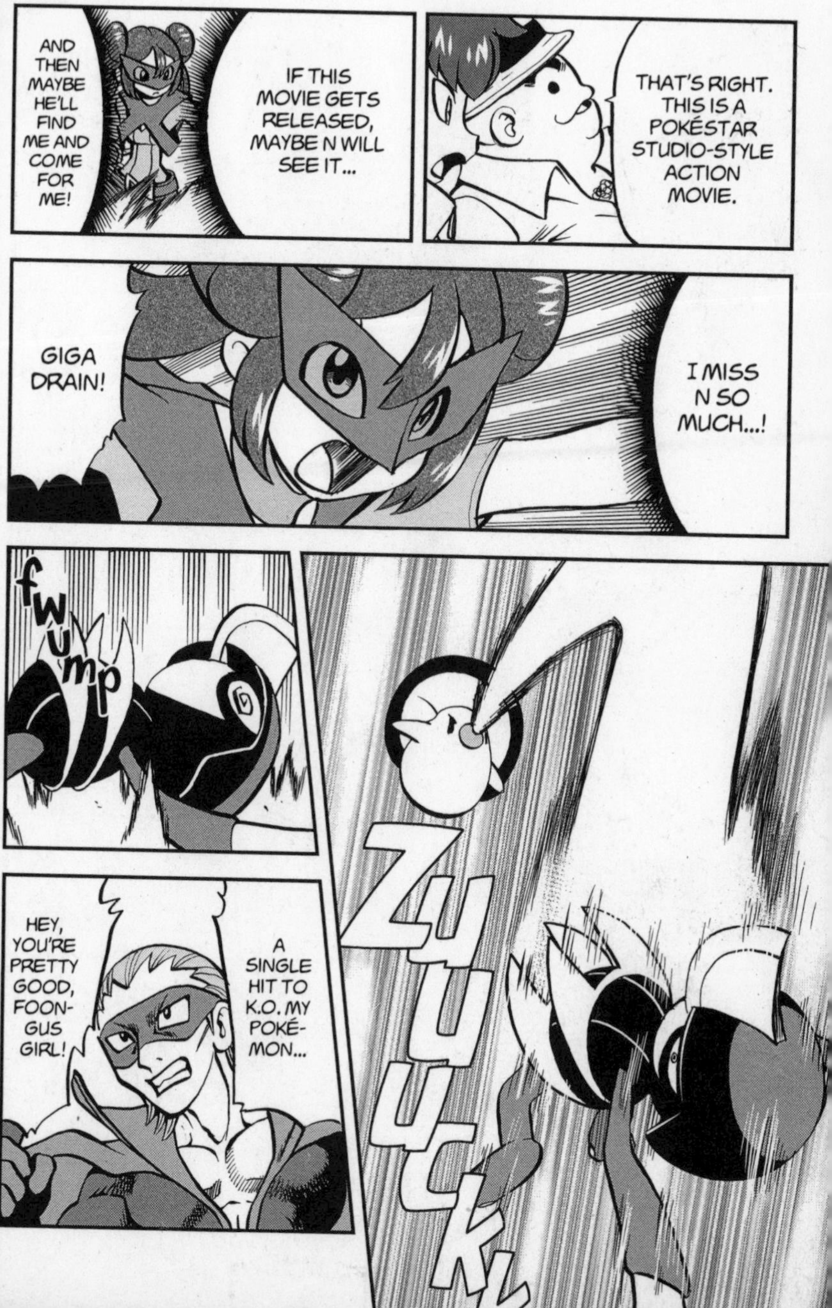
THAT'S RIGHT. THIS IS A POKÉSTAR STUDIO-STYLE ACTION MOVIE.
IF THIS MOVIE GETS RELEASED, MAYBE N WILL SEE IT...
AND THEN MAYBE HE'LL FIND ME AND COME FOR ME!
I MISS N SO MUCH...!
GIGA DRAIN!
ZUUUCK
fwump
A SINGLE HIT TO K.O. MY POKÉ-MON...
HEY, YOU'RE PRETTY GOOD, FOON-GUS GIRL!

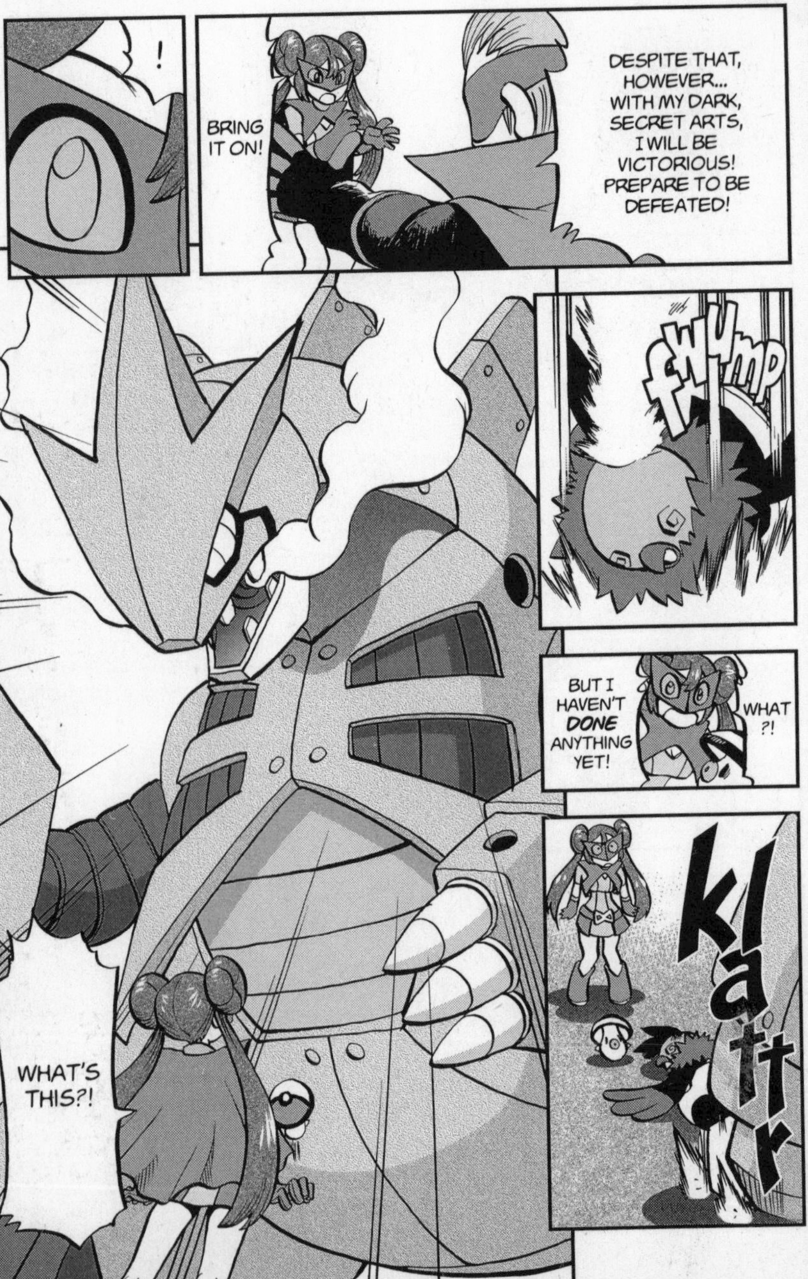
DESPITE THAT, HOWEVER... WITH MY DARK, SECRET ARTS, I WILL BE VICTORIOUS! PREPARE TO BE DEFEATED!
BRING IT ON!
!
FWUMP
WHAT ?!
BUT I HAVEN'T *DONE* ANYTHING YET!
KLATTR
WHAT'S THIS?!

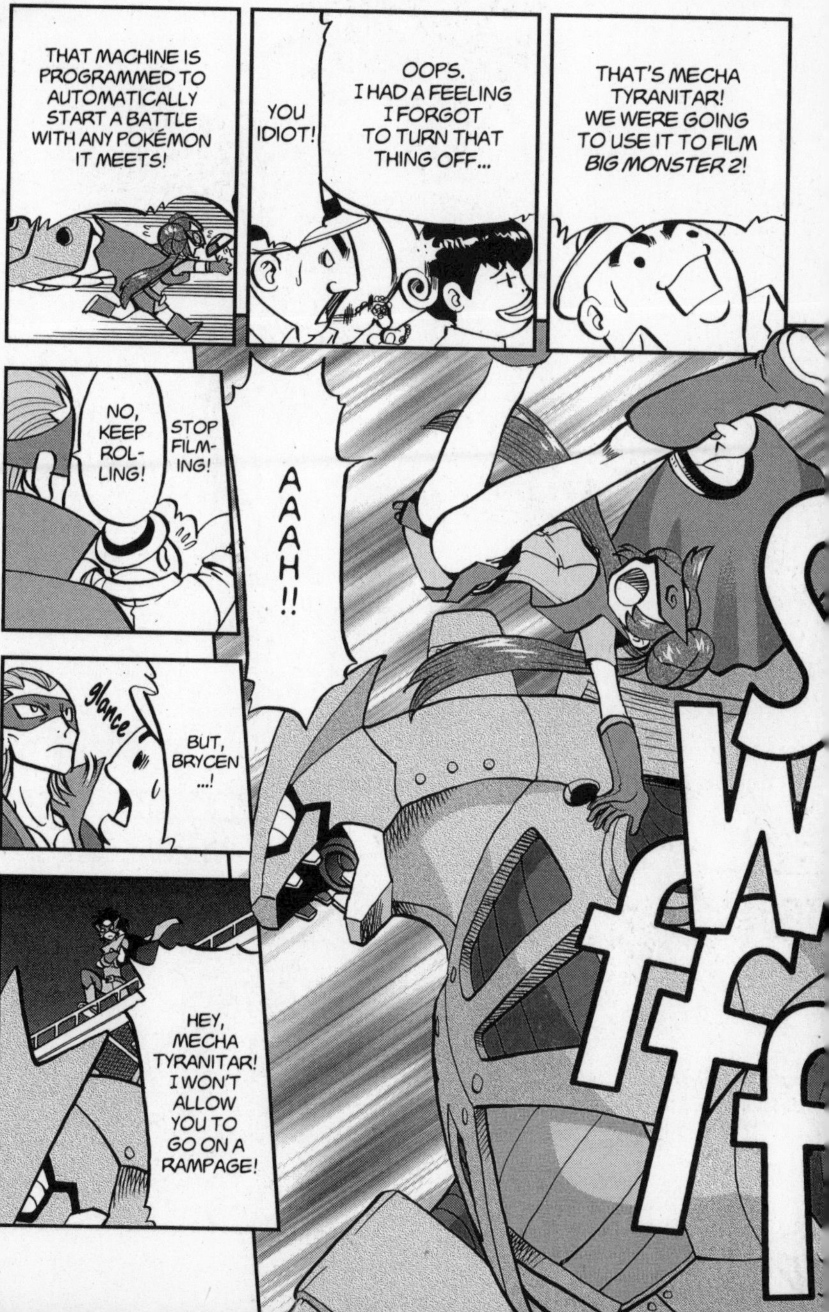
THAT'S MECHA TYRANITAR! WE WERE GOING TO USE IT TO FILM *BIG MONSTER 2*!
OOPS. I HAD A FEELING I FORGOT TO TURN THAT THING OFF...
YOU IDIOT!
THAT MACHINE IS PROGRAMMED TO AUTOMATICALLY START A BATTLE WITH ANY POKÉMON IT MEETS!
AAAAH!!
STOP FILM-ING!
NO, KEEP ROL-LING!
glance
BUT, BRYCEN ...!
HEY, MECHA TYRANITAR! I WON'T ALLOW YOU TO GO ON A RAMPAGE!

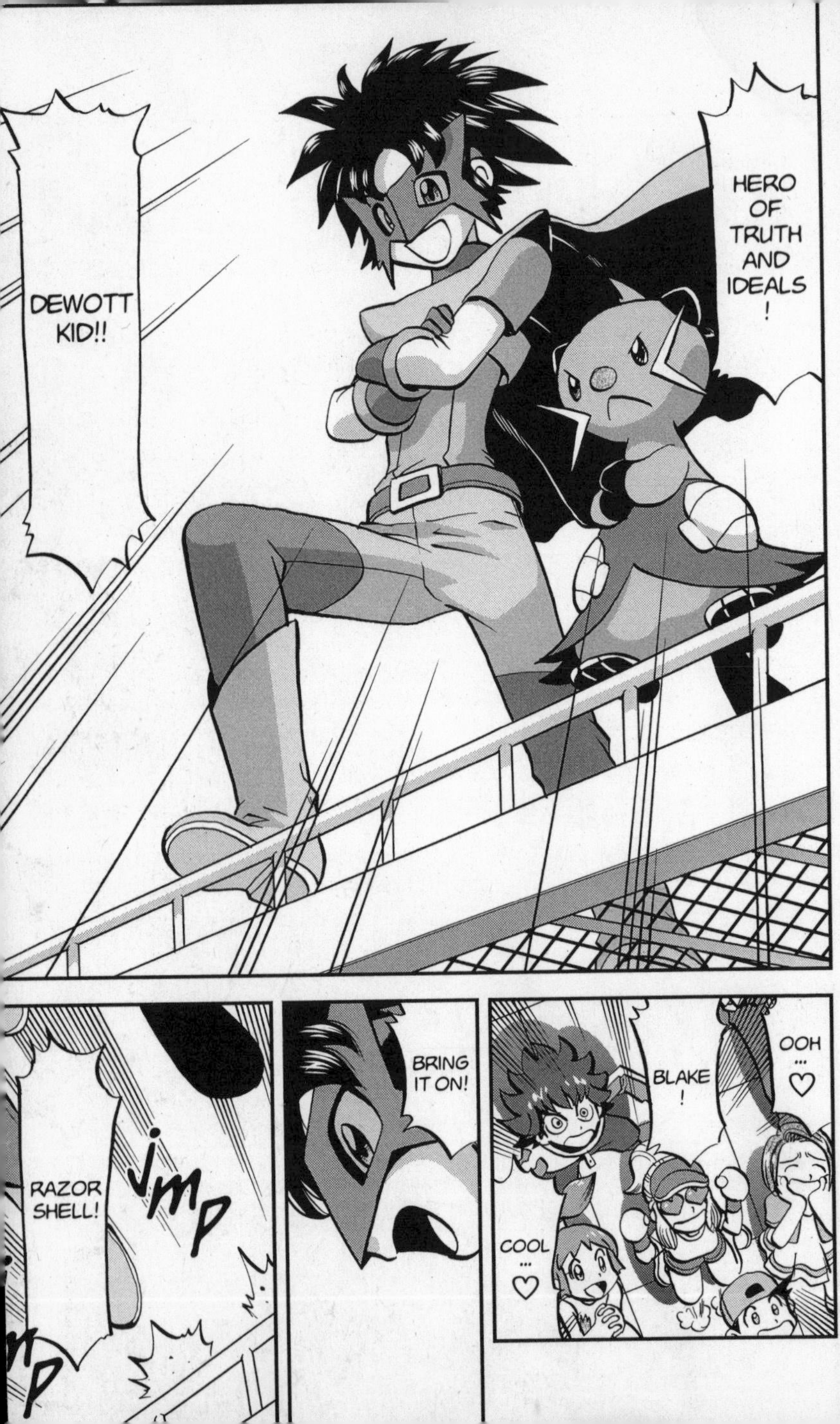
HERO OF TRUTH AND IDEALS!
DEWOTT KID!!
OOH... ♡
BLAKE!
COOL... ♡
BRING IT ON!
RAZOR SHELL!

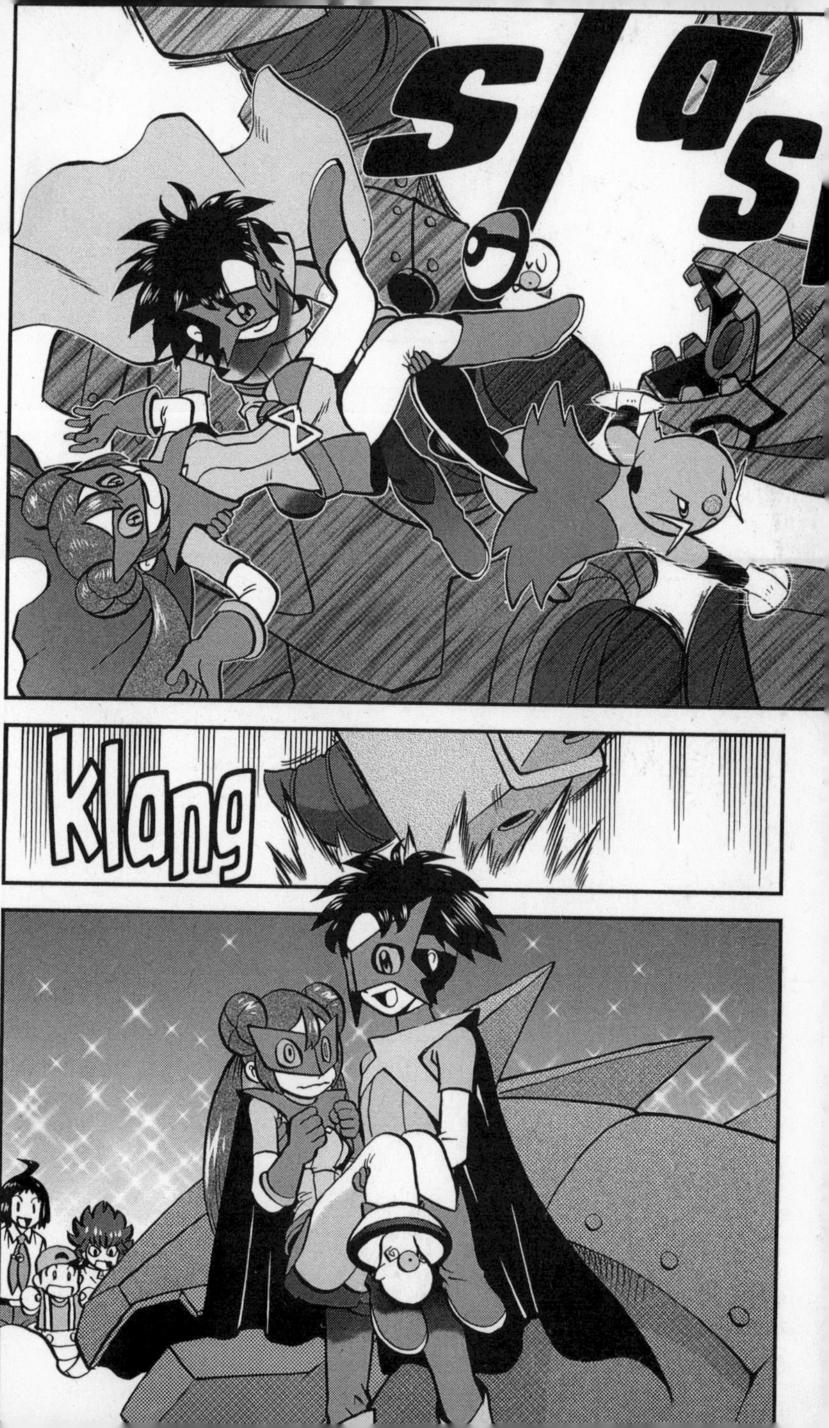

Slas
klang

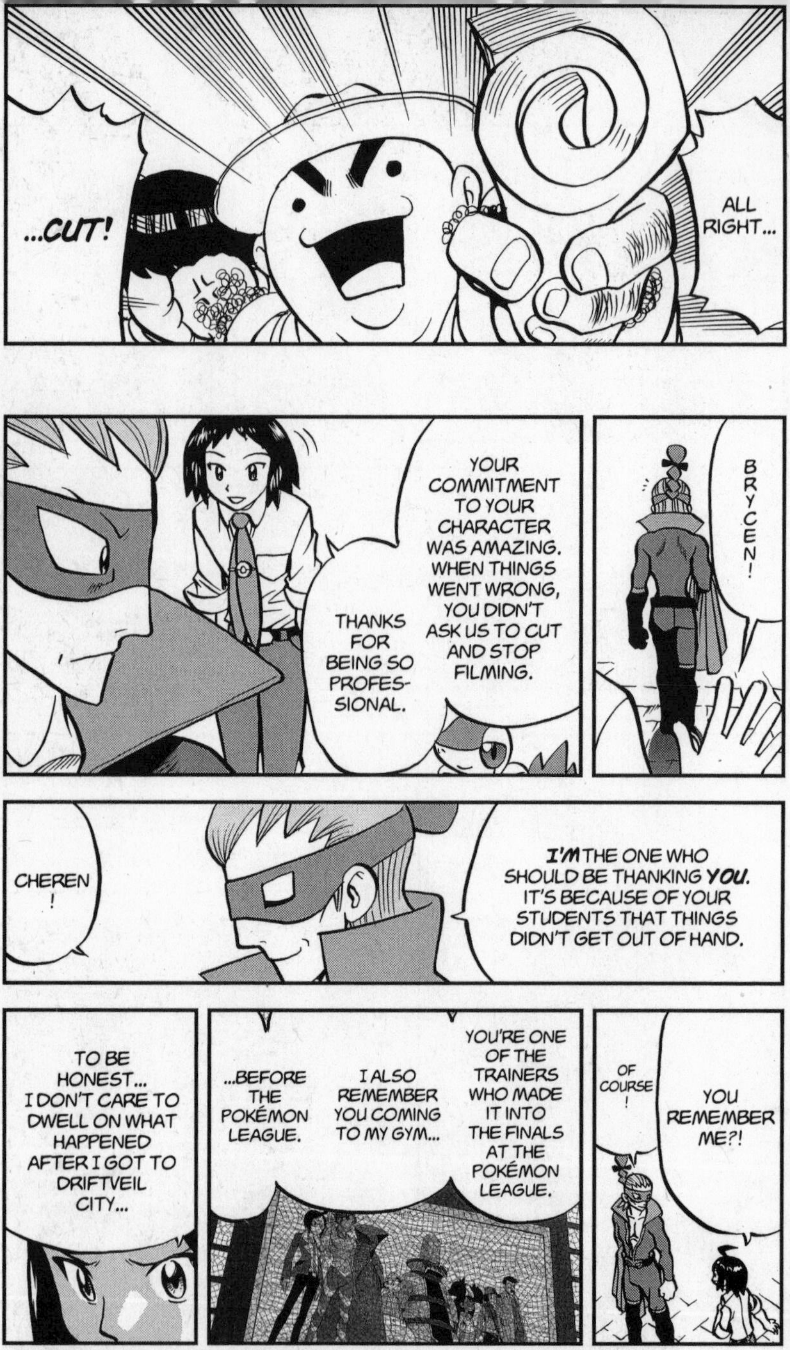

ALL RIGHT...
...CUT!
BRYCEN!
YOUR COMMITMENT TO YOUR CHARACTER WAS AMAZING. WHEN THINGS WENT WRONG, YOU DIDN'T ASK US TO CUT AND STOP FILMING.
THANKS FOR BEING SO PROFES-SIONAL.
I'M THE ONE WHO SHOULD BE THANKING YOU. IT'S BECAUSE OF YOUR STUDENTS THAT THINGS DIDN'T GET OUT OF HAND.
CHEREN!
YOU REMEMBER ME?!
OF COURSE!
YOU'RE ONE OF THE TRAINERS WHO MADE IT INTO THE FINALS AT THE POKÉMON LEAGUE.
I ALSO REMEMBER YOU COMING TO MY GYM...
...BEFORE THE POKÉMON LEAGUE.
TO BE HONEST... I DON'T CARE TO DWELL ON WHAT HAPPENED AFTER I GOT TO DRIFTVEIL CITY...

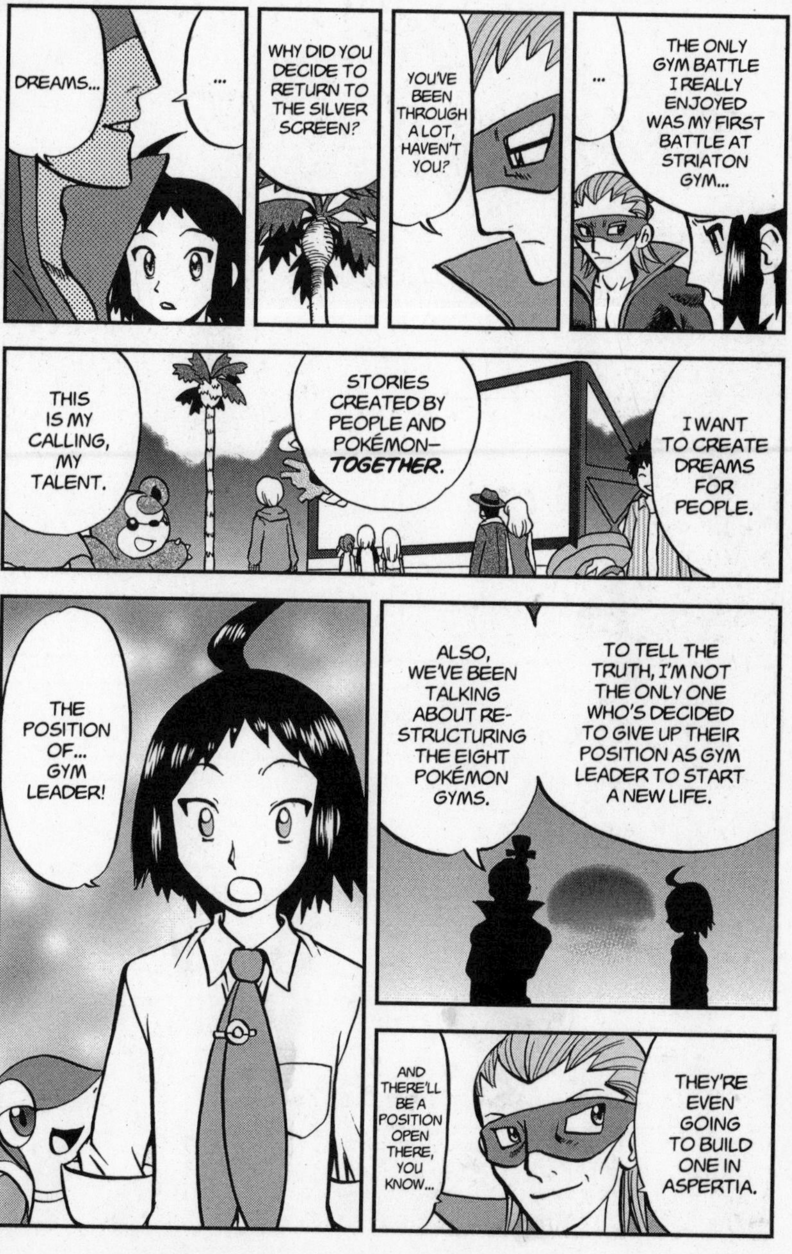
THE ONLY GYM BATTLE I REALLY ENJOYED WAS MY FIRST BATTLE AT STRIATON GYM...
...
YOU'VE BEEN THROUGH A LOT, HAVEN'T YOU?
WHY DID YOU DECIDE TO RETURN TO THE SILVER SCREEN?
...
DREAMS...
I WANT TO CREATE DREAMS FOR PEOPLE.
STORIES CREATED BY PEOPLE AND POKÉMON—*TOGETHER.*
THIS IS MY CALLING, MY TALENT.
TO TELL THE TRUTH, I'M NOT THE ONLY ONE WHO'S DECIDED TO GIVE UP THEIR POSITION AS GYM LEADER TO START A NEW LIFE.
ALSO, WE'VE BEEN TALKING ABOUT RE-STRUCTURING THE EIGHT POKÉMON GYMS.
THEY'RE EVEN GOING TO BUILD ONE IN ASPERTIA.
AND THERE'LL BE A POSITION OPEN THERE, YOU KNOW...
THE POSITION OF... GYM LEADER!

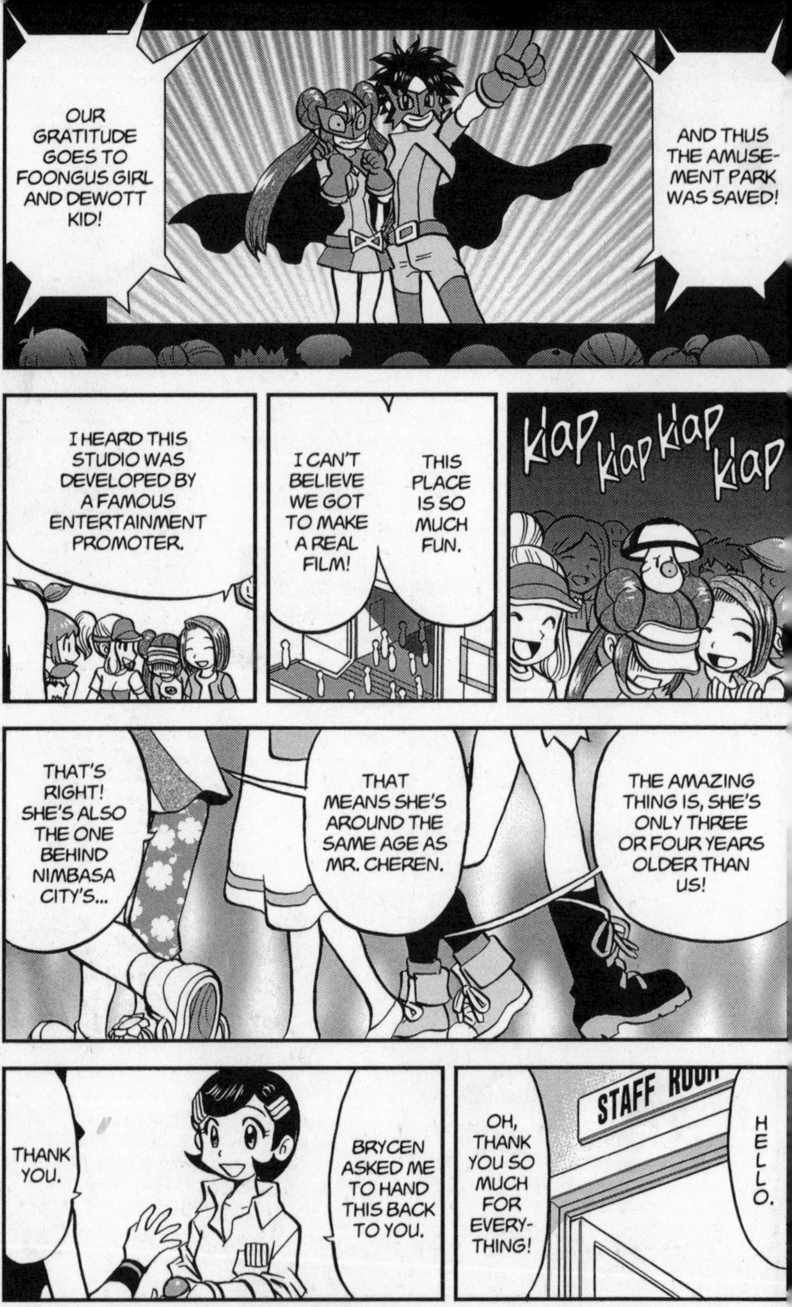
AND THUS THE AMUSEMENT PARK WAS SAVED!
OUR GRATITUDE GOES TO FOONGUS GIRL AND DEWOTT KID!
klap klap klap klap
THIS PLACE IS SO MUCH FUN.
I CAN'T BELIEVE WE GOT TO MAKE A REAL FILM!
I HEARD THIS STUDIO WAS DEVELOPED BY A FAMOUS ENTERTAINMENT PROMOTER.
THE AMAZING THING IS, SHE'S ONLY THREE OR FOUR YEARS OLDER THAN US!
THAT MEANS SHE'S AROUND THE SAME AGE AS MR. CHEREN.
THAT'S RIGHT! SHE'S ALSO THE ONE BEHIND NIMBASA CITY'S...
HELLO.
STAFF
OH, THANK YOU SO MUCH FOR EVERYTHING!
BRYCEN ASKED ME TO HAND THIS BACK TO YOU.
THANK YOU.

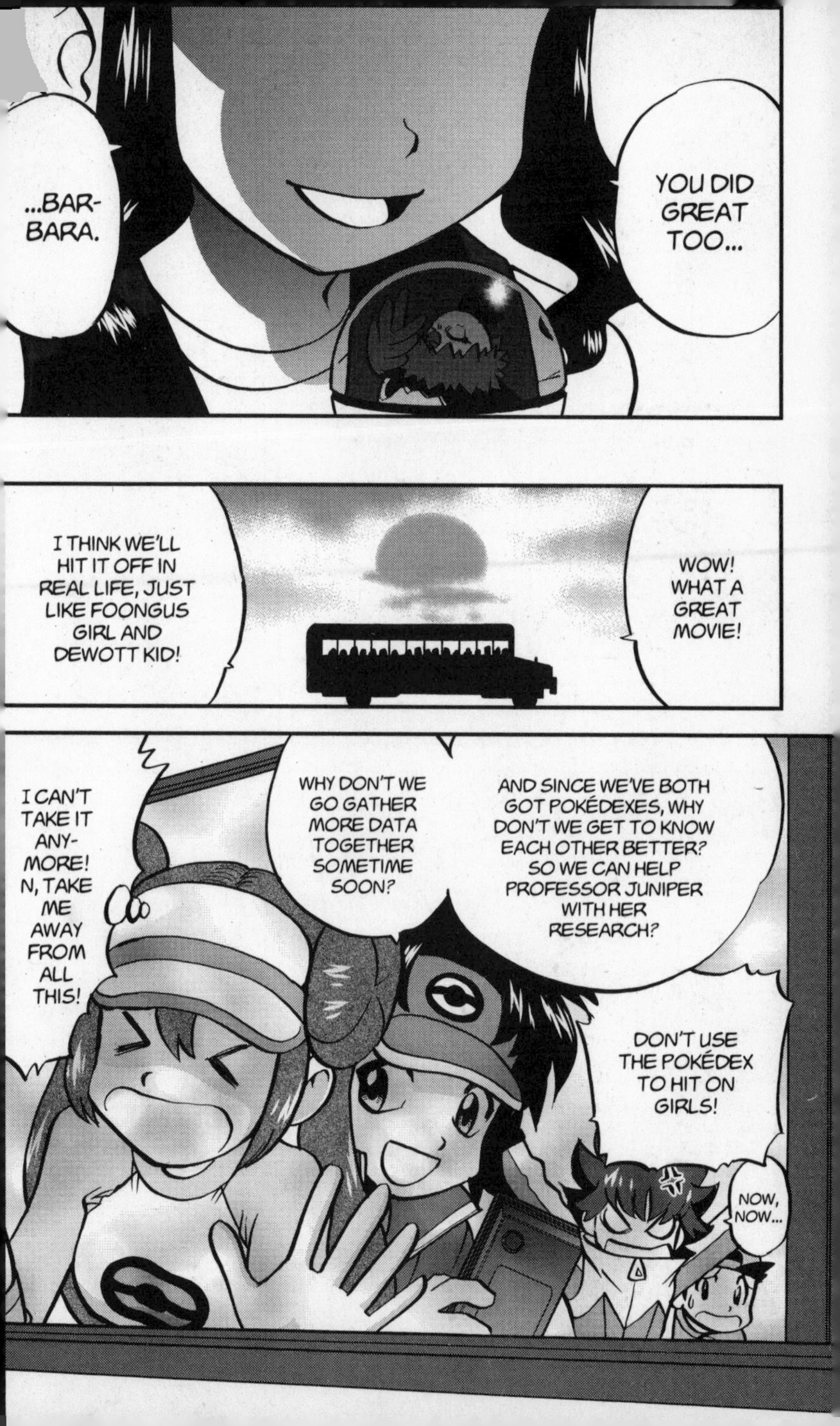
YOU DID GREAT TOO...
...BAR-BARA.
WOW! WHAT A GREAT MOVIE!
I THINK WE'LL HIT IT OFF IN REAL LIFE, JUST LIKE FOONGUS GIRL AND DEWOTT KID!
AND SINCE WE'VE BOTH GOT POKÉDEXES, WHY DON'T WE GET TO KNOW EACH OTHER BETTER? SO WE CAN HELP PROFESSOR JUNIPER WITH HER RESEARCH?
WHY DON'T WE GO GATHER MORE DATA TOGETHER SOMETIME SOON?
I CAN'T TAKE IT ANY-MORE! N, TAKE ME AWAY FROM ALL THIS!
DON'T USE THE POKÉDEX TO HIT ON GIRLS!
NOW, NOW...

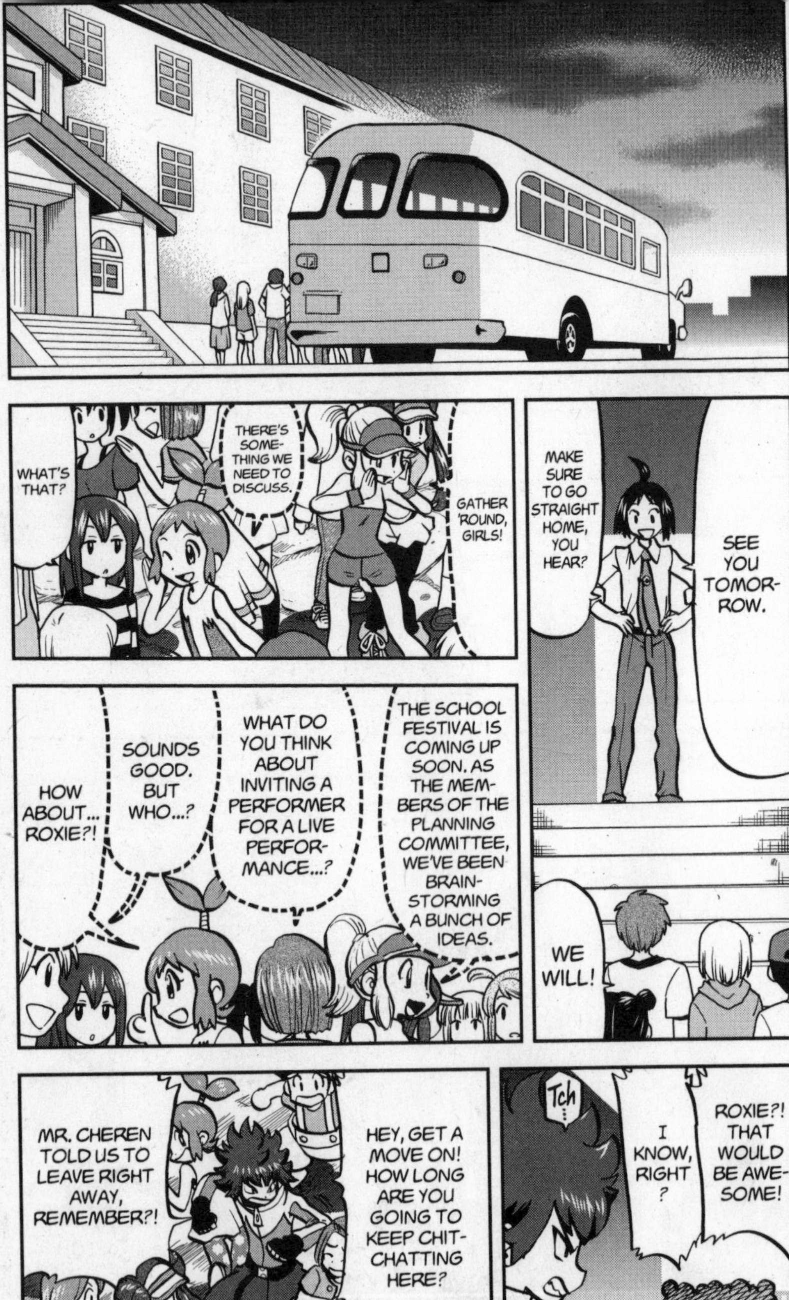
MAKE SURE TO GO STRAIGHT HOME, YOU HEAR?
SEE YOU TOMORROW.
WE WILL!
GATHER 'ROUND, GIRLS!
THERE'S SOMETHING WE NEED TO DISCUSS.
WHAT'S THAT?
THE SCHOOL FESTIVAL IS COMING UP SOON. AS THE MEMBERS OF THE PLANNING COMMITTEE, WE'VE BEEN BRAINSTORMING A BUNCH OF IDEAS.
WHAT DO YOU THINK ABOUT INVITING A PERFORMER FOR A LIVE PERFORMANCE...?
SOUNDS GOOD. BUT WHO...?
HOW ABOUT... ROXIE?!
Tch...
ROXIE?! THAT WOULD BE AWESOME!
I KNOW, RIGHT?
HEY, GET A MOVE ON! HOW LONG ARE YOU GOING TO KEEP CHIT-CHATTING HERE?
MR. CHEREN TOLD US TO LEAVE RIGHT AWAY, REMEMBER?!

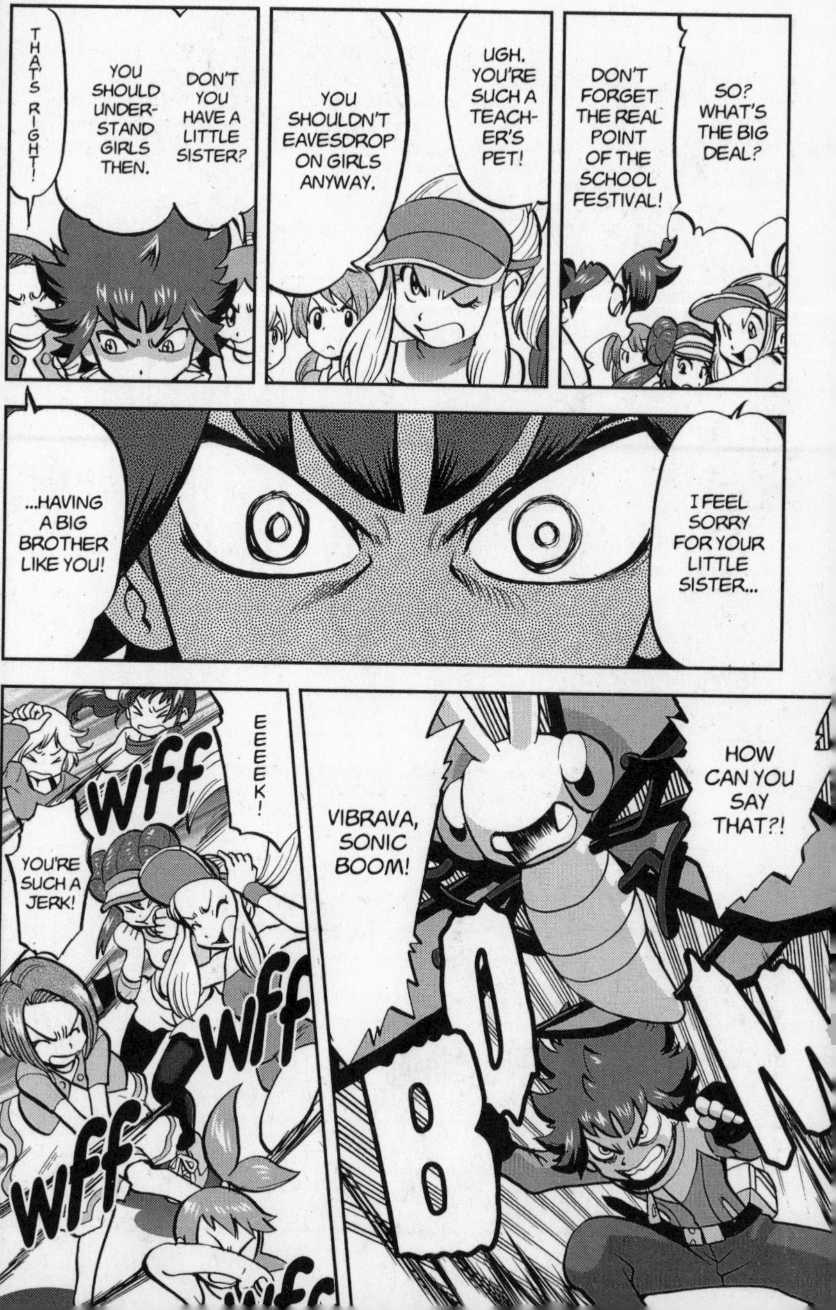
SO? WHAT'S THE BIG DEAL?
DON'T FORGET THE REAL POINT OF THE SCHOOL FESTIVAL!
UGH. YOU'RE SUCH A TEACHER'S PET!
YOU SHOULDN'T EAVESDROP ON GIRLS ANYWAY.
DON'T YOU HAVE A LITTLE SISTER?
YOU SHOULD UNDERSTAND GIRLS THEN.
THAT'S RIGHT!
I FEEL SORRY FOR YOUR LITTLE SISTER...
...HAVING A BIG BROTHER LIKE YOU!
HOW CAN YOU SAY THAT?!
VIBRAVA, SONIC BOOM!
EEEEEK!
WFF
YOU'RE SUCH A JERK!
WFF
WFF

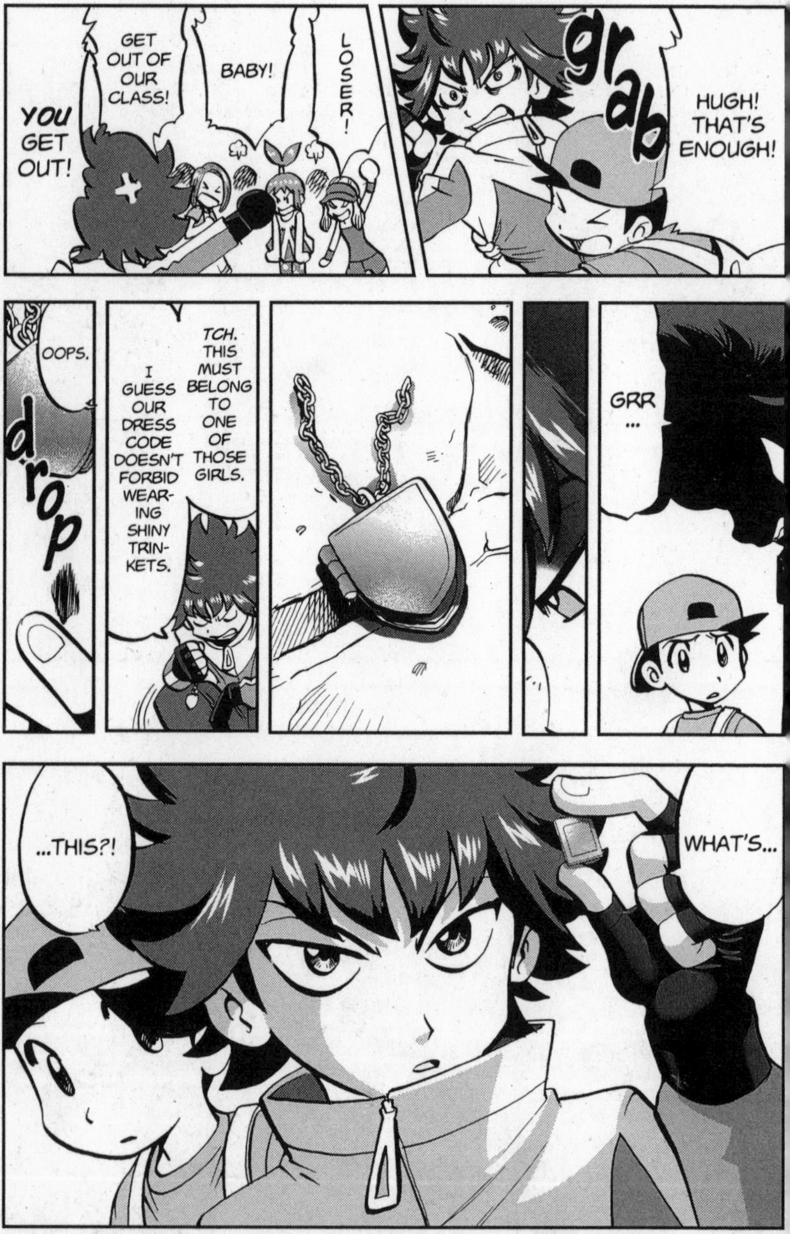
grab
HUGH! THAT'S ENOUGH!
LOSER!
BABY!
GET OUT OF OUR CLASS!
YOU GET OUT!
GRR...
TCH. THIS MUST BELONG TO ONE OF THOSE GIRLS.
I GUESS OUR DRESS CODE DOESN'T FORBID WEAR-ING SHINY TRIN-KETS.
OOPS.
drop
WHAT'S...
...THIS?!

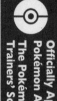

Officially Approved by the Pokémon Association
The Pokémon Trainers' School

Trainers' School Prospectus

The Trainers' School takes pride in their time-honored traditions but has a reputation for innovation as well. One new challenge we have taken on is the establishment of a Pokémon Gym inside the school. One of our instructors will become the Gym Leader and test students' progress through Gym Battles. We are currently working hard on this ambitious project and hope to launch it next year.

After Graduation?

Our graduates have had success in various fields as skilled Pokémon Trainers. Last year, seven graduates entered the PTS. Watching students' progress after graduation is one of the joys of being a teacher here.

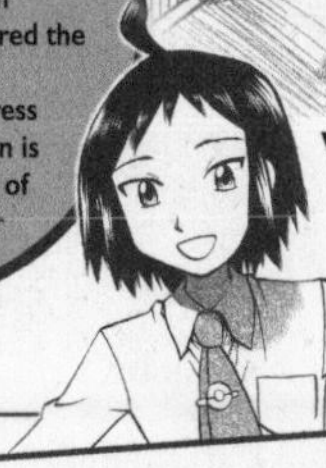

New Teacher:
Mr. Cheren

School Song

Lyrics: **Bon Sazanami**
Music: **Yamaji M. Holden**

[Verse 1]
The hand that holds the Poké Ball...
Shows the strength of our determination!
We shout it to the mountain tops!
We shout it to the skies above Aspertia
and our nation!
We will grow stronger without hesitation...
With our Pokémo-o-o-on...
Our glorious days of trai-ai-aining
at our beloved...
Trainers' School!
Trainers' School!
Trainers' School!
Hail, our alma mater!

[Verse 2]
Freeze, Paralysis, Burn, Confusion,
Poison, Infatuation, Sleep!
Although we can barely move...
We'll take our next step even if
we have to creep!
As the winds of Aspertia City blow...
With our Pokémo-o-o-on...
Our Training skills and strength will grow!
Trainers' School!
School!

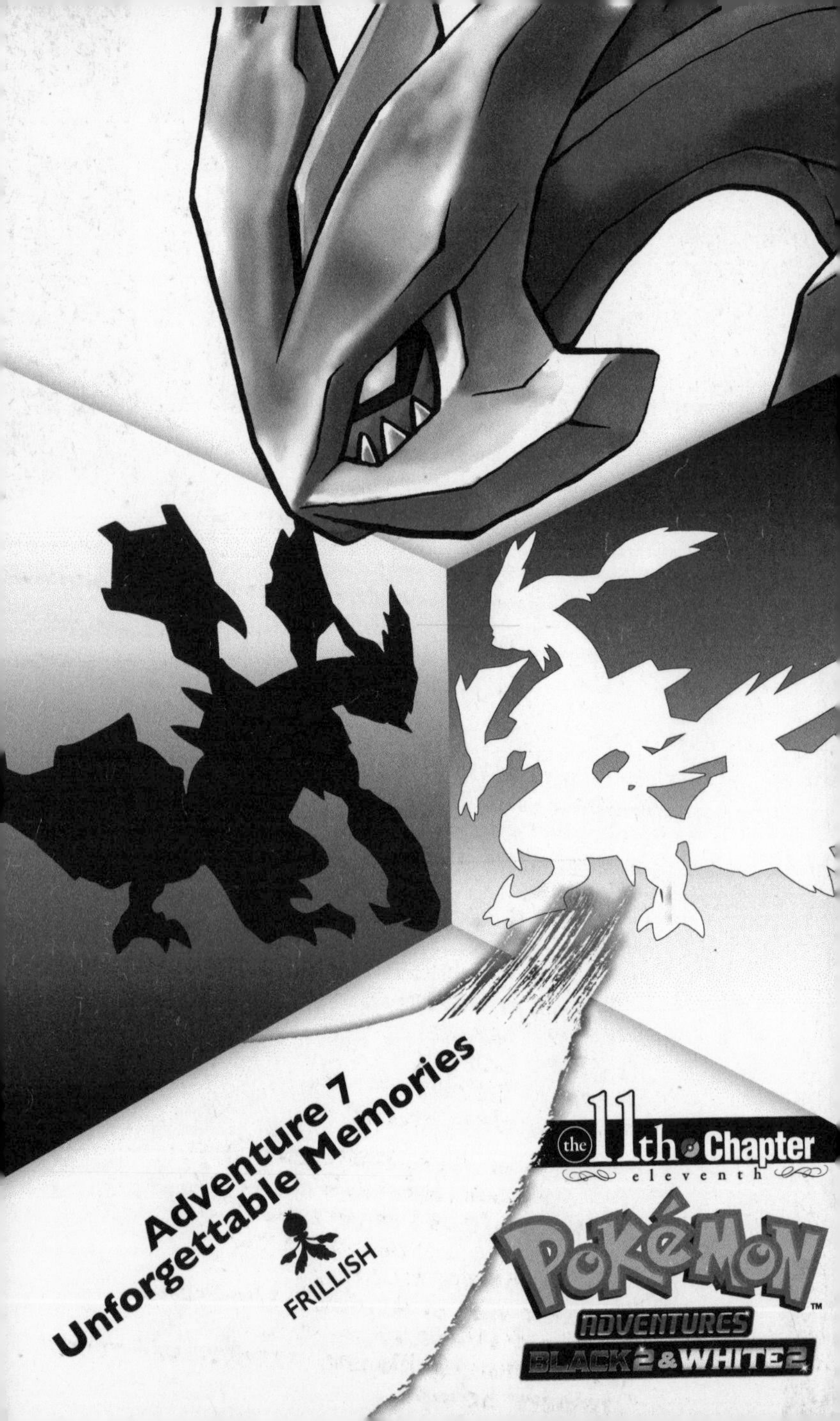
Adventure 7
Unforgettable Memories
FRILLISH
the 11th Chapter
eleventh
POKÉMON
ADVENTURES
BLACK 2 & WHITE 2

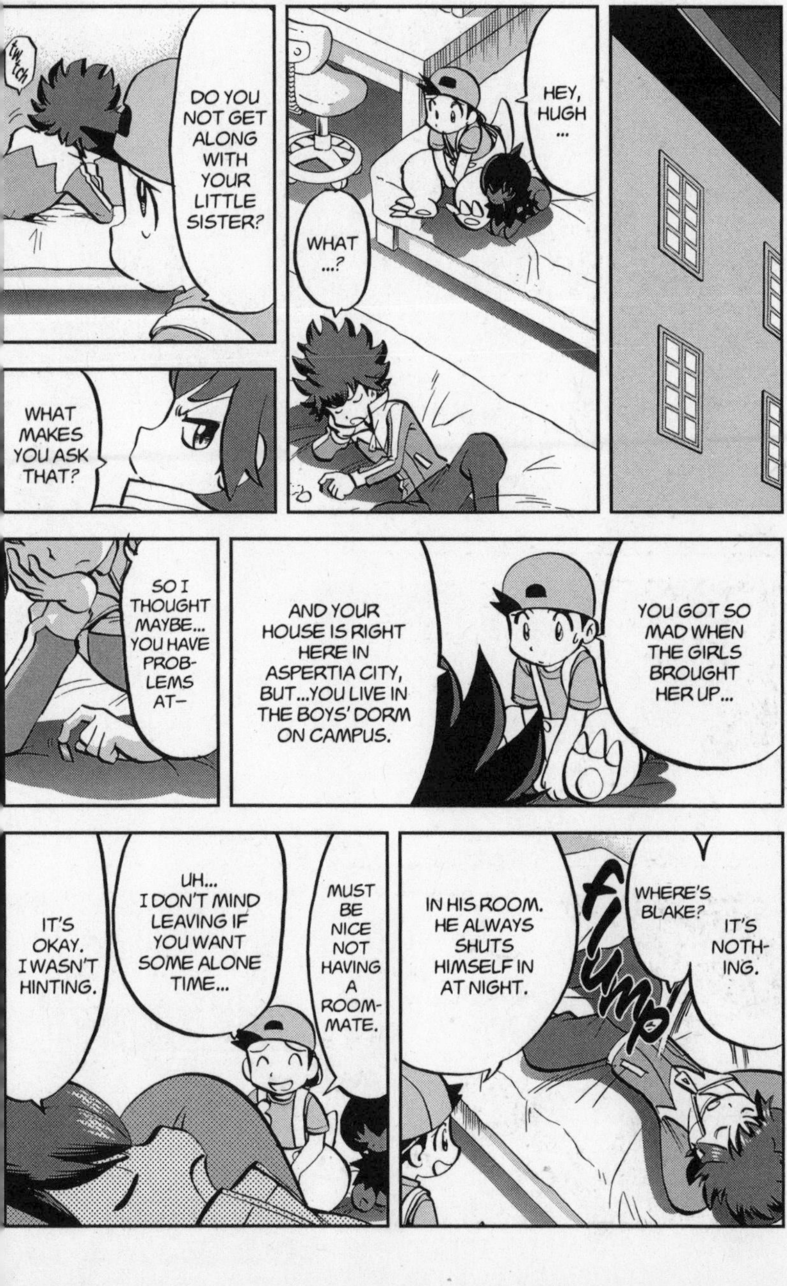
HEY, HUGH ...
WHAT ...?
twitch
DO YOU NOT GET ALONG WITH YOUR LITTLE SISTER?
WHAT MAKES YOU ASK THAT?
YOU GOT SO MAD WHEN THE GIRLS BROUGHT HER UP...
AND YOUR HOUSE IS RIGHT HERE IN ASPERTIA CITY, BUT...YOU LIVE IN THE BOYS' DORM ON CAMPUS.
SO I THOUGHT MAYBE... YOU HAVE PROB- LEMS AT–
IT'S NOTH- ING.
flump!
WHERE'S BLAKE?
IN HIS ROOM. HE ALWAYS SHUTS HIMSELF IN AT NIGHT.
MUST BE NICE NOT HAVING A ROOM- MATE.
UH... I DON'T MIND LEAVING IF YOU WANT SOME ALONE TIME...
IT'S OKAY. I WASN'T HINTING.

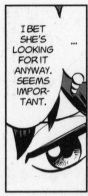

I BET SHE'S LOOKING FOR IT ANYWAY. SEEMS IMPORTANT.

...

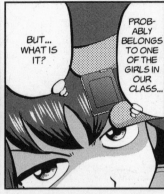

BUT... WHAT IS IT?

PROBABLY BELONGS TO ONE OF THE GIRLS IN OUR CLASS...

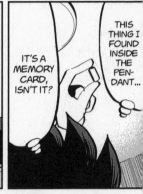

IT'S A MEMORY CARD, ISN'T IT?

THIS THING I FOUND INSIDE THE PENDANT...

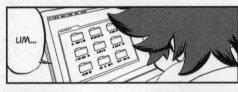

UM...

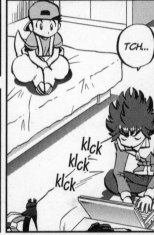

TCH...

klck
klck
klck

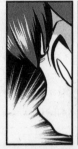

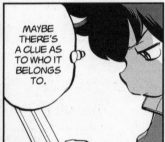

MAYBE THERE'S A CLUE AS TO WHO IT BELONGS TO.

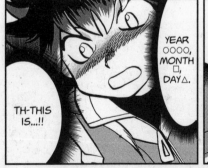

YEAR ○○○○, MONTH □, DAY △.

WHAT'S THIS...?!

TH-THIS IS...!!

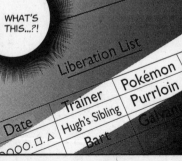

Liberation List

Date	Trainer	Pokémon
		Purrloin
○○○.□.△	Hugh's Sibling	
	Bart	Galvan

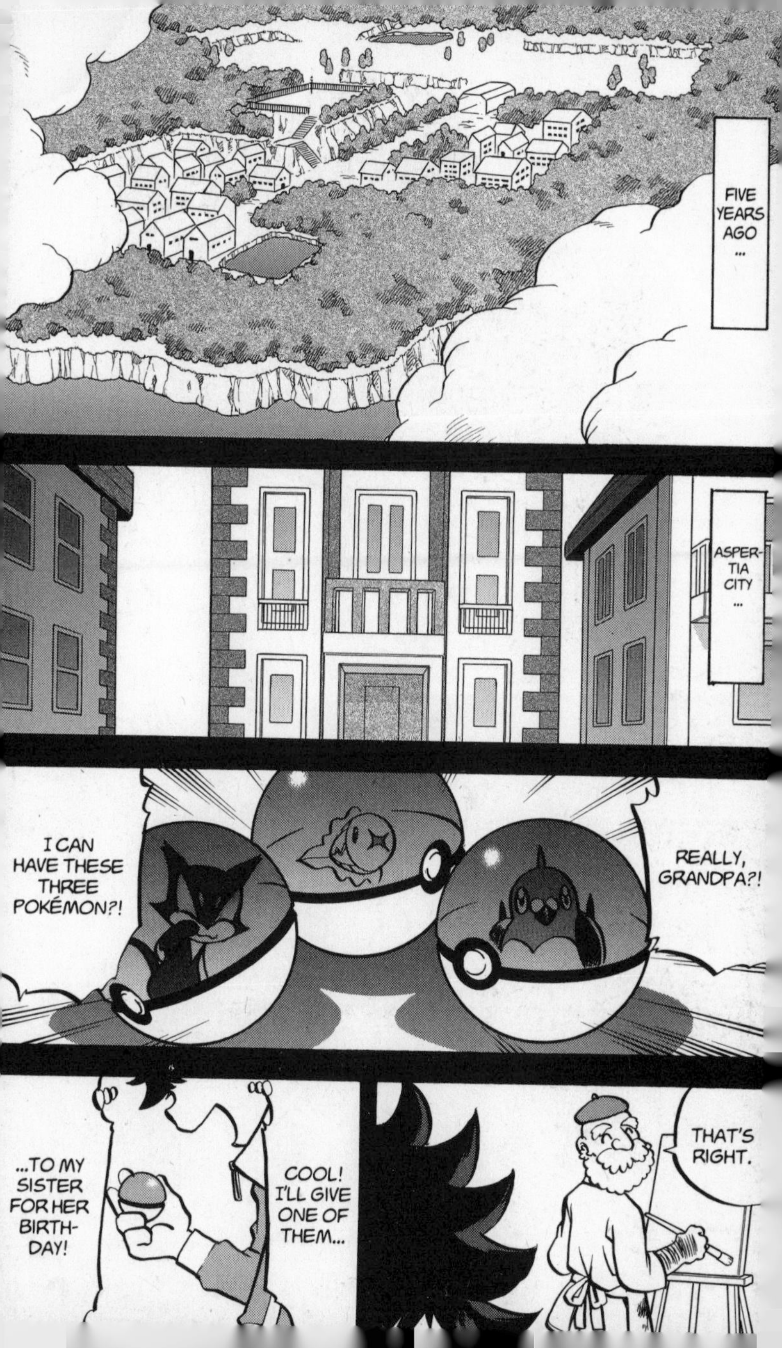
FIVE YEARS AGO ...
ASPER-TIA CITY ...
REALLY, GRANDPA?!
I CAN HAVE THESE THREE POKÉMON?!
THAT'S RIGHT.
COOL! I'LL GIVE ONE OF THEM...
...TO MY SISTER FOR HER BIRTH-DAY!

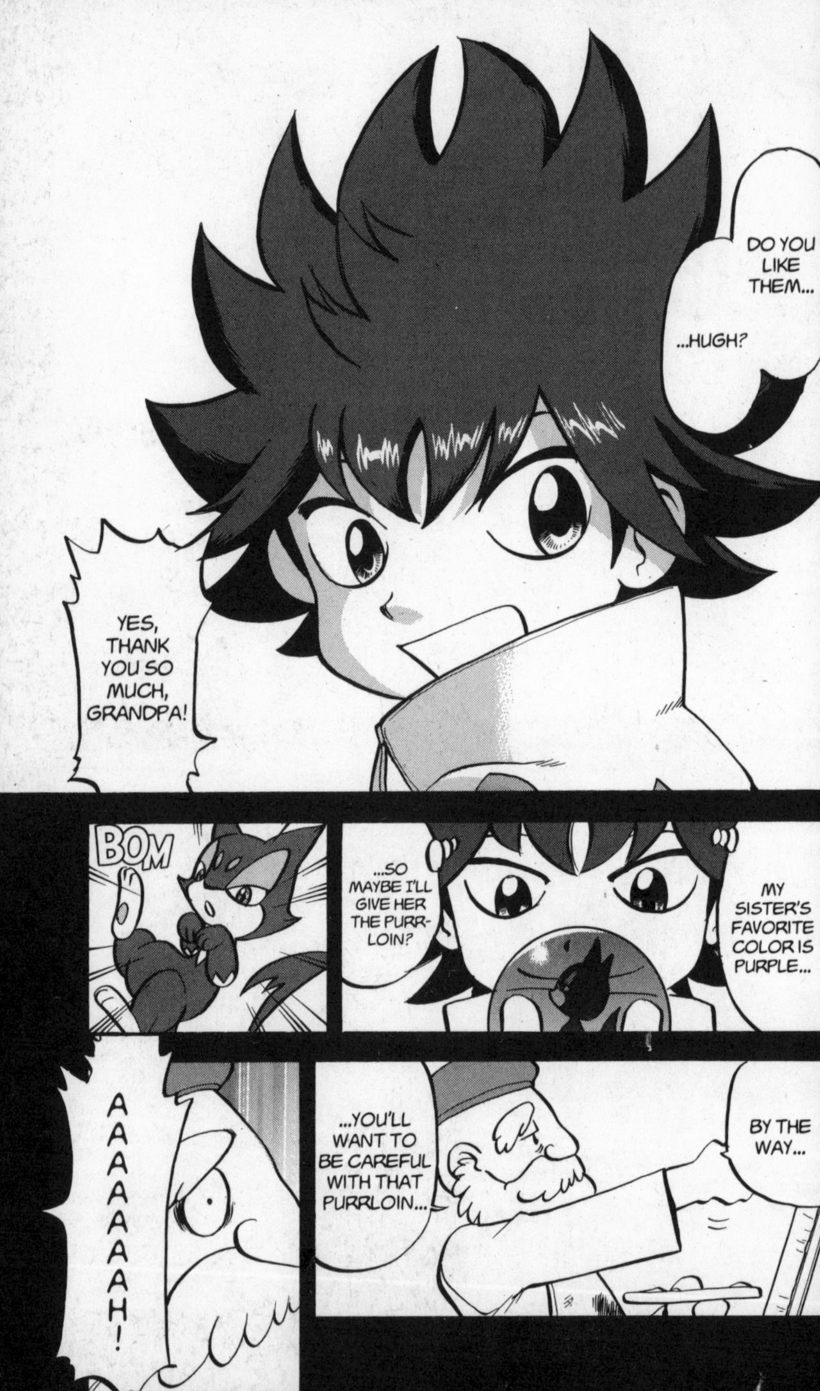
DO YOU LIKE THEM...
...HUGH?
YES, THANK YOU SO MUCH, GRANDPA!
MY SISTER'S FAVORITE COLOR IS PURPLE...
...SO MAYBE I'LL GIVE HER THE PURR-LOIN?
BOM
BY THE WAY...
...YOU'LL WANT TO BE CAREFUL WITH THAT PURRLOIN...
AAAAAAAAAH!

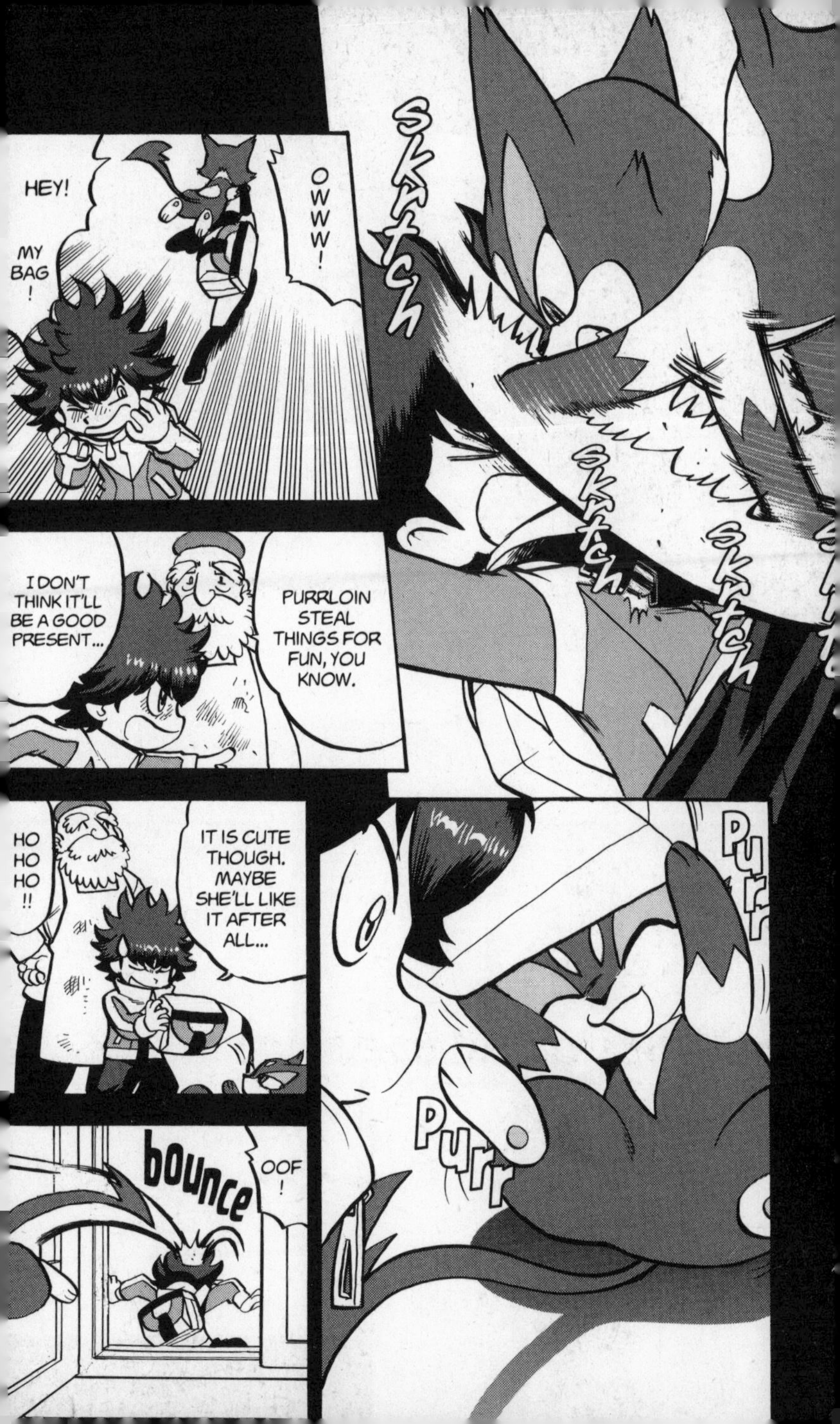
Skrtch
Skrtch
Skrtch
Skrtch
OWWW!
HEY!
MY BAG!
PURRLOIN STEAL THINGS FOR FUN, YOU KNOW.
I DON'T THINK IT'LL BE A GOOD PRESENT...
Purr
Purr
IT IS CUTE THOUGH. MAYBE SHE'LL LIKE IT AFTER ALL...
HO HO HO!!
OOF!
bounce

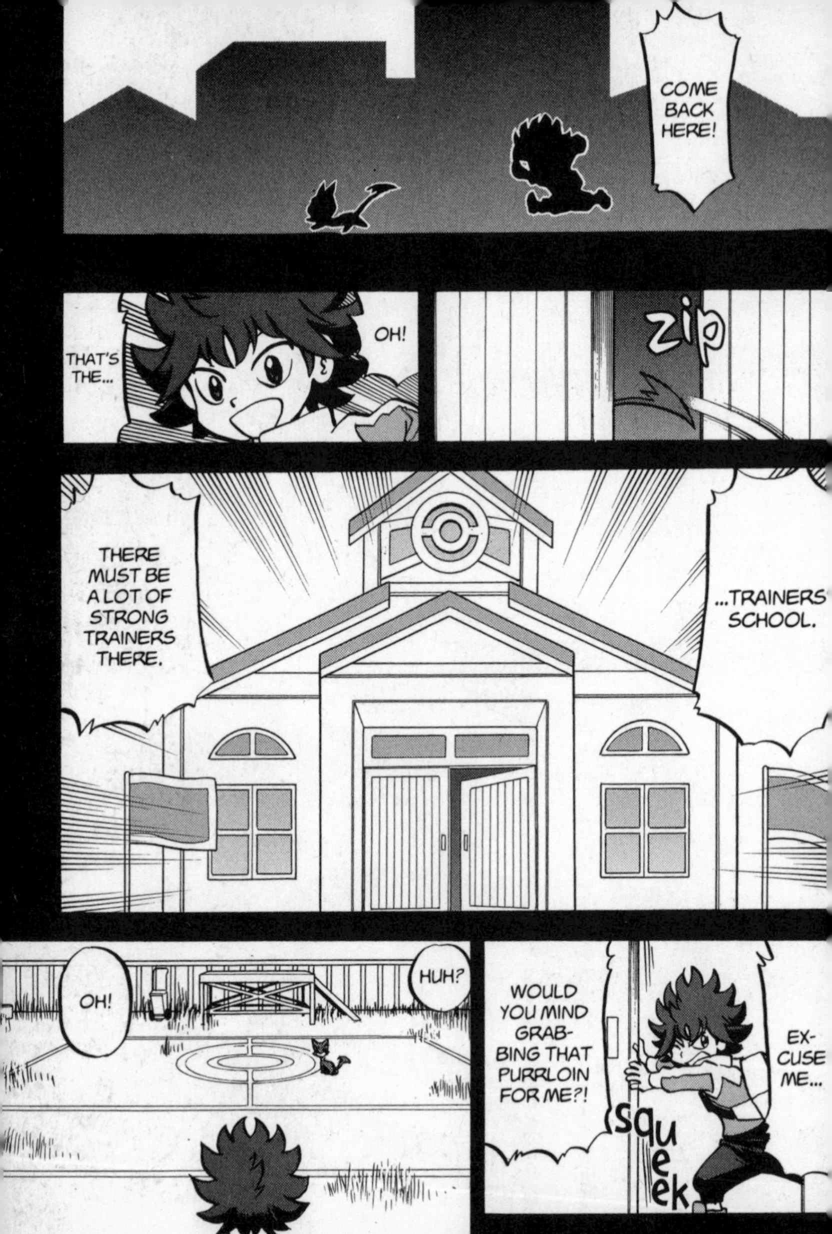
COME BACK HERE!
zip
OH!
THAT'S THE...
...TRAINERS SCHOOL.
THERE MUST BE A LOT OF STRONG TRAINERS THERE.
EX-CUSE ME...
WOULD YOU MIND GRAB-BING THAT PURRLOIN FOR ME?!
squeek
HUH?
OH!

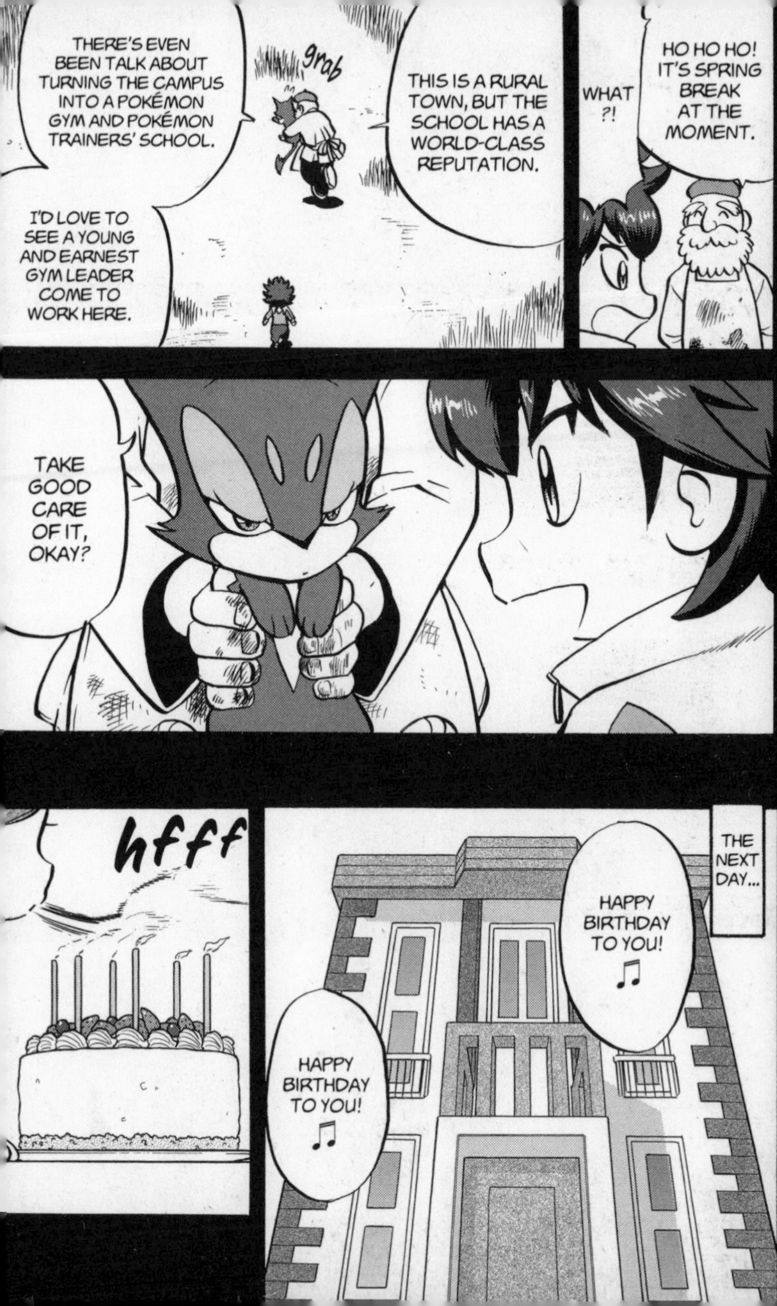
HO HO HO! IT'S SPRING BREAK AT THE MOMENT.
WHAT ?!
THIS IS A RURAL TOWN, BUT THE SCHOOL HAS A WORLD-CLASS REPUTATION.
grab
THERE'S EVEN BEEN TALK ABOUT TURNING THE CAMPUS INTO A POKÉMON GYM AND POKÉMON TRAINERS' SCHOOL.
I'D LOVE TO SEE A YOUNG AND EARNEST GYM LEADER COME TO WORK HERE.
TAKE GOOD CARE OF IT, OKAY?
THE NEXT DAY...
HAPPY BIRTHDAY TO YOU! ♫
HAPPY BIRTHDAY TO YOU! ♫
hfff

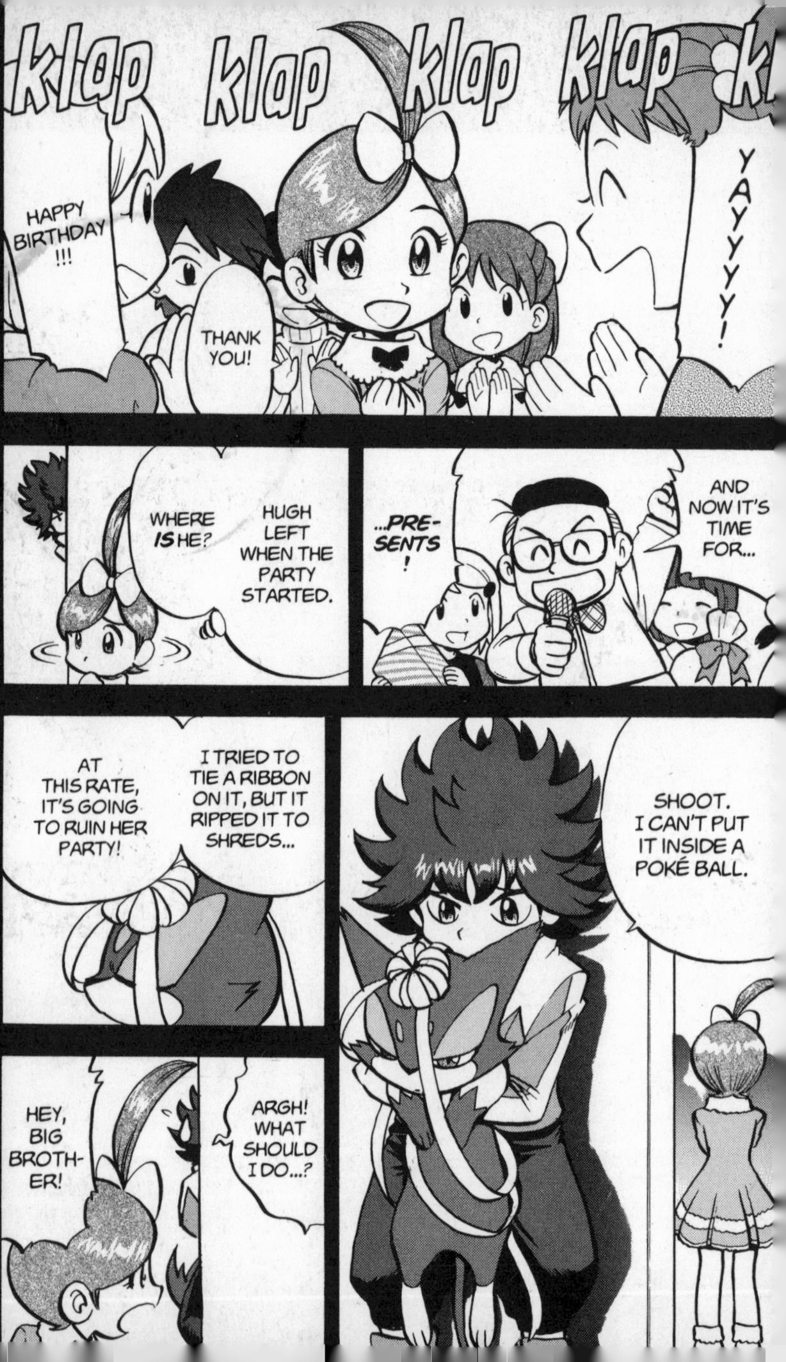
klap klap klap klap kl
YAYYYYY!
HAPPY BIRTHDAY!!!
THANK YOU!
AND NOW IT'S TIME FOR...
...PRESENTS!
HUGH LEFT WHEN THE PARTY STARTED.
WHERE IS HE?
SHOOT. I CAN'T PUT IT INSIDE A POKÉ BALL.
I TRIED TO TIE A RIBBON ON IT, BUT IT RIPPED IT TO SHREDS...
AT THIS RATE, IT'S GOING TO RUIN HER PARTY!
ARGH! WHAT SHOULD I DO...?
HEY, BIG BROTHER!

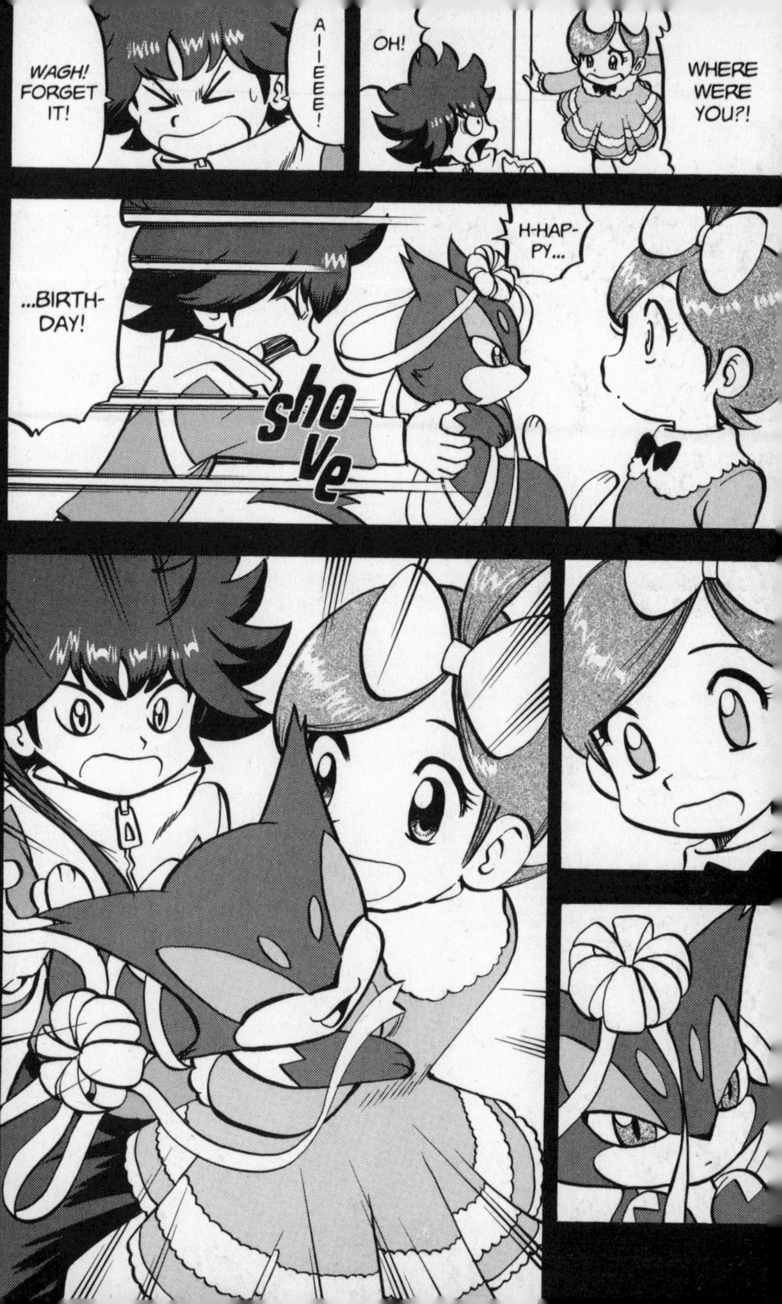
WHERE WERE YOU?!
OH!
AIIEEE!
WAGH! FORGET IT!
H-HAPPY...
...BIRTHDAY!
shove

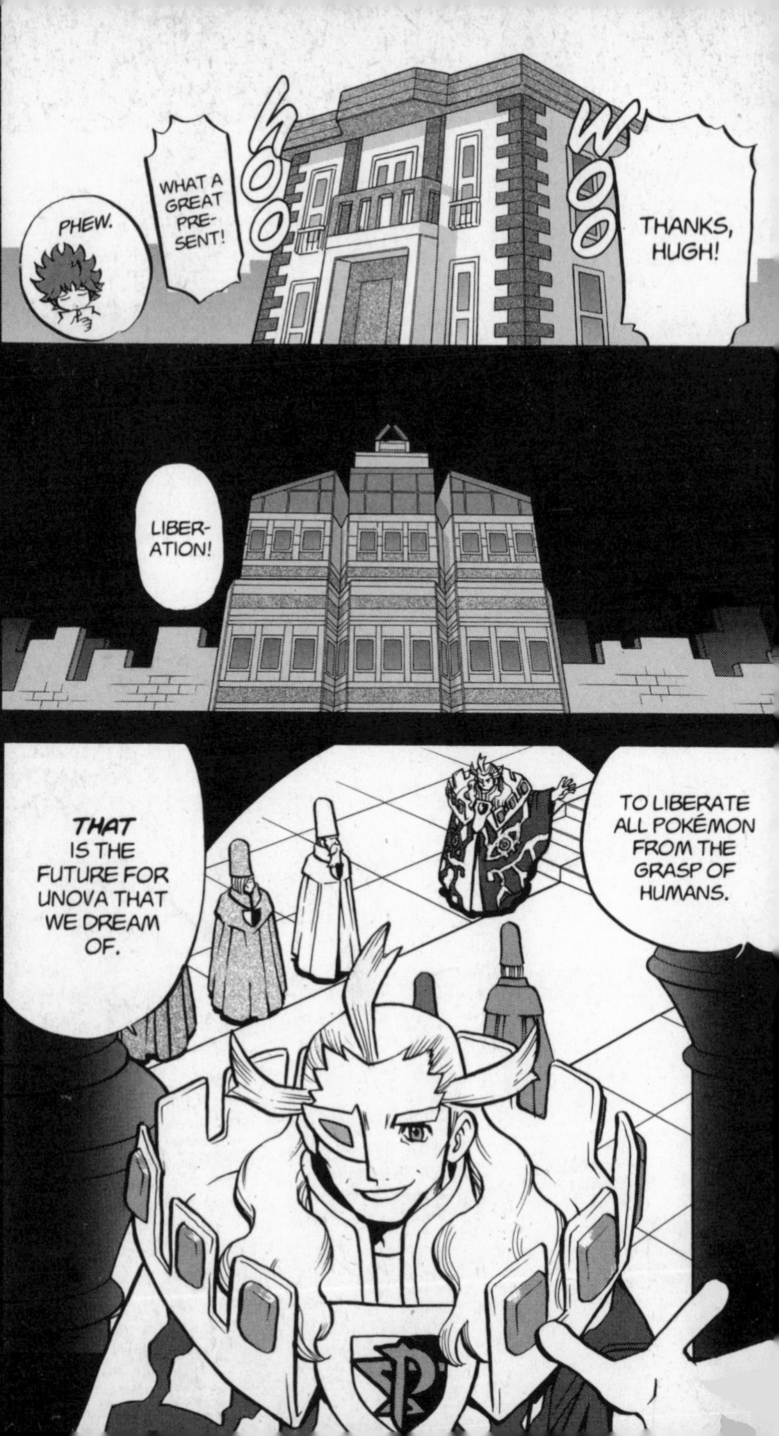

THANKS, HUGH!
WOO
WHAT A GREAT PRESENT!
WOO
PHEW.
LIBERATION!
TO LIBERATE ALL POKÉMON FROM THE GRASP OF HUMANS.
THAT IS THE FUTURE FOR UNOVA THAT WE DREAM OF.

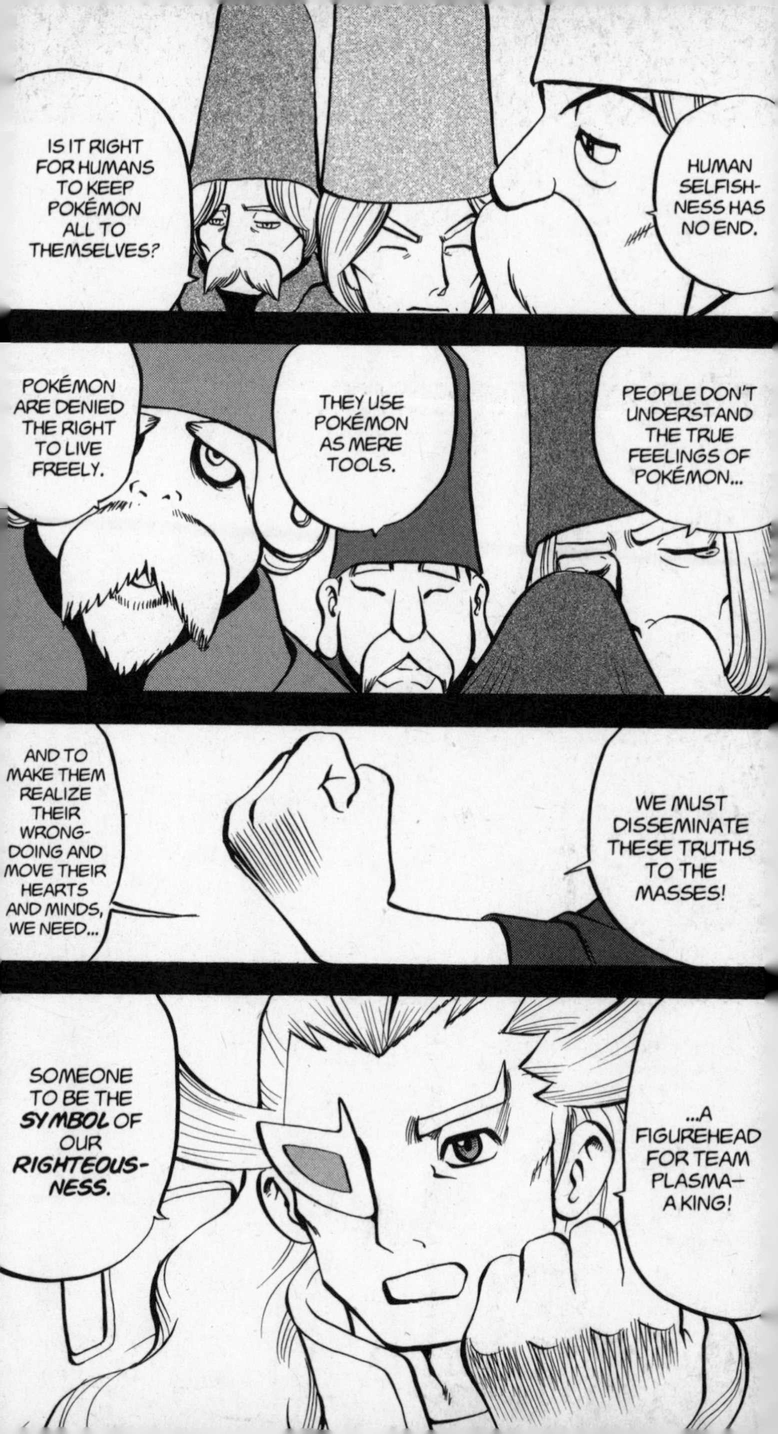
HUMAN SELFISH-NESS HAS NO END.
IS IT RIGHT FOR HUMANS TO KEEP POKÉMON ALL TO THEMSELVES?
PEOPLE DON'T UNDERSTAND THE TRUE FEELINGS OF POKÉMON...
THEY USE POKÉMON AS MERE TOOLS.
POKÉMON ARE DENIED THE RIGHT TO LIVE FREELY.
WE MUST DISSEMINATE THESE TRUTHS TO THE MASSES!
AND TO MAKE THEM REALIZE THEIR WRONG-DOING AND MOVE THEIR HEARTS AND MINDS, WE NEED...
SOMEONE TO BE THE ***SYMBOL*** OF OUR ***RIGHTEOUS-NESS.***
...A FIGUREHEAD FOR TEAM PLASMA— A KING!

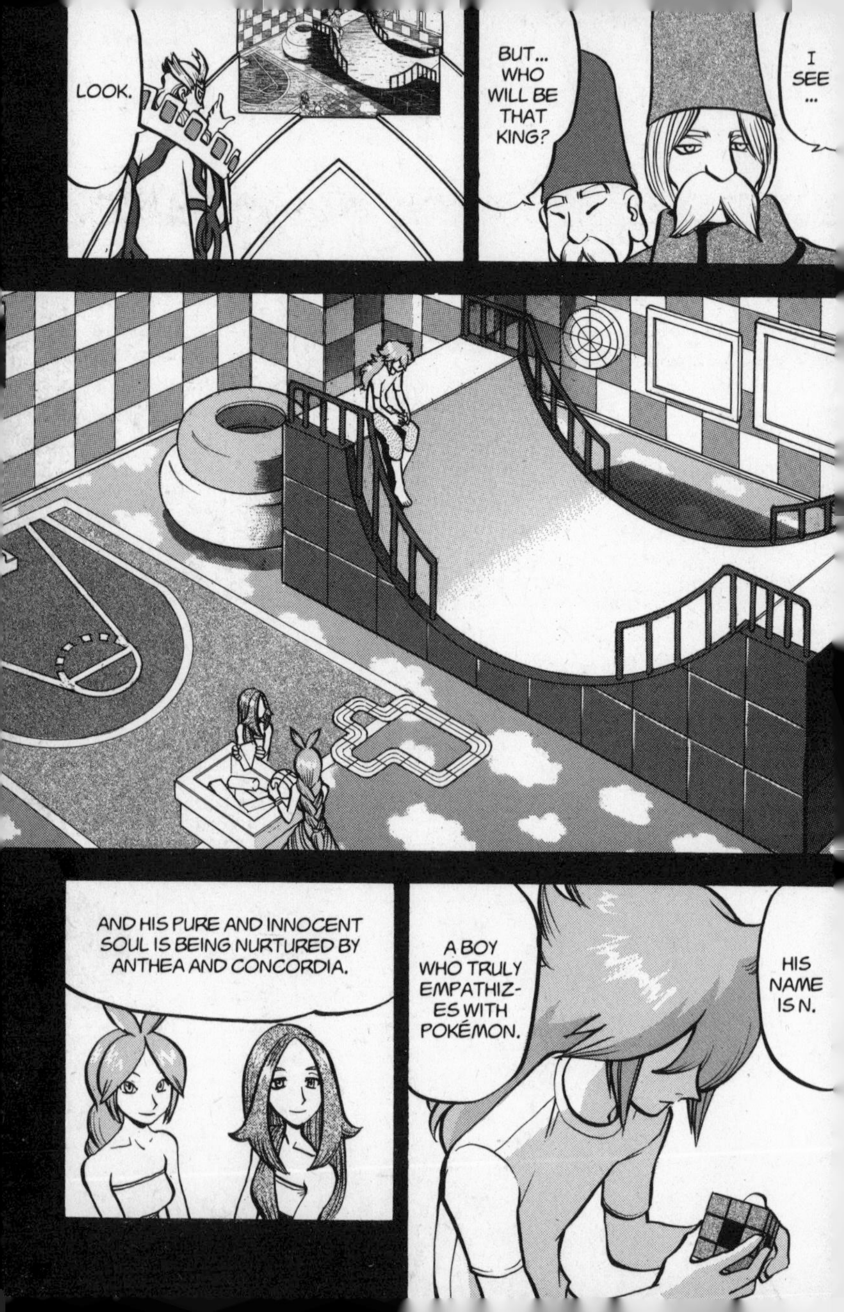
I SEE ...
BUT... WHO WILL BE THAT KING?
LOOK.
HIS NAME IS N.
A BOY WHO TRULY EMPATHIZES WITH POKÉMON.
AND HIS PURE AND INNOCENT SOUL IS BEING NURTURED BY ANTHEA AND CONCORDIA.

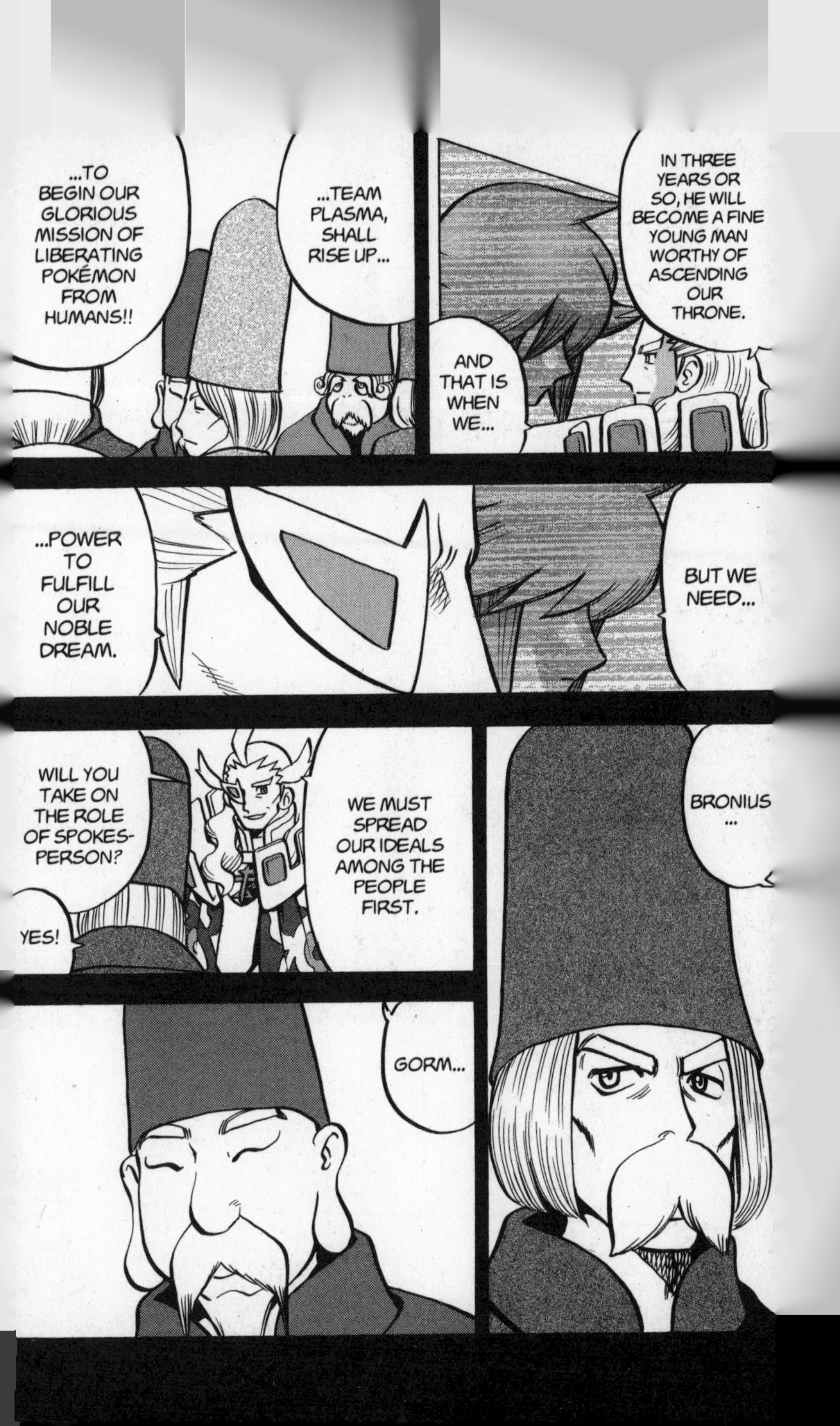
IN THREE YEARS OR SO, HE WILL BECOME A FINE YOUNG MAN WORTHY OF ASCENDING OUR THRONE.
AND THAT IS WHEN WE...
...TEAM PLASMA, SHALL RISE UP...
...TO BEGIN OUR GLORIOUS MISSION OF LIBERATING POKÉMON FROM HUMANS!!
BUT WE NEED...
...POWER TO FULFILL OUR NOBLE DREAM.
BRONIUS ...
WE MUST SPREAD OUR IDEALS AMONG THE PEOPLE FIRST.
WILL YOU TAKE ON THE ROLE OF SPOKES-PERSON?
YES!
GORM...

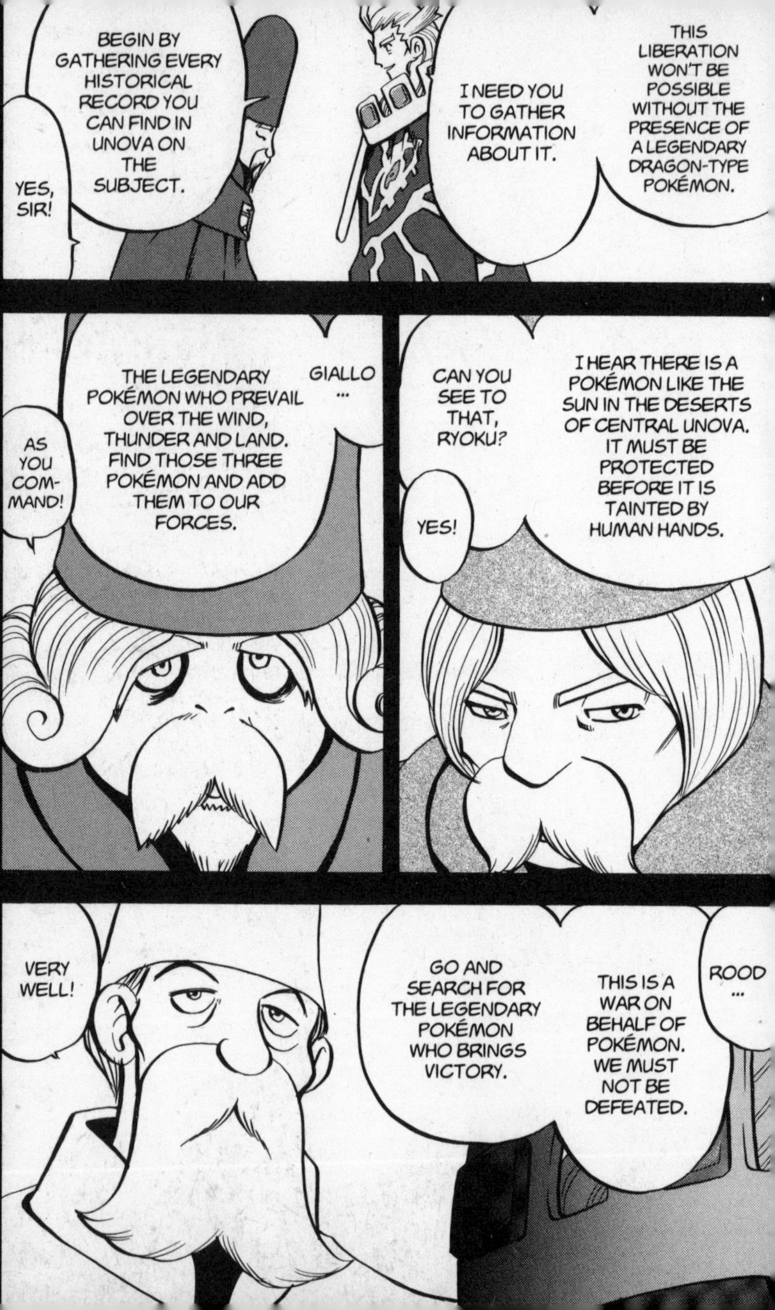
THIS LIBERATION WON'T BE POSSIBLE WITHOUT THE PRESENCE OF A LEGENDARY DRAGON-TYPE POKÉMON.
I NEED YOU TO GATHER INFORMATION ABOUT IT.
BEGIN BY GATHERING EVERY HISTORICAL RECORD YOU CAN FIND IN UNOVA ON THE SUBJECT.
YES, SIR!
I HEAR THERE IS A POKÉMON LIKE THE SUN IN THE DESERTS OF CENTRAL UNOVA. IT MUST BE PROTECTED BEFORE IT IS TAINTED BY HUMAN HANDS.
CAN YOU SEE TO THAT, RYOKU?
YES!
GIALLO ...
THE LEGENDARY POKÉMON WHO PREVAIL OVER THE WIND, THUNDER AND LAND. FIND THOSE THREE POKÉMON AND ADD THEM TO OUR FORCES.
AS YOU COM-MAND!
ROOD ...
THIS IS A WAR ON BEHALF OF POKÉMON. WE MUST NOT BE DEFEATED.
GO AND SEARCH FOR THE LEGENDARY POKÉMON WHO BRINGS VICTORY.
VERY WELL!

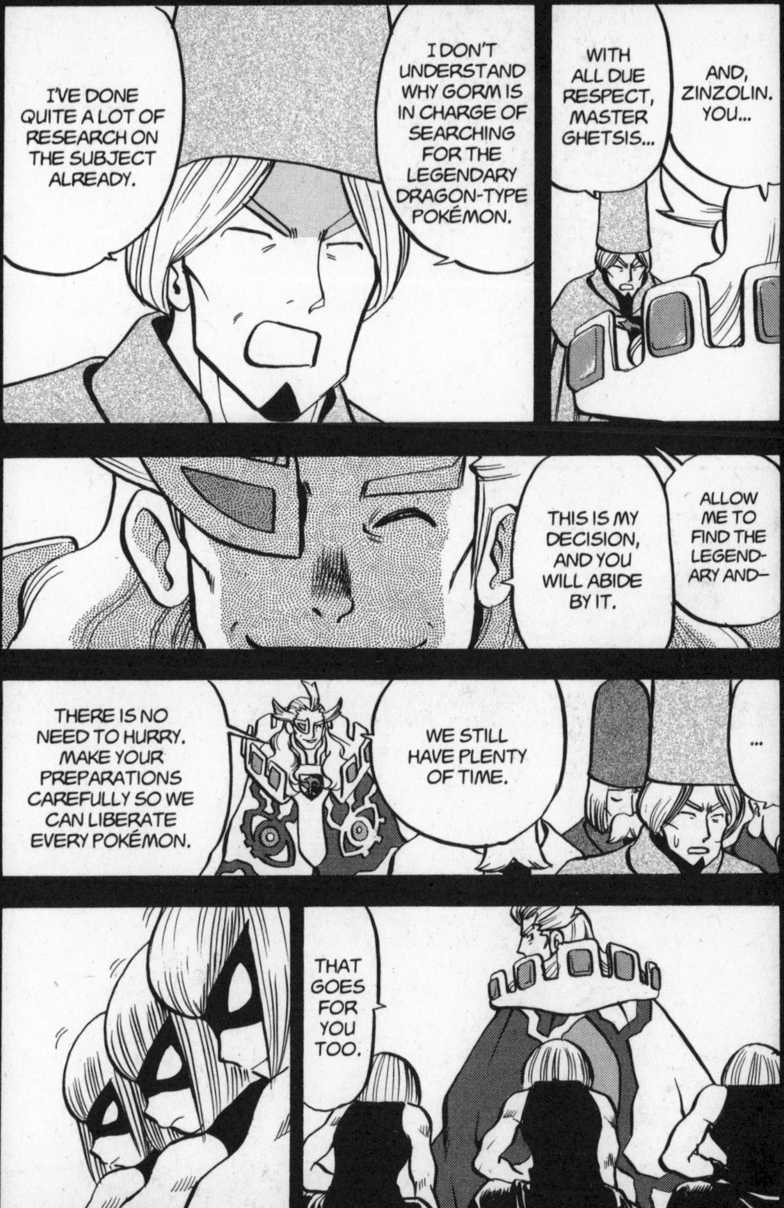
AND, ZINZOLIN. YOU...
WITH ALL DUE RESPECT, MASTER GHETSIS...
I DON'T UNDERSTAND WHY GORM IS IN CHARGE OF SEARCHING FOR THE LEGENDARY DRAGON-TYPE POKÉMON.
I'VE DONE QUITE A LOT OF RESEARCH ON THE SUBJECT ALREADY.
ALLOW ME TO FIND THE LEGEND-ARY AND—
THIS IS MY DECISION, AND YOU WILL ABIDE BY IT.
...
WE STILL HAVE PLENTY OF TIME.
THERE IS NO NEED TO HURRY. MAKE YOUR PREPARATIONS CAREFULLY SO WE CAN LIBERATE EVERY POKÉMON.
THAT GOES FOR YOU TOO.

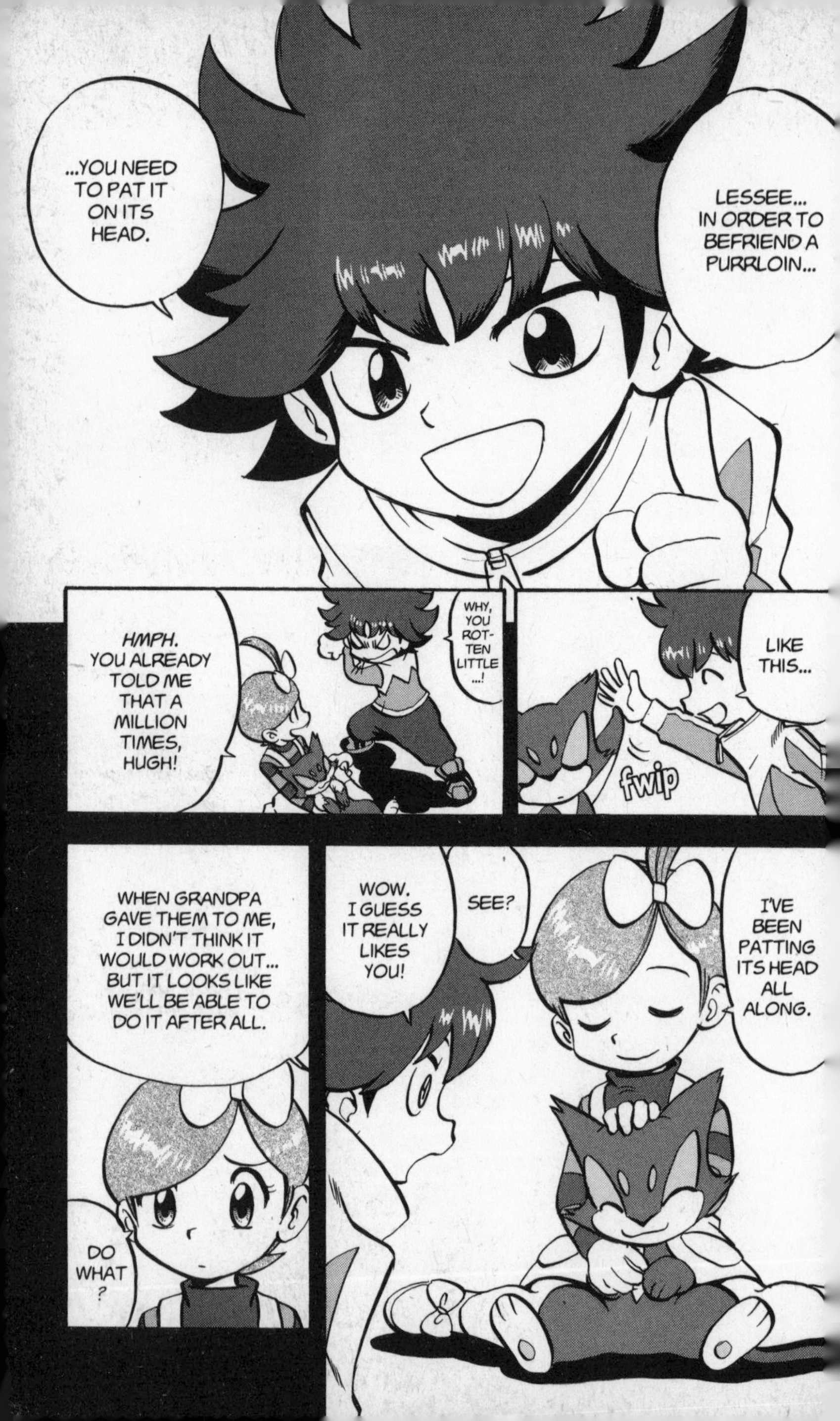
LESSEE... IN ORDER TO BEFRIEND A PURRLOIN...
...YOU NEED TO PAT IT ON ITS HEAD.
LIKE THIS...
fwip
HMPH. YOU ALREADY TOLD ME THAT A MILLION TIMES, HUGH!
WHY, YOU ROT-TEN LITTLE ...!
I'VE BEEN PATTING ITS HEAD ALL ALONG.
SEE?
WOW. I GUESS IT REALLY LIKES YOU!
WHEN GRANDPA GAVE THEM TO ME, I DIDN'T THINK IT WOULD WORK OUT... BUT IT LOOKS LIKE WE'LL BE ABLE TO DO IT AFTER ALL.
DO WHAT?

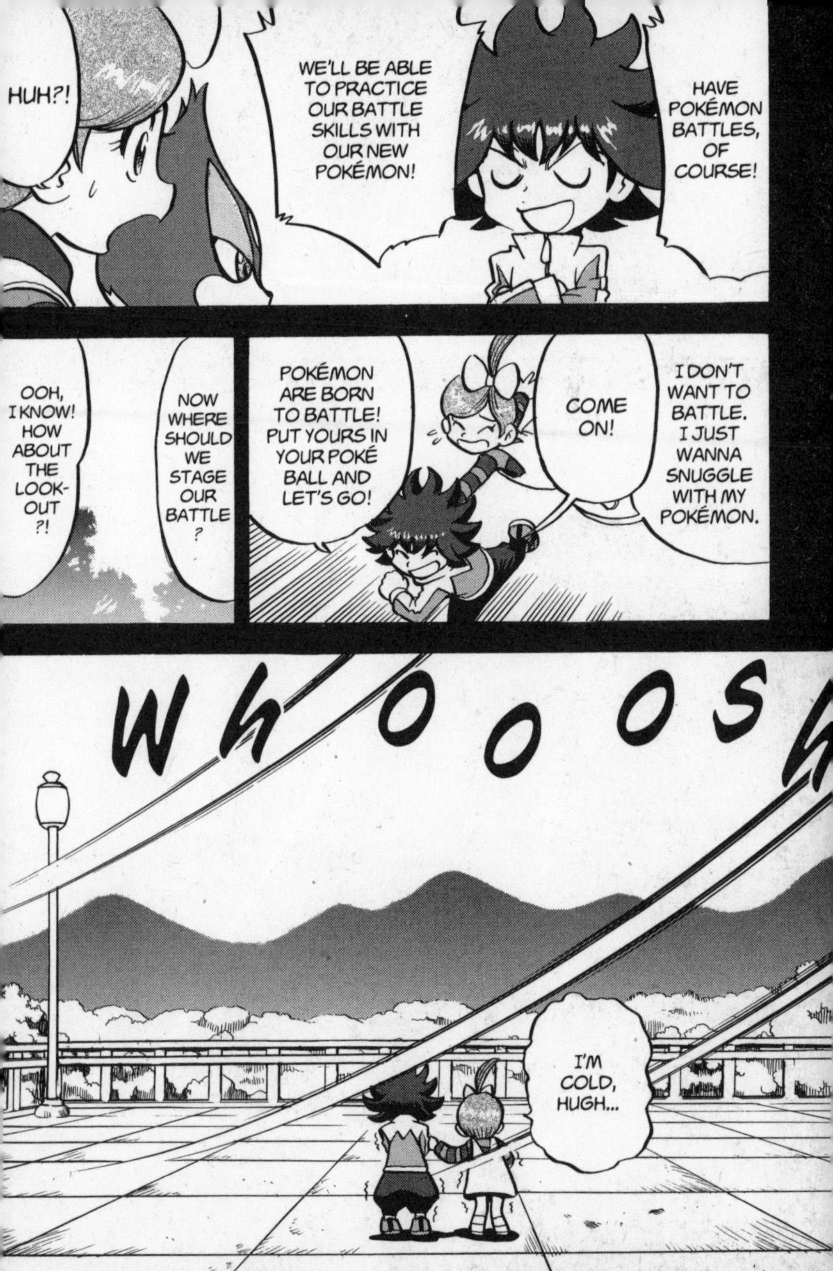
HAVE POKÉMON BATTLES, OF COURSE!
WE'LL BE ABLE TO PRACTICE OUR BATTLE SKILLS WITH OUR NEW POKÉMON!
HUH?!
I DON'T WANT TO BATTLE. I JUST WANNA SNUGGLE WITH MY POKÉMON.
COME ON!
POKÉMON ARE BORN TO BATTLE! PUT YOURS IN YOUR POKÉ BALL AND LET'S GO!
NOW WHERE SHOULD WE STAGE OUR BATTLE?
OOH, I KNOW! HOW ABOUT THE LOOK-OUT?!
WHOOOSH
I'M COLD, HUGH...

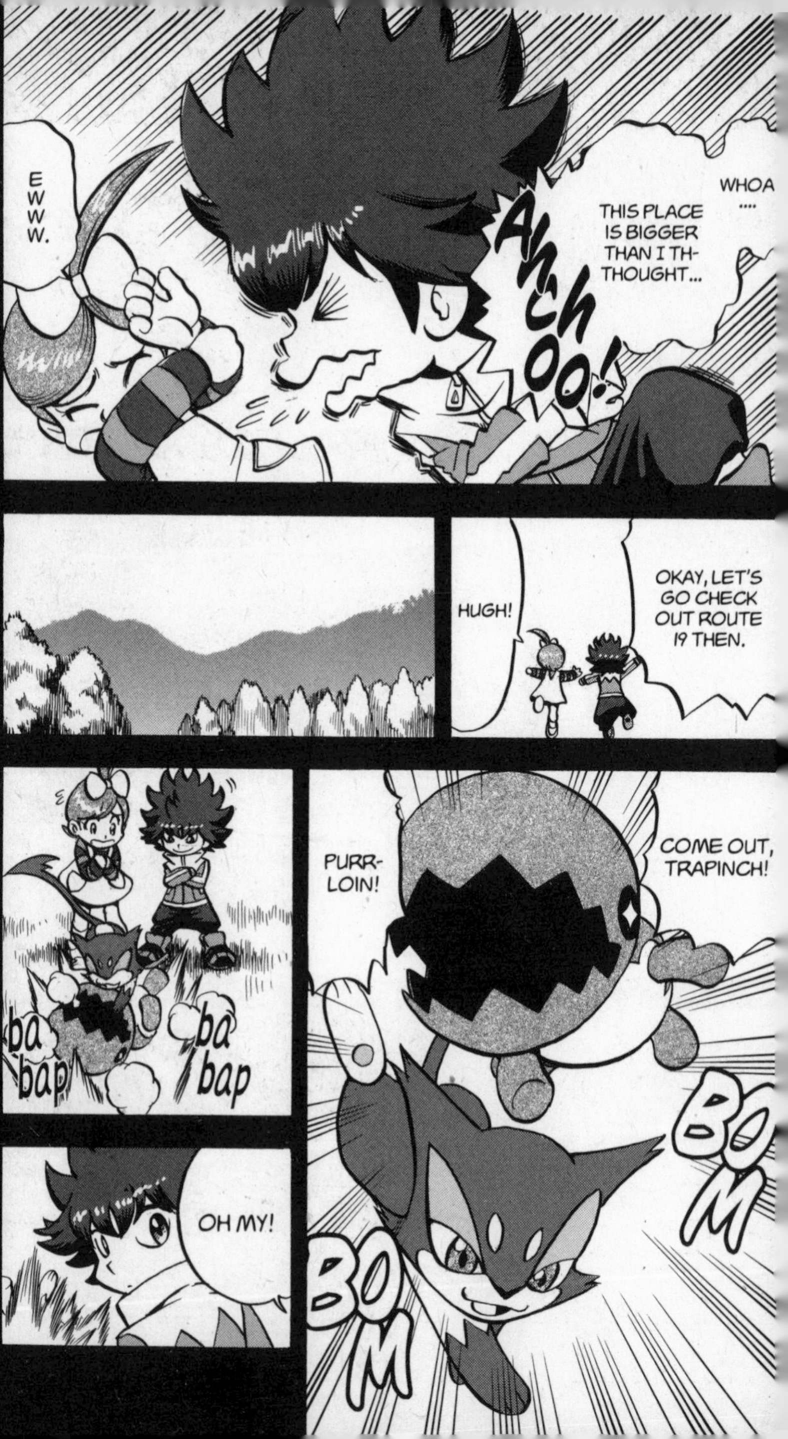
WHOA ....
THIS PLACE IS BIGGER THAN I TH- THOUGHT...
Ahchoo!
EWWW.
OKAY, LET'S GO CHECK OUT ROUTE 19 THEN.
HUGH!
COME OUT, TRAPINCH!
PURR- LOIN!
BOOM
BOOM
ba bap
ba bap
OH MY!

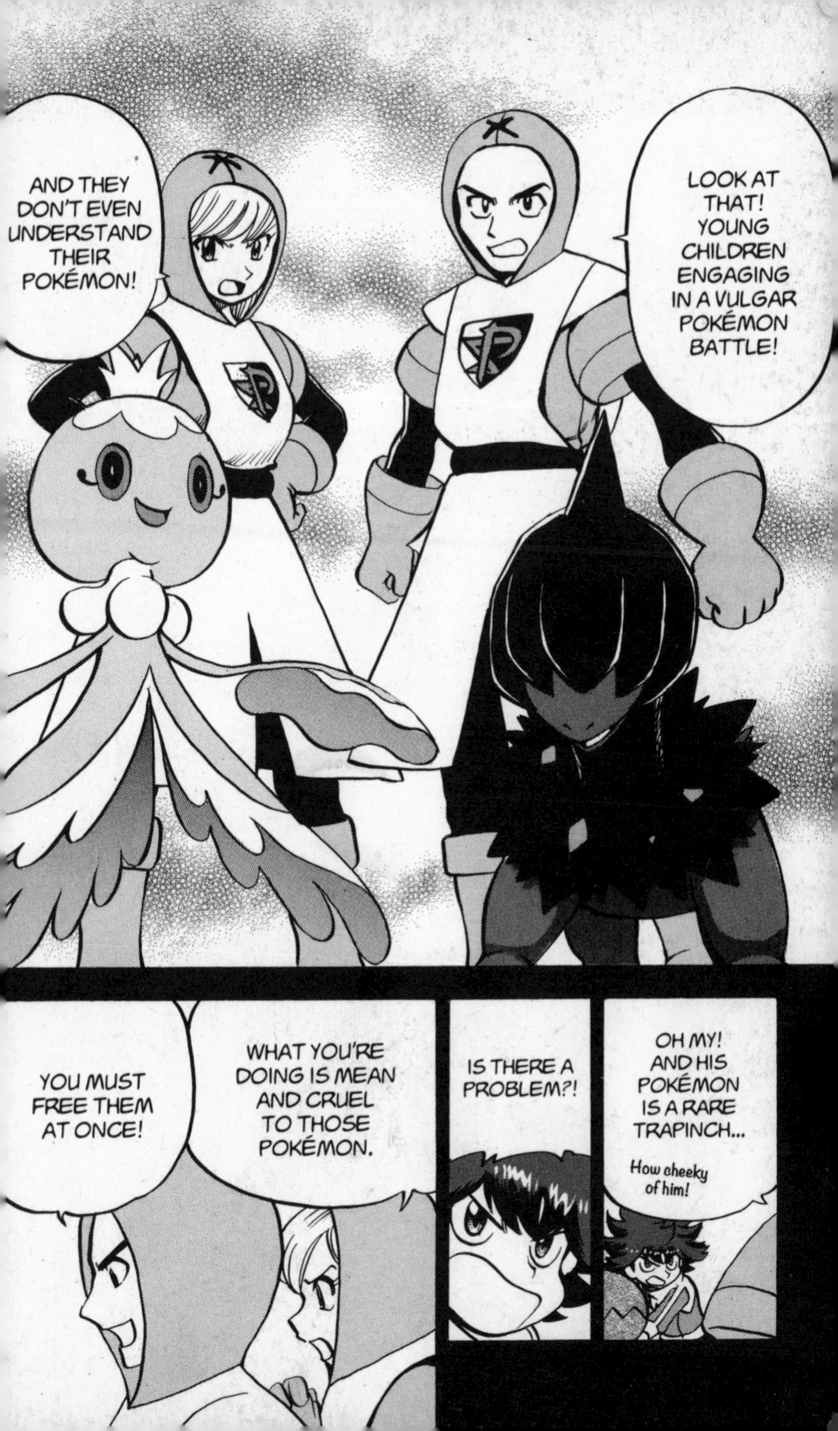

LOOK AT THAT! YOUNG CHILDREN ENGAGING IN A VULGAR POKÉMON BATTLE!
AND THEY DON'T EVEN UNDERSTAND THEIR POKÉMON!
OH MY! AND HIS POKÉMON IS A RARE TRAPINCH...
How cheeky of him!
IS THERE A PROBLEM?!
WHAT YOU'RE DOING IS MEAN AND CRUEL TO THOSE POKÉMON.
YOU MUST FREE THEM AT ONCE!

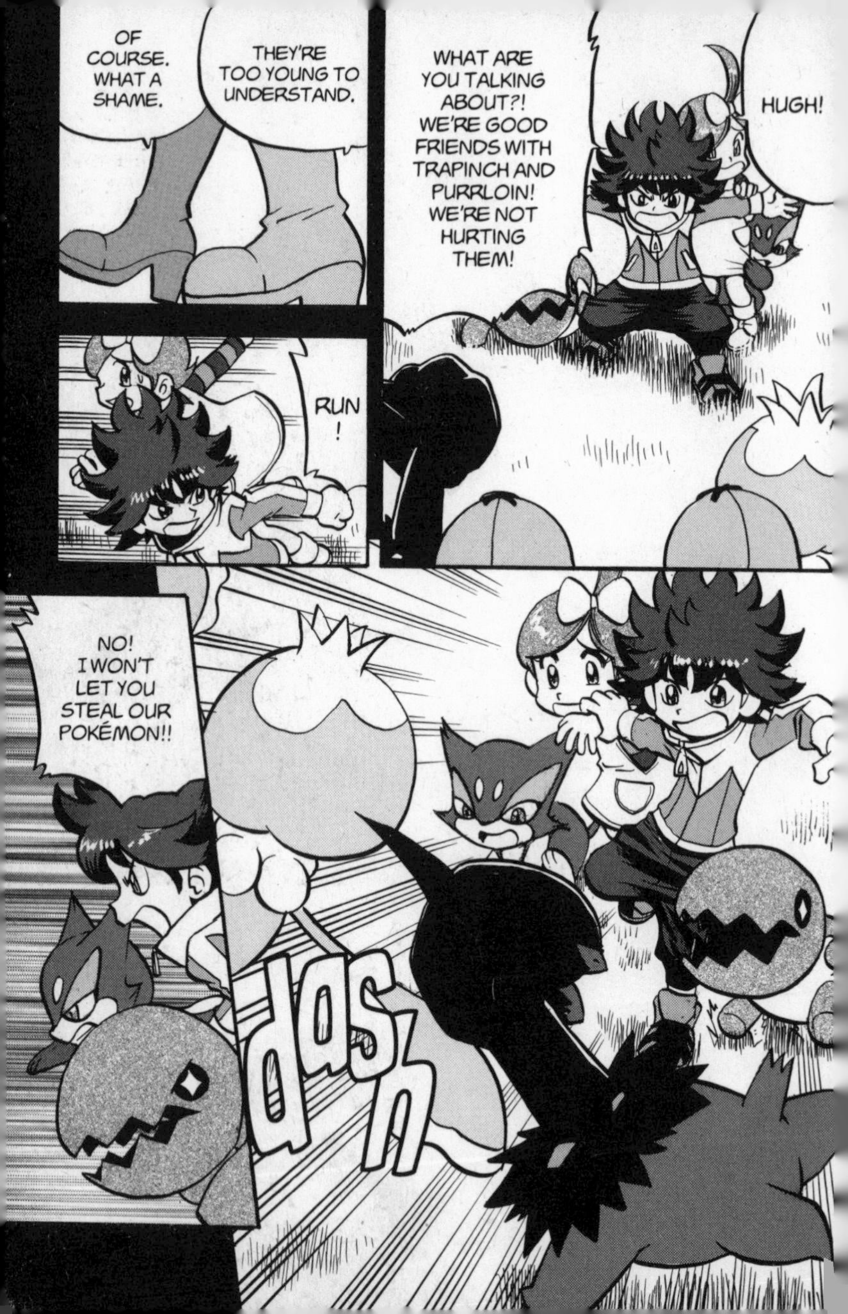
HUGH!
WHAT ARE YOU TALKING ABOUT?! WE'RE GOOD FRIENDS WITH TRAPINCH AND PURRLOIN! WE'RE NOT HURTING THEM!
THEY'RE TOO YOUNG TO UNDERSTAND.
OF COURSE. WHAT A SHAME.
RUN!
NO! I WON'T LET YOU STEAL OUR POKÉMON!!
dash

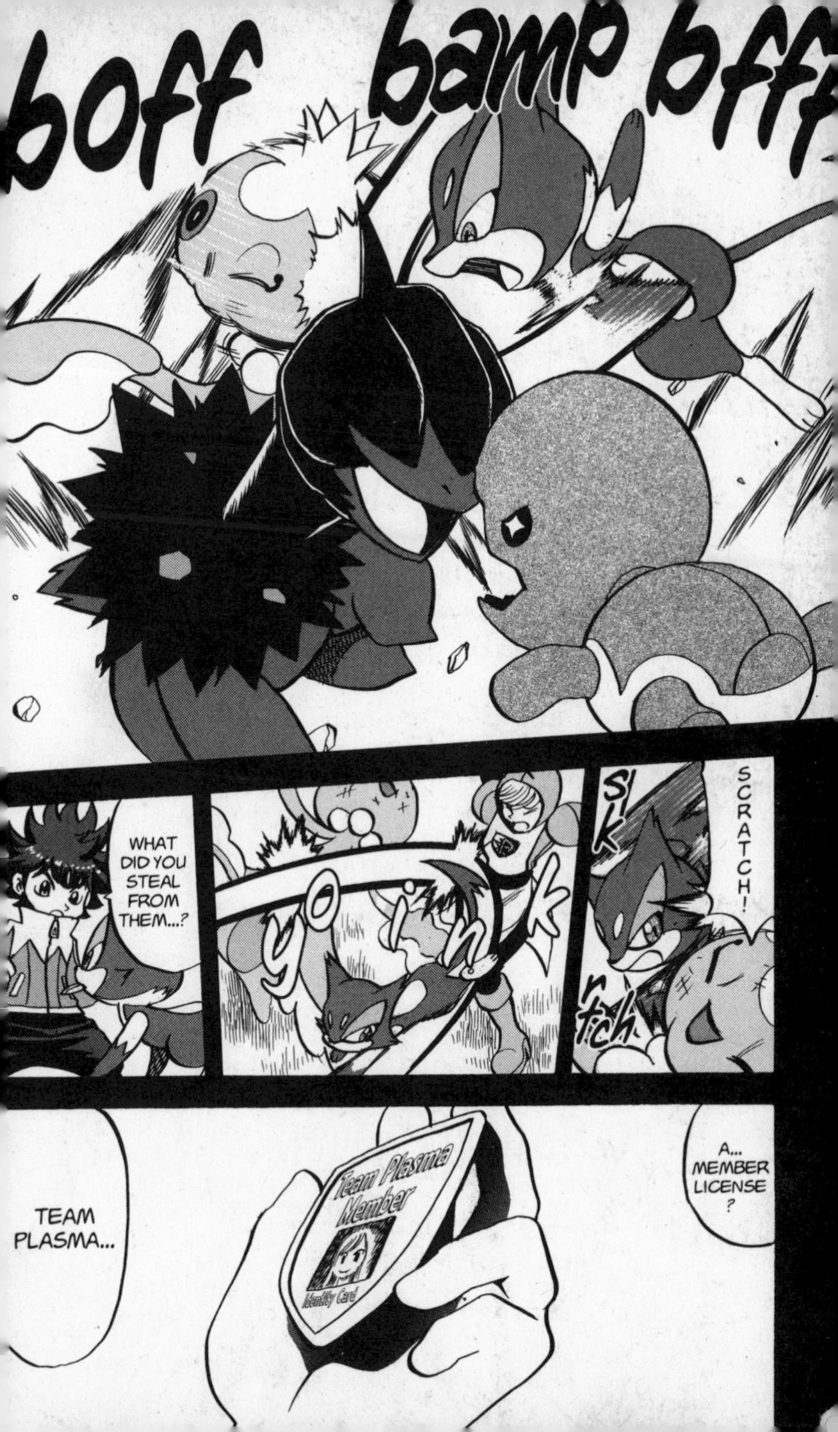
bamp bff
boff
SCRATCH!
sk
rtch
yoink
WHAT DID YOU STEAL FROM THEM...?
A... MEMBER LICENSE?
Team Plasma Member
Identity Card
TEAM PLASMA...

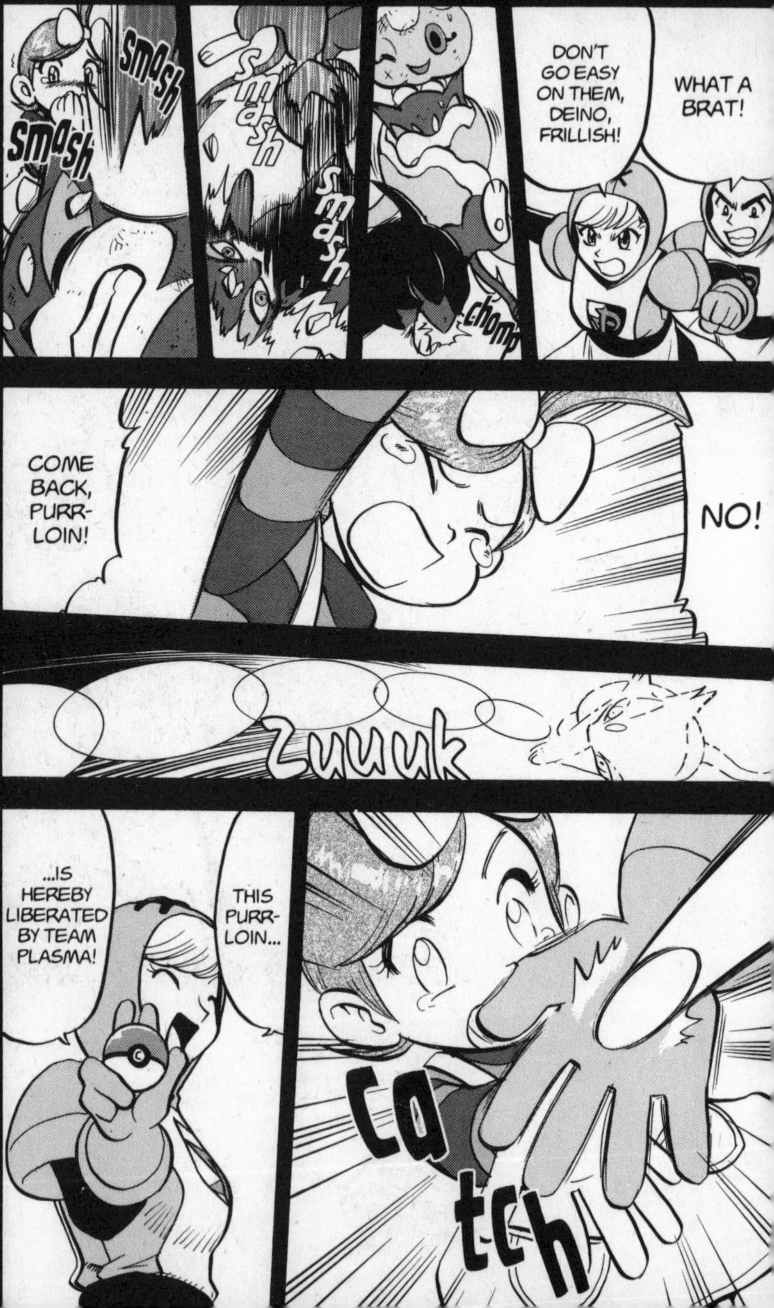
WHAT A BRAT!
DON'T GO EASY ON THEM, DEINO, FRILLISH!
chomp
smash
smash
SMASH
SMASH
NO!
COME BACK, PURR-LOIN!
Zuuuk
catch
THIS PURR-LOIN...
...IS HEREBY LIBERATED BY TEAM PLASMA!

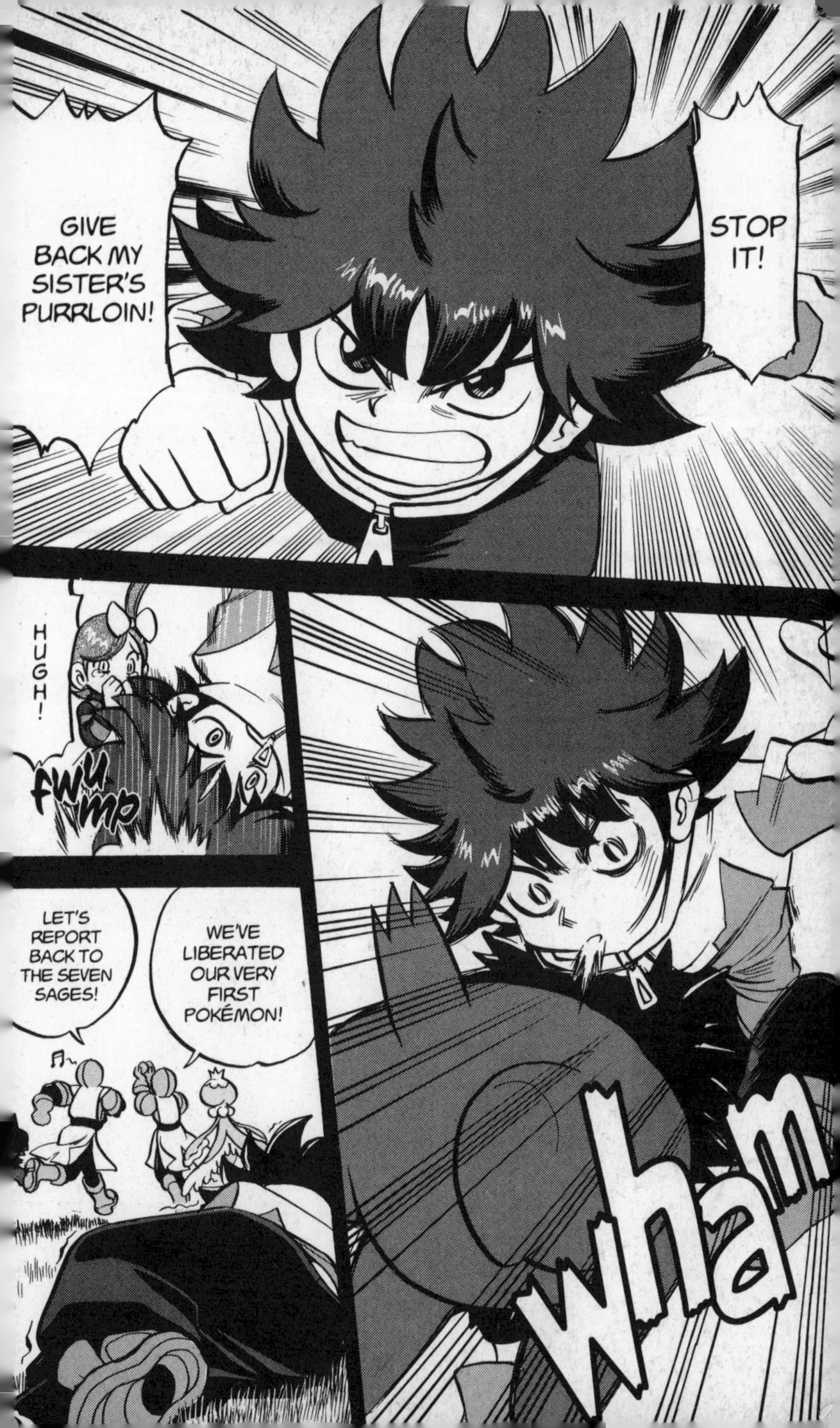

STOP IT!
GIVE BACK MY SISTER'S PURRLOIN!
wham
HUGH!
fwump
WE'VE LIBERATED OUR VERY FIRST POKÉMON!
LET'S REPORT BACK TO THE SEVEN SAGES!

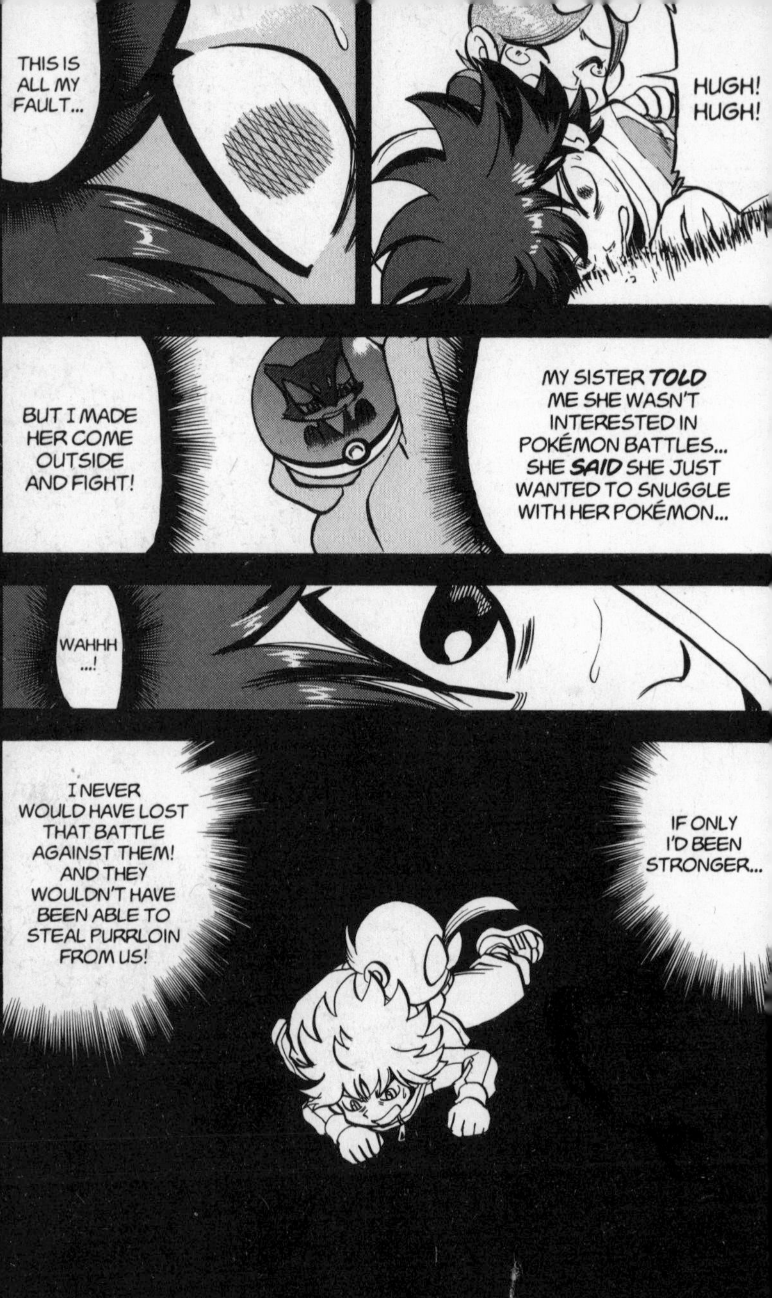
HUGH! HUGH!
THIS IS ALL MY FAULT...
MY SISTER **TOLD** ME SHE WASN'T INTERESTED IN POKÉMON BATTLES... SHE **SAID** SHE JUST WANTED TO SNUGGLE WITH HER POKÉMON...
BUT I MADE HER COME OUTSIDE AND FIGHT!
WAHHH ...!
IF ONLY I'D BEEN STRONGER...
I NEVER WOULD HAVE LOST THAT BATTLE AGAINST THEM! AND THEY WOULDN'T HAVE BEEN ABLE TO STEAL PURRLOIN FROM US!

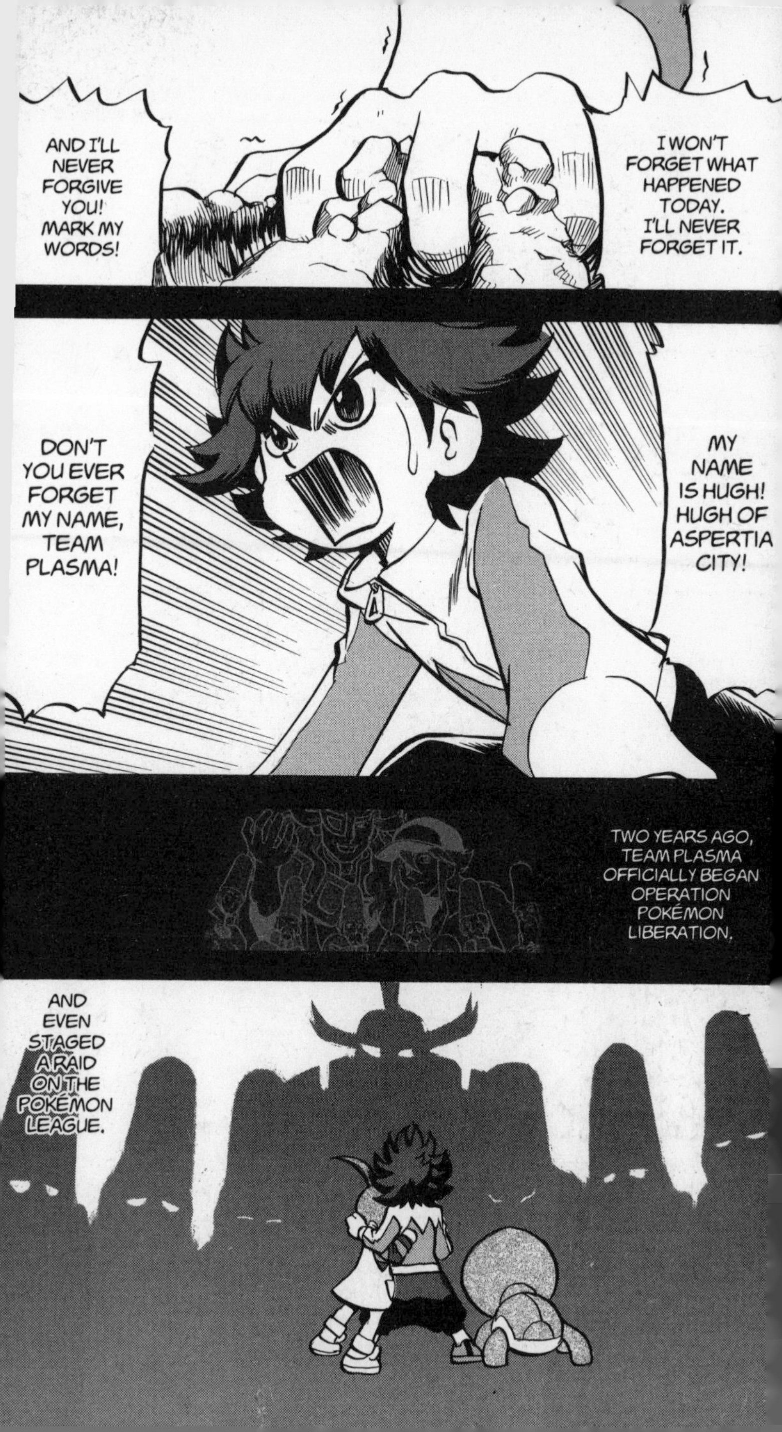
I WON'T FORGET WHAT HAPPENED TODAY. I'LL NEVER FORGET IT.
AND I'LL NEVER FORGIVE YOU! MARK MY WORDS!
MY NAME IS HUGH! HUGH OF ASPERTIA CITY!
DON'T YOU EVER FORGET MY NAME, TEAM PLASMA!
TWO YEARS AGO, TEAM PLASMA OFFICIALLY BEGAN OPERATION POKÉMON LIBERATION.
AND EVEN STAGED A RAID ON THE POKÉMON LEAGUE.

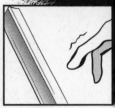

THIS IS A RECORD...

THERE'S NO DOUBT ABOUT IT.

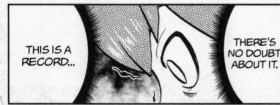

...TEAM PLASMA'S MASS THEFT OF POKÉMON UNDER THE GUISE OF LIBERATION...

...OF...

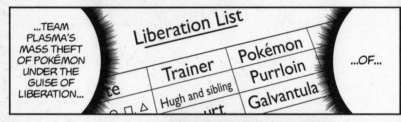

Liberation List

	Trainer	Pokémon
		Purrloin
□ △	Hugh and sibling	Galvantula

I JUST REAL-IZED THAT...

LEAVE ME ALONE, LEO!

HUGH? ARE YOU ALL RIGHT...?

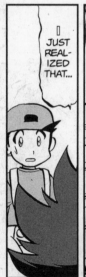

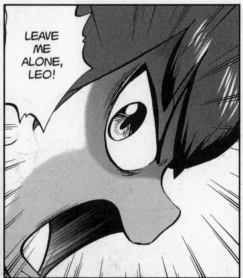

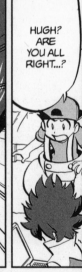

...WITH *MY SISTER'S PURRLOIN!*

...TEAM PLASMA'S LIBERATION BEGAN FIVE YEARS AGO ON THAT DAY...

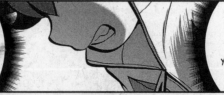

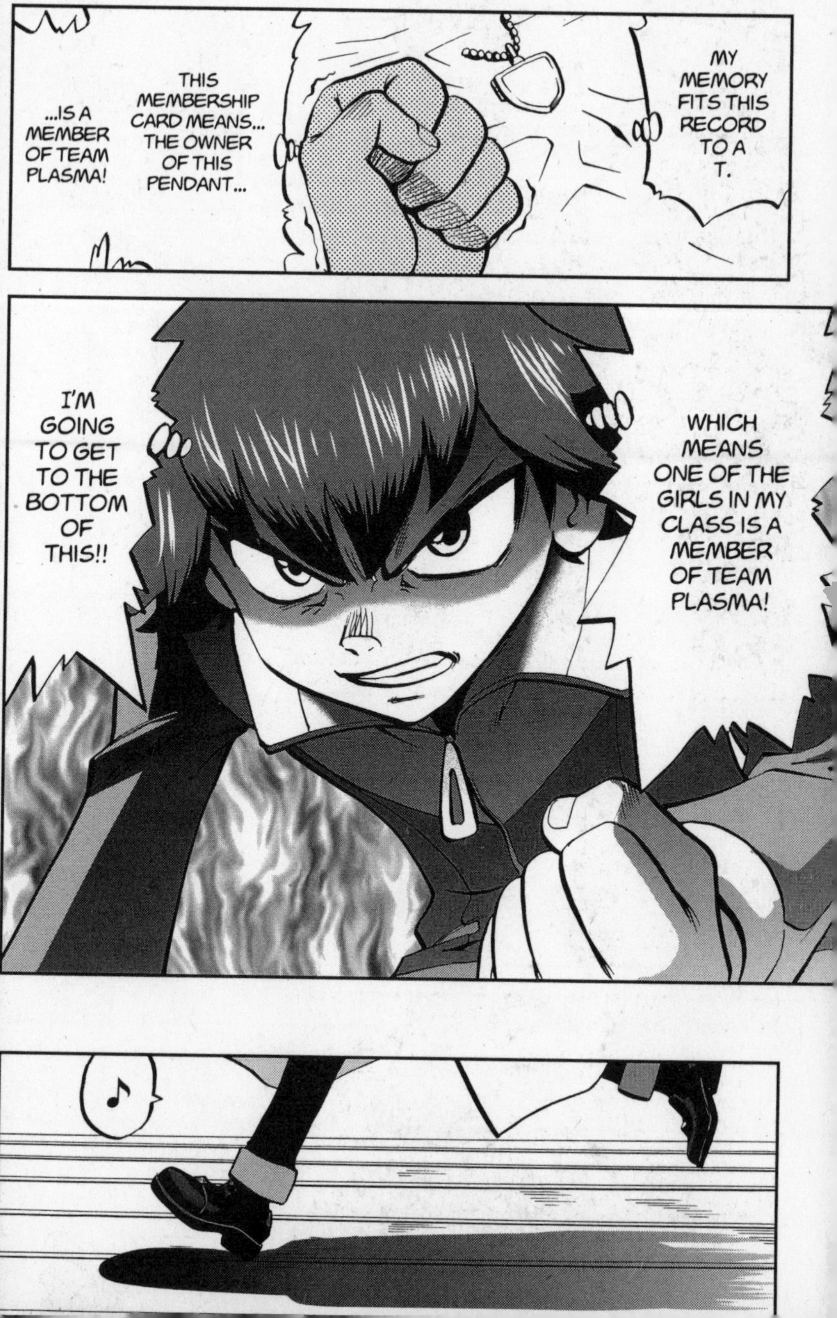
MY MEMORY FITS THIS RECORD TO A T.
THIS MEMBERSHIP CARD MEANS... THE OWNER OF THIS PENDANT...
...IS A MEMBER OF TEAM PLASMA!
WHICH MEANS ONE OF THE GIRLS IN MY CLASS IS A MEMBER OF TEAM PLASMA!
I'M GOING TO GET TO THE BOTTOM OF THIS!!
♪

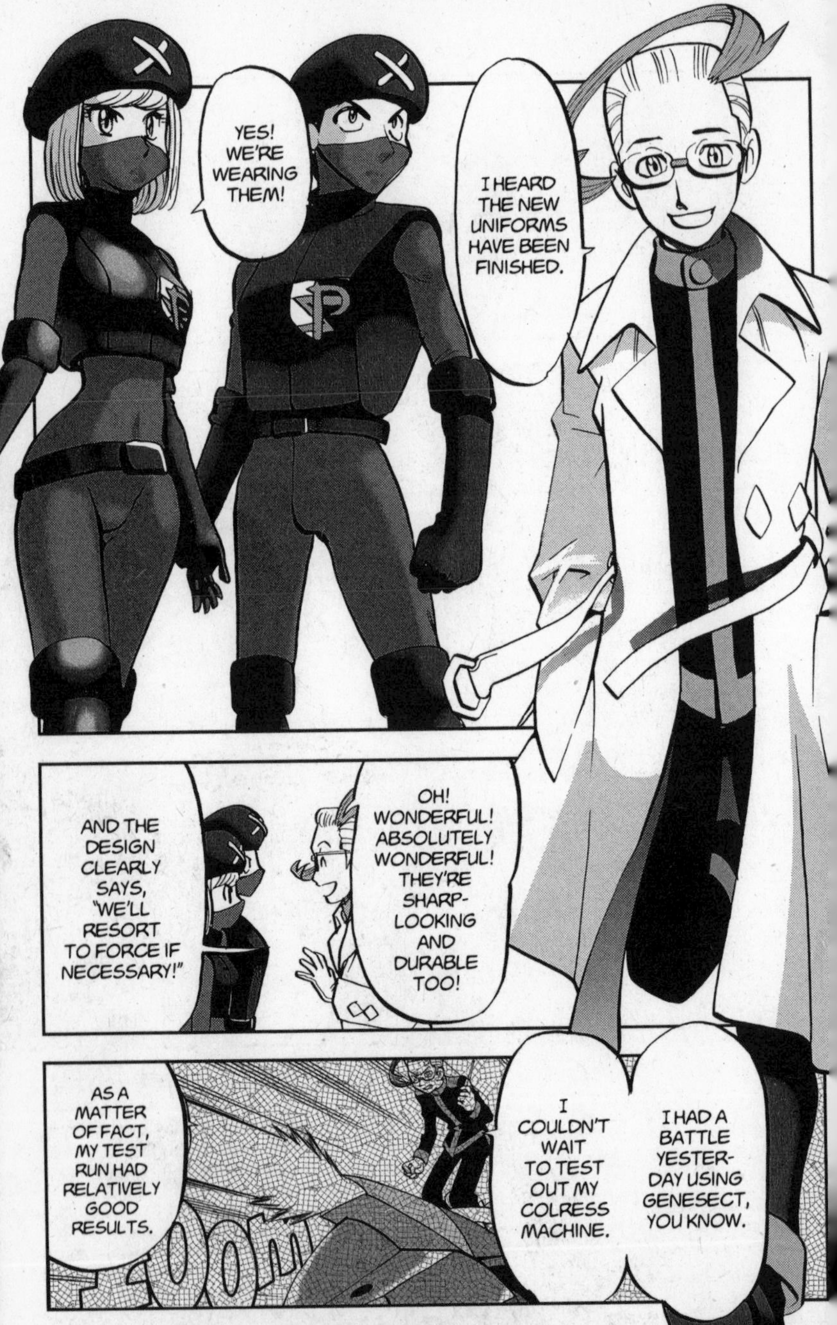
I HEARD THE NEW UNIFORMS HAVE BEEN FINISHED.
YES! WE'RE WEARING THEM!
OH! WONDERFUL! ABSOLUTELY WONDERFUL! THEY'RE SHARP-LOOKING AND DURABLE TOO!
AND THE DESIGN CLEARLY SAYS, "WE'LL RESORT TO FORCE IF NECESSARY!"
I HAD A BATTLE YESTER-DAY USING GENESECT, YOU KNOW.
I COULDN'T WAIT TO TEST OUT MY COLRESS MACHINE.
AS A MATTER OF FACT, MY TEST RUN HAD RELATIVELY GOOD RESULTS.

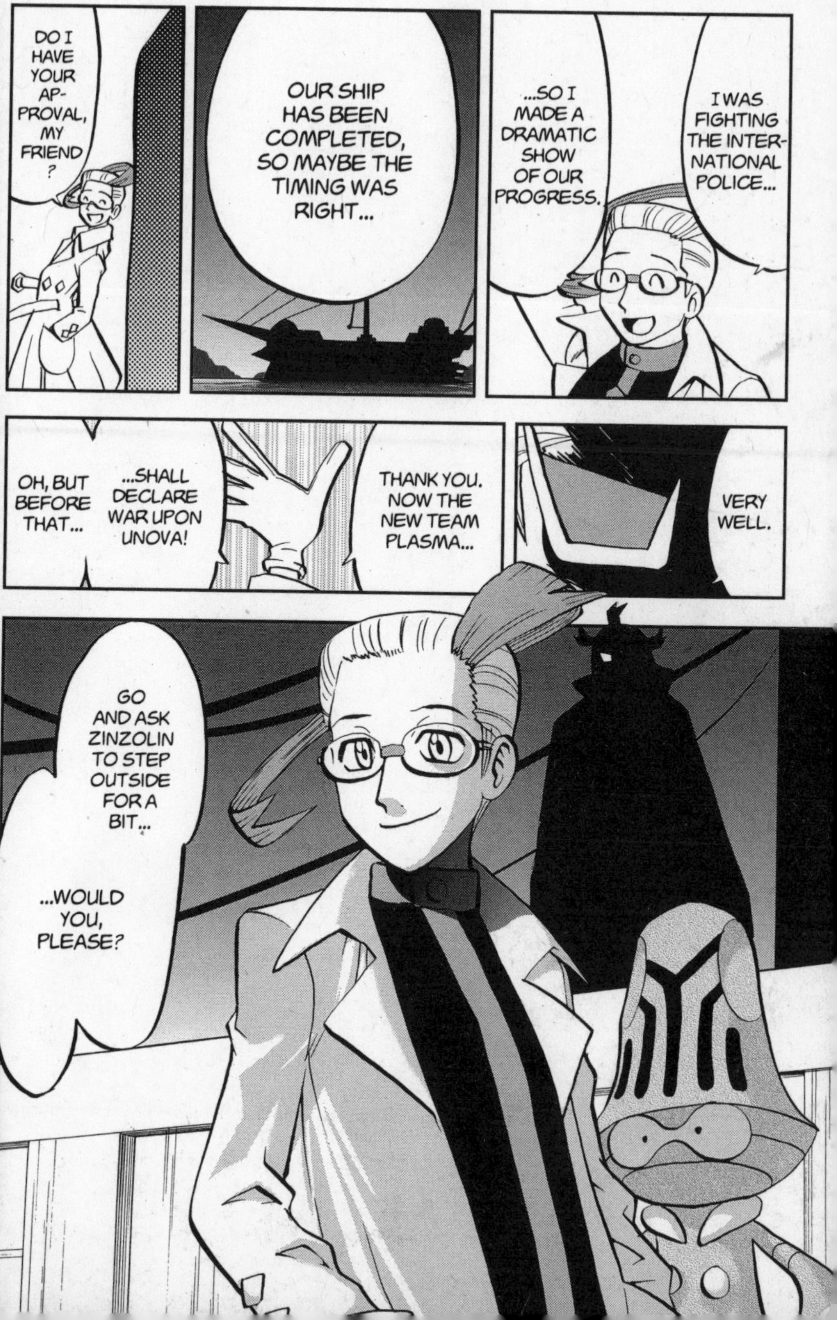
I WAS FIGHTING THE INTER-NATIONAL POLICE...
...SO I MADE A DRAMATIC SHOW OF OUR PROGRESS.
OUR SHIP HAS BEEN COMPLETED, SO MAYBE THE TIMING WAS RIGHT...
DO I HAVE YOUR AP-PROVAL, MY FRIEND?
VERY WELL.
THANK YOU. NOW THE NEW TEAM PLASMA...
...SHALL DECLARE WAR UPON UNOVA!
OH, BUT BEFORE THAT...
GO AND ASK ZINZOLIN TO STEP OUTSIDE FOR A BIT...
...WOULD YOU, PLEASE?

TO BE
CONTINUED

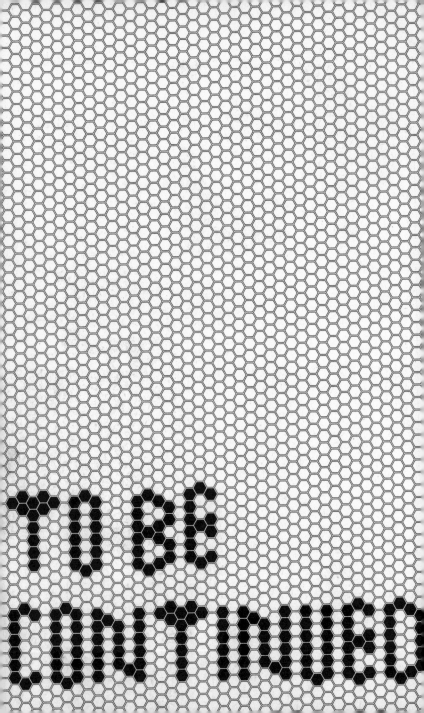

Chapter Title Page Illustration Collection

Presenting title page illustrations
originally drawn for some of the chapters
of *Pokémon Black 2 White 2*
when they were first published in
Japanese children's magazines
Corocoro Ichiban! and *Pokémon Fan*.

Let's take a look back at
Blake and Whitley's journey in pictures...

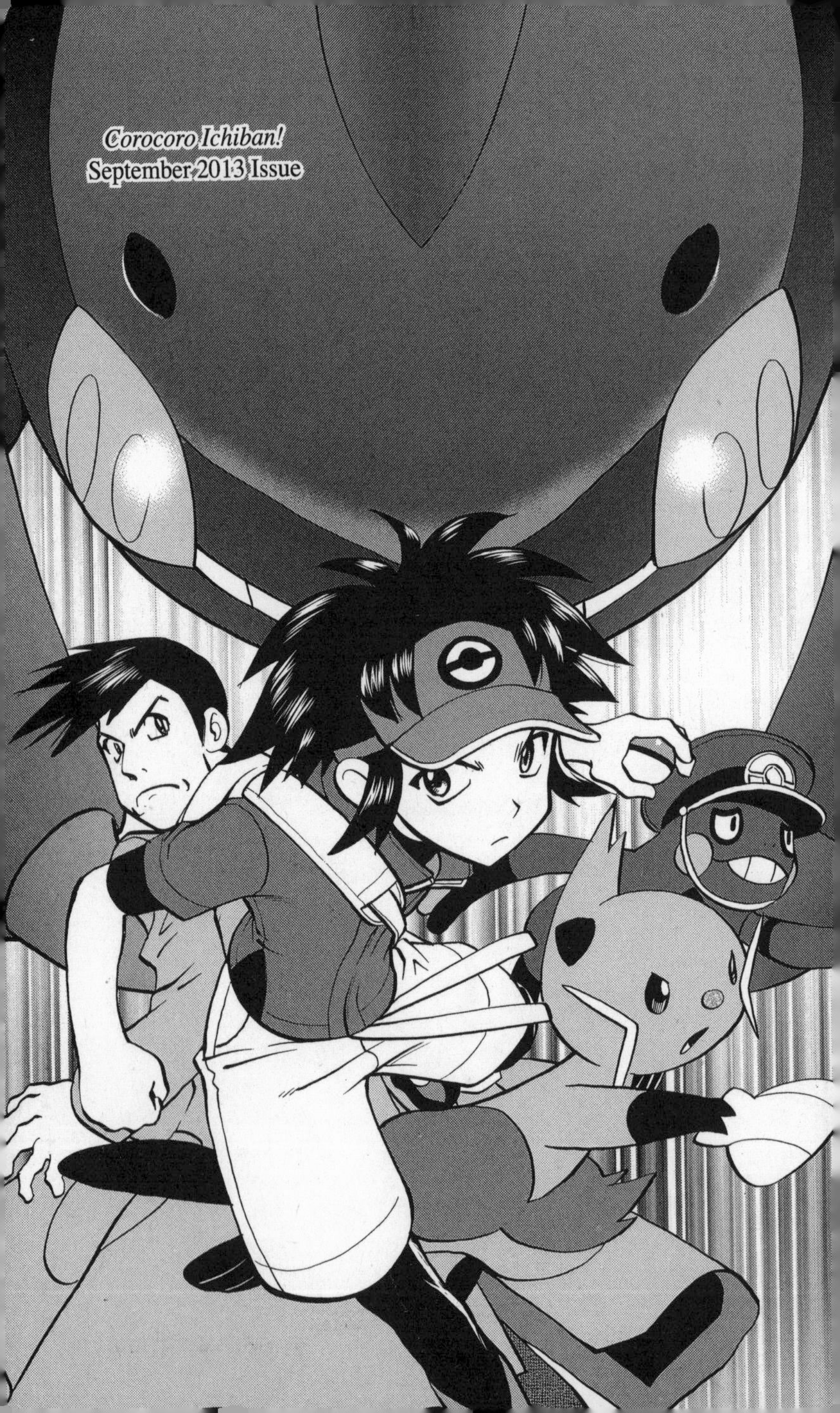
Corocoro Ichiban!
September 2013 Issue

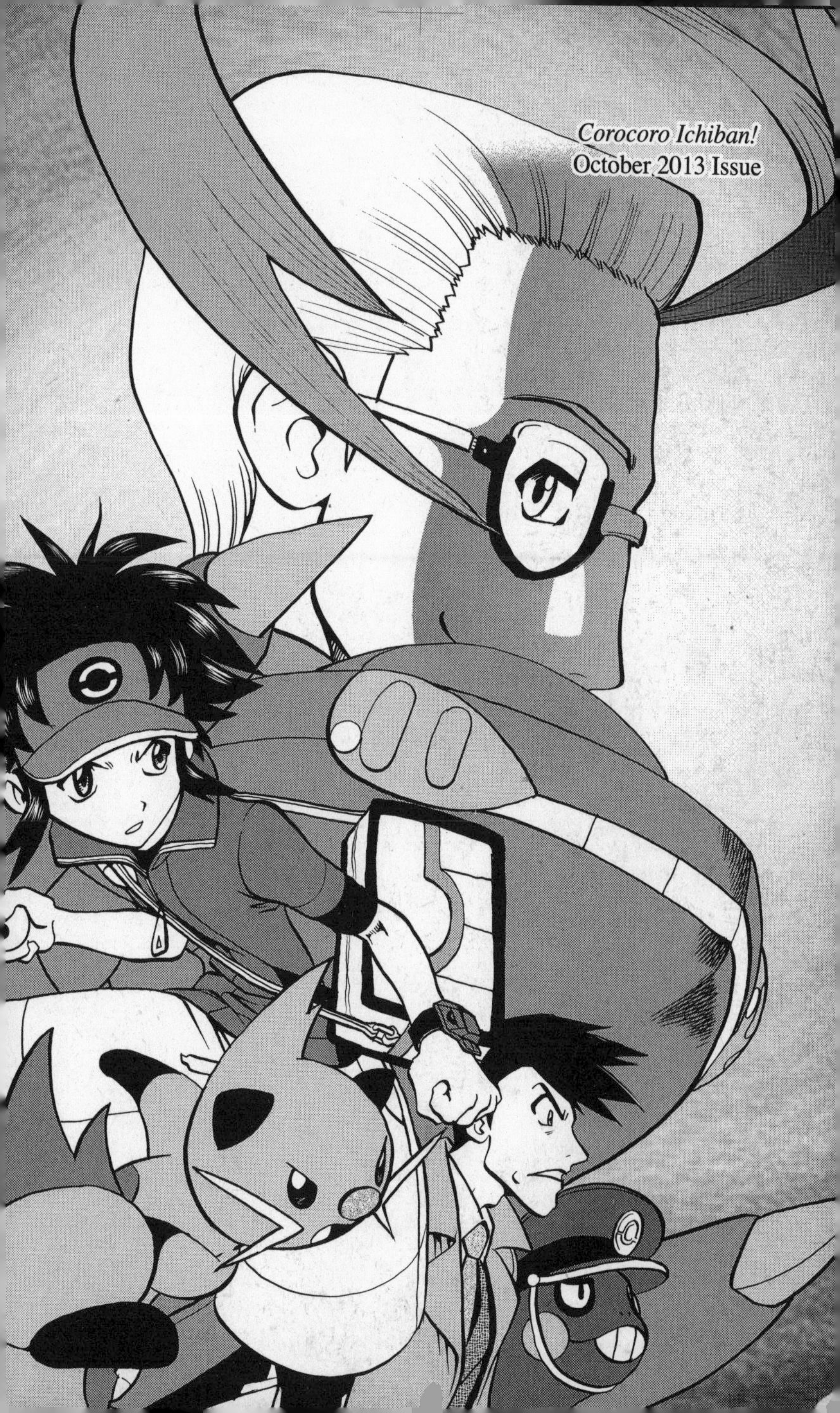
Corocoro Ichiban!
October 2013 Issue

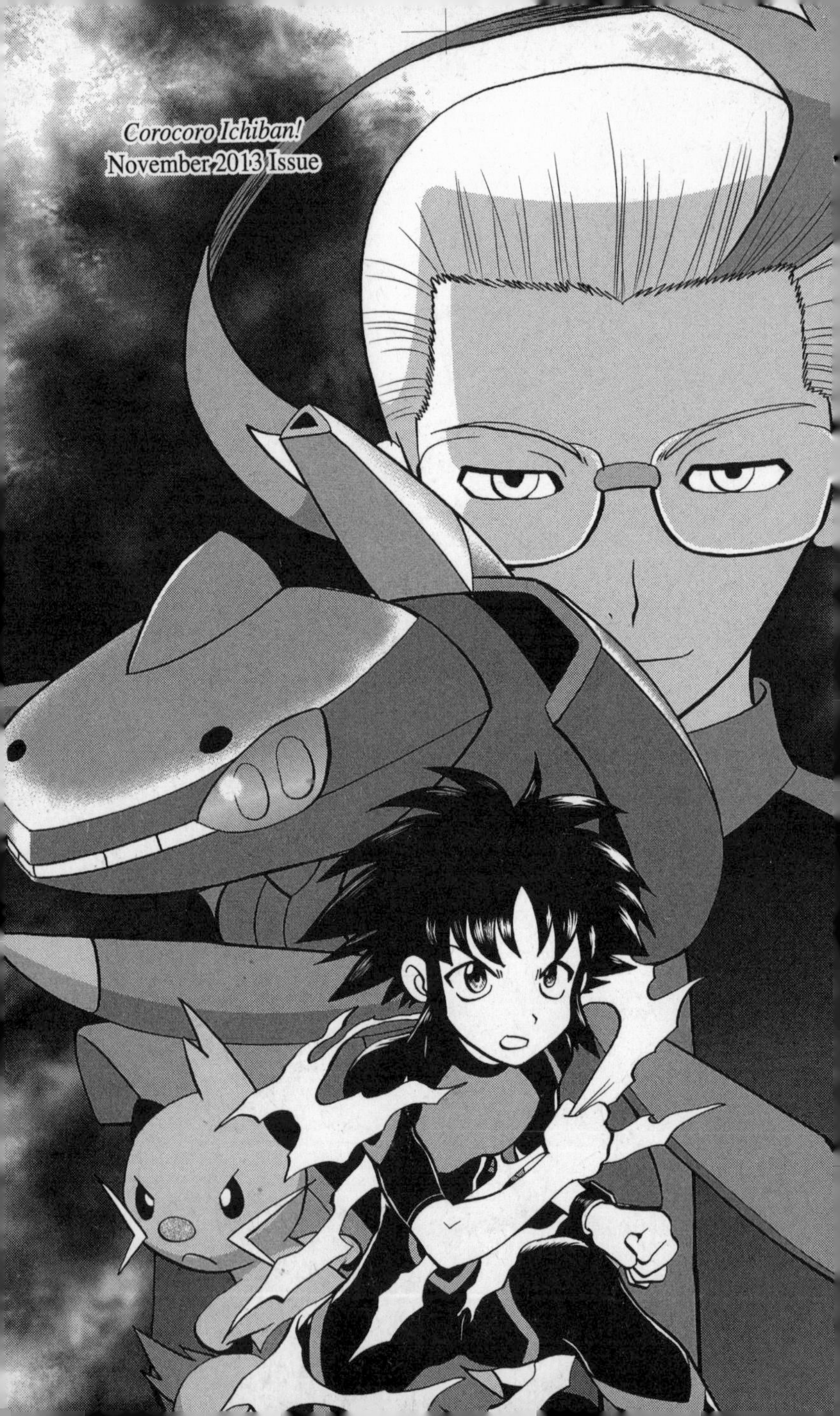
Corocoro Ichiban!
November 2013 Issue

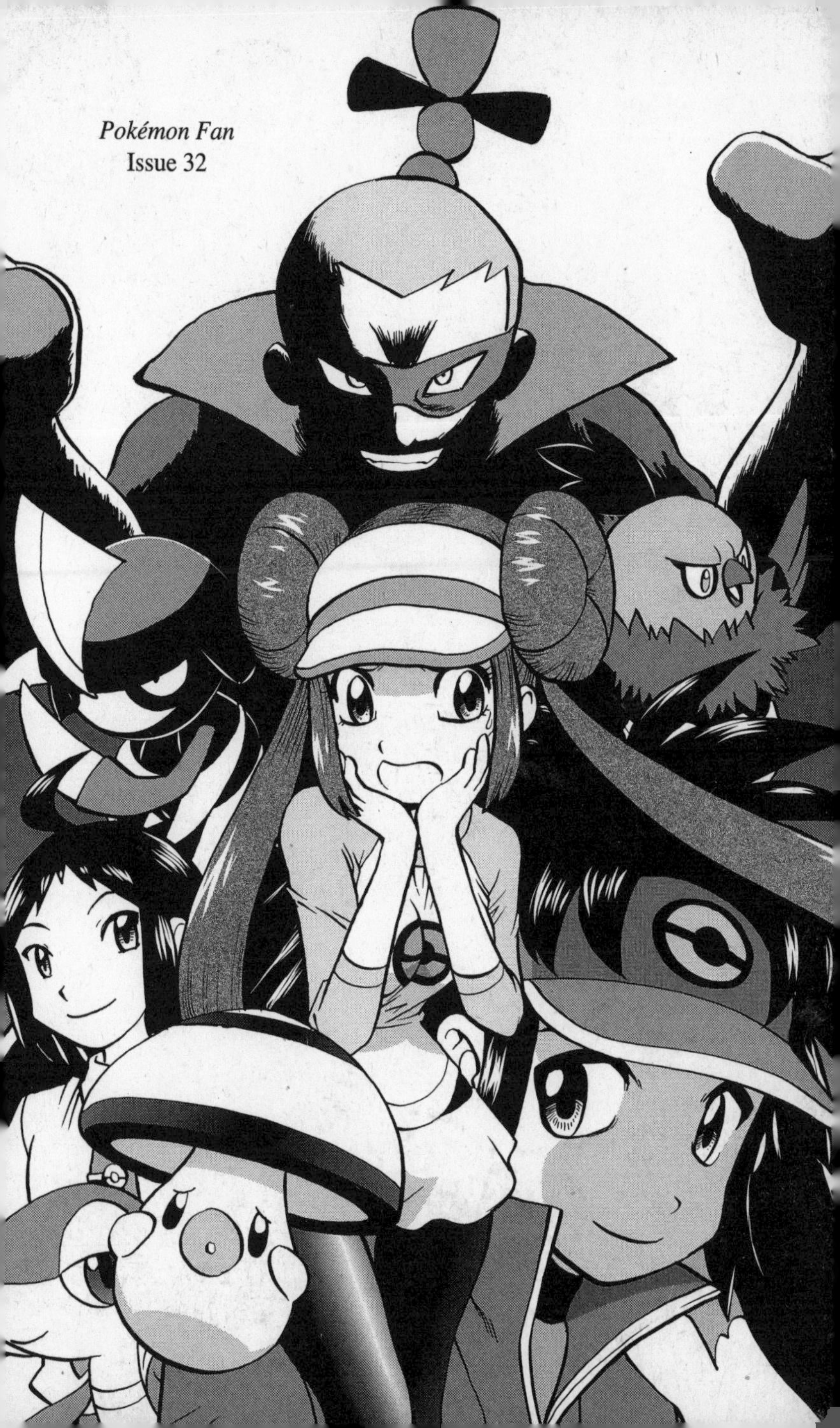

Pokémon Fan
Issue 32

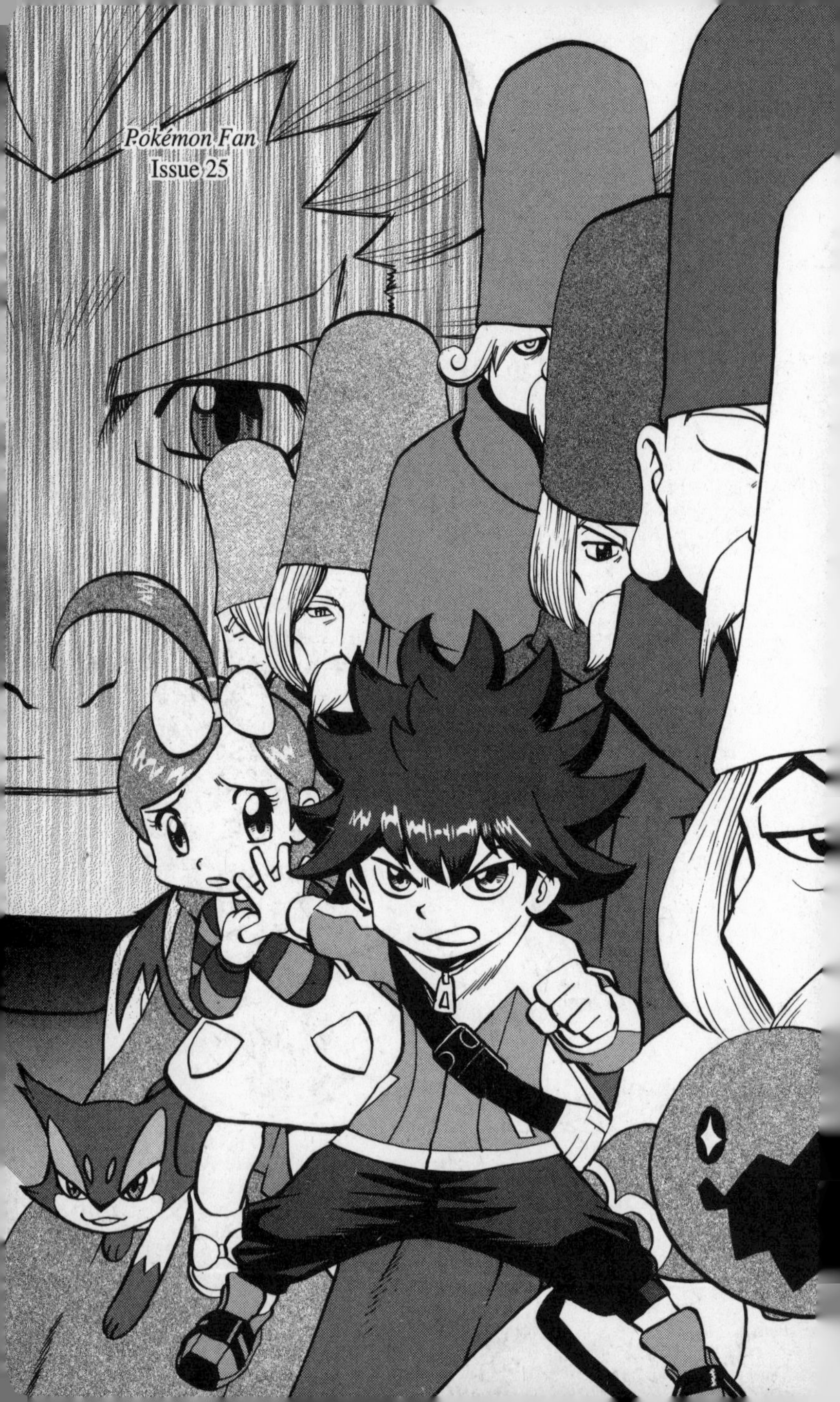
Pokémon Fan
Issue 25

International Police Investigation File (Report)

Unova Region
Legendary Pokémon/Mythical Pokémon

Black No. 2 reporting to headquarters. I have gathered intel on the Pokémon of this region while attempting to track down the identity of the girl in question. This is a report of the evidence and information I've gathered so far.

Black No. 2

[Zekrom, Reshiram]

The officer (Looker) who was dispatched to the scene of the crime two years ago succeeded in taking a picture of them. The existence of these two Pokémon has long been questioned, but we now know for sure that they are real. The black Dragon-type Pokémon Zekrom and the white Dragon-type Pokémon Reshiram each side with a trainer (the legend describes them as "heroes"). These heroes are said to search for an Ideal and the Truth. It has become clear that this part of the legend is also true. In other developments, the two Trainers who fought against each other with Zekrom and Reshiram have disappeared. Looker has reported that their names are "N" and "Black." We must find them, as they are our primary witnesses.

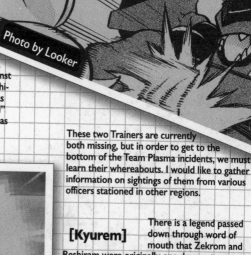

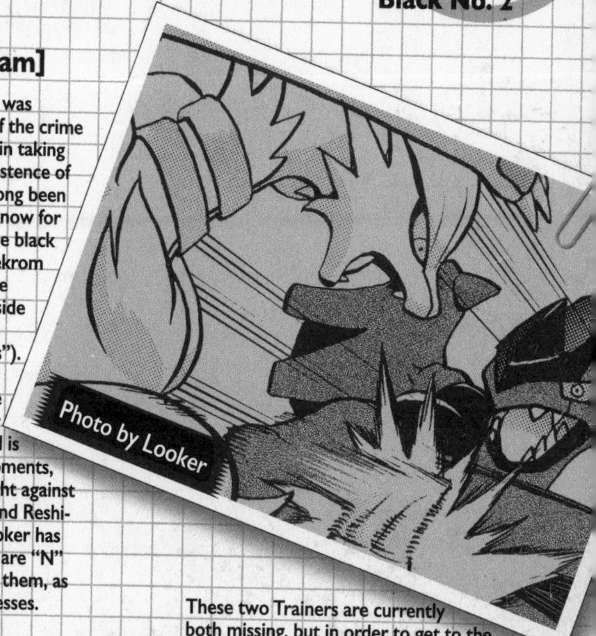

Photo by Looker

These two Trainers are currently both missing, but in order to get to the bottom of the Team Plasma incidents, we must learn their whereabouts. I would like to gather information on sightings of them from various officers stationed in other regions.

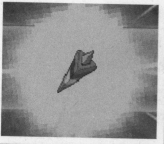

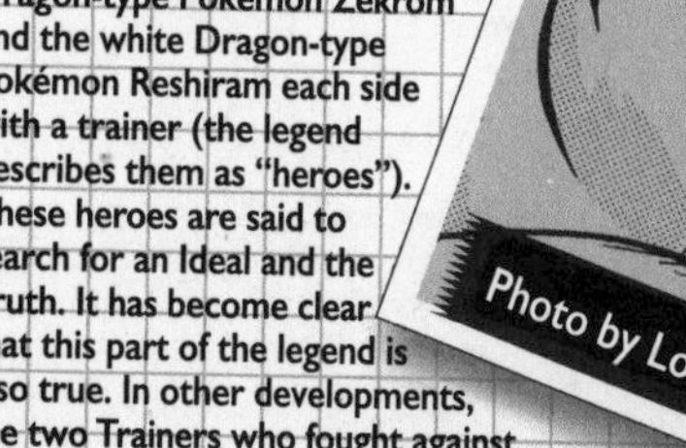

[Kyurem]

There is a legend passed down through word of mouth that Zekrom and Reshiram were originally one dragon-type Pokémon who broke in two, leaving behind an empty shell which developed into an independent Pokémon itself, named Kyurem. That's all I've been able to find out about this legend at the moment, but I discovered this strange item at the Giant Chasm where I learned about the Kyurem legend. I'm currently investigating it to see if it has anything to do with Kyurem.

[Cobalion, Virizion, Terrakion]

The whereabouts of these three powerful Pokémon, known as the Swords of Justice, are currently unknown. But I have discovered a rock with slash marks left by the trio at the Pledge Grove near Floccesy Town, which is close to where I have been stationed. I have verified the marks left on the rock with the International Police data archive and there is no doubt they were made by these three Pokémon.

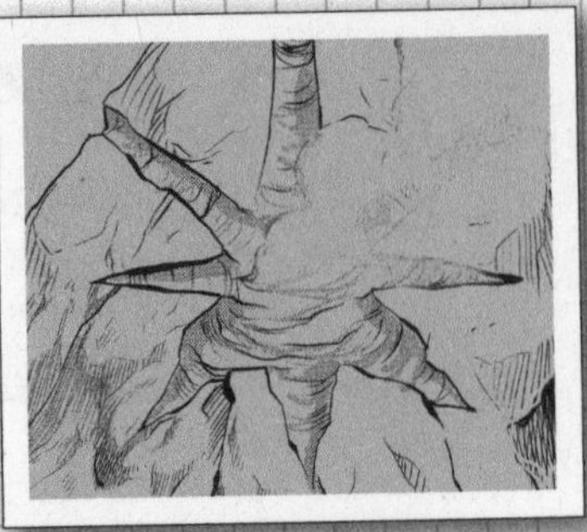

[Keldeo]

I encountered this Pokémon last week at the Pledge Grove. It was near the rock with the marks left by Cobalion, Virizion and Terrakion, so I am currently investigating its connection with them.

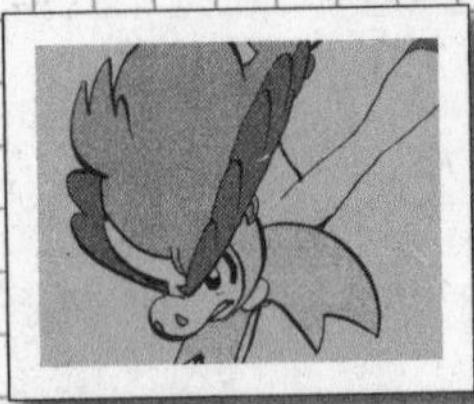

It was a very short battle, but I clearly saw that it had incredible speed and strength.

[Victini]

There have been reports of sightings of this Pokémon near the lighthouse on Liberty Garden.

[Meloetta]

There have been no clear sightings of this Pokémon.

[Tornadus, Thundurus, Landorus]

Like Zekrom and Reshiram, there have been various reports of sightings of these Pokémon at the Pokémon League two years ago. The officer (Looker) who was dispatched to the scene has reported that they were used by Team Plasma. Unfortunately, there is no photographic record of any of the three. Judging from how Team Plasma recently, there is a good possibility that Team Plasma will make use of them again. In case we are to face these Pokémon, I strongly recommend having a prepared in advance.

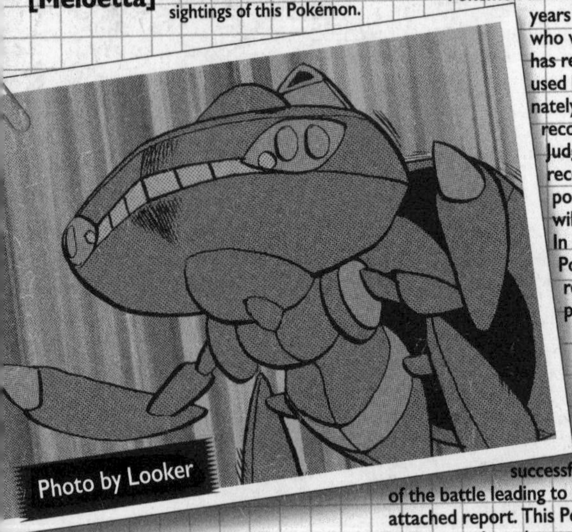

Photo by Looker

[Genesect]

successfully captured. The details of the battle leading to its capture are on the attached report. This Pokémon is highly dangerous and currently under special protective observation at the headquarters' Intensive Analysis Lab.

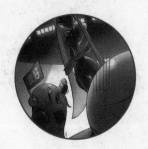

Message from
Hidenori Kusaka

Students, teachers, classes, classmates, field trips, first crushes... School is filled with all sorts of excitement, and that's why the school life genre has become so popular in TV and manga. So...I decided to take on the challenge myself and create a school life story arc for the very first time in *Pokémon Adventures*! It takes place somewhere I'd never written about before...a Pokémon Trainers' School! And now it's time for class! *Ring ring ring ring!*

Message from
Satoshi Yamamoto

I've been working on the *Pokémon Adventures* series for 14 years and have been faced with many challenges, such as drawing machines (which I'm not good at) and drawing hordes of Pokémon. But the *B2W2* story arc will probably be my most challenging yet! "Why?" you ask. Because a guy who is unpopular with the ladies has to draw a guy who is super popular with the ladies! I have no idea how to draw him! (´ Д `)ノ

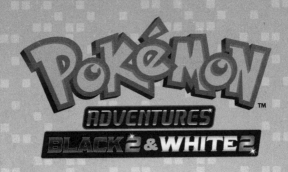

**Pokémon ADVENTURES
BLACK 2 & WHITE 2**
Volume 1
VIZ Media Edition

Story by HIDENORI KUSAKA
Art by SATOSHI YAMAMOTO

©2015 The Pokémon Company International.
©1995–2015 Nintendo/Creatures Inc./GAME FREAK inc.
TM, ®, and character names are trademarks of Nintendo.
POCKET MONSTERS SPECIAL Vol. 52
by Hidenori KUSAKA, Satoshi YAMAMOTO
© 1997 Hidenori KUSAKA, Satoshi YAMAMOTO
All rights reserved.
Original Japanese edition published by SHOGAKUKAN.
English translation rights in the United States of America, Canada,
the United Kingdom, Ireland, Australia, New Zealand and India
arranged with SHOGAKUKAN.

Translation/Tetsuichiro Miyaki
English Adaptation/Annette Roman
Touch-up & Lettering/Susan Daigle-Leach
Design/Shawn Carrico
Editor/Annette Roman

Printed in the U.S.A.

Published by VIZ Media, LLC
P.O. Box 77010
San Francisco, CA 94107

10 9 8 7 6 5 4 3 2
First printing, January 2017
Second printing, April 2017

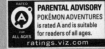

PARENTAL ADVISORY
POKÉMON ADVENTURES
is rated A and is suitable
for readers of all ages.
ratings.viz.com

www.viz.com

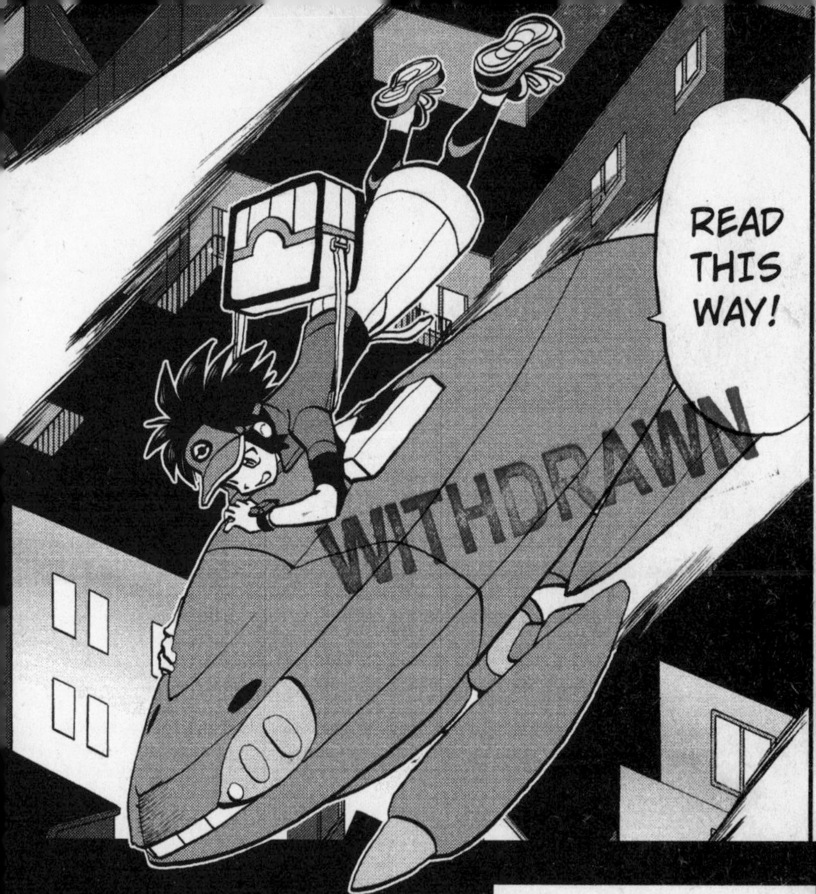
READ THIS WAY!

THIS IS THE END OF THIS GRAPHIC NOVEL!

To properly enjoy th[illegible] graphic novel, please [illegible] and begin reading fr[illegible]

This book has been printed in the original Japanese format in order to preserve the orientation of the original artwork.

Have fun with it!

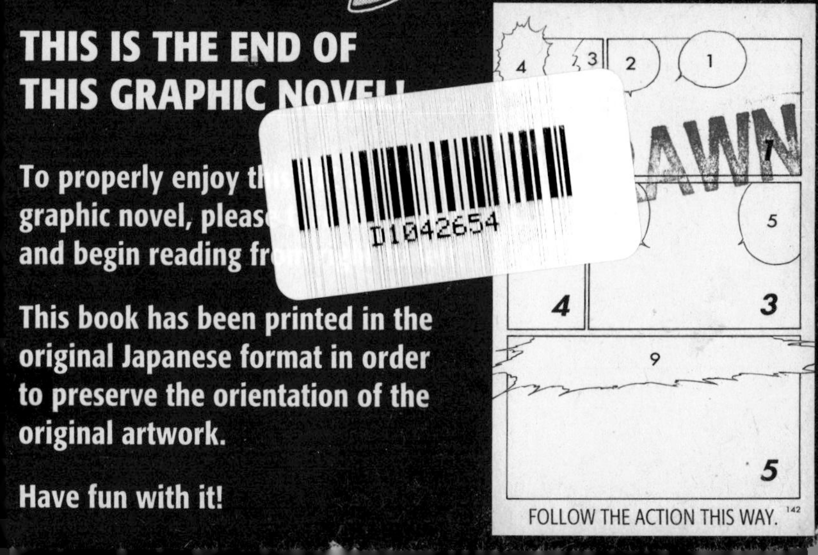
4
3
2
1
1
5
4
3
9
5
FOLLOW THE ACTION THIS WAY.